Fragile Beasts

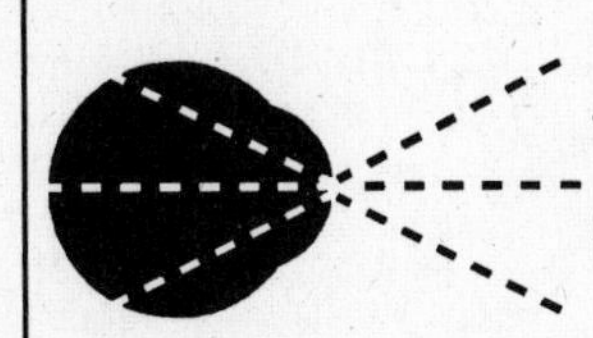

Fragile Beasts

Tawni O'Dell

THORNDIKE PRESS
A part of Gale, Cengage Learning

Detroit • New York • San Francisco • New Haven, Conn • Waterville, Maine • London

Thorndike Press, a part of Gale, Cengage Learning.

Thorndike Press® Large Print Basic.
The text of this Large Print edition is unabridged.
Other aspects of the book may vary from the original edition.
Set in 16 pt. Plantin.

LIBRARY OF CONGRESS CATALOGING-IN-PUBLICATION DATA

O'Dell, Tawni.
Fragile beasts / by Tawni O'Dell.
p. cm. — (Thorndike Press large print basic)
ISBN-13: 978-1-4104-2864-6
ISBN-10: 1-4104-2864-8
1. Teenage boys—Fiction. 2. Older women—Fiction. 3. Coal miners—Fiction. 4. City and town life—Pennsylvania—Fiction. 5. Pennsylvania—Fiction. 6. Large type books. I. Title.
PS3565.D428F73 2010b
813'.54—dc22 2010018192

Published in 2010 by arrangement with Shaye Areheart Books, an imprint of the Crown Publishing Group, a division of Random House, Inc.

Printed in the United States of America
1 2 3 4 5 6 7 14 13 12 11 10

For Tirzah and Connor,
my fragile beasts

Prologue: The Quiet One

Villarica, Spain. June 24, 1959.

Manuel Obrador knew that he was dead but understood he had not yet finished dying.

He lay in a haze of yellow dust on a carpet of glittering sand beneath the blinding white disc of a setting Spanish summer sun. The sky was the same fierce yet tender blue he remembered from as long ago as his boyhood spent in this same town and from as recently as this afternoon when he left his contented cuadrilla smoking their cigarettes after a fine lunch and strolled from the restaurant to his hotel to have his siesta. Grilled fish, cold partridge, lamb chops, a hard, salty Manchego cheese, cake and ice cream, and more than a few bottles of *vino tinto* for him and his men: many toreros found it impossible to eat before stepping into the ring, but the anticipation always made him hungry. He didn't know at the time that it was to be his last meal, but if he had known, he probably wouldn't have requested a different one.

Calladito had been an excellent bull, the kind many toreros spent the better parts of their careers hoping to meet. Manuel had known he was going to be such a bull when he first chanced to glimpse him at Carmen del Pozo's finca more than a year ago standing with a group of five others in an endless field of lavender, his coat a sleek black that shimmered with glints of blue each time a muscle twitched. He was easily over a thousand pounds, his body thick and compactly powerful, his legs slender and delicate in comparison: a heavy-weight fighter with a ballerina's grace and speed.

Manuel and everyone else in the Jeep had sat perfectly still so as not to attract the attention of any of the bulls but despite this, Calladito noticed them.

While the rest continued to graze with the tufts of silky hair at the ends of their long tails flicking lazily at their backs, he raised his head and sniffed the air, and the great mass of muscle on his neck rippled with agitation. Without warning, he began to gallop stiff-legged across the grass toward them, then lowered his head and chopped with one horn at an imaginary foe before coming to an abrupt stop.

For Manuel, it wasn't merely the bull's size, or strength, or majesty that caught his attention. It was his eyes. Usually the eyes of bulls were impossible to read. They were still,

black, and depthless like pools of night water. All toreros agreed that toros were thinkers, but no one could ever know what they were thinking about.

Calladito's eyes held a special light. It wasn't intelligence exactly. Something more basic. Something deeper. It was knowledge.

His hand had been resting on the bare skin of Candy's shoulder, and he moved his fingertips to the lovely curve of her neck where he could feel her pulse beating madly with fear as she watched the bull, too, trying to anticipate what he'd do next and suddenly realizing that if he chose to ram into the side of their vehicle, it would be no different than being hit by a truck but a truck armed with sharp curved horns as thick as a man's forearm and a will to survive.

"Éste es para mí, y yo para él," he whispered to her, not caring that she didn't understand much Spanish yet. *That one is for me, and I'm for him.*

Where are you now, Calladito? he wondered.

By law, another torero would have been responsible for killing the bull since he could no longer do it, but this had been a one-man corrida, a special event held in his honor in his hometown of Villarica on the eve of his thirtieth birthday. There was no other torero.

Instead the bull would be taken to a small enclosure where he'd be dispatched by a

silver-knobbed knife with a thin blade called a *verduguillo. The little executioner.* He would be denied the glory of dying in the ring that he deserved and be slaughtered anonymously, without dignity, for food.

He tried to turn his head to look for Calladito, but he was no longer capable of any movement other than the gagging reflex that continued as his body struggled to clear his throat and prevent him from drowning in his own blood.

His hearing was still fine. He could make out the sounds of moaning and crying and shouting and a few women shrieking, but his vision was beginning to fade. The people crowded around and above him had dulled into indistinct black shadows against the brilliant blue sky.

When he had first fallen and his men had rushed to him, he had been able to make out some of their faces.

One of the first to get to him had been his senior banderillero, Paco, a whip-thin leathery man of impressive speed and indeterminate age who rarely spoke or smiled but whose devotion to Manuel was unquestioned. He was the only member of his cuadrilla who had been with him since the very beginning of his career.

Paco had knelt over him and placed his hand on his wound, and Manuel had glanced down the length of his body and seen scarlet

blood spurt between the old man's long brown fingers.

He had felt the pressure but no pain. Even when Calladito's horn had plunged beneath his rib cage, he hadn't felt pain.

In his mind he could still see Paco's lined face looming over him twisted into a rapture of anguish so keen it could have been mistaken for joy.

"Maestro." The word came from his throat as a sob. "Manolo mío."

He had known then for certain what he had only previously guessed. His prestigious title and the intimate usage of his name would only be uttered together in the ring in a moment of desperation: a soldier's last chance to speak to his leader, an old man's offering of comfort to a young man he loved. Paco was saying, "My prince. My son."

They were not going to be able to save him.

Once he fully understood this, he almost felt like laughing. He felt the giddy relief of being let in on a particularly good secret.

For most of humanity, death was a vague terror that constantly stalked them. How a man would meet his end was an overwhelming, distracting concept because there were literally thousands of ways for him to die; but for a bullfighter, there were only two ways to die: in the ring and out of the ring.

Now Manuel knew his fate and it was a good one, but it had come much too soon.

This was the only thing he would ever know for certain about his own death.

He would never know the exact cause, which would appear over and over again in newspapers around the world the following day along with photos of him stretched over the back of the colossal bull with its massive head buried in his lap looking like he was giving it an awkward hug: Manuel Obrador, the great matador El Soltero, had been gored by the bull Calladito. The bull's right horn had split one of Obrador's ribs and pierced a lung. He had died instantly, the Spanish newspapers would go on to say out of respect for his memory, in an effort to get people to concentrate more on the man and his deeds than the grisly details of his death and also because people wished it for him, but the firsthand accounts from people present at the corrida would spread like fire. These would be the facts the international papers would report, and soon it was all the Spaniards talked about as well.

How the blood sprayed from his nose and gushed from his mouth and bubbled from the long ragged rip in his gold-encrusted jacket with each of his gasps for breath. How he managed miraculously to get to his feet after the bull had been distracted by the other capes, and how he clamped his mouth shut, covering it with his hands, trying to keep back the blood, but he coughed and more red

poured from his nose and mouth. How he fell and his body jerked and shuddered from shock before it finally came to rest.

Even then he was still alive. Even now he was still alive. If someone had told him that this was considered dying instantly, he would have told them it wasn't as desirable an end as people made it sound.

His eyesight was gone now. He could hear noise but not distinct sounds. He continued gagging helplessly on the blood that kept filling his throat. He was suffocating and the lack of oxygen to his brain was making it impossible to focus his thoughts anymore.

He tried to recall again that first time he had seen Calladito. It was the first time he had taken Candy to a breeder's ranch, and the only time he had ever taken a woman along with him.

People who knew him well had been surprised by the gesture. Was it merely part of his seduction of a foreign beauty? they wondered; an attempt to impress her by showing her the size and savageness of the animals he was going to dominate with nothing more than a cape and a suit of crystal and beads? No. This didn't make sense. She had already seen him perform in one of his better corridas. In Sevilla. She had witnessed not only his bravery and his skill but had been exposed to the glamour and pomp of one of Spain's grandest bullrings and had heard the

worshipful shouts of "Olé!" given to him by the crowd, building slowly in ecstasy and intensity like chants in a religious ritual.

Could it have been simply because he enjoyed her company and her obvious female charms and wanted to spend as much time with her as possible? This was true, but he had pursued and been pursued by countless stunning, exciting women and had never felt compelled to take a single one of them to a hot, dusty ranch to be jostled along rutted dirt roads in an old Jeep in order to view animals that could potentially harm them.

He rarely allowed any woman anywhere near the more personal aspects of his life. His nickname El Soltero — the Bachelor — was well deserved.

The reason was very simple. Of all the women he had loved — Spanish and otherwise — he had never known one who understood and enjoyed bullfighting the way she did: a milky-skinned, copper-haired American rich girl whose wealth came from coal mines she said her brother had stolen and who she claimed to have left recovering in a private hospital bed after barely surviving an attack in his office by a starving miner during the height of a particularly long, ugly strike. She talked primly but thought radically, traveled with a friend she claimed she didn't know, and made love with a complete attentiveness and sweet earnestness that reminded him of

his own devotion to bullfighting during his apprentice days as a *novillero.* That's how he teasingly referred to their steamy siestas — her apprenticeship — although he often felt that he was the one who was finally being taught something new.

Unlike most of her countrymen and other Anglo-Saxons he had known over the years, she didn't regard bullfighting as a sport or a contest or disregard it disgustedly as a barbaric form of bloody entertainment. She immediately embraced the almost carnal pleasure and the horror of watching a lone man using elegance and restraint to control a dangerous wild animal, to take the creature's fear and anger and his own fear and anger and turn it into something solemn and beautiful and for one brief shining moment, something heroic for both man and beast. She realized it was a dance but a dance to the death.

Luis had told him the rumors were true. He had seen her in the stands sitting with the breeder, Carmen del Pozo. She had come back to him. She had come back to Spain.

He had decided the moment she left him that if she ever returned, he would make her grovel and beg before he would take her back; but when Luis caught his arm tonight before he paraded into the ring and said her name, all the pain and loneliness of the past months flew away. His wounded pride, his need for

vindication, the heartache he had carried around inside him because he knew he had been unfair to her, because he knew the sacrifice he had asked her to make was one he could have never made himself: none of it mattered anymore. He was going to get a second chance.

The bullring in Villarica was especially dear to him because it was the place he had seen his first fiesta de toros. As a boy, his father took him many times, and the times he couldn't go, he'd pause during his work and look in the direction of the ring whenever the band played and the crowd cheered or jeered and he would think: *This is what a man's life should be: extremes.* He should be adored or hated but never simply tolerated.

The ring was one of the most distinctive in Spain, not because of its splendor but because of its age. It was known for its roof over the last section of seats made of ancient blue, yellow, and white tiles set on top of pink stucco columns, and the rich, golden quality of its sand brought in from a special quarry miles away on the banks of the Tago River. From where he stood in his father's highest field, the town was a honeycomb of tiny orange clay houses clustered up against the ring with the overflow spreading away from it with seeming reluctance. The pale stone church stood on a hill directly behind it. In the setting sun it had a bright coral glow,

almost as if God knew it should wear a festive color this time of day in honor of his two favored beasts: hombre y toro.

As he had stepped into the ring tonight, he'd been flooded with memories of his past and expectations for his future. Never had he felt such potential for the extremes he had always craved. He would succeed with this woman and this bull and know love and adulation or he would fail and know loneliness and shame. Either way Death would be standing nearby, a presence as familiar as the heat and one whose interference he had learned to ignore long ago as completely as he did the nosy old neighbor ladies of his youth shouting after him to put on his shoes.

He had planned on dedicating the last bull of the night to her, an unusual chestnut beauty with a coat the same color as her hair. Later he would ask her to marry him again, but this time he would do it on his knees in his suit of lights, and he would promise they could visit this land of Pennsylvania she loved so much yet needed to escape.

He thought he heard her voice calling his name, sobbing.

"Manuel!"

He felt a weight on top of him and knew it was her. Her hair brushed against his cheek and got caught in the sticky mask of blood on his face.

"Manuel, no!"

Her breath against his ear.

"Manuel."

No longer sobbing. Trying to remain calm. Thinking she could stop him from dying if only she could talk sensibly to him.

"I was stupid. So stupid."

Her voice, high-pitched with grief, shaking uncontrollably but a voice nonetheless forming coherent words while all around him he heard crying, nothing but crying. The screaming and shrieking and wailing was over. The shouts for the doctor were no longer needed. All that was left to do was cry. Men crying. The most defeated sound in the world.

"Please. Don't leave me. I can't . . ."

Her words were cut off from him. He realized they were trying to lift him. He tried to say no. He didn't want to die on a hard white bed in a sterile infirmary surrounded by cold steel surgical instruments. He wanted to die here on the sand in the dying sun.

He barked a thick syrupy cough to try and clear his throat to speak and the action sent a final spray of blood over himself and Candy, consuming the last of his physical life but leaving him with a few more seconds of consciousness.

He saw Calladito's eyes a final time in his mind. The moment when the bull understood there was a man behind the cape. The moment when the coal miner understood there was a rich man behind an office door not pay-

ing him what he was worth. Fatal knowledge for one of them.

"Please, let him live!" she sobbed.

First in English. Then in Spanish.

"¡Por favor, ruego que lo deje en vida!"

He believed she was begging God for his life, and he was moved by her love for him and her American need to believe a man's fate could be changed.

The Spaniards would mourn him for weeks. They would line up for miles to attend his lavish funeral. They would write poems and songs about him. But not a single one of them would have ever pleaded with God for his life, because on some level, they would all be glad that he had died.

Alive he had been a great matador — an artist and a star — but by dying in the ring he had fulfilled a torero's destiny and became the beloved ending to the fairy tale that was Spain.

He didn't know that she and everyone else crowded around his body already knew he was dead. She wasn't begging for his life. She was begging for the life of the bull who had killed him.

Part I
Muerte En El Acto

Chapter One: Kyle

I hope he was drunk. I guess it's probably not the best thing for a kid to wish when his dad was out driving, but I don't care. If he was drunk, he was either happy or mad; he was either singing along with the country-western station while thinking about beer-commercial-caliber women and Klint's future, or he was scowling into the black night muttering about the latest injustice life had dealt him; but either way he wouldn't have realized what was coming.

People are finally starting to leave. I can hear their low voices outside my window and the crunch of gravel beneath their tires as they pull out of our driveway and away from the side of the road.

Red and blue lights flash on my wall for an instant as the state trooper starts up his cruiser. He told me earlier if Dad had been wearing his seat belt he might have lived, which to me was like saying if he'd been a foot taller he might have been a better

basketball player.

He wouldn't tell me if he was drunk or not. He said it didn't matter, and I wanted to yell at the top of my lungs, "It's the *only* thing that matters!" but I knew everyone in the room would look at me like I was crazy. Crazy with grief, they'd say, when all I am is sensible.

A creaking footstep stops outside my bedroom, and I close my eyes so whoever looks in on me will think I'm asleep.

The door opens. It shuts. The footsteps walk away.

I keep my eyes closed not because I'm tired but because everything in my room reminds me of Dad. We didn't have a lot in common; about the only interests we shared were hot wings and Klint. Most of the stuff I own I have in spite of him: my books, my four-foot-high erector set model of the Eiffel Tower I built when I was eight and never dismantled, my art supplies and sketch pads, all my drawings and paintings in various stages of completeness scattered everywhere, all the cool rocks, bird feathers, dead bugs, dried leaves, bones, and pieces of broken glass I've collected on my treks through the woods that Dad called my "nature crap," and my set of Van Gogh playing cards I got on a seventh-grade field trip to the Carnegie Art Museum in Pittsburgh. Everything in this room belonged to a kid with a dad, and those things

are still here and he isn't. I had a dad this morning. I had a dad four hours ago.

How can someone be gone just like that?

He had plans. This is the thing I can't stop thinking about. They weren't big plans. Nothing ambitious or complicated or admirable. Definitely not anything that could ever be considered a goal. His needs were simple, and his desires even simpler.

Take today for instance. After Klint and I started off to Hamilton's farm for their annual September barbecue, we knew he planned to drive to the Rayne Drop Inn for Wing Night. He was going to tie one on with a couple of his buddies and eat greasy chicken drenched in hot sauce. He'd shoot some pool and hope to pick up a woman, but he'd never succeed at it. He planned to drive off into the inky black country darkness in his truck with the new chrome deer antlers mounted on the grill, confident in his ability to get safely to where he was going despite his inability to remember where he was going and why he had left the place he was leaving. He planned to sleep until noon the next day and watch the Steelers game. Then he'd go to a job he hated on Monday because it paid the bills. But, most important of all, he planned on living.

What's the point of even making plans if they can be erased in an instant? What's the point of even getting up in the morning?

I pull my knees up against my chest and try to make myself into a little ball. My jeans smell like dirt and a smoky wood fire, and my hands smell like the hot dog I roasted for Shelby Jack just a couple hours ago.

I pull my T-shirt up to my nose to see if any of Shelby's scent rubbed off on me. She always smells good. I don't know if it's from a soap she uses or a shampoo or perfume or maybe it's just the way she smells naturally. I can't describe it because there's nothing to compare it to. It's purely her.

Talk about having plans. I had plans for tonight, too. Sitting next to her on a log, our shoulders touching, the fire so hot in front of us and the night air so cold on our backs. Her laughing and smiling and smelling Shelbylicious.

It took everything in my power not to reach out and touch her hair. Not because I'm a sex fiend or disrespectful to women or anything like that. My fingers are drawn to it the same way they're drawn to the velvety noses on the Hamilton dairy cows.

It's long, shiny, and dark and in the firelight, parts of it have a reddish glow like there might be a coal smoldering underneath it.

I was planning on kissing her and finally touching her hair. I'd fantasized about it for a while. Then I decided to make it a goal, something I could work toward, something I

was definitely going to do or else feel like a loser.

I didn't even care that she had a thing for Klint. All the girls around here are nuts over Klint. They're always parading around in front of him in tight jeans and short skirts, pretending to stumble in the hall at school so they can bump up against him at his locker, calling their friends to find out if they've heard whether he's going to show up at so-and-so's party or whether he'll be at the football game on Friday or which night he's going to the Laurel County Fair. (And it's always been the same night his entire life: Monster Truck Night.) They can try all they want. They don't know what I know or if they did know, they'd think I was exaggerating.

People say the reason priests don't have sex is because they're married to the church. Klint's married to baseball.

That doesn't mean he loves baseball. I think the love has already gone out of it for him the same way love seems to go out of most marriages. But it doesn't seem to matter to him. He's committed for better or worse, in sickness and in health, 'til death do him and second base part.

I had been ready to make my move on Shelby. I had roasted a perfect hot dog for her: golden, charred just a little, the skin starting to split, and the juices leaking out. I asked her if she wanted me to get her a bun

and she said no, she wanted to eat it off the stick. I told her that's my favorite way to eat it, too, and she gave me a funny look and said, "I know, Kyle. I've known you forever."

I liked the way she said it. I liked that it was true.

I was about to tell her I thought the fire was getting too hot and ask her if she'd like to take a walk, but then Bill came driving up to the barn and got out of his truck, crying.

I get up off my bed and head to my window to look for Mr. B. I know there's no chance he'll come around with all this commotion going on, but I'd like to see him.

Something in the carpet catches my eye, and I stop to pick it up. This used to be my little sister's room, and every once in a while I find some tiny sparkly reminder of her. It's usually a bead from a jewelry-making kit, or a sequin from her dress-up clothes, or a dried dab of glitter glue.

This time it's a little silver high-heeled Barbie doll shoe.

I stick it in my pocket and continue on to the window. I push open the screen and lean out and try to make my mind a blank.

I know I'm not doing the things I'm supposed to be doing.

I haven't prayed for Dad's soul yet. I haven't even thought about heaven and, if it exists, if he's up there lying on a couch made of clouds drinking from a solid gold beer cozy

shooting the shit with Roberto Clemente. Or if it's the kind of heaven where he wouldn't care about beer and baseball and couches anymore and he'd just float around being blissful. I haven't tried to comfort myself by believing that either one could be true and that someday I'll see him again when I die.

I haven't cried yet.

Klint did. He bawled like a baby. I couldn't watch him. I walked away because I knew if I stayed, I'd start crying, too, but I would have been crying because my brother was crying, not because my dad was dead, and that seemed wrong.

I haven't let myself really think about what happened. I haven't asked myself all the important questions, like once he missed the curve and lost control, did he know he was going to die? When his truck started somersaulting down over the mountain, did he have time to understand what was happening? Was he scared? Was he sad? Did he think about us? Was he worried about what would happen to us? Did his life flash before his eyes like it's supposed to? Did he see a movie in his mind where he was a little kid getting tucked into bed by Grandma Bev, and then he was a young man marrying Mom, and then he was a proud father watching Klint get his first Little League MVP trophy?

Did it hurt? The state trooper said he died instantly. Died instantly after having his neck

broken. What about before he died instantly? What about while his neck was being broken?

What if terror, pain, and loneliness were the last things he felt, and now there will never be a chance for him to feel anything else?

I haven't asked myself any of those questions yet.

All I can think about are his plans. He had a lot of plans but no goals. He and Mom used to fight about that, but they used to fight about a lot of things so I never placed more importance on that particular topic than any other. Maybe I should have.

I remember when I started sixth grade three years ago, our new teachers gave us one of those getting-to-know-you forms to take home and fill out. It asked things like: What's your favorite subject? and Do you have any special concerns about integrating into a larger student population? One of the questions was: What are your goals for middle school?

I was reading that question out loud to Mom while I was sitting at the kitchen table and she was trying to tear open a bag of frozen french fries without breaking a nail and without letting the ash from the end of her cigarette fall onto the counter — a feat I always regarded as a skill — when Dad and Klint came through the back door. Dad was all smiles, which meant Klint had a good

night in the cage.

Dad had heard the question and he grinned at me and rubbed his knuckles on the top of my head as he passed by on his way to the fridge for a beer and said, "Goals are what you score in hockey."

Mom had resorted to trying to tear the bag open with her teeth. I saw her give him a nasty look over the top of the bright red Ore-Ida bag before she took it out of her mouth long enough to tell him that just because he was a loser without any goals didn't mean he should try and make his kids losers, too.

He slammed the refrigerator door hard enough to make the dishes in the cupboards rattle. Mom made a motion like she was going to throw the bag of frozen fries at him, but she thought better of it and put it back between her lips and he walked back outside.

I didn't think anything of it at the time. My parents were always loud and violent with each other, even when they weren't fighting.

Sometimes they were loudly and violently in love and Dad would chase Mom around the house roaring about what a lucky man he was, and he would catch her and she would squeal and shriek as he smacked her butt or planted loud sloppy kisses on her neck, and Klint and I would watch gratefully as they went out to the bars to continue celebrating Dad's good fortune before returning home a few hours before dawn and waking us up with

thuds as they stumbled through the house on the way to their bedroom. The rest of the time they were loudly and violently not in love with each other: Mom throwing things and screaming at Dad that he was a loser who couldn't get it up, and Dad kicking furniture and telling her she was a lazy slut whose tits were starting to sag.

A few days after Dad's comment about goals Mom took our little sister, Krystal, and moved to Arizona with some guy we'd never heard of before.

I don't know if it had anything to do with goals. Maybe this guy had some and Mom liked them. Maybe Mom had some goals of her own, and we were all getting in her way.

I never turned in my form. I looked at it one more time and thought they should have included the question: How do you think you'll cope with middle school if your mom leaves?

"Mr. B.," I call out softly. "Where are you?"

I know exactly where he is on a night like tonight. He's out killing something, and even though death is one of his favorite preoccupations, the death of a human means nothing to him.

There's a knock on my door, and I close the window and sit down quickly on my bed.

"Kyle? You asleep?"

It's Bill.

"No."

"You want to come out to the kitchen for a minute? Your aunt Jen's gonna leave."

"Did all the other people leave?" I ask him.

"Yeah. It's just us."

I open the door a crack and see Bill standing in the hallway being careful not to look at me.

He's a big guy, beefy not fat, with shaggy salt-and-pepper hair, a broad, flat face, and small brilliant green eyes set so deep inside the folds and wrinkles of their sockets that they usually go unnoticed but every once in a while they flash like two emeralds lost at the bottom of a craggy canyon of skin.

He's leaning heavily on his cane. He had his leg broken in a mine cave-in six years ago. It was too smashed up to heal properly, and it still gives him problems. Some days he can't walk on it at all. Most days he talks fondly about J&P Coal and how he wishes he could be back on his crew. Every day he drinks. He says it's for medicinal purposes, but I think he does it to make the boredom go away as much as the pain.

He's been our next-door neighbor for my entire life. Before tonight, I've seen him cry exactly twice: once when Jerome Bettis fumbled in the final moments of the Steelers playoff game against the Colts a couple years ago and once from laughing so hard when my dad cut off the top part of his pinkie while trying to install his new chrome grill with the

deer antlers on the front of his truck.

They put the amputated part of his finger in my dad's beer cozy and took it to the ER, but it was impossible to reattach it, so Dad brought it home and set it on the front porch in a coffee mug and declared it to be a conversation piece.

People came from everywhere to see it. Dad would tell the story, then stick the nub of his pinkie up his nose. It looked like he was pushing a regular-sized pinkie much farther than it was supposed to go, and it never failed to gross out Klint's friends and make girls shriek and giggle.

Klint never laughed about it. Not once. He and Dad had some ugly fights over that stupid pinkie. Klint told him there was nothing funny about making people think he had so little inside his head that he could stick an entire finger up inside it, but like all their fights, what he was really saying was please stop drinking.

I knew something was terribly wrong when I saw Bill standing next to his pickup truck at the Hamiltons'. Even worse than the tears streaming down his face was the fact he had taken off his ball cap and was clutching it in both hands in front of his big belly.

Crying was one thing, but I'd never seen him take off his hat.

"It's your dad," he said.

We didn't need to hear anything else. I looked at Klint and he looked at me, and I could see myself in his face. It's the worst kind of fear, free-falling, no way to be saved, no way to turn back, like being pushed from an airplane.

We knew what the next words were going to be.

If Dad had broken his leg or been arrested or lost his job, Bill would have been smiling. Even if Dad had slipped into a coma, Bill would have made a joke about it.

Only one thing could have made him cry and take his hat off.

I was still staring at Klint as his lips started to tremble and his eyes turned glassy with tears.

This was Klint: a guy who could step up to a plate with a full count hanging over his head, two outs, a man on base, a tying run at stake, and smash a triple over the right fielder's head with the same calm he would have hit a practice ball with my dad in the backyard; this was a guy who could play four tournament games in a row on a ninety-degree Saturday and never complain and never make an error in the field; this was a guy who had broken his nose, his left thumb, pulled a tendon in his foot, and had a stress fracture in his shoulder by the time he was fourteen and each injury just seemed to make him stronger.

And now he was going to cry.

I covered my ears and closed my eyes and backed away. I was more scared of seeing Klint fall apart than hearing the next words out of Bill's mouth: "He was in an accident. In his truck."

"No," Klint said.

"I don't know how to tell you."

"No, no, no," he repeated, shaking his head.

"I'm sorry, boys."

"No!" he shouted. "No!"

That's when he started to cry, and I ran away down the road toward our house.

Bill reaches out and puts a hand on my shoulder, but he still doesn't look at me. He talks to the floor.

"You feeling any better?"

"No."

"Course not. That was a stupid question. I just meant . . . did you get any sleep?"

"I'm okay," I tell him, mostly to make him feel better.

It seems to work. He takes his hand off my shoulder, sighs, and starts limping into our living room.

It's empty except for Klint, who's sitting on Dad's easy chair, leaning forward, his elbows on his knees, his hands clasped together, staring into space, like he's listening intently to some invisible person's confession.

His eyes are raw and red from crying and

there are gray shadows of exhaustion beneath them but otherwise he looks like himself. Relief sweeps through me. I want to hug him. I want to feel his physical body and know that he's real, but Klint doesn't hug. Not even when he wins. He stopped hugging years ago. It wasn't a big deal for me or Dad to abandon the practice. Our hugs had been nothing more than pats on the back after a game. Mom took it much harder, though, and continued wrapping Klint in her arms even after it was obvious he was never going to return her embrace.

He glances my way.

"You okay?" he asks me.

"I'm okay. You okay?"

"I'm okay."

Aunt Jen is standing in a corner, smoking. She's Mom's sister. She's our only family around here, and I suppose it was good of her to come so fast on a Saturday night, especially since she never liked Dad except for when she tried to date him back when he was dating Mom.

Dad's only sibling is a half-brother who's a lot older than him and lives all the way in California. He's some kind of junior executive (even though he's over fifty). He doesn't drink, his kids all went to college, and, according to Dad, his wife thinks her shit doesn't smell.

He and Dad never had much to do with

each other as adults, not because of any profound dislike but more from mutual disappointment.

Dad's parents are both dead. He was a late-in-life baby, and his mom was a late-in-life wife for his dad. My grandfather was dead before I was born, and Grandma Bev died a couple months before Mom left with Krystal.

Mom's dad ran out on them when she was ten, and she's never been able to talk about him without her eyes going eerily blank, like the only way she can force herself to talk about him is by making herself not think about him. Her mom died of some kind of female cancer the year I was born. Mom and Aunt Jen have never provided more details than that to any of us, but sometimes they used to get together and discuss Grandma's condition for hours in intense hissy little whispers over a bottle of Tequila Rose and would always end up with their arms around each other crying before the alcohol fully kicked in, and then they'd remember all the jealousies and grudges they still held against each other, some going all the way back to grade school, and they'd start fighting.

Aunt Jen is pretty in a mean, skinny girl kind of way. There's nothing wrong with her face except the lack of anything soft or inviting about it. She reminds me of a viper I saw once at the Pittsburgh Zoo on a school field trip. It was covered in a geometric pattern of

sleek, bright colors. I thought it was beautiful until it woke up and fixed its beady eyes on me, and I realized there was nothing in them except self-preservation and poison.

"So I guess I need to call your mom," she says between puffs, "unless one of you boys would like to do it."

Klint slowly turns his head and fixes her with the same calm blue stare that makes all the high school pitchers within a two-hundred-mile radius quake in their cleats. It's the serenity behind the intensity that makes his gaze frightening. Everyone knows once he's in the zone, nothing can deter him from his mission. He will hit the ball, and he will hit it far.

I wonder what he's thinking about Aunt Jen, if she's the ball in this situation.

I try to see her through his eyes. He wouldn't equate her with a pretty, deadly snake. The sharp angles of her body and the coffee-stain color of her tan would probably make him think of a spider.

"There's no reason to call her," he says.

She stops smoking and matches his stare with one of her own, but her heart doesn't seem to be in it. She stalks over to the coffee table and grinds her cigarette into the lid of an old Skoal tin that's doubling as an ashtray.

"Of course there's a reason to call her. She's your mother. She's the only parent you got now."

"What are you saying?" Klint asks her. "Now that Dad's dead, she's gonna want us?"

"She's always wanted you. She left because of your dad not because of you boys."

"She left because she's a slut."

Aunt Jen whirls around on him, her snake eyes flashing.

"Don't you talk about your mother that way, boy."

"She's right," Bill pipes up from his corner of the couch. "You shouldn't talk that way about your mom."

Klint snorts disgustedly at Bill.

"I didn't say you were wrong," Bill defends himself. "You just shouldn't say it out loud."

"You would take Carl's side," Aunt Jen turns her wrath on Bill. "You always did."

"He's dead, Jen," Bill cries out. "For Christ's sake, the man's dead. Could you leave him alone for one goddamned minute?"

His outburst shuts up Aunt Jen and seems to take all the life out of him. His head droops from his wide shoulders, and I think he might start crying again.

I don't want to see it. I walk over to the front door. Someone's propped it open. The room was probably stuffy with all the people coming and going and everybody smoking. I went to my room pretty fast, so I don't know for sure what happened out here.

I wasn't here when Coach Hill showed up. I feel sorry for Klint that he had to go

through that. The only thing worse for Klint than finding out Dad was just killed in an accident would be having Coach Hill see him messed up.

I'm sure Coach came because he thought it was his duty. He needed to show that he's a caring guy who realizes his players have lives and emotions that extend beyond the bleachers even if he doesn't understand why.

Maybe he even thought Klint might need him, not to provide any emotional support but simply as a reminder that there were more important things in life than life and death. There was next season.

I only stayed in the living room long enough to see Shelby. I knew she would come right away, zipping along the road from Hamiltons' in the new convertible her dad just bought for her.

She's a year older than me, a sophomore, and already has her permit. She's not supposed to drive without an adult, but she doesn't care since her dad's Cam Jack, the J in J&P Coal, and there isn't a cop anywhere around here who'd give her a ticket.

She doesn't live here or go to school here, but she willingly spends most of her summers and some of her weekends here with her aunt Candace, who's supposed to be one of the meanest, ugliest, weirdest, richest old ladies to ever live. She calls our crappy little town "her country escape" and defends her

aunt by claiming she's misunderstood.

Shelby sees greatness in small things and beauty in wreckage, and that's why I love her.

She only stayed a few minutes but cried hard the whole time and seemed more upset than I was.

I don't think losing Dad has become real to me yet. It's still too easy for me to tell myself I'll see him in the morning. We'll make our regular Sunday brunch of eggs and sausage and bacon and ham steaks and Tater Tots and more eggs. I'm the cook, but Bill always brings the ham and sausage and Dad brews the coffee. Klint will eat everything I fry up along with a big bowl of Wheaties and a couple bananas, and Dad will make his joke about him being a friggin' health nut because he ate a piece of fruit, but he'll say it with a gleam of pride in his eyes. Afterward Dad and Bill will aid their digestion by driving to the beer distributor and then we'll watch football for the rest of the day until I say I've got to go do my homework, even though I already did it and I really just want to be alone and draw for a while, and then Dad will make his joke about me being a friggin' Rembrandt except there won't be any gleam in his eyes this time.

I could still believe that it would all happen again except for Shelby. She saw everything like she was watching a movie. She knew the plot. She knew there would be no regular

Sunday for me tomorrow; she knew there would be no regular Sunday for me ever again.

"Well, I'm gonna call your mom tonight," Aunt Jen announces.

I can't help feeling a little excited. Mom will have to come for the funeral. I haven't seen her for over two years. She's only come back for one visit since she left, and it was a disaster. I talk to her on the phone now and then, but it's not the same as seeing her. She's always distracted on the phone.

Maybe she'll move back now. Maybe we can live with her again.

I cross the room to Aunt Jen. It's the closest I've been to her all night, and the combined scent of her sugar cookie perfume and cigarette smoke makes me feel sick to my stomach.

"I suppose she'll come and take you boys back to Arizona with her," she continues and my heart plummets.

"What do you mean?" I cry out. "This is Klint's junior year. There are gonna be scouts looking at him. He's gonna get scholarship offers."

"So what?" she says. "He can play baseball in Arizona."

Klint flicks me an astonished look. I know for him she might as well have suggested that he could play baseball on Mars.

"You don't understand," I begin.

"They just lost their dad," Bill helps me out. "Don't start talking about taking them from the only home they've ever known. Their school and all their friends."

"And the team," I add.

She steps closer to me, and I smell sour sweat beneath the smoke and perfume.

"What do you boys think you're gonna do? Live here by yourselves?"

"Why not?" I ask.

"You're kids."

"Klint turns seventeen in a couple months. Next year he'll be eighteen. He'll be an adult."

She throws back her streaky blond head and eyes me critically.

"And what are you gonna live on? Is he gonna quit school and get a job? Are you?"

I don't have an answer for her. All I know is I can't quit school and I can't move. I have goals. I want to kiss Shelby Jack. I want to go to college even though I've never told anyone. I want to study art, not just think about it. I want to travel to other places, but Arizona's not one of them.

"It's up to your mother," she says. "You got no say in the matter."

I reach inside my pocket and finger Krystal's shoe.

I want my sister back but not at the expense of my brother.

Klint stands up.

"We're not going anywhere," he says. "If you talk to her, you can tell her that. Now why don't you leave?"

"Are you kicking me out?"

"It's my house."

She laughs sharply.

"It's gonna be the bank's house in a couple days."

"Until then, it's mine."

She grabs her purse and shakes it at him before sliding it over her bony brown arm.

"You got some nerve little boy, talking to me like that."

He doesn't respond. He stands his ground and looks right through her.

She won't fight him. Klint has an aura about him, the righteous power of the wrongfully condemned. Everyone recognizes it and respects it, but they don't understand where it comes from. I do.

He's been held captive his entire life by something more precious and terrible than any of Dad's lost plans or my stupid goals. Klint has a destiny.

CHAPTER TWO

I've never been to a funeral before. I guess that's because I've never known a dead person before besides my grandma Bev who died when I was eleven. I probably should've gone to her funeral but I didn't. Klint was playing in a tournament that weekend and even though Dad did everything he could to postpone the burial, he finally had to give in. "You can't fight nature," Bill had pointed out to him over a couple of beers on our back porch.

Klint got a ride with his best friend, Tyler, and his family, and Dad made me go with him. I've never missed one of Klint's games so it wasn't exactly a strange request. He told me I shouldn't feel bad about missing Grandma's funeral. He said she'd want me to be with Klint because it was important for Klint to know he always had someone from the family there rooting for him. I almost laughed when Dad said that, but then I realized he was serious. I knew that Klint could care less

if any of us were there. Half the time I don't think he noticed if anyone was in the stands. Jessica Simpson could have strolled in front of the batter's box, whipped her shirt up and flashed him, and Klint would have told her to "Move."

But Dad wanted me to go and I couldn't say no. He took Grandma Bev's death very hard, and the fact that he missed the tournament to see her get buried was one of the most powerful displays of love I'd ever seen. Even Mom was touched by it.

Mom's here. She got in last night. I thought she might come and see us right away but she didn't. She just showed up at the funeral.

She smiled at me when I went over to her, and gave me a hug, and ran her hand through my hair the way she used to, and told me she couldn't believe how tall I was getting. I expected it to feel good, but the touch of her fingers on my scalp sent shocks of pain down my spine.

I couldn't help remembering the last time I saw her before she left. I was on my way to the school bus. I had slung my backpack over my shoulder and stopped to give her a hug while she held her cigarette and coffee cup up in the air trying not to get ashes on me.

"I can't believe you still want to hug me every morning," she said. "I guess I should enjoy it 'cause in another year you'll be a teenager and you won't want me anywhere

near you."

I don't think that would've been true. I think I would've kept hugging her all my life, but even if I didn't want to, it would've been nice for me to have been able to make the decision.

She didn't want to make small talk. She didn't want to know about school or anything. All she wanted to do was smoke, and she had to go outside to do it so I followed her.

She had lost some weight and she was skinny to begin with. Her hair was blonder and puffier than before, and she had traded in her pink frosty lipstick for something orange and alarming. I told her she looked good. She smiled again and smoothed her short black skirt over her hips and said it's too hot to eat in Arizona.

We stood outside the funeral home for a little while. It's the most impressive building in town, which isn't saying much because most of the buildings are boarded up. Dad said when he was a kid — back before Lorelei, J&P Mine #5, closed — downtown was a happening place with stores and a restaurant and even a movie theater and a bank with brass handles on the doors and marble floors. Now the only places still open are a couple of bars, an old white church with stained-glass windows badly in need of a wash, a Kwiki-Mart, and this big funeral home.

I guess it's a crummy-looking town on the surface, but I always try to look deeper. Everything is sturdy and patient, soundly and sensibly built of wood and brick but decorated here and there with little touches of art like the bald eagle carved into the stone above the abandoned bank's doors and the gingerbread trim hanging in pieces from the eaves of an old dress shop like torn lace. All the place needs to make it nice again is a good cleaning and a purpose.

People started filing in past Mom and me. They all stopped to talk to me. Men shook my hand. Women burst into tears and hugged me. Kids from school who knew me muttered "sorry" and made some sort of brief physical contact whether it was punching my shoulder or brushing a hand against my arm or giving me a quick embrace. Kids from school who didn't know me, but were there for the spectacle and would spend tomorrow missing all their classes while they sat in the guidance office sobbing with the grief counselor, avoided me. Klint's teammates were somber and respectful in their dark sports banquet suits and all of them told me what a great guy my dad was and how they were going to miss him, even Brent Richmond, who was probably wishing Dad could've got killed during the upcoming season so Klint's batting would've suffered and he could be top man. Then came Coach Hill, who was prob-

ably thinking how relieved he was Dad didn't get killed during the upcoming season so Klint's batting wouldn't suffer. Klint's teammates shook me up the most. I'd never seen any of them in a group when they weren't in uniform, wisecracking, spitting tobacco, and calling me faggot and shit-for-brains.

Nobody talked to Mom.

I know it was awkward for her, but she had to have known it was going to be like this. It was Dad's funeral after all. These were Dad's friends. They all knew what she'd done to him and even though people like Aunt Jen said he deserved it, hardly anybody thought she went about it the right way.

It had come as a complete surprise to me. I think the only person more surprised was Dad. I knew my parents' marriage wasn't perfect, but at least it had been consistent. Dad drank a lot but not more than most guys. He held down a job. He never hit Mom. When he wasn't fighting with her, he was all over her. He brought her flowers for no reason and told her she made his life worth living. I've never understood what happened to make it so bad all of a sudden that she couldn't stay anymore or was it that this other guy offered her something so good she couldn't stay anymore?

But why no discussion? No warning? And even if she wanted to leave Dad, why did she leave me and Klint? What did we do that was

so wrong?

Standing there watching the grief parade troop past me, being clasped and grabbed and cried on and offered worthless words of advice and commiseration, I kept glancing at Mom smoking and pretending that she didn't care that everyone was ignoring her, and all I could think of were those questions and why I couldn't ask her any of them, especially the last one.

I look over again and she's gone. I don't know where she went. She probably got sick of the dirty looks and wandered off. I don't care too much because here comes Shelby Jack.

She's wearing a black dress and high heels and big black sunglasses and has her hair slicked back in a ponytail with a black bow.

I imagine rich people have the perfect outfit for every occasion. She probably has a charity luncheon outfit and one for watching tennis tournaments, so it would only make sense she'd have a funeral dress. I think she goes to a lot of old rich guy funerals. I know their family went to Ronald Reagan's funeral. Ten million other people did too, but they were actually invited.

I wasn't sure she'd come. She's missing school to be here.

She starts up the steps, sees me, and comes toward me, slipping off her sunglasses.

She's been crying again.

"Kyle," she says, then puts her arms around me and gives me a hug.

I let my hands lightly touch her back and her hair while she presses against my chest.

God, I'd give anything to be able to do this without someone having to die first.

"How are you doing?" she asks as she pulls away from me.

"I'm okay."

She takes my hand and squeezes it.

"I guess that's a really stupid question to ask someone at their father's funeral."

"It's okay. I know what you mean."

"Where's Klint?"

Klint. Of course, Klint.

"He's off somewhere with Tyler. He'll be back in time."

She keeps holding my hand.

"I saw your mom," she says with a frown.

Shelby knows all about Mom leaving us. She hates my mother, pure and simple. She won't accept any excuse for a woman leaving her children.

It hits me for the first time that the way I feel about Dad dying is pretty much the same way I felt about Mom leaving. Except I cried when Mom left. I cried every day for a month.

"Did you talk to her?" Shelby asks me.

"A little."

"And?"

"We didn't have much to talk about."

"What about Klint?"

"He left with Tyler as soon as he saw her."

She nods her understanding. I know she thinks Klint is acting the way he should, and I'm not.

"How did you feel? Seeing her again?"

"Good," I tell her.

I'm not lying, exactly. It's one of those things I can't explain to someone else.

I thought I'd be happy to see her again and I am, but it's a sick kind of happy, like what a wounded soldier must feel when he wakes up and finds out he's going to live but without his legs.

"Why is she here exactly?"

"I don't know," I answer her honestly.

I know what she's trying to ask. My heart beats faster thinking back to the night when Aunt Jen said Mom would make us move to Arizona with her.

I glance at Shelby's pretty face, then at the hills behind her. The green of summer has begun to fade and soon the bright colors of fall will appear in patches of orange, red, and yellow. The air smells like damp earth and dry leaves. It's warm and cool at the same time, like a breath.

What do I know about Arizona? It's hot. It's a desert. I imagine the air burning as I swallow it and cooking me from the inside out. Barren, treeless, huge white sun blazing down on tiny white houses, dry red dirt instead of moist black soil, horizons that

stretch on forever instead of comforting, worn-down old mountains surrounding us on all sides.

"Are you going to have to move?" she whispers.

"I hope not."

"What does Klint say?"

I sigh, irritably.

"Klint's not saying anything. He's spent the past two days hanging out with Dad's truck at Sledziks' junkyard. Bill says it's so smashed up you can't even tell what it used to be. Last night he came home with the chrome deer antlers off the grill, and his hand was all cut up and bloody."

"He's upset," Shelby interrupts me. "People do strange things when they're upset."

Her eyes stop me from saying more. There are tears shimmering in them again. I realize I've said more to her in the past few minutes than I've said to everybody else combined in the past two days. I feel embarrassed until I remind myself that she doesn't know this.

"Yeah, I guess so," I tell her.

She gives me a final squeeze of her hand and goes inside.

Bill comes and gets me a few minutes later. Bill in a suit and tie with no ball cap: the sight is so bizarre I can almost convince myself that none of this is really happening, that it's all a dream, but then he opens his mouth and says my name and I know it's real

because that amount of sadness can't be made up.

I follow him inside and sit beside him in the front row. Bill made all the arrangements. He's been taking care of everything. Last night while I sat with him at his kitchen table poking listlessly at the franks and beans he made for dinner, he told me with a certain amount of shame in his voice that he wished Klint and I could stay and live with him, but he didn't see any way he could afford to feed two teenage boys.

Klint wasn't even there. He was hanging out with Dad's mangled truck.

I told him we would've liked to live with him, too, that he was almost like a dad to us. He pulled the bill of his cap down lower over his forehead, stared at his beans for a moment, then got up and went and stood at the counter with his back to me.

For the first time since Dad died, I realized what a loss it was for Bill, too. He and Dad did everything together. They were drinking buddies and fishing buddies. They watched football and NASCAR together and went to all of Klint's games together. But probably most important of all, they hung out with each other almost every single night after Dad got home from work. The weather didn't matter. It could be pouring rain or bitter cold or stinking hot, and they'd stand on Bill's back porch, throwing back a few beers, shoot-

ing the shit, and bitching about life in the good-natured way of guys who don't mind the problems because they know overcoming them gives them something to do.

The worst part about someone dying is his eternal absence. I'll never see my dad again. I'll never talk to him. I'm going to have a big hole in my life now that can't ever be properly filled by anyone else. Maybe over time I'll forget the feel and smell and sound of him, the same way I am starting to forget Mom, but I'll never be able to forget that he should've been here.

All this funeral stuff — people dressing up, bringing casseroles and pies to the house, standing around casting pitying looks at me and Klint, whispering behind our backs — is meaningless to me. It has nothing to do with the reality of Dad's death. Even the casket sitting ten feet away from me has nothing to do with it. I know Dad's body is inside it but he's not. There's not a man in there, just a corpse.

We weren't allowed to see him. I don't know who made that decision but Bill stood by it. No one's going to see him again. It's a closed casket.

Apparently as Dad's truck was somersaulting down over the mountain while he was dying instantly, he crashed through the windshield, face first.

It's the kind of detail Dad would've loved

hearing if it had happened to someone else.

The funeral home director comes over and says a few words to Bill. He's asking about Klint. I glance around behind me, searching for him, and catch sight of Aunt Jen walking through the doors holding a little girl's hand. It takes me a second to realize the girl is Krystal. I haven't seen her for two years, and she's changed a lot. She's taller and thinner, and her hair is lighter. It used to be really long and she always wore it in a braid down her back; now it's cut to her shoulders and she has feathery bangs.

She's wearing a dark blue dress and I want to call out and make fun of her because she always hated dresses, but the way she's walking so straight-backed with a sort of snooty expression on her face makes me think she doesn't hate this one. She's clutching a matching purse in the hand that isn't holding on to Aunt Jen.

I smile and wave at her.

She gives me a startled look, then squints at me like she's trying to figure out who I am. Finally, she surrenders a little smile; it's not the kind of smile I expected, but it is a funeral after all. I wonder how Krystal is taking Dad's death. We used to talk on the phone. She used to talk to Dad, too, but about a year ago she stopped being available. That's the way Mom always put it: Krystal isn't available, like she was some kind of hot-

shot bank executive instead of a nine-year-old little girl with freckles.

They find Mom and just as they're all sitting down together, Klint and Tyler come walking in.

Tyler takes a seat with the rest of the team and Klint strides up the aisle, not looking at anybody, especially not Mom, and sits down next to me.

I try to zone out during the speeches. They're either too heartfelt and painful or too phony and disgusting for me to listen to. Dad would've liked some of them and would've laughed at others, especially the one from the minister who hadn't seen Dad inside his church for over ten years and probably wouldn't have recognized him even before his face went through a windshield. He called Dad an "occasional Christian," which I think was a nice way of saying he needed to tend to his hangover every Sunday morning instead of going to church.

I try to put my mind somewhere else, but all I come up with is thinking about the dead chipmunk Mr. B left for me this morning. I found it on the porch when the first lady from the casserole brigade arrived at the front door. She was standing as far away from it as she could get, and Mr. B was staring at her with his completely bored yet wholly alert cat gaze from his perch on his favorite tree branch. If she had gone anywhere near the

chipmunk, he would have sprung to the ground and scooped it up in his mouth and trotted off with it, but there wasn't any chance of that happening.

I let her in and as soon as she was gone, Mr. B joined me, purring ferociously and rubbing against my leg. I reached down and scratched him behind his ears to let him know I appreciated his thoughtfulness, then waited to see if he wanted the chipmunk for himself. He gave his paw a lick and walked off with a flick of his orange tail, which meant it was all mine.

I went and got a shovel and slid it under the limp little body and dumped it into the trash can. I used to bury everything he killed, but he would always dig it up and bring it back to me. Eventually I realized he expected me to eat it. The bodies were gifts. I could tell because he never purred so loudly as when he watched me encounter the latest clump of bloody fur or feathers he had left for me to find.

Even though my heart wasn't in it, I always tried to look happy and make my voice sound pleased as I thanked him, just like Mom used to do whenever I'd give her one of my construction paper Valentines.

Klint tries not to pay attention to the speeches, either. At one point I think he's fallen asleep, but he's only staring intently at a blue bead sitting near his foot on top of the

funeral home's stiff mustard-colored carpet. I wonder if it came off a lady's dress and if she was alive or dead at the time.

Finally the talking is over and everyone starts to get up. Klint and Bill and I are riding together to the cemetery.

I tell Bill I'll meet him at the car. I want to say hi to Krystal.

I manage to catch up with her outside on the sidewalk where she's standing with Mom and Aunt Jen.

"Hey," I call out to her happily, maybe too happily under the circumstances.

I stoop down and hold out my arms.

"Aren't you gonna give me a hug?"

She looks up at Mom, and Mom nods her head.

"Give your brother a hug," she commands and Krystal does but not very enthusiastically.

"I almost didn't recognize you. You look all grown up in that dress."

She looks at Mom again, and Mom nods again.

"Thanks," she says.

I'm beginning to get this creepy feeling that she can't say anything to me without Mom's okay. It's a stupid idea. It wouldn't make any sense but I can't help feeling it.

"Can I talk to you for a minute?" I ask. "Just the two of us?"

She flashes Mom a look of panic. Mom

shrugs and nods while she lights up a cigarette.

I take a few steps away. She hesitates, then catches up to me.

"You sure got quiet since the last time I saw you."

She doesn't say anything.

Her whole manner has changed. She doesn't smile, and she's lost her spunk. Maybe it's all part of the growing-up process for girls but when I think back to girls I knew when I was ten, they were some of the bounciest, chattiest, craziest creatures I ever knew.

"So how do you like Arizona?"

"We have a pool," she says flatly.

"That sounds great. If I had a pool I'd swim every day. Do you remember going swimming in the pond at the Hamiltons' farm? You used to love to jump off the tire swing into the water. You used to scream so loud."

"Our pool is clean," she states.

"Yeah, well, I'm sure it is."

I'm starting to get even more creeped out and also a little annoyed.

"So how do you like living with what's-his-name?"

This topic wakes her up. She opens her eyes wide and throws her head back.

"Mom told me you'd ask that."

"It's just a question."

"Jeff's nice. Much nicer than Dad."

Her words feel like a punch in the gut.

"You shouldn't say stuff like that. Dad was always nice to you."

The color starts rising in her pale cheeks. I hadn't noticed before but her freckles are gone. It doesn't make sense. They always got darker in the sun. After a summer of sitting on the steel bleachers at Klint's games, they used to stand out against her skin like a spattering of cinnamon.

"Do you remember that time he wouldn't let me go horseback riding with Ashley Riddle?"

I do remember because I had to sit in the backseat of a car with her for two hours while she cried and screamed about it.

"You were too little to go, plus Klint had the Dog Days doubleheader that weekend."

She screws up her face triumphantly.

"He always loved you and Klint more."

"That's not true."

"Mom told me you'd say that."

"It's not true. Dad loved you very much. He missed you like crazy."

"Then why'd he kick us out?"

Another punch to the gut.

"Dad didn't kick you out," I cry. "Mom left."

"Mom told me you'd say that."

"I was there Krystal. I know what happened."

I saw the look on Dad's face when he found her note. I even saw the note. It said: "I've

found someone else. Krystal's with me. If you know what's good for you, you'll leave us alone." She didn't mention me and Klint at all. Dad left it sitting on the kitchen table for a week before Bill made him throw it away. Dad wasn't embarrassed by it. He didn't care who saw it. He constantly wandered into the room and picked it up and just held it. I couldn't tell if he did this in order to make himself believe it was real or if it was because it was the last thing she had touched.

"You don't know for sure," Krystal says. "You only know what Dad told you, and he was a liar."

I can't have this conversation anymore. I'm starting to feel sick. I reach into the pocket of my suit pants and bring out her silver Barbie doll shoe.

"Here. I found this in the house. I thought you might want it."

She takes it, looks at it, and flicks it away into the street.

"Thanks," she says, "but I don't need it. I have tons of new ones."

"Krystal, honey." I hear Mom's voice.

She joins us and Aunt Jen slithers up alongside her. She's dressed entirely in black: black shoes, black stockings, black dress. She's got black liner around her eyes and has extra thick black lashes. Her hair's pulled up in a big messy yellow knot with two black sticks stuck in it. She's even wearing black

nail polish.

"Where's your brother, Kyle?" Mom asks.

I search the crowd milling around behind us, heading for their cars.

"I don't know."

"I need to talk to you boys."

"Can't we talk later?"

"We're not going to the burial. Krystal's too young to see something like that."

Mom notices Bill and Klint and calls out to Bill.

He turns her way and she waves at him.

"Bill! Bring Klint over here."

I wonder if Klint will come. So far his method of choice for dealing with Mom has been staying as far away from her as possible, but he surprises me by heading this way the moment Bill talks to him.

Bill ambles along behind with his rolling limp.

Klint arrives and stands at attention in front of her. When Dad died he fell apart at first because he was blindsided but now that he has it together, nothing will rattle him. Standing here in his dark suit and tie with his black shoes shined to perfection, he looks like he's the adult who should be telling everyone what to do.

"I'm going back to Arizona in two days," Mom announces from behind a veil of smoke, "and you boys need to be ready to leave with me."

"You're doing this now?" Bill asks.

"I don't need any shit from you, Bill," Mom snaps at him.

Klint laughs.

"We're not going anywhere with you."

"I told you," Aunt Jen whispers to my mom.

"I'm your mother. Your father's gone now, and you're going to live with me."

Klint laughs again. I know he's not much of an actor so he must genuinely find her suggestion funny.

"We don't have a mother," he replies, all the humor suddenly draining from his face.

"I told you," Aunt Jen says again, louder this time.

She puts an arm around Mom's shoulders sympathetically.

"I told you what he's done to them."

The devoted sisters: they only support each other when they're both fighting against someone else.

"You have to come with me," Mom repeats. "You have no choice."

Klint crosses his arms over his chest.

"Why is it so important to you? You didn't want us before."

"I did. Your father wouldn't let me take you."

He drops his arms and takes a step back from her.

"Your lies won't work on us."

He raises his hand and I see it trembling.

He jabs a finger in the air at her.

"There's no way you can make us live with you. We'll run away. We'll drop out of school and get jobs and live on our own."

"You can't do that. I'll send the cops after you."

"Send all the cops you want. Drag me back as many times as you want. I'll die before I'll live with you again."

People have come to a standstill and are gawking at us.

"And so will Kyle. Right Kyle?"

"Huh?"

"We'll drop out of school," Klint repeats. "We'll run away. We'll die first."

Everyone looks at me. Bill comes to my rescue.

He clears his throat and shifts his weight on his cane. I know his good shoes have got to be killing his feet.

He shakes his big shaggy head.

"I'm putting a stop to this right now. This is not the time or place to be having this conversation. Come on, boys. We have to get to the cemetery."

We turn to go.

"Dad was a drunk," Krystal pipes up in her high-pitched voice.

The hostility and inappropriateness coming from such a little kid makes us all stop and fall silent. Even Mom and Aunt Jen look shocked.

A mix of grief and revulsion passes over Klint's face like he can't decide if he wants to bawl or puke.

"Yeah, he was," he tells Krystal while staring straight at Mom with tears glittering in his eyes. "And Mom's a slut. One big happy family."

I hear Mom gasp, but we've already turned to go again, and this time we won't be coming back.

I want to run. I feel like if I took off and started right now I could run for the rest of my life. Never stop. Never talk to anyone. Never worry about having a home. Never care about anything except the weather.

People are staring at me. I try not to catch anybody's eye, but I can't help noticing Shelby. I let her catch up to me.

"You heard all that?" I ask her.

She nods.

"I wasn't spying. I swear. I was just standing there."

"It's okay. Pretty embarrassing, though."

She frowns.

"You should hang out with my family sometime."

I study her face to make sure she's serious. I can't imagine anything in her life being less than perfect.

"Do you think Klint's serious? Do you think he'd really drop out of school and run away?"

"I don't know."

Before today I would have said definitely not. I couldn't imagine Klint jeopardizing his golden future for any reason, but now I realize there's something inside him that's just as powerful as his desire to play ball and that's his hatred for Mom.

"Would you go with him?" she asks.

"I couldn't let him go by himself."

She nods slowly.

"I don't know what's going to happen," I tell her. "No one around here's gonna take us in. Who wants two instant kids who aren't even little and cute anymore? And who has the room or the money to feed us? You've never seen Klint eat. And even if someone wanted to do it, they'd probably have to fight Mom."

"Kyle!" Bill shouts at me.

"I gotta go."

"Okay."

She gives me a hug and walks away. She looked really sad. I want to believe it's because she might miss me — not because her sense of justice has been offended or, worse yet, because she might miss Klint — but I don't dare.

A glint of silver catches my eye mixed in with the cigarette butts and gravel next to the curb. I bend down and check it out. It's Krystal's Barbie shoe.

I pick it up and put it back in my pocket.

Bill and Klint are waiting for me inside the long black funeral car. As we're driving away I hear the sound of high heels clattering on the sidewalk, and I lean out of the open window and look behind us.

Shelby's hurrying after the car.

"Kyle," she calls out breathlessly, smiling and waving. "I'll call you tomorrow! I have a great idea!"

Chapter Three: Candace Jack

Shelby has just come to me with the most ridiculous idea.

Not only was the entire scheme absurd and indecent (I call it a scheme because that's what it sounds like to me, a scheme cooked up between two lovesick teenagers), but she seemed to feel I couldn't possibly say no, that it wasn't really a request at all but one of those "done deals" I've heard her discuss with her friends usually pertaining to romantic couplings and uncouplings or the buying of concert tickets.

I told her it was completely out of the question and she responded with such a look of wounded incredulity that I wondered for a moment if we were discussing the same thing. Her shock quickly turned to anger, and she accused me of never doing anything nice for anyone.

This simply isn't true. I do many things for people, although I detest the word *nice.* I hate anything vague. I prefer to say I sometimes

provide monetary assistance where needed and deserved, and I do it discreetly, so I may not seem nice to the general public, but I've never cared one iota for the general public's opinion.

What upset me most about her outburst was the underlying message that what she wanted from me was so commonplace that I would have to be a monster to refuse. Imagine asking a seventy-six-year-old single woman to provide a home for two teenage boys she's never even met!

What is this world coming to? When did children start running it?

Apparently, these boys have suffered a tragedy. Shelby told me the whole story about their father and their mother and how the boys don't want to leave their friends and their school. Well, of course, they don't. But they're children. That decision isn't up to them, and it certainly isn't up to me.

I think the man's obituary was in yesterday's paper. Yes, here it is.

I fold the paper and spread it out flat on my desk in front of me and put on my glasses.

Carlton Ray Hayes: the name speaks volumes, doesn't it? Age, forty. Born here. Died here. I assume he lived here in between. A graduate of Centresburg High School. Employed by Burke Pharmaceuticals as a custodial supervisor; in other words, head janitor. Survived by three children: Klinton, sixteen;

Kyle, fourteen; and Krystal, ten. Look at that . . . he and his wife managed to misspell two of their children's names. Member of the Crooked Creek Sportsman's Club and Lucky Lanes Bowling League. He enjoyed hunting, fishing, and playing horseshoes.

What? No mention of his favorite beer?

I glance at his picture. A not-bad-looking man. In his youth he was probably a handsome boy, but decades of drink and fried food had softened and discolored him. Alert eyes and a genuine smile, not the idiot grin or macho smirk a man usually wears when posing for a photo but an expression verging on authentic happiness. Wearing a Centresburg Flames ball cap and his gray work coveralls. A white patch over his heart reads: Carl.

I shouldn't be so cruel. The man is dead. He may have been a perfectly fine man. Not everyone is meant to be a captain of industry or a good speller. The world needs people to clean up, too.

I close the paper and leave it there, being careful not to cover up Rafael's letter. I received it yesterday but haven't been able to give it my undivided attention yet.

I walk over to the window, pull back the curtain, and look out at the front drive.

Shelby went running off after our argument. I'm not concerned. Her car is still here. It's a beautiful day. I'm sure she's sulking in the woods or hiding in the barn.

She went to this man's funeral yesterday and came here afterward and asked to spend the night. She missed school today as well. I called her mother to ask if she was allowed to do this and in typical Rae Ann fashion, she told me Shelby was already doing "too well" in school and could use a few days off to "lighten up." Rae Ann is a former Miss Florida runner-up who wanted to work at Sea World, but married a very rich man with the sexual maturity of a thirteen-year-old instead. Her aspirations for her daughters are just as high.

Cameron never returned my calls.

I think I'll go look for my grandniece and Ventisco, too. I haven't seen him for a few months despite my lengthy walks and drives in the Jeep with Luis hoping to catch a glimpse of him. He's wandered far, which is not surprising this time of year. The weather is perfect for him. The sun doesn't get too hot during the days, and the nights aren't cold yet. The grass is in its final lushness, and the air has a slight fall nip to it that makes every creature want to frolic. He's having a good time and doesn't want to be anywhere near the scent of man.

I walk to the front door and slip on my shoes and my scarf. I won't need a coat.

Yesterday Shelby told me I dress like the Queen of England (she had just watched the film *The Queen,* with Helen Mirren), and she

obviously didn't mean the comment to be a compliment.

I told her the Queen of England is one of the wealthiest women in the world, she's over eighty and still walks several miles a day, and she has her own navy. That shut her up.

However, I do not dress like the Queen of England. I do favor sensible shoes because at my age I have no choice, and I do prefer to wear simple, well-tailored dresses and skirts rather than pants. I also have an ancient, olive drab, waterproof overcoat with plenty of pockets and a favorite silk scarf I tie over my hair whenever I walk my property, but these are superficial similarities. Our styles are nothing alike. Her hats; dear God! Not to mention, I've always been slim.

From the front porch, I can see down the white gravel drive to the point where it disappears into a copse of large maples with broad pointed leaves beginning to turn a dusky red. The hills roll away from the house in waves, reminding me of the sea, only this sea is grass green and solid. They end calmly at the foot of the humble mountains that surround all in this valley. This time of year they look subdued and patchy, almost like a shabby old couch, but this is only temporary before they will explode into a carnival of fall colors.

I never tire of this view, and I never tire of this porch. It's one of my favorite places. It runs the entire length of the house and is

fully wide enough to drive two cars, side by side, from one end to the other. The white stone columns set in square bases of red brick reach to the second story.

I have it furnished eclectically with various odd wicker and rattan pieces I've collected over the years, which are scattered with plump cushions and draped with fringed Spanish shawls.

My brother built this house more than fifty years ago. He chose basic red brick and white mortar, designed it simply and impressively. It is enormous and imposing and unlike many of the mansions I've visited in my lifetime, it still looks and feels like a home, not a palace or a tomb or a Marriott.

We lived here together for close to five years before he married the Mouse and brought her here to live also. It was understood I would stay on not only because the house was more than big enough but because of Calladito.

Even though the bull caused one of the worst fallings-out Stan and I ever had, he allowed me to keep him here. I could be cynical and say it was because after the prodigious amount of money I spent on him, Stan regarded him as an investment and felt he needed to keep an eye on him, but I think it was his way of trying to be good to me.

Stan was incapable of expressing compassion with words or caresses or even overt acts

of kindness. He could only show he cared by putting you into his debt and then allowing you to be thankful to him.

Life with the Mouse never bothered me. I was deep into my mourning and barely noticed her existence.

I knew he would eventually marry — despite his unabashed womanizing — because I knew he wanted a son, but considering the number of beautiful women he'd had in his bed it was nearly impossible to imagine him inviting the Mouse into it and keeping her there for the rest of his life. She was such a strange choice.

But I suppose that's often the case with men like him. They marry the dowdy ones. They don't want pretty, active wives they have to keep happy and entertained or ones who other men might find attractive. They want someone to share their lives who will be unobtrusive, blindly devoted, tied to the home, and who will keep her mouth shut. The Mouse was all this and more; she also gave him the all-important son.

When Cameron was born, Stan was the one who decided he didn't want to live in "the goddamned sticks" anymore, as he put it. He built another mansion closer to Centresburg — which is still very much the goddamned sticks in my opinion — where J&P Coal had its headquarters and moved the Mouse and the Turd with him.

He gave this house to me. It was the beginning of my fortune.

I decide to look for Shelby in the barn first. I'm on my way there when I come across Jerry tinkering with one of the tractor mowers.

"Hello, Jerry."

"Afternoon, Miss Jack."

"Have you seen Shelby?"

He straightens his long thin frame slowly from a crimp in the middle like the unbending of a stubborn wire. His gray work pants, shiny at the knees with age, and his red-and-black-checked flannel shirt are speckled with grease and dirt.

In the past I've offered to replace his old work clothes since he wears them out in my employ, but he always took offense at the suggestion and acted as if I intended to dress him in the full regalia of a servant to an eighteenth-century duchess. Eventually we agreed that I would add extra money to his paycheck twice a year as part of a clothing budget. I have no idea what he does with this money.

He takes off his ball cap, folds the bill in half, and stuffs it into his back pocket. His hair is white and thinning, and his face is sunburned the deep dark red of a farmer and heavily lined.

I've never been able to imagine Jerry as a boy and I even find it difficult to remember

him as the dark-haired, monosyllabic, rustically appealing victim of my brother's mines who came to me forty years ago offering his services as a handyman.

Instead I think of him springing fully formed from the earth exactly the way he is now: an old man but not old in human terms. He's as strong as an ancient tree, as permanent and weather-resistant as a boulder that's been lying in a field for centuries, and as patient as a river carving a canyon.

"Saw her in the barn a few minutes ago," he says.

"Thank you."

I start on my way again, then think to ask, "Oh, Jerry. There was a man in town who was killed a few days ago in a drunk driving accident."

"Carl Hayes," he says, nodding.

"Did you know him?"

"Some. Not well."

"What can you tell me about him?"

"Well, let's see."

He scratches at the white stubble on his cheek.

"Think he worked pushing a broom over at Burke's. Think he worked in Lorelei before the layoffs started. His wife left him a few years back for another man. Took his little girl and left him and the two boys high and dry. The oldest one is a heck of a ballplayer from what I hear. He used to talk about those

boys all the time. Loved those boys."

"I thought you said you didn't know him well."

"It's a small town, Miss Jack. Not knowing someone well means you know basically everything about 'em but you've probably only talked with 'em once or twice."

"I see. Any word on Ventisco?"

He begins scratching the other cheek.

"Talked to Luis couple days ago. Said he saw him over near Spring Creek when he was out riding."

"That's strange. He didn't say anything to me."

Jerry slips his cap back on, his sign that he's used up his quota of words for the day.

"Thank you," I tell him again and walk on.

I don't have to go far before I see Shelby walking toward me coming from the barn.

She's changed her clothes since we talked this morning. She's wearing a flannel shirt that's threadbare enough and large enough that it could belong to Jerry. Her jeans are baggy and torn at the knees. She's wearing a pair of black work boots, caked in mud, with the yellow laces untied. Her lovely auburn hair, so like my mother's, is pulled back in a ponytail and covered with a dusty blue ball cap.

She's staring glumly at the ground, kicking at stones and watching them skitter away from her oversized boots.

She's a capricious girl: sweet and appeasing one moment; stubborn and cocksure the next. It would be easy to label her as moody or emotional, but I've observed her around others and she's entirely in control of herself. Of the three sisters, she is my favorite. However, all three of them are dangerously volatile when pushed out of their roles. That whole family is entirely too thin-skinned and excitable. Spending a day with them, I feel like I'm surrounded by little yappy lap dogs with expensive clothes and good haircuts.

I wonder if Shelby's outfit was put together for my benefit. She knows I don't approve of girls dressing sloppily or masquerading as boys.

She'd be an absolute picture on a day like today wearing a sundress and sandals and a shawl. What a shame.

She looks up, catches my eye, and pulls her cap lower.

"A pretty young girl like you should not dress like a hobo," I tell her sternly.

"Hobo?" she wonders.

"Yes, hobo," I repeat impatiently. "Tramp, bum, derelict, vagrant, vagabundo. What is the politically correct term these days: housing challenged?"

"That's not funny, Aunt Candace."

"Shelby, I think you owe me an apology."

"For what?"

"For saying that I never did anything nice

for anyone."

She drops her head and begins kicking at the whitewashed gravel again.

"You know what I meant."

"No, I don't know what you meant other than what you said."

She sighs.

"I just meant that you have *so* much. You have this huge house and all this land and so much money, and there's only you. Don't you ever feel like sharing it? And I don't mean sharing it with charities and foundations. That's being nice, too, but I mean sharing it with someone you love."

"But I don't love these boys. I don't even know them."

"Then would you at least meet them?" she asks, a smile lighting up a face so full of innocent benevolence that I can't help but wonder at its true intent.

"No, I most certainly will not meet them."

The smile is gone.

"See, that's what I mean. You won't even consider it. Why not?"

"Shelby, this is ridiculous. It can't happen. You have to understand. Even if I wanted to do it — which I absolutely do *not* — old women can't walk around picking up teenage boys off the streets and installing them in their guest bedrooms."

"You can do whatever you want. You're Candace Jack."

"Shelby, please. You sound like your father when you talk that way."

"Dad says I sound like Grandfather when I talk that way."

"It's true that my brother might have said the same thing, but he would have meant that I can accomplish whatever I want because of who I am. He wouldn't have been implying that just because I'm wealthy and respected . . ."

"And feared," she says under her breath.

". . . I'm exempt from following the same moral guidelines that everyone else does."

"Dad says that's one of the perks of wealth."

"Yes." I rub my temples. One of my instantaneous Cameron headaches has arrived. "I'm sure he does say that. Legally, I simply couldn't do it."

"I see what you mean. You'd have to get permission from their mother."

The smile returns, and she rushes to my side and takes my hand.

"I have a better idea. Instead of meeting them, meet their mother."

I shake my head at her.

"Come with me," I tell her. "Let's take a walk."

We start down the drive toward the road. She keeps her hand in mine and begins to swing it the way she used to as a little girl when we'd take these same walks together, and for a moment my eyes sting with tears

that I don't want or understand.

I've been entirely too emotional lately, and I fear it's one more uncontrollable, annoying aspect of aging.

"You don't understand about their mother," she goes on. "She's awful. She's . . ."

"She can't be that bad."

"She is!"

"I know that she left their father for another man and left the boys with him, but you don't know the circumstances."

"It's not just that." She shakes her head vehemently. "I knew her before she left. And I just saw her again at the funeral."

"What exactly did she do that was so terrible? Did she beat them? Did she fail to feed them or get them their booster shots? Is she an alcoholic?"

"I don't really know about any of that. I don't think so. She's just mean and selfish."

I laugh.

"You've just described the majority of the human race."

"No." She continues shaking her head. "I wish I could make you understand."

She looks up at me and pleads with her dark eyes.

"You're the only one who could put her in her place."

"Don't try manipulating me."

"Okay," she says with a pout, "it's just hard to see someone you like have a bad mother.

Especially when you have a good mother."

I think about Rae Ann, pretty, vacuous, annoying, affected, misguided, overindulged Rae Ann. She has her flaws. She has many flaws, but neglecting her children is not one of them.

"You understand what I'm saying, right?" Shelby asks. "You had a good mother, didn't you?"

"Yes, I did."

"What was Great-Grandma like?"

Her question catches me off guard. I don't think she or her sisters have ever asked me about either of my parents. Cameron used to ask me about them when he was a child because his own father would never talk about them.

"You know she died when I was young. Not quite as old as you are now."

She nods solemnly.

"That must have been the worst thing in the world."

"It was."

I pause for a moment to gather my thoughts.

My mother has long ceased being a person whom I can describe to others. I can't remember the sound of her voice or the smell of her skin or even any of her physical characteristics other than a pink scar on her hand I used to trace with my finger when she would hold me on her lap and rock me to

sleep and the long hair she used to unpin from the top of her head every night before bed and I'd watch pour down to her waist like a copper waterfall.

She represents a certain time to me, a time when my life was filled with hardship and hunger, yet it was somehow more peaceful and enjoyable than any life I've known since, a time when I felt safe and could still hope.

"We were very poor," I tell Shelby. "What I remember most about her was that she was always working and she was always tired."

"But you knew she loved you?"

"Yes, I knew she loved me."

We walk on in silence for a while. I scan the green hillsides looking for Ventisco even though I know my search will be in vain. We won't see him near the house. He's a wild thing living among tamed people. He stays away not out of fear or even dislike but simply because he has no use for us.

"Do you like this boy?" I decide to ask her.

"We're friends. That's all," she answers, but I detect a slight blush to her cheeks.

"Do you like the other one?"

The blush deepens.

"I like both of them."

She stops suddenly and looks me directly in the eyes. Hers are genuinely pleading.

"Aunt Candace, I can't explain it to you. It's just that . . . I know if they go live with her, she's going to destroy them."

I'm listening to her and watching her face, when something beyond her in the field catches my attention.

A heavy black shadow emerges from the tree line, tosses its head several times, then bounds forward at a slow, rollicking gait.

"Look," I whisper to her.

She follows my line of vision and turns around at the fence to face the hills sloping upward and away from us.

"I see him," she says excitedly.

The bull, silvered by the sunlight, raises his head as if he heard her. He stands perfectly still, a magnificent broad-shouldered ebony creature who obeys nothing but his own will.

"He's beautiful," she breathes.

He is so reminiscent of Calladito I can't help but recall the first time Manuel pointed him out to me at Carmen del Pozo's finca. "Éste es para mí, y yo para él," he said. *That one is for me, and I'm for him.*

In his heavy, muscled body was such a concentration of unthinking power that the only word that came to my mind was "beast." Here was the beast of all beasts. What creature could possibly threaten him? I imagined it would be easier for a man to chip away at a wall of coal with a toothpick than to try and conquer this dense, black mass with only grace and a cape.

I had seen bulls in America, but Calladito was my first exposure to El Toro.

"How long will he pose like that?"

"He's not posing. He's seen us and he's deciding if he's going to charge or not."

As if on cue, he takes a step backward, lowers his head to show us his horns, and paws the ground several times.

Shelby grabs my arm and pulls us back from the fence.

"Oh my God," she gasps.

I can feel her heart beating in her hands.

"Don't move. If you don't move, he can't see you. We're far enough away that we must be a blur to him."

"Could he break through the fence?"

"It's possible."

He decides not to charge. He snorts a warning in our direction, then walks back into the trees, taking his time, slowly bobbing his majestic head from side to side like a king acknowledging his subjects.

"That was intense," Shelby says.

She loosens her grip on my arm and while I watch her begin to calm down it strikes me that although fear and love can be faked like any other emotion, they are the only two, when genuinely felt, that can't be hidden.

Chapter Four

My brother grew up poor and determined while his son grew up rich and useless.

I've witnessed this phenomenon many times, and I've never quite understood how these dynamic, driven, visionary self-made men can fail so miserably and consistently at raising their children.

I think a large part of the problem comes from the fact that they're torn between the values that made them capable of becoming successful and the values they've embraced since their success. They preach one set and act out the other set, and as everyone knows actions speak louder than words, especially when the words are critical and the actions are a never-ending stream of undeserved rewards.

Any sensible person would realize a man can't expound upon the ethics of hard work and the necessity of making his own way in the world and then buy his son an extravagant sports car when he turns sixteen and expect

the boy to care at all about making his own way. He can't preach about moral decency and honesty and then when his son comes to him because he forced himself sexually on the underaged daughter of one of his father's coal miners the father responds by giving the miner a great deal of hush money. Months later when evidence of the boy's crime is gone, the father lays off the miner and blackballs him so he and his family are forced to move away. He can't stress the importance of education, then allow his son to spend his college years drinking and whoring and barely maintaining a C average. He can't lecture about the need to understand the world community and then lead his son to believe that a spring break spent in the Bahamas and a cruise ship stop in Cozumel constitutes "going abroad."

But probably the most insurmountable difference between these generations is that the principle that drove the fathers the most is completely absent from their children's lives: survival of the fittest.

My brother wasn't a saint. He made his money on the backs of other men and was indirectly responsible for many of their deaths and directly responsible for two in particular. Yet he worked harder than any man I've ever known, took care of his family, and gave generously to his community.

Can killers have ethics? I believe so, just as

I believe a mother — a giver of life — can have ice in her veins.

I understand that Cameron was not brought up well and that all his faults are not of his own making, but there comes a point when a boy must take on the responsibilities of manhood, and the first one he must tackle is choosing what kind of man he will become.

Cameron chose wrongly.

I've been blessed by his presence this evening. He and Rae Ann have just arrived.

I'm not happy about this. I suspect Shelby had a hand in it, but I'm not sure why she would want them here.

She claims this was her mother's idea, that she suddenly realized coming to my house this evening would be a convenient opportunity for her to see Shelby, who attends a private boarding school that is a ninety-minute drive west from her parents' home and a twenty-minute drive northeast from my own. Rae Ann has calculated that by coming here to see her daughter she will save herself some time; exactly how much she's not sure. The inability to do the math sounds like Rae Ann, but paying an impromptu, non-obligatory visit to me does not.

Yet here they are, the two of them emerging from Cameron's big black Cadillac.

Shelby's sisters are away at their respective colleges.

The oldest, Skylar, is a self-absorbed, stun-

ning blonde with the vulgar vocabulary of a cranky pop star.

Starr is the middle daughter, the troublemaker, the car crasher, the marijuana smoker, the caught-naked-with-a-boy-in-her-parents'-bed-all-before-the-age-of-seventeen daughter. She shares her father's tendency to pick fights and Rae Ann and Skylar's fair coloring but not their shiny glamour. She's the final member of the blond trifecta: mother, daughter, and holy terror.

"Hi, Aunt Candy," Rae Ann calls out, waving wildly with one hand and clutching her hideous Chihuahua with the other.

I try to arrange my features into something approximating a smile, but I'm afraid the best I can do is a grimace.

There have only been three people in my life whom I've allowed to call me, "Candy." Rae Ann is not one of them, but over time I gave up trying to get her to call me Candace because I realized she's simply incapable of it. She's one of those people who must give everyone a nickname.

Shelby bounds down the steps, squealing, "You brought Baby."

I can't watch. I greet my nephew instead.

"Hello, Cameron."

" 'Lo Aunt Candace."

He comes lumbering toward me. His gait is less plodding than it used to be now that he's lost weight due to his recent illness, but he

will always have the slow, heavy stride of a man who feels he's too important to hurry for anyone.

He underwent a kidney transplant last year, and his recovery has gone well. He came to see me here a few days before his surgery. It was the only time I can remember seeing fear in his face since he was a boy, and I was pleasantly surprised to realize that it wasn't death that frightened him but what was to become of his father's empire. He didn't want to leave it to me because he doesn't like me and because he believes Stan has already given me more than I deserve. Leaving it to Rae Ann would be like leaving a vineyard to an Eskimo. Shelby is the only one of his daughters who's showing any promise, but she's much too young to manage such a far-reaching fortune. Besides, like any king, he has always regarded his daughters as nothing more than bait to lure other rich men's sons into his family to help manage his affairs until his grandsons can take over. He's never considered any of the girls potential queens.

He gives me a doughy hug.

"You're looking good, Aunt Candace."

"So are you. How are you feeling?"

"Never better," he replies, slapping his barrel chest in a pastel-striped polo shirt I'm sure Rae Ann picked out for him along with the khaki pants.

He smiles and for a moment, I see Stan in

his face. In the past I was never able to completely hate him because of that resemblance; now it's one of the reasons why I do.

"That's good to hear. Come and sit down."

We make ourselves comfortable on the porch.

Dusk is settling over the valley. The sky is streaked with pink and primrose. I've already had Luis light the many candles I keep on the porch. Their flames flicker inside their jewel-tone mosaic globes, casting shards of bright color everywhere like a shattered church window.

Shelby and Rae Ann join us, Rae Ann resplendent in a short-sleeved, mint-green pantsuit with white piping that shows off her tan and her figure.

She leans forward to give me a hug, and I come face-to-face with Baby hanging limply from her well-manicured hand, shivering and bulbous-eyed.

"Here," she extends him toward me once she stands upright again. "Speak to him in his native language."

"I don't speak rat."

"I mean Spanish," she laughs.

"Tu eres el bicho mas feo que hay en el mundo."

Shelby frowns at me. She's had enough Spanish to have some idea of what I said.

"What did you say?" Rae Ann asks.

"Good doggie."

"Ooooh," she coos, pressing the dog against her neck. "Hear that? You're a bee-show mass fay-o. Now go play but don't go too far."

She sets him on the floor and he teeters uncertainly before walking off.

Luis appears from inside the house dressed in cabana boy attire. He's wearing a bright red Hawaiian shirt covered in white lilies, white pants, and sandals. He won't make eye contact with me because it will make him laugh.

"Buenas noches, señor Jack, señora Jack."

"Buenas whatever to you too, Louis," Cameron replies disgustedly.

"Cam," Rae Ann says as she swats him playfully on his pudgy knee. "Be nice."

Rae Ann loves to hear Spanish. It reminds her of her homeland: Miami.

"Buenas noches, Luis," she replies with a lovely smile that isn't lost on Luis.

"Can I offer anyone a drink?" He switches to English but maintains a thick accent for Rae Ann's sake.

"Listening to you always reminds me of home," she gushes. "Let's celebrate! I'll have a mojito."

Cameron screws up his face as if he might spit.

"Bourbon, Mr. Jack?" Luis asks.

"Yeah."

"¿Y usted, señorita?"

"Can I have a mojito, too?" Shelby asks her mother.

"No, they're much too strong. Have a daiquiri."

"And you, Miss Jack?" he asks me while still unable to look me in the eyes. "Can I bring you some warm milk?"

I watch his lips tremble beneath his bushy gray mustache as he tries to restrain his mirth.

"Bourbon for me, too, Luis. A double."

"Bueno."

"He's the cutest little old man," Rae Ann comments after Luis leaves.

I smile to myself. Her comment about his age and size serves him right.

Luis brings us our drinks, some of his homemade allioli with ciabbata bread ripped into chunks, and a small blue bowl of olives, and we commence chitchat.

Rae Ann's centers almost completely on their homes. They have three: one here, one in New York, and one in Florida. She agreed to Cameron's desire to continue living in a small town in rural Pennsylvania in the house where he was brought up and close to where his father established the family fortune only if they could also live part of the year some place where "other rich people live" and some place where there's "tons of sun." To Rae Ann's credit, of all the truly horrid places in this country where rich people gather, she chose the only interesting one: New York.

And as for her other choice, she's one of a rare breed, a native Floridian. I can't blame her for needing to migrate back to her original nesting grounds from time to time. She's guided by an instinct stronger than common sense and good taste; she has Coppertone in her veins.

Shelby sits cuddled up next to her mother sipping at a red frothy daiquiri Luis prepared especially for her with little rum, not saying much, which is unusual for her. This was supposed to be a visit between her and her parents but that particular exchange never gets under way.

She dunks bread in the allioli for herself and her mother and pops one olive after another into her mouth.

Cameron doesn't eat. He doesn't talk either. He's tense, distracted, and fidgety.

Eventually, he turns his oily charm on me and asks with his best salesman's smile, "So what have you been up to, Aunt Candace?"

"I've been keeping busy in my way."

"Right. In your way."

He runs his hand through his hair, then pats it down on all sides into a perfectly smooth pewter cap, a nervous gesture of his.

"I hear you had a bit of a tragedy around here recently."

I rack my brain. I can't come up with any recent tragedy other than this visit.

"And what would that be?"

"That guy. The one killed in a drunk driving accident."

"Oh, yes. The man whose funeral Shelby attended."

"That's awful. Drunk driving." Rae Ann shakes her head as she reaches for her third mojito. "He's lucky he didn't kill anyone else. Did he kill anyone else?"

"No," Shelby answers.

"You didn't go to the funeral, too?" Cameron asks me.

"Absolutely not. I didn't know the man at all."

"Interesting. You didn't know him at all?"

"Of course not. Shelby is friends with his sons."

"Shel said something about you taking these boys in. Letting them live here."

I flash Shelby a disapproving glare. She withers noticeably.

"That's nonsense. Shelby may have brought up the subject, but I told her it could never happen. I believed it was a conversation strictly between the two of us."

I glance her way again. She shrugs.

"Shel seemed to think you're considering it."

"That's ridiculous."

"Good. I mean, good." He signals to Luis for another drink. "Can you imagine anything worse for two teenage boys than living here with you?"

I sit up in my chair, stiff-backed, holding my drink in my lap, and give him my undivided attention.

"Yes, I can imagine worse things."

"I just mean . . . what would they do here? It's like a convent but without the nuns."

"And would nuns make the convent better or worse?"

He stares blankly at me. I've stumped him.

"I mean, the rules," he rallies and continues. "The lectures. This weird Spanish obsession you have with bulls and this eye-olly shit and little old Spanish men. And your coldness and bitterness. They're boys. If they're going to live with a woman, they need one who's going to take care of them and love them, someone who's affectionate. Not you, for Christ's sake."

"Dad, stop it," Shelby interrupts. "Klint and Kyle aren't little kids."

"You can't even be nice to a dog," Cameron practically bellows and gestures toward Baby who's now curled up in Rae Ann's lap. "An innocent little dog."

"Cam, I think you're being a little hard on Aunt Candy. Hard on Aunt Candy," Rae Ann giggles drunkenly. "I almost said hard candy."

I smile at him.

"Your concern for these boys is admirable, Cameron. Possibly you'd like to provide a home for them."

"Oh, no," Rae Ann objects, giggling again.

"I wouldn't have any idea what to do with boys. Well, I know what to do with boys. But that would be illegal. Wouldn't that be illegal?"

"Stay out of this," Cameron snaps at her and turns back to me. "I just wanted to make sure we're on the same page here."

"And what page would that be, exactly?"

"The page where you don't let those boys live here."

"And the reason is simply that you don't feel I could provide a healthy environment for them?"

"It's not something we do, all right? Take in homeless white trash kids. It doesn't look right."

"And there's no other reason?"

"Look. It doesn't matter what my reasons are. I don't have to explain them to you. Those kids aren't living here. I forbid it."

"What did you say?"

"I forbid it. I'm the head of this family. And I forbid it."

Silence falls suddenly and very heavily. No one moves or speaks. Even the frogs and the crickets cease their musical chirping.

I stand up slowly. I have arthritis in my knees and can no longer stand quickly. The pain aside, it has caused me to adopt a more regal mode of movement.

"Cameron, your position in this family could certainly be described using a body

part, but I don't think it's the head. Now if you'll excuse me, I'm old and tired and I'm going to bed."

I may be old but I'm not tired and I'm not going to bed, but one of the advantages of getting on in years is that you can use your age to excuse just about any indiscretion, whether it be something trivial like a desire to leave a social gathering early or a need to wear paisley or something a little more dramatic such as driving your car into someone's living room or shoplifting a clock.

Rae Ann won't stand up because she doesn't want to disturb the rat in her lap, and Shelby won't dare come near me after what just transpired. Cameron simply has no manners.

"Just remember what I said," he calls after me.

"I promise you, I'll never forget it," I reply.

I make my way through the foyer to the bottom of the staircase where Luis is standing with his tray acting as if he hadn't been standing in the doorway a moment ago listening to our conversation.

I say nothing to him.

"Aunt Candace," Shelby cries out from behind me.

She has followed me after all. She has more courage than I thought.

I ignore her, turning my back on both of them, and start up the stairs, glancing over

my shoulder only once.

Luis whispers something to her.

She gives him a brilliant smile and makes a small curtsy.

"Muchas gracias," she whispers back.

Chapter Five: Kyle

She's going to ask us how we're doing, this crazy, mean, ugly aunt of Shelby's. She's going to give us a pitiful look like we're skinny stray cats and then she's going to form the words very slowly and obviously like we're kids who ride the short bus, "How are you boys doing?" Maybe she'll even try and touch us: squeeze our shoulders or pat our hands or, holy shit, give us hugs.

I don't know what I'm going to do because I've already decided if one more person asks me how I'm doing, I'm going to lose it. How am I doing? Well, I'm doing lousy, of course. My dad's dead. My mom's dragging me off to live with her in a crappy place while the whole time she acts like she hates me. Like I've done something wrong to her, and this time I'm sure I haven't. My brother's gone completely nuts, talking day and night about running away and kissing his dream and his future good-bye. My baby sister looks at me like I've committed some terrible crime I

don't even know about. Bill hobbles around with a face as long as a horse's and sits for hours on his back porch doing nothing, not even drinking beer, which is very worrisome.

I can't concentrate in school. I can't even watch TV. I'm going to have to leave everything I love and everything I know. Mom won't even let me take Mr. B. She says Jeff's allergic to cats.

I know Bill will take care of Mr. B for me, and that way his life will change very little. Not like my life. But even though it might sound stupid, I'm sure that cat's attached to me. I know he'll miss me and even worse, he'll wonder why I left. He'll think he did something bad to make me hate him. Otherwise, why would I leave him? You can't explain things like Arizona and Jeff to a cat.

So how am I doing? I'm doing okay, I tell the people who ask because that's what they want to hear. They don't want to hear the truth. They're not asking because they care. Most of these people don't even know me. If it wasn't for the fact my dad just died in a well-publicized accident, they still wouldn't know I exist. They'd walk right by me in the halls like they used to.

The day the vice principal made the announcement at school about our dad, there was a line a mile deep outside the guidance counselors' offices with students needing to talk to someone about their "grief." Appar-

ently they were so torn up about what had happened to Klint and me that they weren't able to go to their classes, which turned out to be okay because most of the teachers were too upset to teach anyway. They spent the day in the teachers' lounge drinking coffee, eating doughnuts, and gossiping with their other devastated colleagues while trying to regain their composure and find the strength to carry on.

I'm really starting to hate all this phoniness. Most people are always pretending to be something they're not, and I don't understand why. If you're going to pretend to be one way, then you must think that's the right way to be so why not just be that way to begin with?

But then there are certain people who are so great and make you so happy that you don't care about all the jerks. It's really amazing that a couple decent people can protect you from millions of idiots. Sometimes I wonder what it would be like not to have any good people in your life at all, not even one. I think that's how psychos are made.

Klint and I are supposed to leave with Mom the day after tomorrow. She rented a little U-Haul trailer we're hitching to her car, and she said this is our only chance to take our stuff with us. Whatever we leave behind will be gone for good. Bill is going to take care of Dad's personal effects and sell the furniture

and the TV and microwave and give the money to us. Aunt Jen has volunteered to help.

Part of me wants to leave everything behind and try to forget that the first fourteen years of my life ever happened, but another part of me knows I'll go crazy without my stuff and my memories. Still, I haven't packed anything. Neither has Klint.

Klint's actually pushing in the other direction. Instead of condensing his possessions into the empty boxes from Bi-Lo Aunt Jen dropped off for us, he's spreading out. He's left clothes and dirty dishes in the living room. He even set a pair of reeking gym socks and a jock strap right in the middle of the coffee table next to the twisted chrome remains of the antlers from Dad's grill: a definite statement if I've ever seen one, except I don't know who he's trying to impress. It's only us now.

None of this seems real. Tomorrow will be my last day of school at Centresburg High, and I only just started here a couple weeks ago. I asked Mom if our transcripts should be sent to another school, and she said we'd take care of it when we got to Arizona. I didn't like the sound of that. I don't want to miss too much school. I don't want to fall behind in my classes and mess up my grades.

It's not that I'm a teacher's wet dream or anything like that. I'm no Honor Society geek

or an ass-kisser. I get good grades because I can't help myself. I happen to be smart. Plus I kind of like school. I'd never tell anyone, especially not Klint who hates school except for baseball, or my friends who hate school except for lunch and wood shop, or Dad who hated school when he was in it except for baseball, or Mom who hated it, too, except for the boys who played baseball and one particular math teacher who she never had for class because he taught the advanced students but apparently he was good-looking and she and Aunt Jen both dated him. (This would definitely get him canned nowadays but to hear them talk, it was pretty common back then.)

The simple truth is I like to learn things. I admit most classes are boring and most teachers don't teach well, but sometimes when I least expect it, I encounter a new idea or a historical event or a scientific fact that blows me away.

Unfortunately for me, though, doing well in school is not something that's admired by the people I live with. Everyone I know equates being smart with being stuck-up.

I used to hide my report cards from my parents not because they were bad but because they were good and I knew I'd get teased and accused of thinking I was better than everybody else. It also gave them an excuse to start reminiscing about their own

failed school careers, things like how Dad showed that son of a bitch Mr. Hickey how much he hated him by ditching the final and flunking his class and having to take it over the next year and how Mom got a D in English because it was during eighth period and she always skipped it to go smoke with her friends and she had to go to summer school because of it.

I was always troubled by the glee and pride in their voices that accompanied these tales. I couldn't understand how making their lives more difficult and limiting their futures could be considered a triumph.

Eventually I figured out that the reason they seemed pleased about being screwups and disappointed in me for doing well was because it was easier to make people who do something better than you feel bad about themselves than it is to admit there's something wrong with you and maybe you should try and fix it.

But realizing this didn't change anything for me. I just became more committed to hiding myself.

Klint still insists he's not going with Mom. He says unless she's developed a really good right hook, there's no way she's getting him into that car. He already has a part-time job after school working at Hamilton's Dairy. He says if Bill will let him bunk with him for the time being, he should be able to make enough

money to pay for his food and chip in some rent, and if Mom causes him any problems like involving cops or social services, he'll run away and no one will ever hear from him again.

He doesn't include me in his plans, but he also never talks about me leaving with Mom, either. I think he's giving me the power to make my own choice, and I appreciate this because he's never treated me like an adult before. The problem is, he's given me an impossible choice. If I go with Mom, he'll never speak to me again. If I stay here, we're going to end up running away and Klint's going to screw up his chance to keep playing ball. Mom would never let us live with Bill or anyone else. It's gone well beyond maternal concern at this point. She and Klint are out for each other's blood.

Shelby has a plan. It's one of the weirdest things I've ever heard, but since nothing seems real right now, I figure why not try one more thing that can't possibly work out? Besides, there's a home-cooked meal involved and the chance to hang out with Shelby.

The plan itself sort of creeps me out. She wants Klint and me to live with her aunt. Now even if I can pretend that there's any way in hell to get Klint to agree to this, I've heard enough strange things about Candace Jack to make me not so keen on the idea myself.

She's old and mean and lives all by herself in a huge mansion and hardly ever goes out because she hates just about everybody. She's never been married or had kids and people say it's because no man would ever go near her because she's hideously ugly.

She's filthy rich. Her nephew is Cam Jack, Shelby's dad, the guy who owns J&P Coal, and he's not exactly popular around here. There have been a lot of accidents in his mines. When I was a little kid, there was an explosion in Beverly that killed eighteen men, and a couple years ago five miners were trapped in Josephine near Jolly Mount. They were rescued and were pretty famous for a while. There were rumors they were going to sue him, but they didn't end up doing it. Nobody seems to know exactly why, but everyone seems pretty sure it's because Cam Jack did something sleazy that only a rich person with a ton of lawyers could get away with.

Lorelei, the J&P mine in our town, closed a long time ago. Dad worked in it for a couple years. Bill worked in it until he messed up his leg. It was the biggest source of employment around here and things have been really depressed since it closed, but I'm still relieved it did. It means guys have to leave when they get out of school and go find jobs somewhere else, but at least they're jobs that don't kill or cripple them.

That's what I know about Candace Jack, that and the rumors about her bull.

Some people say she's had the same bull for fifty years. Other people say that's not possible and she just gets a new one whenever the old one dies. Other people say he's a demon bull she conjured up with the help of Satan. He's gigantic, black as coal, and has killed lots of kids who have crawled over her fence and tried to cross her land. Nobody knows who these kids are. Mostly they're supposed to be from other towns. No one ever finds their bodies because after the bull kills them, Candace Jack plucks them off the ends of his bloody horns and takes them back to her house where she eats them and then throws their bones in a pit in her cellar.

But tonight Shelby says we're having chicken.

We've borrowed Bill's pickup for the occasion. Dad and Klint had both been saving money to get Klint his own truck. Dad had a special savings account with several thousand dollars in it, but now that he's dead we've been told we can't get the money because Dad died without a will. Now the government gets hold of all his bank accounts first (the savings account and a checking account with $524.66 in it), takes out a bunch of taxes, and then decides what Klint and I get.

He had a retirement plan with Burke Pharmaceuticals but since he died at forty instead

of retiring at sixty-five, Burke gets to keep all the money. Besides a will, he also didn't have life insurance or mortgage insurance on the house. I guess those things seemed like a waste of money to him while he was alive.

Klint hasn't said a word for the entire drive. I haven't either. I'm gloating in silence. I was able to do the impossible and convince him to have dinner with Shelby and her aunt. I told him I knew he didn't want to go because he was afraid of her because he believed all those stories about her eating kids.

At first he just denied it and tried to ignore me, but the more I ragged on him about it, the angrier he got and before long he smacked me and I smacked him back and we got into it pretty good.

In the end I think he agreed to go mostly for the same reason I did: it's something bizarre and totally unexpected that gets us out of our depressing house for a night and distracts us from thinking about our impending doom.

Candace Jack's house turns out to be as huge as everyone says it is, but it's nothing like I imagined. I thought it might be like a movie star's mansion with everything polished and glittering, or maybe a cold sinister stone castle like they have in England, or a haunted house with turrets and gargoyles and tons of dark windows.

Instead it's red brick with white trim like a

lot of houses around here and even though it's bigger than my elementary school, there's nothing fancy about it. I get the feeling the guy who built it was only interested in impressing himself, not anybody else.

It sits on a hillside about a mile off the main road at the end of a white gravel driveway that seems to go on forever beneath a tunnel of gigantic trees.

There's a red barn a little ways off behind the house. I think it might be the first barn I've ever seen that doesn't have peeling paint or a hole in it somewhere.

Shelby's sports car is red, too, but a flashier shade. It's parked in front of the house: small, scarlet, shiny, and rounded like a drop of new blood.

Back by the barn I spy a beat-up Dodge Ram pickup and an old Jeep with no top. I point it out to Klint and tell him maybe we should park back there.

We do. As we're getting out of Bill's truck I notice one side of the Jeep is completely dented in and has ragged holes in it like it's been stabbed with a spear or blasted with a shotgun.

We're on our way to the house, walking as slow as we can without going backward, when a tall, skinny, old man comes walking toward us in a John Deere ball cap and a checked Woolrich coat carrying a rifle at his side.

"We're not trespassing," I volunteer without

being asked, and Klint gives me a disgusted look.

"Good, then I won't have to shoot you," he says without any sign of humor on his leathery, lined face.

"You the Hayes boys?" he asks.

We nod.

"Knew your dad," he says. "My condolences," he adds while taking a quick tug at the bill of his cap.

This is exactly the kind of guy I needed to run into: the kind of guy who's never going to ask someone how he's doing.

"You knew Dad?" Klint asks.

"Saw him around town. In the bars. Exchanged a few words now and then."

He extends his hand.

"I'm Jerry."

Klint takes it first. Then me.

"Where are you going with the gun?" I ask, and Klint gives me another dirty look.

"There's a doe been spotted 'bout five miles up the road from here. Got an arrow in her neck. Bleeding out. Some idiot with a crossbow. I'm gonna go put her out of her misery."

"Are you with the park service?"

"Nope. It's on Miss Jack's land so I'm gonna take care of it for her."

"Five miles from here? How much land is hers?"

He turns slowly in a full circle looking out

toward the mountains, then at the fields and forest behind the house and barn, then at the trees lining the driveway.

"Pretty much all of it," he says.

"Can I ask you something?"

"Shoot."

"What happened to your Jeep?"

He looks briefly at the damaged door.

"Bull," he says simply.

"Kyle! Klint!" I hear Shelby call out.

She's standing on the porch waving at us.

"There's little Miss Jack," Jerry comments. "You better get going."

I don't need to be told twice.

Shelby's beaming. Her face is always pretty, even when she's frowning, but when she's happy, she's almost too pretty to look at. She's like the sun.

She has on a blue dress made out of some kind of gauzy material that sort of floats around her as she hurries down the porch steps to meet us. The bottom of her dress is sprinkled with sparkly beads and her bare toes in a pair of sandals peek out from underneath the hem. Her toenails are painted blue, too.

She told me that Klint and I should "dress nicely." We've responded by wearing jeans without grass stains, gym shoes without rips down the sides, our cleanest flannel shirts over T-shirts without curse words or beer slogans on them, and ball caps without

grease, mud, blood, or paint spattered on them.

She doesn't look very pleased by our outfits. Her smile falters for a moment as her eyes travel from the tips of my shoes up to the top of my cap.

She doesn't give Klint the same thorough going-over. She can only manage a glance at him while he looks away from her, and she blushes. Same old shit.

"You look nice," I tell her.

"Thanks. You look . . . better than usual."

Her smile returns, and I relax a little.

"So this is the place, huh? Where's the bull?"

"Ventisco? He's out there somewhere."

"Ventisco?" I repeat.

"What kind of a name is that?" Klint snorts.

"It's Spanish. It means tempestuous one."

"Give me a break," he mutters.

"We've known each other for a long time," Shelby says to me while leading the way up to the front door, "and you've never asked me about Aunt Candace's bull before."

"So it's real?"

"Of course, it's real. Why wouldn't it be real? It's just a bull. Lots of people have bulls on their farms."

The door is almost twice my height and has a border of small square windows all around it. A gold knocker the size of my head with the name JACK etched into it is anchored

in the very center.

Shelby pushes the door open and we follow her into a huge entryway that reminds me of entering a church. The wood floors are the color of honey, and the staircase is carpeted in plush chocolate, mustard, and orange flowers curving off to one side. The walls are hung with paintings and mirrors in ornate frames, and a gold chandelier as big as our kitchen table hangs from the ceiling.

One of the paintings in particular catches my eye. It's a bullfighter dressed in sky blue and gold with socks the color of Pepto-Bismol and a cape of yellow and purplish pink raised above his head as a bull charges past him. Plaza de Toros Madrid, Gran Corrida de la Prensa is written in bold black letters along the bottom and beneath it the name, Manuel Obrador, and in quotation marks: "El Soltero."

I'd like to get a closer look, but Shelby ushers us into an adjoining room to meet her aunt.

I know instantly that there's no chance Candace Jack's going to ask me how I'm doing. There's not going to be any hugging or phony sympathy of any kind. I'm relieved about that, but it's not the kind of relief that allows a person to relax.

She stands very tall and straight, all alone in the middle of the room, nowhere near a chair or couch even though she's surrounded

by tons of furniture, looking like she'd choose to stand for the rest of her life rather than accept the comfort of a seat.

She's wearing a long black skirt, a silky gray blouse tied in a bow at her neck, and black boots, the pointy-toed, lace-up kind that witches wear, and I can't help thinking about all the kids she's supposedly eaten. She has glasses but she's not wearing them; they hang from a gold chain around her neck.

She's definitely scary but not because she's ugly. She's not bad-looking for an old lady and the moment I think that, I cringe inside myself just imagining what would happen if Klint could somehow read my thoughts. I'd spend the rest of my life hearing about how I'm hot for a granny. Grannyfucker: that would be my new nickname. Every high school baseball player in the state of Pennsylvania would know it in a matter of days.

It's true, though. She's not bad-looking. Her hair is white and smooth and has a snowy glimmer to it, and it must be long because it's rolled up into a fat coil on the top of her head.

I can't figure out what color her eyes are. They're greenish gray, kind of beautiful but terrifying like the sky gets at sunset on a stifling hot, perfectly still summer day right before a thunderstorm.

She keeps her hands clasped in front of her and stares directly into my eyes. Hers aren't

kind but they're also not mean. They're watchful like Mr. B's. I understand why she scares people, but it's not her face; it's her presence. She takes up all the space in a room.

"Aunt Candace, this is Klint and Kyle Hayes," Shelby introduces us.

Miss Jack doesn't make a move toward us, and we don't make a move toward her. We all seem satisfied with our mutual decisions on the matter.

"I'm pleased to meet you both," she says. "Welcome to my home."

"Thanks," Klint and I mumble.

She waits and when we don't say more, she says, "I thought since Shelby has to drive back to school tonight that we should eat dinner early. Does that suit you?"

Klint replies with a shrug.

"Sure," I add.

She fixes us, in turn, with her stare, and I can tell we've both just failed Beginning Conversation 101.

She brushes past us out of the room. Shelby makes a face at me, but I can't tell what it means except that we've done something wrong.

Everyone else walks quickly through the entryway, but I stop in front of the picture of the bullfighter. I can't help it.

Mom used to tell me I asked too many questions. I guess when I was a little kid, I

never shut up. I wanted to know everything. How far away is the moon? Why don't grape Popsicles taste like grapes? Do plants have feelings? How do you make cardboard? Why do people say "nervous as a cat" when cats seem pretty calm?

I think the reason I learned to read before I was even in kindergarten is because I wanted answers, and I could only get them from books. Mom got mad when I asked her too many questions. Dad, on the other hand, was always willing to answer me, but it didn't take me long to figure out his answers were usually wrong.

Mom said I drove her crazy. I thought it was just an expression. If I had known it was the truth, I would've kept my mouth shut and maybe she would've stayed.

"Excuse me," I speak up. "Can I ask a question about this painting?"

Everyone stops and turns around and stares at me. Shelby looks angry. Klint shakes his head.

"Of course you may," Miss Jack replies. "But it's not a painting. It's a poster advertising a corrida, a bullfight. What is your question?"

"Why's the cape pink and yellow? Isn't it supposed to be red?"

"A torero uses two capes. First, the capote" — she points to the fabric billowing out behind the man like a sail on a boat — "then

later, the muleta. That's the red cape you're referring to. It's much smaller than a capote. The red color is a matter of tradition. Bulls are color-blind."

"No way."

"Yes," she says.

"Speaking of color-blind," I hear Klint comment from behind me, "check out the guy's socks."

Miss Jack ignores him, but her lips flatten with disapproval.

"Then why do bulls charge when you wave something red at them?" I keep going.

"The color has nothing to do with it. They attack moving objects. The color is simply tradition."

"Is this the bullfighter's name? Manuel Obrador?"

"Yes."

"And what about this part? El Soltero?"

"His nickname. Most toreros have nicknames."

"What does it mean?"

"Think about it," she instructs me. "It's not that different from the English equivalent."

"Soltero." I repeat the word. "Soldier? Solid? Solemn? Solar?"

"Solitary," Klint interrupts.

Miss Jack turns and looks at him.

"And what do you call a man who chooses to be solitary, to live alone?"

"A hermit," Shelby volunteers.

"A bachelor," Klint says.

"Yes," Miss Jack agrees and heads toward the dining room again, "Manuel Obrador was the Bachelor."

Shelby gives Klint an admiring glance. How did he figure that out and I didn't?

I lag behind and watch the two of them walk side by side behind Miss Jack.

Why am I even here?

I look back at the poster. The bull, on all fours, is almost as tall as the matador who's standing upright on two feet. The animal's back is about as high as his shoulders, and its horns are as thick as his arms.

The little black shoes he's wearing look like ballet slippers. I can tell there's no cleats on them, and I wonder if that's done on purpose to make things more difficult for him. It occurs to me that some traction might be helpful when a guy's running around a dirt ring with a bull chasing him.

He has his feet close together, planted flat on the ground, with his arms reaching high over his head holding the cape, his entire body stretched out in a graceful curved line, his face full of concentration but no fear, looking more like he's about to launch himself off a cliff into a lagoon in a swan dive than he's trying to prevent a huge, pissed-off animal from charging at his balls.

If I had to pick one word to describe him

besides "stupid," it would be "vulnerable."

I catch up with the others. We're eating dinner in a cantaloupe-colored room with a whole wall of windows and smooth, blue ceramic tiles on the floor, each one painted with a design of green curlicues and yellow flowers. The table and chairs are made of a dark wood with green-and-gold-striped satin cushions on the chairs. The tablecloth is pale green with pink roses embroidered all over it.

This room is covered with paintings, too, all different styles and all kinds of different subjects, but my eyes are instantly drawn to one of a bullfighter again. I can't tell if it's the same guy who's in the poster. The brushstrokes are smudgy — impressionist stuff, I think — and he's wearing a white suit this time and using a red cape. On the opposite wall is another painting that looks like it was made by the same artist. It's of a woman dancing in a tight red dress that flares out at the bottom in frothy layers of ruffles. She has slicked-back, black hair and big hoops in her ears. Her back is arched slightly and her arms are stretched above her. The pose looks familiar and I realize her body's making the same line that El Soltero's body makes in his poster.

I know the type of dancing she's doing, but I can't think of the word then it comes to me all of a sudden: flamenco. It's a kind of Spanish dancing.

I don't know where I picked up the word. Probably from a movie or TV. Not from school. We hardly studied Spain at all. Once we memorized the names of all their explorers, our teachers seemed to think there was nothing else worth knowing about it. Instead they're hung up on countries we've beaten in wars, like Germany, or countries we've saved in wars, like France, or countries we've beaten in one war and saved in another, like England; and of course they all love Italy because just about everyone in America has some great-great-grandfather Vincenzo who came over on a leaky boat and cried when he saw the Statue of Liberty.

Miss Jack tells us to take a seat, then she excuses herself for a moment.

The three of us look at one another. The table's not as big as I expected. There are only eight chairs sitting around it. I thought we'd eat in a cold, gloomy room the size of a school gym with one of those long tables that seat a hundred people and Klint and I would sit at one end and Shelby and Miss Jack at the other, and whenever we wanted to talk to each other we'd have to cup our hands and shout, "I say, my dear, could you be a good chap and please pass the caviar?"

The table's set for four: two on one side and two on the other. Klint and I take seats beside each other, and Shelby sits across from me.

The whole room's not what I expected. It's kind of wild. Nothing matches but still everything seems to go together.

Most of the mothers I know would freak out in a room like this. Everything in their houses has to be color coordinated.

Aunt Jen's house is that way. The carpet is dark purple. The furniture is light purple. The walls are white with purple flowers. The curtains are white lace. She has white lace all over the place: on the coffee table, on the arms of the chairs, on the back of the couch.

She has a statue of a ballerina in a purple tutu, a purple glass bowl filled with fake grapes, and a bunch of white candles in purple holders that smell like vanilla. She has a painting of a field of violets and another one of a litter of kittens with purple fur.

All of it's very girly stuff. I think she picked the style on purpose not because it suits her but because she's trying to make people think she's a real woman. It's like laying palm leaves across a pit for a lion to fall into, only she lays a trap of doilies and cookie-scented candles for men to fall into.

"Your aunt has a real thing for Spain," I say to Shelby after we sit down.

"You have no idea," she says, shaking her head.

"Why?"

"I guess she spent some time there when she was young. She doesn't talk about it, and

my dad says Granddad never talked about it, either, except to complain about Calladito."

"Who's Calladito?"

"On one of her trips she brought back a bull named Calladito. According to Dad, she paid a fortune for him and she and Granddad had a big fight about it and didn't speak to each other for a long time. But when it turned out she could make a ton of money from breeding him, then Granddad didn't hate him so much."

"What happened to Calladito?"

"He got old and died. But Aunt Candace has always kept one son from each generation. Ventisco is Calladito's grandson."

She opens her napkin and puts it on her lap. Klint and I do the same.

We hear the click of Miss Jack's boots on the tiles heading in our direction.

"What's Calladito mean?" I whisper across the table to Shelby.

"The Quiet One," she whispers back.

"Excuse me," Miss Jack says as she returns and takes a seat. "I had something I needed to attend to in the kitchen."

Following at her heels is a short, brown man in butter-colored pants and a turquoise shirt carrying a basket of bread and a big glass pitcher of water with ice and lemon slices in it. He's bald except for a ring of gray hair around the top of his head that's the same color as the bristly mustache covering

his upper lip and drooping down both cheeks. His face is shiny, smooth, and round like a Buddha's face, but his body isn't fat at all. His eyes are black and friendly.

"Luis," Miss Jack says to him, "this is Klint and Kyle Hayes."

He nods at each of us, smiling.

"Mucho gusto," he says.

He sets down the bread, pours water for all of us, then disappears and comes back right away with four bowls of soup and another bowl of olives on a tray.

"Sopa crema de tomate," he announces.

He puts a steaming bowl in front of each of us. It looks like tomato soup, but it has a white swirl of something in it and a bunch of green leaves on top.

Shelby sticks her face near the bowl, closes her eyes, and takes a big sniff of the soup. She looks up at me smiling dreamily.

"I love Luis's homemade tomato soup. It's so good."

She picks up her spoon and stirs it slowly until the white stuff disappears.

"I never thought about anyone making tomato soup from tomatoes before," I say. "I guess I always thought it originated in nature as a red blob of paste in a soup can."

Shelby laughs at my joke.

I look over at Klint, who's staring at the leaves in his soup like they're turds.

"What's this on top?" I ask for him.

"Some sour cream and fresh basil. Try it. You'll love it."

I stir it the way she did and take a bite.

"She's right," I tell him. "It's great. It doesn't taste anything like Campbell's."

"I like Campbell's," he grumbles.

"This is a nice house," I say to Miss Jack, in an attempt to change the subject from food.

"Thank you," she replies. "It was built by my brother, who was also Shelby's grandfather."

"But Aunt Candace did all the decorating," Shelby chimes in.

"You have good taste," I tell her.

Klint kicks me under the table.

"So tell me about yourself, Klint? What do you do for fun?" Miss Jack asks.

He takes a break from glaring at his soup and looks up at her.

"I don't know," he says.

"How interesting."

"Aunt Candace can relate to what the two of you are going through right now." It's Shelby's turn to try and change the subject. "She lost both her parents when she was thirteen."

Miss Jack glances disapprovingly at Shelby. I get the feeling she didn't want her niece to tell us this or she didn't want Shelby assuming any of us can relate to each other.

"A fire in our home," Miss Jack explains.

"My father was able to save my brother and me. He went back in to save our mother and never came out again."

"That's terrible," I say.

"Yes, it was terrible. It's very hard to lose someone you love and depend on."

"Was it a house like this?"

She laughs, a happy, genuine laugh that sounds a lot like Shelby's. Hearing it come out of her is like hearing merry-go-round music coming from inside a prison.

"Certainly not," she tells me, suddenly turning serious again. "My father was a coal miner."

"What? I don't get it. I thought you owned the coal mines?"

"My brother was very ambitious," she replies, abruptly ending the conversation with the tone of her voice.

We all start eating. I check on Klint, who finally dips his spoon in the soup, being careful to avoid the leaves.

"I don't enjoy small talk," Miss Jack announces after a few minutes of silence.

"Neither do we," I tell her even though I do kind of enjoy small talk. Talking about big things usually depresses me.

"Especially Klint," I add.

"I see. So Klint's reticence comes from a disdain for discussing trivialities, not from rudeness or ignorance."

Klint and I look at each other trying to

figure out exactly what she said. I think Klint may have been insulted, but I'm not sure.

"Right," I answer.

"What is your situation now?"

We don't say anything.

"Now that you no longer have your father," she further explains.

We still don't say anything.

"Your father didn't leave you well provided for?" she assumes.

"No," I answer.

"Shut up," Klint says.

"Why?"

"It's none of her business."

"But it's true."

"That doesn't make it any of her business."

"And obviously it's very inconvenient that he wasn't able to provide for you," Miss Jack continues.

"Yeah," I say.

"No," says Klint.

"A little," I explain. "But he wasn't old. Why would he be thinking about dying?"

"Anyone can die at any age. That's not the issue here. The issue is whether a man was responsible enough to make sure that his children would be taken care of if something should happen to him."

I wish I could make her understand about Dad. He wasn't irresponsible; he just never worried about anything. It's a quality in him I envied even though it didn't always turn

out to be the best quality for a dad to have. I can't imagine what it would feel like to only live in the moment, to think everything important was out of your control so you shouldn't care about it, to see the future as a simple collection of plans to tackle household chores and make beer runs.

"He took good care of us," Klint jumps in angrily. "He worked hard. He would've never left us."

"The way your mother did."

"This is so messed up," Klint goes on, his rage deepening. "I don't need to sit here and have some old lady I don't know say bad things about my mom."

"But Mom did leave us," I remind him. "And you hate . . ."

"Shut up!" he screams at me.

Luis shows up in the doorway.

"Is there a problem with the soup?" he asks.

"No, Luis," Miss Jack replies calmly. "The soup is excellent."

"It's really good," Shelby adds nervously, her eyes darting back and forth between her aunt and Klint, who's staring a hole through his bowl.

"What is your situation now?" Miss Jack repeats as soon as Luis leaves.

I check on Klint again. The tips of his ears are bright red, a sign that he's boiling mad. Whenever he strikes out, he rips off his batting helmet, throws it on the ground, and

stalks away from it like it's the root of all his troubles, and I swear I can see his ears glowing all the way from the stands.

No matter what I do or say at this point, he's going to be pissed at me. I convinced him to come here. It's my fault.

I consider Miss Jack's question. I think about all the phony "How are you doings?" I've had to listen to for the past week. I think about the teary faces peering into mine, how everybody gets worked up when they see us not because they care about us but because they're excited by the drama we provide. Having me and Klint around is better than watching reality TV; we're actual reality.

Now someone is asking me a specific question about my life in a detached way like she's giving me a test about myself, and even though I don't know why she wants this information, I feel like giving it to her.

"We can't stay here on our own," I begin hesitantly, glancing at Klint whose ears get redder. "We wish we could, since this is the only place we've ever lived. All our friends are here and our school . . . and Klint's team," I add.

I wait for a reaction from him but get none.

"Our mom wants to take us to live in Arizona where she's living with this guy . . . our sister's there, too, but she . . . she's different now."

I stop. Explaining our situation is harder

than I thought.

"Have you kept in close contact with your mother since she left?" Miss Jack asks.

"We've seen her once."

"Once? In how many years?"

"Three."

"Did you want to see her more?"

"Sure."

I look at Klint. Nothing.

"Why do you think she wants you to live with her now?"

I shrug.

"We are her kids. I mean, what is she going to do? Let us starve in the streets?"

"You don't think she's happy to have you come live with her?"

"I think she feels like she has to take us. It's her obligation."

"Why wasn't it her obligation to take care of you before your father died?"

"I guess she thought Dad would take good care of us and he did."

"So she simply decided you didn't need a mother anymore."

Maybe that was it. Maybe she thought I didn't need her anymore. I get a sick, panicky feeling in my stomach as I think about that morning on my way to the bus when I had my last conversation with her before she left. She said soon I wouldn't hug her anymore. It wasn't true, but she thought it was. Did she think it was a sign I didn't need a mother?

Do human mothers make that decision? I know animal mothers do. Bird moms push their babies out of the nest. Wolf moms snap and growl if grown pups come back to bug them. Sea turtles don't even wait around to see if their babies are born. But I thought human moms understood they were in it for the long haul.

What if she left because she thought I wanted her to? Was there a part of me that did want her to go?

After she had been gone awhile and Dad and Klint and I had settled into our bachelor lifestyle and weren't too miserable, I'd still have sad moments when I'd wish I had a mom around to ask me about my day and actually listen to my answer, or notice it was cold and make me wear a hat even though I'd take it off as soon as I was out of sight of the house, or cook me one of my favorite dinners when I seemed down, or defend me against Dad and Klint and say things like, "Now, Carl, you're being too hard on Kyle. He's a wonderful boy," or "Klint, being a good baseball player is not the most important thing in the world. Your brother has many fine qualities, too," or do little feminine things like put air fresheners all over the house and make sure there were always clean towels in the bathroom, but then I'd realize I was thinking about things moms did on TV, not what my mom did.

Some nights when we were sitting at the table eating spaghetti for the fourth night that week, I almost felt relieved that she wasn't around to yell at us and complain about how her life sucked, but I hated myself for feeling that way.

"Did you know that El Soltero guy?" I blurt out instead of answering Miss Jack's question.

She sets her spoon down so quickly she gets soup on the table.

"I was just wondering. I mean, I have a poster of Miss February 2006 in a Bud Lite T-shirt and red high heels sitting on the hood of a pickup truck and I don't know her, and Klint has a poster of Roberto Clemente and he was dead before we were even born. But I don't know how it works with bullfighters. Can anyone get a bullfight poster or are they special? Do you have to know the bullfighter?"

She clears her throat.

"Yes, I knew him."

"You never told me that," Shelby practically gasps.

"You never asked," Miss Jack replies.

"Why would I ask something like that? I always thought it was just another piece of Spanish art."

"He thought to ask," she says, looking at me, then Shelby, then at the drops of red seeping into the tablecloth.

Miss Jack clears her throat again.

"If you felt differently about your mother, would you be willing to leave your school and friends and go with her?"

I take a deep breath and let it out slowly. I give up. Miss Jack is obviously not going to let the topic of our situation drop. The price of a dinner with Shelby is going to be total, excruciating soul-baring.

"I'd probably go. I mean, if Klint would go, too."

"What about you, Klint?"

"No," he says darkly. "I would never go."

"Why not?"

"Because I can't imagine feeling differently about my mother."

"Why do you hate her so much?"

He finally looks up at her.

"You're a bitch," he hisses across the table.

"Oh my God," Shelby cries, and covers her mouth with her hands.

He slams his fists down on the table, making soup slosh out of all our bowls.

"No, this is stupid," he shouts. "This is totally fucked up."

He jabs a finger at Miss Jack's unyielding figure.

"She just wants to screw with our heads."

He pushes his chair aside and storms out of the room.

The stained tablecloth looks like the scene of a knife fight.

"Sorry," I say.

I start after Klint, then turn back.

"Vaya con Dios," I tell Miss Jack.

It's the only Spanish I know. I heard it in a Clint Eastwood western I watched once with my dad.

Chapter Six

Another silent drive — only this one is worse because there's nothing to anticipate at the end except a dark, empty house full of packing boxes and maybe getting my head smacked.

Klint never loses his temper, especially around strangers. He loses it around me all the time, but I don't mind. I find it kind of flattering. It means he can relax around me and reveal his true emotions. I just wish occasionally he'd have an emotion other than anger.

I've seen him take abuse that would reduce a lot of guys to tears. I've watched Coach Hill get so close to him when he was bawling him out that the bills of their caps overlapped. Veins standing out in Coach's neck, spit flying from his mouth, fists clenched at his sides while kicking dirt on Klint's shoes, his face turning as red as the symbolic flames on the front of their school jerseys — Coach Hill has to destroy in order to rebuild — but Klint

just stands there, unflinching, staring past him until Coach realizes the futility of screaming at someone who's not there.

I've heard Mom tell him she wished she'd never gotten pregnant with him because it ruined her life, and how he's a pig and a selfish jerk like all men. I've seen her smack his head with a pound of frozen ground chuck and do this thing with her finger where she flicked her long nail at the side of his face and sometimes it left a little cut. Through it all, Klint never reacted.

I was surprised by the way he talked to Mom at the funeral home, but I chalked it up to the stress of the day and everything else going on in our lives. He was mad, but even then he didn't freak out. He told her off, but he didn't scream. He didn't run. He didn't spill soup.

Miss Jack really got to him, and I don't know why.

Klint parks Bill's truck in his driveway and walks to his door. The outside porch light comes on and I see Bill peer out. I get out of the truck, throw a wave in his direction, and head to our house while Klint talks to him for a minute, both of them doing it out of loneliness, not because they have anything to say to each other.

Mr. B darts out of a bush in front of my feet, and I practically trip over him. He flies to the top of our porch, stops in an orange

streak, then sits there licking a paw, waiting, and watching me with fierce, golden eyes.

I sit down next to him and scratch him between his ears. He purrs and butts his face against mine. I saw a show on the Learning Channel that said this is how cats give kisses.

I grab him, flip him over on his back, and hold him like a baby. He squints his eyes at me and keeps purring. He'd never let anyone else do this to him. He's a wild, tough cat who only comes inside to eat in the morning and sometimes to curl up on my bed for a few hours on a winter night.

He just showed up one day in our backyard. He was good-sized but painfully skinny and had caked blood on the end of his tail and around one eye. I started feeding him without telling anybody. He wouldn't let me touch him so I couldn't clean off the blood, but it ended up falling off on its own.

Mom started noticing him around the house and said we couldn't keep him. She claimed if we had a cat it would mean more work for her. The woman was always responsible for everything, she said, and she couldn't cope with the burden of another life.

Dad didn't mind him hanging around as long as he stayed outside, but he made it clear he wasn't a fan of cats. It wasn't until Mr. B started depositing dead mice, voles, and chipmunks on the porch steps that Dad

finally brought home the first bag of Cat Chow.

He filled out nicely in no time and started letting me pet him, but he never warmed up to anyone else in the family.

Dad used to call him that "big frickin' cat." It was the only way he ever referred to him. He'd say, "Look what that big frickin' cat killed last night," or "Get that big frickin' cat out of my house." I started calling him Mr. Big and eventually shortened it to Mr. B.

I can't believe I'm never going to see him again.

These past few days I've discovered possessions are meaningless. I can't think of anything I own that I care about. Not a single video game or board game. Not the iPod Dad, Bill, and Klint got me for my birthday last year. Not my concert T-shirt from the Lynyrd Skynyrd/Hank Williams, Jr. Bad Ass Tour or my poster of Miss February. Not my books or my art supplies. Not even my collection of "guys" I've had since I was a kid: aliens, pirates, dinosaurs, soldiers, farm and jungle animals that came in plastic tubes I got in my Christmas stockings, Pokemon characters, knights, robots, rainbow-colored rubbery frogs I got out of bubblegum machines, a set of bendable monsters I got in a goodie bag at a Halloween party, a set of peanuts painted to look like Steelers that Dad found at a flea market up in Cameron County

when he was on a fishing trip with Bill, and a bunch of random cartoon and Disney figures I've accumulated from Happy Meals. I've used them my whole life to wage battles and populate imaginary cities, and now I'm suddenly looking back on all those safe, lazy afternoons as a waste of time.

If I could take Mr. B with me, though, things wouldn't be so bad.

I keep holding him and enjoying sitting outside. After the long sticky summer we had, these first cool nights have a clean brightness to them. The white moon and stars look like they've been freshly polished and stuck into the dark violet sky, and the stillness in the air is so complete it's more like a calming presence than a lack of movement.

If I could take this Pennsylvania night with me, things wouldn't be so bad, either.

Klint comes walking across our yard, and I quickly set down Mr. B. He gives me an indignant look, then notices Klint and disappears into the bushes.

Klint picks up one of the dozens of baseballs that are always lying around our house and starts absentmindedly tossing it one-handed in the air and catching it again. He thinks better with a ball in his hand.

Klint's not stupid; he just doesn't want to be smart.

A lot of people think baseball players are dumb, and I don't blame them if they're

watching a game without any real knowledge of what's going on. It seems the players spend most of their time sitting in the dugout and standing in the field, and while they're waiting around for something to happen they're usually wearing dopey expressions on their faces and occupying themselves by spitting and scratching.

When there is action, it's over so quickly it appears effortless. It only takes a few seconds to hit a ball four hundred feet or to gun someone out from deep in the hole at shortstop. It seems to barely require any physical exertion, let alone mental power.

What people don't understand is the whole act of hitting the ball is a lesson in physics and once that ball is hit, a hundred different scenarios can unfold and the players in the field have to be able to respond correctly and instantly.

A dumb guy can't do it.

Klint sits down next to me on the steps, still tossing the ball. I take out the pocketknife Dad got for me when I was ten, find a branch, and start paring away strips of the wood until I come to the tender green center.

We sit that way for a while until I can't stand it anymore.

"Are you ever gonna talk to me again?" I ask him.

"Why do you need me to talk to you?"

"I don't."

"Then what do you care?"

We sit for a while longer, Klint with his ball and me staring at the stars. Less than a week ago I was looking up at those same stars through the ragged pattern of leaves made by the Hamiltons' towering oaks and maples. I had a dad and a home then and Shelby Jack nuzzling up next to me in front of a fire instead of looking at me across her aunt's table with horror in her eyes.

"That woman was messed up," Klint says out of the blue. "Asking us all that shit about Mom and Dad."

"She was thinking about letting us live with her," I explain feebly. "Maybe she wanted to know something about us."

"She was never gonna let us live with her," he growls at me.

"Then why did she invite us to dinner? Why would Shelby lie?"

"You don't understand anything about people. Especially rich people."

It's true that Klint has more experience with rich people than I do. He's been to Brent Richmond's house a couple times for team-related functions. Brent's dad owns Sunny Valley Homes. He rips up quiet green hillsides and slaps together identical, prefab houses and fills them with poor young families with screaming kids and frustrated, yelping dogs, and poor single people who play really loud music with their windows open in

the hopes someone will think they're cool and want to hang out with them. Aunt Jen lives in one of his developments: Sunnybrook Estates.

Klint also got to go to the home of the dean of a university when he was invited down to a special batting camp sponsored by a group of Florida colleges last December. It was a huge coup for a sophomore to be asked to attend, and Dad talked about it for the entire off-season.

One of the schools hosted a reception for the ballplayers at the dean's house. All Klint remembered about the house was that there was an aquarium full of colorful fish as big as an entire wall, and that there was a fountain with two gold dolphins spouting water in their front yard. The only thing he ever told me about Brent's house was that he had a huge hot tub with a TV mounted above it and that his mom had a sunken bathtub that looked like a gigantic clamshell.

Apparently for Klint, one of the most striking differences between poor and rich people is a more creative use of water.

"We were a diversion for her," he goes on.

"A diversion?"

"Yeah, you know. An amusing distraction from her boring rich old lady life."

He's definitely let his guard down when he starts using big words and then providing definitions.

I spy Mr. B sitting on his favorite tree branch, watching Klint intently like he wants to be prepared in case my brother suddenly shrinks down to small rodent size.

All of a sudden his gaze turns wary, and he slinks off his perch into the dark leaves.

A moment later we hear the sound of the car engine that he heard first.

A big black SUV comes rumbling down our road. We both know who it is before it comes to a stop.

"Shit," Klint says.

"I'll leave you guys alone," I say gladly, and go inside.

My bedroom's in the front of the house and my window's right next to the front porch. I keep my lights off and sit on my bed where I can hear everything.

"Hey, Klint."

"Coach."

"Hope you don't mind me dropping by like this. I had something I wanted to discuss with you, and I didn't feel like using the phone."

I sidle up next to the window and peer out the screen.

Coach is wearing his gray Centresburg Flames windbreaker and ball cap. He has his hands stuck in his pockets and is working a piece of chew inside his lower lip.

The skin on his face, neck, and arms is the consistency of beef jerky from all the days spent standing in the sun. He teaches tenth-

grade history at the high school and his evaluations from the students every year always say his class is a great place for a nap. He's the kind of guy no one notices except for when he steps on a baseball field; then something electric happens to him, and he becomes the guy everyone needs to look at before and after every single play.

Coach glances down at the ball in Klint's hand.

"So what's going on?"

"Not much."

"How are you doing?"

"Okay."

"Mrs. Hill and the girls wanted me to tell you that they hope you're feeling better. They're all very concerned about you."

No one's ever seen Mrs. Hill but the coach often relays messages from her: "Mrs. Hill says good luck," or "Mrs. Hill is home rooting for us."

There are two types of coaches' wives: the type that's almost as involved as the coach, who shows up at every game in sunglasses and a team cap, greased with coconut oil, toting a cooler full of Gatorade and a clipboard, who knows the RBIs, allergies, names of girlfriends, and shoe sizes of every player; and the type who wouldn't be caught dead at a game. Mrs. Hill appears to be the second type.

She and the coach have three daughters and

no sons. The middle one is a year older than Klint and the youngest one is my age. They both have things for Klint. They cheer wildly for him at the games and try to talk to him when he's waiting to bat.

The oldest daughter is away at college on a track and cross-country scholarship. Because of the coach's well-known disdain for girls' sports — he was quoted once in a newspaper interview as saying the school board should take the money they spend on girls' softball and hire a new sex ed teacher — she was able to have a flourishing high school running career without any pressure put on her by her parents.

Probably the worst thing that ever happened to Coach and the best thing that ever happened to his kids is none of them were born male.

At the mention of the girls, I make a kissy noise at the window and Klint whips the ball so hard at me it rips through the old, rusty screen and bounces off my wall.

"What the hell?" Coach shouts at him.

"I saw a bug," Klint says.

Coach Hill regains his composure by concentrating on his chewing and then spitting a long stream of tobacco in our yard.

"As I was saying, they're concerned about you."

"That's nice," Klint says.

"I heard you're not real excited about go-

ing to live with your mom in Arizona."

What he means is everyone is talking about Klint's outburst in front of the funeral home.

"Of course, I don't have to tell you how much the team would miss you."

What he means is he's going to have to kiss his shot at the state championship title good-bye.

"Mrs. Hill and I discussed it."

What he means is I discussed it with myself.

"And we know it might be a little bit presumptuous and of course we'd have to talk to your mom about it, but we'd like to have you come live with us."

Live with Coach Hill: it takes a minute for the idea to sink in.

I wonder if he screams and his face turns red if you don't clean your room. I wonder if Mrs. Hill can cook. I wonder if Klint and I would have to share a room. I've gotten used to having my own room since Mom and Krystal left, but I suppose I could go back to bunking with Klint if I had to.

The daughters aren't bad-looking. The youngest one, Katy, was in my English class last year. We talked sometimes. Most of our conversations were about Klint and the team, but every once in a while I'd try discussing a movie or an assignment with her and it always went well. She said hi to me at the games.

I think I could do it. I could probably live

with them.

"I don't know," Klint says. "It's nice of you and Mrs. Hill to make the offer. I'll have to talk it over with Kyle."

"Yeah. About Kyle," Coach says. "I know you boys are close. I don't think he's ever missed a game. He's practically like a mascot."

"My brother's not a mascot," Klint says roughly.

"You know what I mean. The problem is we don't really have the room for both of you. I thought he could go with your mom. He's younger. He should be with her."

I feel like I've been sucker punched in the gut. I can't listen to any more. I roll off my bed and wander through the dark house.

I tell myself deep down I don't care. The crucial thing right now is finding a good environment for Klint's ballplaying and what could be better than living with a guy who eats, drinks, and sleeps baseball and wants him to succeed just as much as Dad did and even for the same reason, so someday down the road he can point and say, "That's my boy. I made him what he is today."

This will be Klint's most important year of high school ball. College scouts will be watching him extrahard during the upcoming spring and summer seasons, and he'll get his offers next fall.

College isn't his only option, though. He

could go for the draft his senior year. That's what Dad would've told him to do because Dad was blinded by Klint's potential. The golden glow coming from Klint's dream future made it impossible for Dad to see the equally possible nightmares: injuries, burn-out, drugs, alcohol, bad breaks, breakdowns; there are lots of reasons why guys don't make it.

I'm the one who convinced Klint he needs college. I've done my research, plus like I said, Klint's not dumb. He knows the road to the majors is paved with the bodies of players who were drafted in the thirty-fifth round and went on to play farm ball for their entire careers, never making any money, never once setting foot on a major-league field, and having nothing to fall back on once they couldn't or wouldn't play anymore.

I'm starving. A couple bites of soup wasn't much of a dinner. I head for the kitchen.

The countertops and the table are covered with half-eaten, dried-out casseroles and lasagnas and rubbery Jell-O molds we forgot to put in the fridge. The moon shines through the window over the sink and lights up the dishes with an eerie glow, each one like a miniature alien landscape full of crumbling canyon walls, craters, caves, and lakes of grease.

The light splashes across the red-and-white tile floor Mom wanted desperately, and Dad

worked overtime to afford and installed for her one sunny spring weekend years ago while she fluttered around him smiling prettily and bringing him beers. It's filthy, scratched, and faded now, more the color of rotten hamburger meat than the candy cane it used to resemble.

The moonlight stops on the wall next to the back door where our calendar hangs. September is pretty empty. I wrote down "SCHOOL STARTS" on our first day and Klint wrote over it "SCHOOL SUCKS." I also wrote down the date of the Hamiltons' party, which is now also the date of my father's death.

Dad wrote down the date of a meeting at the high school next week. I remember the yellow flyer Klint brought home from school for him:

ATTENTION PARENTS OF STUDENT ATHLETES INTERESTED IN THE COLLEGE SCHOLARSHIP PROCESS. DON'T MISS THIS INFORMATIVE MEETING!

I remember how excited he was. I knew he was already picturing himself strutting into the auditorium. He'd be royalty there — King Carl, the father of the Prince of Diamonds — his gray janitor coveralls a distant memory sitting at home in a wet ball in the washing machine.

I fix myself a bowl of cornflakes and milk and go sit on the back stoop.

Bill's house is dark, too. On a night like tonight he and Dad should be sitting on his back porch shooting the shit. Right about now I'd come outside and yell over that I'm going to bed, and they'd both smile and raise their beers in a good-night salute.

Klint would already be asleep. He keeps farmers' hours. I'd lie awake until I heard Dad come back inside and turn on the TV. He spent a lot of nights on the couch after Mom left. The garbled sound of the TV voices and the clink of Dad's whisky bottle hitting the rim of his glass over and over again would make me drift off. Eventually we'd all be asleep, safe and sound, together in our aloneness.

Dad's not on Bill's porch tonight. He's not on the couch. Where is he? That's what I can't wrap my head around. His body's rotting in the ground, but where is he?

From the front of the house I hear a car door slam and an engine start.

A few minutes later the front door opens and closes, then the back door screen squeaks open.

"What are you doing?" Klint asks, standing behind me.

"Nothing."

"How long you been here?"

"Awhile."

I stare out at our backyard. In one corner I can barely make out our old sandbox in the

shadows. In another corner is a big oak with boards nailed to the trunk as steps going up to our tree house. All that's left of the house is the floor. We can't use it as a hideout anymore, but it's still a good place to sit.

Our rusted swing set stands in the middle of the yard. The swings are long gone. For a while Klint used it as a bar to do chin-ups but now he does his workouts at the school gym or the Y.

Krystal and I used to play with the slide sometimes. I showed her how she could fill a bucket with water and set it at the bottom and send her Barbies down the silver chute. I told her it was The World's Biggest Barbie Water Slide.

She loved doing that.

I set down my bowl, stand up, and face Klint.

"Will you take Mr. B?" I ask.

"What?"

"Will you take him when you go live with Coach Hill?"

"What are you talking about? Why would I take that piece of crap old cat with me? Cats are for girls and faggots."

"How would you know? You don't know shit about girls, although I guess you know plenty about faggots."

He gives me a two-handed shove in the chest, and I fall backward off the steps onto my ass. He's on top of me before I can react,

and we go rolling around the yard.

He's bigger than I am and has more muscle on him, but I'm fast and wire-tough and have the advantage of having been beaten on my whole life by an older brother while he's never been beaten on by anyone other than his mom and she doesn't count because she fights like a girl.

We pound on each other until we're winded. I've torn the knee out of my only good pair of jeans, and my right arm feels like it's been wrenched out of its socket.

Klint's lip is bleeding, and he has a clump of muddy grass in his hair. He sits up and brushes it away.

I lie on my back, cradling my arm at my side, and try to catch my breath.

"You're gonna go live with him?" I ask the stars.

"No."

I look over at him to see if he's watching me. I don't want him to see the relief on my face. I feel bad for feeling it. I should push him to go live with Coach. It would be best for him.

"Why not?"

"Shit. You think I want to live with my coach?"

"His daughters aren't bad-looking."

"They're all right."

His tongue darts out of his mouth and licks at the blood.

"What are we gonna do?" I ask him.

"Run away, I guess."

"Where?"

"I don't know yet."

"What about ball?"

"A lot can happen between now and spring."

He lies back on the grass next to me.

"It might have been interesting to see what Mrs. Hill looks like," he says a little regretfully.

"You mean to see if she's real?"

He smiles.

"Yeah."

"I still say she's his alter ego. He puts on a dress and a wig like that Norman Bates dude in *Psycho* and talks in a woman's voice."

"Mrs. Hill, we have a game tomorrow," I say in a low voice imitating Coach.

"Tell the boys I'm rooting for them," I say in a high, cackly voice.

Klint cracks up.

Besides being the only person he gets mad at, I'm also the only person who can really make him laugh.

Chapter Seven: Candace Jack

How do you begin a conversation with a woman you've never met with the intention of asking her if she'd give you two of her children?

I've been through many difficult and emotionally taxing experiences in my life and managed to survive all of them with my dignity intact, yet this particular task proved to be more daunting to me than informing my brother some forty-odd years ago that I'd just paid almost a million dollars for a cow.

I made the call last night after the boys and Shelby left.

In a fit of optimism before dinner, Shelby had given me a phone number where the mother could be reached. After dinner, she wouldn't have dared.

She left the table crying and crushed, giving me a terrible stare filled with pain and humble regret. I knew she needed comforting, but I let her suffer because she needed that more.

I spent a good hour preparing what I was going to say to this woman. I had been told she was horrible. I had witnessed with my own eyes the condition of her sons, both of them trying to act like nothing was wrong: one with stoicism, cynicism, and eventually rage; the other with a puppy dog eagerness to please.

They upset me at dinner, but they didn't disappoint. If they had cried, if they had asked if I have a swimming pool or a big-screen TV, if they had answered all of my questions politely or unemotionally, I would have fed them, sent them on their way, and would have never given them a second thought. But this wasn't to be the case.

They are damaged but not ruined.

As for the mother, I was still willing to give her the benefit of the doubt.

This was our conversation:

"I'm trying to get in touch with Rhonda Hayes."

A woman's voice tells me, "Just a sec," and then the name, "Ronnie!!!!" is screamed next to the phone receiver.

"Yeah?"

"Is this Rhonda Hayes?"

"Not anymore. I'm divorced. Thank God. I went back to my maiden name, Welty."

"But you are the mother of Kyle and Klint Hayes?"

"Yeah. Who are you?"

"My name is Candace Jack. My niece, Shelby, is a friend of your sons."
"Never heard of her."
"Regardless. She *is* a friend, and she's very concerned about them."
"Is this about their dad dying? Does she want to say she's sorry?"
"She already did. She was at the funeral."
"Oh."
"This goes beyond offering condolences. We've heard that you're planning to take the boys with you to live in Arizona and that they would rather stay here."
"Where'd you hear that?"
"It doesn't matter. If you'd be agreeable to my proposition, I'd like to provide them with a home here. They could live with me until they're finished with high school."
(A sharp laugh.)
"What kind of perv are you? You think I'm gonna let my boys go live with some lady I don't even know? Are you an old lady? You sound like one."
"I'm seventy-six."
"Seventy-six? Are you crazy? What's some seventy-six-year-old woman gonna do with two teenage boys? That's disgusting."
"I have ample space and ample means."
"Jesus Christ. Ample space and ample means. Are you crazy?"
"That's the second time you've asked me that, so I'll assume that means you're expect-

ing an answer. No, I'm not."

(Silence.)

"Rhonda . . . May I call you that?"

"I guess."

"It was just a thought. I didn't mean to intrude or presume. Obviously you're anxious to have your sons live with you again despite the expense and responsibility."

"What do you mean?"

"Well, the cost alone of feeding two teenage boys must be very great. They'll need clothes and school supplies and money for the never-ending list of things children demand these days. I believe your car insurance will go up quite a bit, and you'll probably need another car unless you're planning to drive them around yourself. They'll need health insurance, too. I imagine they were covered by a plan through their father's employer.

"But as you know, you can't put a price tag on familial joy. I'm sure there's not going to be any tension or unpleasantness when the boys move in with you. I'm sure they'll adjust happily to their new school and from what I've been told, it sounds like they're going to get along wonderfully with your new husband."

(More silence.)

"We're not married."

"All the better. That way if he decides he can't stand living with your sons, he can just leave and you won't have to go through

another divorce."

(More silence.)

"Rhonda, I realize this was a very sudden and unorthodox offer, and I apologize for catching you off guard. I assure you I was only trying to help. I'm going to leave you the name and number of my lawyer in case you'd like to discuss this further. Do you have a pen?"

"What'd you say your name was?"

"Candace Jack. You may be familiar with my last name. I believe all three of your children were born in my brother's hospital."

The phone call is playing in my head as I wake up this morning.

It went about as well as I expected. I never thought for one moment that any mother, no matter how selfish and irresponsible, would simply give up her sons to a complete stranger. She would have to be convinced that to do so would be in her best interest yet would appear to the world to be in the boys' best interest.

I lie in bed for a few minutes gathering my strength. The arthritis in my knees and hip has advanced to a point where the simple act of getting out of bed is excruciating. My doctor has given me pills and injections, but nothing seems to help anymore.

My body has been aging and deteriorating, untouched and unloved, for so many years now I sometimes think of myself as an aban-

doned house. Echoes of laughter, hurried footsteps, and bright peals of music still resonate inside me, but my exterior is bleak and forbidding.

When the younger Hayes boy began asking me questions about Manuel last night, it was like someone had finally ventured up the sagging front porch steps of my soul and shouted through one of my broken windows, "Hello, in there!"

I sit up slowly as I do every morning and look in amazement at the bony, wrinkled arms and gnarled hands roped in blue veins and wonder how they came to be attached to my body.

I used to be an attractive woman, but I make the claim without the least bit of pride or vanity. My beauty was given to me, not earned. It made the people around me behave either foolishly or dishonestly. The supposed rewards that came with it — the desire of men, the envy of women, the attention of strangers — were of no interest or value to me. I didn't want to be watched or coveted or disliked on sight. I wanted to be anonymous and left alone.

However, I won't go so far as to say I wished I was unattractive instead. I'm human. I'm drawn to pretty things. I took pleasure in my reflection in the mirror, in my nicely formed figure and the features of my face, in my green eyes and full lips and

my flawless complexion. I loved the way sunshine turned my hair the color of a freshly minted penny. I loved the silky feel of it in my hands as I brushed it.

I had many men in my life, but I never cared about any of them except for Manuel, and I make this claim, too, without the least bit of pride and vanity, or guilt, or embarrassment. Men wanted me, and I let them think they could have me. Occasionally one did have me, but my heart was never in it.

I slept with four men before I met Manuel. I can give an exact reason for each escapade: in chronological order they would be curiosity, pity, three thousand shares of Peppernack Steel stock, and a bottle of Wild Turkey.

My brother saw beauty as a commodity. When I reached a certain age and it became clear I was going to possess this particular asset, he was thrilled that I would eventually be able to help him in his business dealings in ways other than typing, filing, and accounting.

I was intelligent and did very well in high school, so well that I won a scholarship to a secretarial school in Lancaster. Stan let me go with the understanding that I'd put my newfound skills to use in his fledgling business once I acquired them.

After graduation, I helped him in the front office of J&P Coal for several years until he and his newfound partner, Joe Peppernack,

became successful enough to hire their first perky blonde and to let me go to college, which had always been a dream of mine. Stan had no use for school, as he put it, and dropped out in the tenth grade; but he was proud of my education and the fact that he was able to finance it.

I spent all my breaks and summers with him and he put me to work in a different way than before. There was never anything overtly sexual in the instructions he gave me for entertaining men who could be of some help to him. He never said anything to me other than, "Be nice," yet I knew those two little words implied a wide range of activities.

Stan wouldn't have been the least bit upset to find out I had slept with a man to get him to sell the mineral rights to his family's land for far less than they were worth or if I had slept with him to get him to buy me a new refrigerator. This attitude didn't arise out of any lack of respect or fondness for me. Stan simply did not see sex as an act of love or intimacy and couldn't for the life of him understand the romantic and sentimental hysteria it inspired. Like hunting, he believed it was done for pleasure or to put food on the table.

I dress and make my way downstairs, stopping by my study to pick up Rafael's letter.

It's another lovely, crisp fall day. The sky is a sharp, flawless blue with a few puffs of

bright white clouds. I wrap myself in a heavy, buff-colored silk shawl embroidered with flowers of the palest pink and tell Luis I'll have my breakfast on the porch.

He brings me my coffee, fresh fruit, and one egg with toast, then shows no signs of leaving.

I ignore him and concentrate on slowly spreading his lemon marmalade on my toast. He watches, pretending he's waiting for me to tell him what I think when he knows perfectly well how much I love his marmalades. He wants to talk about last night.

"I think it's a shame," he finally says.

"What is?"

"Those boys. I think it's a shame what happened to them."

"I think it's a shame what happened to my tablecloth."

He frowns at me from beneath his impressive mustache.

"He didn't want to talk about it. You can't blame him. Do you think it's easy for a boy to hear bad things about his mother?"

"Of course not, but the other boy was able to handle it."

"Miss Shelby likes them."

"Miss Shelby likes the older boy too much. She could barely look at him without blushing."

"The younger boy likes Miss Shelby."

"And I don't like any of them."

I take a bite of the bread and savor the tart sweetness of the jam while Luis belligerently plunges his hands into his pants pockets. Since we're alone and he has no role to play, he's wearing jeans and a white corduroy shirt.

"You shouldn't be mad at Miss Shelby. She's just trying to help."

"She's just trying to get what she wants, and she's going about it by being sneaky and manipulative. Don't think for one moment that I didn't realize what she was up to when she invited her father here. What I want to know is if you were in cahoots with her?"

"Cahoots? I'm afraid I don't know this word. What is cahoots?"

"Did you conspire with her?"

"Ah, conspire. That word I know. No. I had nothing to do with it."

I pour steamed milk into my coffee, add two lumps of sugar, and stir it with the air of someone who's not convinced.

"I'm getting old, you know," he tries another route.

"I've noticed."

"Jerry, too."

"Jerry will still be able to chop firewood when he's a hundred and ten."

"We could use some help around here. A couple young strong backs."

"What are you saying? I should think of them as slaves instead of charity cases? You're even worse at this than Shelby is."

He pouts. I sip at my coffee and let him suffer for a few more moments.

"It's all beside the point," I tell him as I take Rafael's letter from the envelope, a signal that this conversation is coming to an end. "I spoke to their mother last night."

"No," he exclaims, his dark eyes flashing. "You didn't."

"Yes, I did."

"What did she say?"

"She thinks I'm crazy. More specifically she called me a perv. I think it's short for pervert."

He looks absolutely stunned for a moment — a man who's been shot in the back and has just begun to feel the pain — then his incredulous expression turns into a grin and he bursts into laughter. He laughs until tears stream down his cheeks.

I can't help but smile a little, too.

He's still laughing as he turns and goes back into the house with his tray.

I finish taking Rafael's letter out of its envelope. As usual, he's enclosed several clippings describing his latest corridas. Manuel disliked the powerful and esteemed bullfight critics and ignored their opinions of him while Rafael claims to not care about the critics yet I know he reads every word written about him.

I settle happily into his words. He writes to me in English. I write to him in Spanish.

Dear Aunt Candy,

I was happy to get your letter. It came at a frustrating time for me when I needed something to make me feel better.

The season is coming to an end, and I'm afraid it's not going to get better for me. A few short months ago the critics were praising me for my exquisite style. Now these same critics are back to saying I only have a career because of my pretty face and the fact that a certain starstruck segment of the public will always pay to see a bullfighter who shares the blood of Manuel Obrador. The crowds have turned irritable and bored. I should be used to the ups and downs by now, but I fear I never will.

The bulls have been bad these past few weeks, but I won't blame them for my own failures. My performance has been fine technically. It's emotion I'm lacking. I'm losing my joy in front of the bull. It's becoming a chore.

Part of the problem might be my distraction. I'm beginning to think I shouldn't have agreed to be the consultant on this movie I told you about.

The actor playing the torero is an American. I don't know who he is, although everyone working on the film tells me he's very famous and I must be mistaken. (Americans think the entire world

knows all their movie stars and other countries don't have movie stars of their own.)

When they asked me what I thought of him, I told them he could never do it. I explained an American could simply not understand what it is to be a torero. They thought I was naive about what acting was all about and also prejudiced. They said it was the job of an actor to be able to portray people unlike himself. I still said it couldn't be done. I told them even in Spain there are very few movies about toreros. No Spanish actors want this role. The Americans said these actors are afraid. I said no, they are respectful. They persisted and said they're afraid they will fail. I said, no, they know they will fail. And you will, too.

I've done my best to try and explain toreo to them, but they aren't open to learning the truth. In the director's first interview here, he tried to distance himself from the very subject he wants to show. He said, "By making this film, we're not taking a stance on whether bullfighting is morally right or wrong." I read these words and wanted to beat him. Morally right or wrong? There are no morals in art.

These people are cowards and hypocrites. The animals they eat live unnatural

lives full of pain and confinement and are killed in terrible, shameful ways. This is okay. Toros have the best lives of any creature. They are left to run wild and do as they please. They spend their last living moments surrounded by people who respect and revere them. They die heroic deaths. But this is not okay?

Is it better to be a man who lives a shabby, wasted, little life until he dies anonymously at the age of eighty or is it better to be a man who lives a large, passionate, meaningful life and dies a glorious death at half that age?

Most men would pick the first choice because they are men, and think like men, and men fear death. Toros think like toros and don't know what death is. Toreros think like toreros and know death so well, we don't regard it as an enemy or an end but a simple fact of our existence.

Try putting that in your film, Mr. Director. They can't. Still, I'm helping them because I need the money, and the lead actress is very beautiful. She understands nothing about anything but thinks she knows something about everything. A typical American. (You are not typical, Aunt Candy.) I'm having a good time with her. She's exactly the kind of woman I like. One I could never fall in love with.

Last week at Valladolid I had three toros

in a row with no pride in them. The last one was the weakest. I ran him with some success, but there was no emotion in him, or me, or the crowd. After a few sets of naturales that earned me a few "Olés," he came to a stop and stood before me with his sides heaving and his tongue lolling out. I clearly heard an old lady shriek, "Matalo! Matalo!" Kill him. Kill him. For a moment I thought she meant for the bull to kill me! Maybe she did.

Love,
Rafi

I fold the letter and tuck it back into its envelope. I have over fifty of them in a box I keep in my bedroom closet beginning with the first one he wrote to me as a ten-year-old boy in an effort to find out as much as possible about his famous great-uncle whom he worshipped and emulated.

He's the grandson of Manuel's only sister and an accomplished torero in his own right but one who's been burdened with a weight his peers don't have to bear.

His uncle Manuel was a magnificent bullfighter and this would have been the extent of his reputation, but by dying in the ring, he became a legend. Rafael could try to live up to his skill and his grace, but he could never live up to his death.

I smile at Rafi's transparency and wonder if

he knew when he wrote about the choice between an old man dying anonymously and a young man dying gloriously that he was so obviously trying to convince himself that we shouldn't grieve for Manuel.

I eventually had to come to the same realization myself. I still sometimes wish Manuel could have led a quiet life and lived to be a man of eighty and still be with me, but that would have required him being someone he wasn't and I wouldn't have loved that man.

I must have fallen deep into my own thoughts because I don't notice Luis's return until he holds a phone under my nose.

"Call for you from a lawyer."

"A lawyer?" I ask.

He shrugs.

I take the phone from him and he strolls away from me, pretending to tend to a potted plant while straining his ears to hear every word of my side of the conversation.

"This is Candace Jack."

"Hello, Miss Jack. This is Attorney Edgars, here. Chip Edgars."

An attorney named Chip? A very specific breed of man.

"Hello, Mr. Edgars. Do we know each other? Your name sounds familiar to me."

"I don't think we've ever met personally, but a lot of people see my ads on TV."

An attorney named Chip who advertises on

TV: an even more specific breed of man.

"Of course. I've seen your commercials. You have very catchy slogans. I especially like, 'However you were hurt, someone, somewhere owes you money.' "

"Hey," he laughs. "That's pretty good. A direct quote."

"What can I do for you, Mr. Edgars?"

"I'm calling on behalf of my client, Rhonda Welty."

"She has a lawyer?"

"As of this morning. We'd like to meet with you to go over what you discussed with her on the phone last night and the sooner, the better. Miss Welty is pressed for time and has to return to Arizona in two days."

"I see. I'm sure she's very busy. Can I get back to you, Mr. Edgars?"

"Sure, that's fine."

I hang up the phone. Luis turns my way, his palm cupped and full of dead leaves.

"Luis, I may need a ride into Centresburg later."

"Por qué?"

"I may be going into battle."

He raises his thick gray eyebrows in mild surprise.

"It's been a long time," he says.

"I know."

"Just don't expect me to be your Sancho Panza."

"I'll expect you to be my Luis Martinez."

He takes his orders seriously. He tosses the leaves off the side of the porch, squares his shoulders, and walks back inside the house with the cocky strut of El Soltero's aide-de-camp.

Chapter Eight

Over forty-five years in this country and Luis still drives like a Spaniard. They have no regard for speed limits or respect for the laws of physics, and they view every driver in front of them as a personal affront that should be immediately passed, oncoming traffic be damned.

I'm perfectly capable of driving myself, but I no longer have the desire. My reflexes have dulled over time while awareness of my own mortality has become extremely keen. Death itself doesn't bother me. I'm weary and frequently in pain. I have no spouse or children or any unfulfilled plans to live for. I've had moments when I've been sure I'm ready to go, and the thought hasn't frightened or saddened me but filled me with a satisfied serenity that I can only describe as coming to the end of a long race. It's the manner of my death that concerns me, and I can say for certain that I don't wish to die crushed beyond recognition in a heap of mangled

metal. The irony in all this is that while I don't trust my own abilities, I will put my fate in the hands of a man who drives like a panicked chipmunk.

It takes me a few minutes to get my bearings once Luis comes to a stop in the parking lot across the street from Chip Edgars's office, a squat, yellow brick building with a life-sized cardboard cutout of himself propped up in the lobby.

My attorney, Bert Shulman, is standing next to it. When he sees me come through the door, he strikes the same ridiculous pose, his arms crossed over his chest, his head cocked to one side, his brow furrowed with concern for my litigious needs.

I shake my head at him and smile.

"Candace," he says, warmly, coming toward me with his hand outstretched. "How are you?"

I give him my hand and he clasps it.

Bert has been a fixture for my entire adult life. My brother hired him when he was only a few years out of law school and already making a name for himself working in the legal department of a large exporting firm in Philadelphia. His father was the owner of the only department store in Centresburg at the time, and they were one of only two Jewish families in the area. Bert was the second son. It was understood his older brother would inherit the family business, which was fine

with Bert, who equated the mental complexities of selling retail with those of heating a can of soup.

He's younger than I am, but I've always considered him older and wiser. He used to be dark-haired and dashing with a sharp wit and a love of yellow roses, which he would bring me by the dozens when I'd return home on my breaks from college.

Now he's an equally dashing man in his seventies with a silver pompadour, a pencil-thin mustache, and sparkling blue eyes behind a pair of octagonal wire-rimmed glasses. His wardrobe is legendary in these parts: seersucker suits in summer, natty tweed blazers in autumn, a midnight blue cashmere overcoat and Russian sable hat in winter, all of it worn with one of his dozens of colorful bow ties.

My brother met him purely by chance in a bar. Bert was home visiting his family. They had an immediate rapport, and Stan claimed he knew instantly that Bert had exactly the kind of legal mind he needed to help him expand his business.

Bert had wanted to stay in his hometown and set up a private practice, but he feared a Jewish lawyer wouldn't be able to build a clientele. He knew of people who refused to shop at his father's store — despite his reasonable prices and the largest housewares

department in the county — because of their faith.

Stan didn't care that he was Jewish. He saw Bert's potential for helping him to make money or save money. This was always his uppermost concern. J&P Coal was the first mining company in the state to employ a black pit boss, a Chinese accountant, and a second-generation East Indian doctor during a time where any of them would have had difficulty finding a restaurant in town that would have served them. My brother was the least racist man I've ever known. When evaluating men, he saw only one color: green.

"I appreciate that you're making time for me on such short notice," I tell Bert.

"Anything for you," he replies with a wink, "and besides, I wouldn't miss this for the world."

We're shown into Chip Edgars's office, a surprisingly spacious, tasteful room with a subtle color scheme, an attractive mahogany desk dominating one end, and the kind of brick-red leather furnishings found in the libraries of English manors.

The walls are covered not with obligatory framed diplomas but with photos of Chip posing with what I assume to be his satisfied customers: a woman in a wheelchair, a man with one arm, a woman sprouting tubes lying in a hospital bed, a man on crutches posing next to a wrecked car, another man with an

eye patch, to name a few. All of them are holding checks and smiling deliriously, their expressions a testimony to the efficacy of pain medication.

Chip Edgars grabs my hand and shakes it vigorously. The man is a definite step down from his office. He's wearing a cheap gray suit, a gaudy neon pink tie, and an obvious toupee. He should let his interior designer dress him.

"I'm Chip Edgars," he shouts at me.

I'm used to it. I'm old; therefore, I must not be able to hear.

"Yes, I recognize you," I reply, pleasantly. "We passed one of your billboards on the drive here. Your mother must be proud."

He continues smiling and shaking my hand until I introduce him to Bert. They know each other. It's a small town.

Next he guides us to a far corner of the room to a few chairs and a sofa situated around a coffee table. Cups and a pot of coffee are sitting on it. I'm surprised, again, to see the cups are china, not Styrofoam, plastic, or chunky mugs with his law firm's logo written across them.

As we walk, he tells me about the few times he's had the privilege of meeting Cameron and what a "great guy" he is. I let him prattle on and don't bother correcting him.

Sitting on the sofa are two skinny, hostile, middle-aged, chain-smoking bleached

blondes who exhibit all the female charm and enthusiasm of a pair of retired anorexic strippers. They're both sitting upright with their legs crossed, holding a cigarette in one hand and a huge Starbucks cup in the other.

One is wearing skintight jeans tucked into white cowboy boots, and a tiny low-cut, cropped red sweater that looks like it was purchased at Petco. The other is wearing a bejeweled lavender sweat suit and flip-flops.

There are two very specific physical species of women common to this part of Pennsylvania. I like to think of them as the cow, and the hardscrabble chicken. The second category can be identified by their darting movements, their screechy voices, their beady predatory eyes, and their scrawny corded necks.

These two women are indisputable examples of the latter group. They are undoubtedly sisters. Along with their stunning fashion sense and apparent need for a constant infusion of caffeine and nicotine, they also share the same mannerisms and lack of a chin.

"Candace Jack, this is Rhonda Welty" — Chip makes the introductions, gesturing at the woman in the cocker spaniel's sweater — "and her sister, Jennifer."

They're stumped for a moment as they try and decide which they can more easily part with, the coffee or cigarette. The sister who is able to make a decision first puts down her

cup and gives me her hand.

"You can call me Jen," she says like she doesn't mean it.

Bert and I take our seats. The two women eye us up and down: me in my cream-colored bouclé suit, brown suede pumps, and ropes of pearls, and Bert in his impeccably tailored trousers, herringbone jacket, and goldenrod-yellow bow tie. As I watch them watching me, it strikes me that I probably have more in common with actual chickens.

"Would you like some coffee?" Chip asks.

I decline but Bert has a cup.

"So," Chip announces as he takes his own seat and claps his hands on his knees, "should we make small talk or get right down to business?"

"I think business would be best," Bert answers him.

"Okay, then. I think we all know why we're here."

"I have no idea," I tell him.

He smiles at me with a patronizing air.

I'm old; therefore, I'm slow.

"We're here to determine what's best for Rhonda's sons, Klint and Kyle Hayes," he explains. "We're all familiar with the circumstances surrounding the tragic death of their father."

"Tragic," Rhonda snorts. "It's amazing he didn't kill himself years ago."

Bert leans over to me and whispers into my

ear, "After seeing this ex-wife of his, I'm inclined to think the same thing."

"The boys have lived here all their lives," Chip goes on. "They have strong ties to the community and they don't want to leave, which is understandable. Miss Jack has made a very kind offer to provide them with a home so they can continue to live here."

"Yeah, I still don't get this," Rhonda breaks in. "Why are you doing this? You don't even know my boys."

"I've met them."

"You didn't tell me that."

"You didn't ask."

"When did you meet them?"

"They came to my house for dinner."

"What'd they say about me?"

"Very little. Only that you left them several years ago."

Her eyes spark angrily, and she bristles with indignation.

"Did they tell you why I left?" she practically shouts at me. "How their father was a drunk and a loser and how he abused me?"

"No, they didn't tell me any of that. You must have been the only one who had a problem with your husband. From all accounts the boys were very devoted to their father and he to them. They both seemed healthy and relatively stable and not the least bit terrorized."

She stabs her cigarette in the air at me.

"Don't you believe anything Klint says about me."

"He was the one who defended you."

She falls silent and looks completely baffled.

"Are you sure? Klint? The big one who glares at you like he wants to rip your head off?"

"The one who regarded a sprinkling of fresh basil as an attempt to poison him? Yes. He's the one."

"Ladies, ladies. Let's not get off the track here," Chip interrupts us. "Miss Jack has made a generous offer, and after giving it much thought, Miss Welty has decided to consider it for the good of her boys even though it will be extremely painful for her."

"Painful in what way?" I wonder.

"She was looking forward to having her sons live with her again."

"I don't understand," Bert joins in. "If she wanted her sons to live with her, why didn't she take them with her three years ago?"

"Because they were on Carl's side," the sister blurts out.

Rhonda nods vehemently.

"On his side?" I exclaim. "Are we talking about a family or a game of dodgeball?"

"Go to hell," Rhonda spits at me.

"Ladies!" Chip says more forcefully.

Call-Me-Jen puts an arm around her sister and says, "Come on, Ronnie. Chill."

Then she looks at me.

"This is very hard for her," she explains.

"Yes, I can see."

We all settle back into our chairs in silence. Bert sips at the coffee cup balanced on his knee, and Rhonda slurps at hers through a straw.

Suddenly she tells me, "You can have them but I want punitive damages."

"Punitive damages?" Bert chokes on his coffee.

"Miss Welty needs to be compensated for her emotional suffering," Chip further explains.

Bert finishes coughing, and we look at each other. I know we're both thinking the same thing. The idea is so appalling, I can barely form the question I need to ask.

"Are you trying to sell me your children?"

"For a certain sum of money, Miss Welty would be willing to let her sons live with you," Chip answers for her.

"In other words, she's selling her children," Bert counters.

"She's not selling her children. She'll still be their mother. We're only talking about several years."

"With Miss Jack covering all their expenses?"

"Right."

"And on top of that Miss Welty feels she should also be paid?"

"Right."

"Excuse us for a moment. I'd like to have a private word with my client."

I get up and join Bert near the windows.

"Candace, don't make any snap decisions here. You need to think long and hard about this. These are the kinds of people who never go away."

I glance back at the two women perched on the edge of the sofa — smoking, slurping, and scheming — and wonder what kind of creature raised them.

I don't think I can make Bert understand what I'm feeling since I'm not exactly sure I understand it myself.

I came into this meeting still full of doubt about what I was going to do, but now I understand what Shelby was trying to tell me. I've only spent one brief, awkward, somewhat disastrous evening with these boys. I barely know them, but I feel an irrational, uncontrollable urge to snatch them away from this woman, no different from the reckless instinct that makes a person dive into a storm-tossed sea to save a stranger's child.

"And what would be a fair price for your grief?" I ask from where I'm standing.

Chip and the sisters exchange knowing glances. They've obviously discussed a figure.

"Fifteen thousand dollars," Chip says.

"You must be joking," Bert sputters.

I stare directly at Rhonda.

"If I make it an even twenty, will you throw

in your sister?"

She meets my gaze and gives me a smirk.

"You're so funny. You think you're so much better than me 'cause you got money. Well, I got something you want, and you're gonna have to pay me for it. And you can get off this moral superiority trip of yours. If I'm selling my kids, then you're just as sick as me 'cause that means you're buying them."

"I assure you I'm not buying your sons," I respond to her baiting. "I'm paying you to stay away from them."

I feel Bert's hand on my arm.

"Are you sure you know what you're doing? Two teenage boys? With that for a mother?"

I turn away from him and confront her a final time.

She and her sister are whispering excitedly, probably making plans for their windfall.

"I don't understand why you didn't just come to me and ask for the money. Why involve a lawyer?"

She looks up at me and smiles. It's not an attractive expression for her. Bitterness suits her better.

"I want it to be all legal so you can't change *your* mind and kick them out. I gotta protect my boys."

They go back to whispering.

I catch sight of one of Chip's photos where he's standing with a woman and a grossly

handicapped child slumped in a wheelchair, drooling, with braces on his legs and no life in his eyes. The mother holds a check, and she and Chip grin for the camera.

I don't know which will prove to be more damaging for these boys: the fact that their father has died or that their mother continues to live.

Chapter Nine: Luis

I knew everything about Manuel Obrador long before I ever met him. To me and the people of my town, he was much more than a brilliant artist, a celebrity, a man of stature and courage, a stunning figure in his glittering suit of lights parading around the ring in the wake of the flowers, shawls, and flasks of wine the adoring crowd threw to him. He was our son and brother. He represented us to the world. Few of us would ever see Madrid, let alone the world, but it didn't matter. We knew if we ever ventured away from home and said the name, Villarica, we would be regarded with esteem and awe. His glory would make us shine like we'd been touched by an angel. As they say in America, he put us on the map.

I know Americans love their hometown heroes, too. An example is our sheriff, who was a football star at Centresburg High School and almost played professionally. People living here can recall the exact details

of a game he played twenty-five years ago but can't name the president of the country where their sons and daughters are fighting a war.

Klint Hayes is another example. I didn't mention it to Candace but I knew who he was before he came to dinner, not because he was a friend of Shelby's or because I had heard of his father's death but because he's often in the local sports pages.

(Candace never reads the sports pages. She regards sports as a "pastime for the mentally deficient" along with going to church and watching TV, although she watches a little herself. She says one of the plights of the elderly is that sometimes they have nothing else to do since they can't be as physically active as they used to be, and extensive reading is hard on their eyes, and by the time they reach her age, there are very few people they can stand to talk to. She admits to liking *Law & Order* and once I caught her watching *The Simpsons.* She claimed she was just flicking through channels but I know better.)

I've also overheard conversations about Klint in the grocery store, the drugstore, Sam's Club, and even once while waiting for Candace at her doctor's office. People are impressed and proud, yet their praise is tainted with jealousy and resentment. For every man sitting at a bar telling glowing tales

of Klint Hayes driving in the winning run in the district championship game and guessing at how much money he could make as a pro, there's another one claiming he's a stuck-up kid who thinks he's better than everyone else and that his success comes from luck.

In Villarica, the love we felt for Manuel was a pure love. We didn't judge his human failings or begrudge him his successes. We expected nothing from him, so we could never be disappointed. The very existence of this kind of man brought us happiness, and we repaid him by letting him live his life his own way. Like the bulls he met in the ring, we kept our distance and only approached him on special days with pesetas in hand to see him perform. We let him run free and took great joy in watching him chase his destiny.

This is not to say he didn't rub some people the wrong way. He had a famous temper and when he wasn't in the ring, his desire for excitement and need for control sometimes got him in trouble. He left a path of wrecked cars, ruined women, frazzled priests, frustrated reporters, and pleading letters from his mother wherever he went.

For six months out of the year, the life of a torero is filled with travel, none of it glamorous. Even today there are no jets or bullet trains that can get them, their team of assistants called a "cuadrilla," and all their

equipment from one fiesta de toros to the next. They must drive from town to town, usually in the middle of the night, over rural, twisting roads, some that haven't been widened or improved for hundreds of years.

During the winter, they rest and practice and usually live in one place. Manuel tried living in Madrid but got into too much trouble. By his twenty-fifth year, he had moved to a finca about eighty kilometers southeast of the city. Villarica was about the same distance from Madrid but in the opposite direction. This put him far from his hometown but he still visited several times a year.

These visits caused uproars in our town. The girls dressed prettier; the men stood straighter; the nuns living in the convent on the hill crossed themselves more often. Even the little dogs that roamed our streets yapped louder than usual.

The few businesses in town made sure to have all his favorite things on hand. The tobacco shop ordered boxes of his favorite cigars. The *panaderia* baked dozens of *marquesitas,* and as dawn broke the day of his arrival, the mouthwatering smell of sweet buns and almonds filled all our homes. On the chalkboards hung outside their doors, the restaurants advertised *perdiz estofada con alubias,* the traditional partridge stew served

with white beans that he loved. The bars stocked bottles of his favorite whisky, a Scottish malt that was almost impossible to get during these closed-off times during Franco's regime when very little was imported; but a local merchant had connections and was always able to supply the bars with enough bottles to keep Manuel happy.

The Obrador farm on the outskirts of town became a temple where people went to worship. After siesta, men wandered down the frozen dirt road bordered on both sides by rows of slumbering olive trees and gathered with Manuel's father outside his humble stone house where they stood smoking and stamping their feet to keep warm and discussed predictions for the quality of bulls next season. Women brought gifts of food and wine to his mother knowing she would be doing much entertaining and hoping they'd be invited.

Every unmarried girl between the ages of sixteen and thirty made a pilgrimage, all claiming the visit was done out of friendship for his younger sister, Maria Antonia, but mother and sister knew the allure of their Manolo and were highly suspicious when it came to female maneuvering. They knew these women were only trying to determine what his exact movements would be during his visit, and they divulged very little.

With her true friends Maria would sit

shiny-eyed, her dark, lovely face animated with laughter and rapid-fire chatter, and wonder about the new dress or piece of jewelry Manuel would bring her from Madrid and which members of his cuadrilla might pay a visit while he was here.

Within my own family, Manuel's visits were always of great importance, too. My father owned the most popular restaurant in town and we also rented the rooms above it. During the bullfight season we did a healthy business, but in winter, things got slow. Manuel's homecomings always guaranteed a crowd of people every night, some hoping to catch a glimpse of him because it was well known he loved my mother's cooking, and others simply because knowing he was back put everyone in a festive mood.

I was ten years younger than Manuel, a boy of fifteen when he came home for a week in early February 1955. I was the fifth of eight children. As in all large families, each sibling had a well-defined role to play and a label to go with it: the responsible one (the eldest); the spoiled one (the baby); the smart one; the pretty one; the lazy one; the funny one; and the bad seed. I was the invisible one, but if anyone had ever noticed me long enough to find out anything about me, I would've been called the dissatisfied one.

I can't say that I hated Villarica or my life, and I certainly didn't hate my family. We were

a loud, boisterous, combative bunch, constantly at odds with one another but as tightly connected as the stitches in the clothing my mother sewed for us. We weren't well-off by any means, but we weren't starving either. Considering the size of our family and the times we lived in, we couldn't complain.

I don't know why I wanted to leave. I wasn't a dreamer or a thrill seeker. I was very levelheaded. I had no grand delusions about being rich or famous or waking up one day and discovering I had a great talent like Manuel Obrador. I didn't know what I wanted or why I wanted it; I only knew I wanted something else, and this something else gnawed at me day and night.

Manuel had been home for two days according to gossip but had yet to make his way into town. He hadn't been to the bakery for his *marquesitas,* or the tobacco shop for his cigars. He hadn't been spotted strolling through the plaza or going to confession. Both days my mother had killed and plucked a dozen partridges just in case. Manuel's *estofado* was so popular that customers asked for it days, even weeks, after his visits and so she needed to add more meat to the giant stew pot every day.

It was siesta and I'd been sent to fetch fresh goat's milk from a nearby farm.

I had made the journey countless times

during my life. When I was a young boy, I used to think the distance would get shorter as my legs grew longer but this never happened. Instead, as I got older my thoughts grew larger and the distance seemed to double.

The town was completely deserted except for the silence. Not the soft, muffled silence I've come to know after a Pennsylvania snowfall but the hard, shiny silence of winters in central Spain.

Every shutter was closed. Every door locked. Every child and dog subdued. Every cage of birds covered. Even the wisps of white smoke crept reluctantly from the chimneys as if they feared they might make a noise if they rushed too quickly and crashed into the wall of bright blue sky.

I was concocting a story in my head where I was the only person left alive on the earth and the best thing about it would be that I'd never have to wait my turn to use the bathroom when my thoughts were interrupted and the silence was shattered by loud slapping sounds coming from behind me.

I turned around and saw a man running toward me down the cobblestoned street in his bare feet!

Even in the height of summer no one ever went in their bare feet. Part of the reason was common sense. The ground was simply too hot. But the other reason was shame. Going

barefoot was a sign of poverty and a reminder of the harsh times of the Civil War, a memory still fresh in all our minds. If a child was seen without shoes in town, the fact would be shouted from one house to the next by the female in charge and within minutes, a mother would be dragging her scandalous child back home by the ear.

The only person I'd ever heard of who openly flouted this convention and got away with it was Manuel Obrador, who not only went barefoot as a boy but used to yell back at the old ladies who chastised him that it was none of their business (when everyone knew everything was their business).

In the ring he'd been known to throw off his shoes in disgust when a bull was being difficult and finish his capework in his bright pink socks.

"Chico!" the man cried when he spotted me. "Help me!"

He was upon me in a matter of seconds.

"You have no shoes," I sputtered.

"It's okay. I can run faster."

"But it's freezing cold."

"Then take me someplace warm. Please." He glanced wildly behind him. "You have to hide me."

As if to show me the truthfulness of his words, the quiet street erupted into a clatter of running feet in shoes and a storm of angry bellowing I wasn't sure was human.

"Quickly," the barefoot man pleaded with me.

"My father's restaurant," I told him and set down the sealed pails of goat's milk in a doorway, knowing I could come back for them later. "This way. It's close."

We took off and were in the dining room in a matter of minutes. I never stopped once to look behind me.

"Is there another way out?" he asked me, his dark eyes filled with panic.

Before I could even answer him, we heard his pursuer shouting outside our door.

I rushed him to a back table. He crawled underneath and I positioned the chairs around him so it would be next to impossible to see him even though the tablecloth didn't quite reach the floor.

Our front door burst open and a crazy man holding a knife came charging in.

"Where is he?" he screamed at me. "Where is that *chulo?* I will kill him."

A girl came running in after him. She was dressed, but I could tell by her flushed face and tousled hair that she'd been recently undressed.

"No, Papa! No!" she screamed and threw herself on him.

The man pushed her onto the floor and came toward me waving his blade, his face purple with rage.

"He thinks because he plays with bulls he

can do whatever he wants? He thinks he owns everyone? He thinks he runs this town like a king? There is no king in Spain anymore, and there will be no king in Villarica. I will chop off his head myself."

"Papa, please," the girl continued pleading from a sobbing heap on the floor.

The man grabbed me by the front of my shirt and shook me.

"Where is he? Are you hiding him? That makes you guilty, too. I'll cut off your ears like you're one of his bulls and parade around the town with them."

I'd never been so scared in my life but at the same time, I felt electrified. I didn't believe he'd cut me but if he did, I'd die a noble death.

I realized who was hiding under my table. I'd be the boy who saved El Soltero. All of Spain would write songs about me, and the pope would declare me a saint. My face would be on holy cards, and beautiful women would cry for me on the steps of the church. My mother would be sad to lose me, but she'd be proud of my sacrifice. I'd become the favorite child, and none of my brothers and sisters would ever be able to topple me from my martyr's throne.

"You have to get out," I told the man, my voice shaking a little and sounding much quieter and meeker than I wanted it to. "You have no right to be here."

He let go of me and put the tip of his knife blade against my throat.

"I'm going to search every inch of this place. I'm going to turn it upside down. You can't stop me. You're a mouse."

My entire body was instantly covered in sweat, even parts of me I didn't know were capable of sweating: my elbows, my ears, the backs of my knees, my butt cheeks.

I swallowed hard and felt the cold metal nick into the skin of my neck.

"I can wake up my father and four brothers," I told the man and looked above me at the rooms upstairs as if we lived there when actually we lived a few blocks away and there wasn't anyone nearby to help me. "They won't like it."

Some sanity began to slowly return to his eyes.

He lowered his knife.

"This isn't over, *ratero!*" he growled at me.

He turned and on his way out, he grabbed the girl's arm and yanked her up from the floor. He dragged her out of the restaurant and I was frightened for her, but as they passed our front windows, she smiled at me and mouthed the word, "Gracias."

I was still watching them when the sound of chairs scraping on wood made me turn around.

Manuel Obrador emerged from beneath the table.

Seeing him now, no one would have ever guessed that he was a man who'd just been pursued barefoot through the frozen town by a knife-wielding lunatic intent on murdering him.

He pushed his thick black hair out of his eyes and smoothed it back on his head, then brushed at the dust on the knees of his pants and straightened his shirt.

He wasn't much taller than I was but he had a presence that filled the large room. He had a taut, athletic body and a natural cockiness that came from self-awareness, not arrogance. He was almost too good-looking. I fell in love with him at first sight, and I was a boy. I couldn't imagine what happened to girls when he crossed their paths, but then again, after what I'd just been through, I had some idea.

"Do you know who I am?" he asked me.

"El Soltero," I said with something close to awe in my voice.

He laughed.

"Under the circumstances, I guess it only makes sense you'd choose to call me 'the bachelor' instead of by my Christian name. Right now I'm much more the first than the second."

He looked all around him. He knew where he was. He'd been here many times.

"Who was that man?" I asked him.

"I can't say for sure," he replied lightly. "We

were never properly introduced, but I have a feeling he's the father of the girl who was with him. She I know very well."

"Is she your *novia?*"

"My fiancée? No, nothing like that. I didn't say I've known her long. I said I know her well."

He began to walk to the bar. I watched him, transfixed. It was as if a rare, beautiful animal had stepped unexpectedly from a forest and passed by me close enough that I could reach out and touch him but I knew I would never dare.

He turned and offered me his famous, captivating smile that I'd seen many times in newspaper photos after his better corridas.

"I could use a drink," he said.

His request jolted me out of my reverie, and I hurried behind the bar.

I knew exactly where my father had put the special bottles of Scotch whisky.

I opened one and poured him a drink over ice.

He took it without showing any surprise at all that we had this expensive, imported whisky that was impossible to get outside our major cities.

He drank in silence while I worked up the nerve to ask him more about his pursuer.

"Why did that man want to kill you?"

He pondered my question for a moment.

"He would probably tell you he was protect-

ing his daughter's honor, but he wasn't. His daughter's honor, belongs to his daughter, and she should be able to do with it what she wants. He was protecting his own reputation in this backward little town. He was saving face."

"By keeping his daughter from being with you?"

"Something like that."

"But you're a great artist."

"That doesn't mean fathers want me to love their daughters."

"Why not? They should."

He laughed again.

"What's your name?" he asked me.

"Luis."

"I like you, Luis. You're very brave. How old are you?"

"Fifteen."

"Have you seen me in the ring?"

"Of course."

"How many times?"

"Every time you've performed here."

"That's not enough."

"How could it be more?"

"You've never been away from Villarica?"

"No," I admitted, reluctantly.

"Not even to Toledo?"

I shook my head in embarrassment.

"Do you have some paper and a pen I could use?"

I went to my father's desk in the small of-

fice off the kitchen and returned with both.

He began writing.

"Can you get a note to my mother?" he asked me.

My heart swelled with pride. Manuel Obrador liked me, and thought I was brave, and now he was asking me to deliver a message to his own dear mother.

"Of course."

He finished the first note and started on a second one.

"And one to the girl if I tell you where she lives?"

"The girl!?" I cried in amazement. "Are you going to see her again?"

He put down the pen, folded both notes, and handed them to me, smiling.

"Not this time. It's better to go away. But I'll find a way to see her again someday. I can't stand to leave a work of art unfinished."

For the next few days, I walked on air. I never told anyone about how I saved El Soltero, partly because I didn't want to be responsible for spreading bad rumors about him and partly because I didn't think anyone would believe me, especially not my brothers and sisters.

I didn't have to worry about the first part because by the next day the entire town knew what had happened, except for what unfolded inside my father's restaurant. As for the second part, telling my tale would have been

like an American boy claiming Superman had dropped from the sky and asked him for assistance in saving the world.

It didn't matter that I had proof. My mother noticed the little cut on my neck and asked me about it. I told her I got it wrestling with my brother Jaime, the bad seed. She told me I needed to grow up. I had to bite my tongue to keep from telling her that Manuel Obrador thought I was grown up enough to take secret, crucially important messages to his mother and lover.

I also kept the glass he drank from.

Time passed as time does and soon it was hard even for me to believe my adventure with Manuel had ever happened.

Before I knew it summer had arrived and the bullfighting season was well under way. One day in July after spending a precious hour hanging out with my friends between siesta and starting my work in the kitchen, I was walking slowly across the plaza when I noticed a commotion going on in my father's restaurant. It was far too early for customers yet there were dozens of people milling about among the outdoor tables and chairs.

I quickly walked inside where there were even more people. An excited buzz of conversation filled the air. My father and my oldest brother, Miguel, were busy pouring drinks for people.

One of my younger sisters, Teresa, the smart

one, grabbed me by the arm.

"Luis, have you heard?" she asked elatedly.

Teresa never got excited.

"Heard what?"

"Come quick," she told me. "Mama has the letter."

I followed her to where my mother was sitting at a table surrounded by a pack of women all talking at the same time. My older sister, Sofia, the pretty one, sat next to my mother looking absolutely dazed. Her face was flushed a dark pink and she had a glass of water sitting in front of her. One of the ladies stood beside her and fanned her with a folded newspaper.

My other younger sister, Ana, the lazy one, was busily folding a stack of cloth napkins on the table next to us with a look of determination on her face I'd never seen before.

The world had been turned upside down.

"Luis," my mother said happily when she noticed me. "It's unbelievable. What a happy day for us."

She stood up and kissed me.

"I don't understand," I said. "What's going on?"

"Your father received a letter today from Manuel Obrador asking if he and his cuadrilla can stay in our rooms when he comes for the fiesta de toros in August."

When she finished speaking, everyone standing near us cheered, laughed, and

clapped, even though I knew all of them had probably heard these same words repeated countless times in the past half hour.

Now I understood the fuss. This was huge news for my family.

Toreros had their favorite lodgings in every bullfighting town. Here, for Manuel, it had always been Hotel Villarica.

My father never took offense at this. We were a restaurant first and foremost. The Hotel Villarica was a true hotel. It was better equipped to care for overnight guests and had a widespread reputation, but with one simple letter, we were about to become a more coveted inn. There would be no limits to our fame.

"Isn't it a miracle?" my mother asked me. "No one knows what changed his mind."

"He finally came to his senses. That's all," Miguel shouted, happily. "He's a man who recognizes quality."

My youngest brother, Javier, squeezed out of the crowd and gave my mother a hug around her waist.

"It's because of Mama's cooking," he cried.

Everyone cheered and clapped again.

He gave me a big smile, and I smiled back because I knew the truth. My mother wrapped her arms around him. He was the spoiled one.

Manuel and his men arrived in the middle of the night the day of the corrida long after

I'd been sent to bed. My father and Miguel were there to greet them. At breakfast they narrated all the details while the rest of my usually loud, animated family sat perfectly still in enraptured silence. Even Felipe, the funny one, never cracked a joke.

Manuel didn't leave his room until he came downstairs to join his cuadrilla for lunch. I fully intended to approach him. I had planned what I was going to say — I had even predicted what his responses would be — but each time I tried to leave the kitchen, I was overcome by doubt.

They had grilled trout, and *escabeche* — another partridge dish where the bird is served cold with onions, tomatoes, and peppers — and *cuchifrito,* pieces of lamb fried in olive oil, then slow cooked with spices, garlic, and dried peppers. It was a dish typical of the Toledo region and one of my mother's specialties. Some people said it was originally brought to Spain by the Arabs, but I never believed this.

They drank beer and wine and finished the meal with cheese and *bizcocho borracho,* drunken biscuit, a cake soaked with rum.

Manuel ate well but not nearly as much as the rest of his party. Most toreros hardly ate at all before entering the ring. Fear prevented some, and others wanted to be sure they had an empty stomach in case they had to be rushed into emergency surgery. Manuel was

one of the few who didn't skimp on his lunch, and inevitably accounts of his appetite were greatly exaggerated. In Sevilla it was once reported he ate an entire baby goat by himself.

Eventually I got up the nerve to go into the dining room, but I still wasn't able to go near him. I lingered at the far end of the bar pretending to dry glasses.

I caught his eye at one point, but he ignored me and I was crushed.

As the hour drew near for Manuel to depart for the plaza, townspeople, tourists, and reporters began to fill our restaurant in the hopes of catching a glimpse of him as he passed through our front doors resplendent in his *traje de luces,* the lavish embellished suit that is a bullfighter's traditional costume.

I waited with everyone else, but my heart wasn't in it. My sisters wore their best dresses, and my brothers strutted around with a newfound dignity. Men stood at the bar drinking cold beers, and women sat at the tables with their fans fluttering in front of their faces.

I sulked near the windows, occasionally casting a glance down the street where six months earlier Manuel and I had run from the man with the knife. Now it seemed like a dream.

The roar of conversation suddenly began to lessen as one of Manuel's errand boys come

bounding down the stairs and walked into the crowded restaurant. By the time he arrived in front of my father's bar, the noise level had dropped to a hum.

"Señor Martinez," he said to my father. "Manuel would like to speak to Luis."

My father's face clouded over with worry.

"Has he done something wrong?"

"No, no," the boy told him. "Luis is a friend of Manuel's."

Everyone turned to look at me.

My father's face was a comical mask of astonishment, but it quickly softened and he nodded proudly.

Just like that, I was no longer the invisible one.

I followed the boy upstairs. He knocked on Manuel's door, and his manservant came out. It was time for Manuel to leave, so I knew the man had just finished helping him dress. He looked at me sternly, said nothing, and trotted down the stairs.

The door was open a crack. I put my eye up next to it.

Manuel was standing at the foot of his bed with his back to me. He was completely in costume, from his bullfighter's black skullcap and fake pigtail attached to the hair at the back of his head to his salmon-pink socks and black leather pumps with bows over the toes.

His bedclothes were rumpled from his

recent siesta. The shutters had been thrown open. Sunlight flooded the room and glinted off the golden embroidery, crystals, beads, and baubles encrusted on his sky blue suit. I knew the name of the color. "Celeste," I whispered to myself. *Heavenly.*

"Come in," he said.

I pushed the door open but only took one step inside.

He turned around and the motion sent darts of light bouncing off the walls and ceiling.

"I've been thinking about you, Luis."

I was speechless.

"Have you thought of me since that day we met?"

"Yes," I managed to stammer out.

"What did you think?"

"I wondered if you saw the girl again."

He laughed, a sound that never failed to cheer me. I would find out soon that he had two laughs: a harsh, derisive one he used for the press and when he was put on display at parties and events, and this genuine one. Whenever he used the second, you knew you had amused or pleased him and you felt like the most important person in the world.

"Yes. I saw her."

"Are you going to marry her?"

"And lose my name? Then I'd have to be called El Esposo. *The Husband.* Bah. Never."

We both laughed at the thought of this.

"What do you think of school?" he asked me while crossing the room to check his reflection in the mirror above the dresser.

"It's boring."

"Why is it boring?"

"Because we don't learn anything interesting."

He adjusted the collar of his ivory tuxedo shirt and picked at a gold tassel on one of his epaulettes.

"What do you think of this town?"

"It's boring, too."

"When you think about how a man should live his life, do you think the most important thing is that he should never be bored?"

I took a moment to contemplate his question.

"Yes," I said, a smile of discovery lighting up my face. "I do."

"Good."

I watched him examine his nails. He would have clipped and filed them earlier to make sure there weren't any ragged edges that might catch on his cape.

I marveled at his composure. He was about to face one of nature's most powerful, fiercest beasts while alone and unarmed and here he was serenely checking for hangnails dressed in a costume so ornate and flamboyant that even a king or sultan wouldn't dare to wear it.

I had replayed our first meeting over and

over again in my mind since it happened, and each time I ended up wondering how a man who wasn't frightened by bulls could be frightened by another man. Seeing him now and hearing his questions, I suddenly realized he had never been afraid that day. What I mistook for fear and panic in his eyes and voice had been exhilaration. Running for his life had been fun for him.

"How would you like to work for me? You could be one of my errand boys; then if things work out, maybe someday my *mozo de espada.*"

I was struck dumb by the suggestion. El Soltero's *mozo de espada?* His sword page? The boy in charge of carrying and taking care of the swords and many other vital tasks like getting the *traje* ready?

Errand boys were as common as dust but the *mozo de espada* was the torero's right-hand man, which made him formally a part of the cuadrilla.

"I'll have to ask my father."

"Your father will not object."

"But I don't understand. Hundreds of boys would give anything to work for you. Why me?"

"I'm very particular about the kind of people I surround myself with. You're the right kind of person."

"But you hardly know me. How do you know I'm the right kind?"

He walked over to me and patted my cheek. "Because when you took her the note, you also took her a flower."

At that moment his manservant returned to the room and held the door open for him. Manuel's entire demeanor changed. His face became deadly calm and serious. He squared his shoulders and held his head high with a slight upward tilt to his chin.

An absolute silence descended over the room, one that didn't come from a lack of sound but from an abundance of respect.

He walked out and I stood there indefinitely, paralyzed with shock and joy. Long after he'd gone, the room continued to glitter.

To say that Manuel Obrador changed my life would be a vast understatement, like saying air is good. I would only spend four years with him before his death and if someone had told me during any of that time that because of him I'd end up spending my adult life living in America far away from my family and my country taking care of a woman I loved but could never be romantically involved with and protecting descendants of the bull that killed him, I would have run screaming in the opposite direction. Yet I don't regret anything.

I was able to be friends with Manuel in a way that the other members of the cuadrilla could not because I was much younger. He

was free to take me under his wing and treat me like the little brother he never had. The others were grown men. When they weren't working, he could care for and socialize with them, but like a prince among his soldiers, there was always a natural, necessary distance between them.

During our time together, I got to know him very well and came to love him deeply. Every night in my prayers I would ask God to protect him but also to bring him peace. I knew his outer calm and focus in the ring was in direct contrast to his inner turmoil away from the ring. I often thought if he hadn't found toreo, he would have destroyed himself with his violent longings. The art tamed his mind and body, but when he was away from it, his heart was like a wild thing released from a trap.

Until he met Candy Jack.

She rarely talks about Manuel with me and never talks about him with other people. It would be too simple and melodramatic to say she stopped living the day he died. What is the definition of "living" in the figurative sense? Is it being able to get out of bed in the morning, dress yourself, and go to your job? Is it the ability to laugh at a joke? To appreciate a sunset? To enjoy your time on earth without being consumed by bitterness and apathy? If it's the last one, then every day I see people who are dead and not because

they suffered a great tragedy.

She didn't stop living or feeling or caring after she lost Manuel. She stopped participating. For forty-seven years, she's been watching the world from inside a velvet-lined glass case. She's not hollow, broken, numb, or hardened; she's simply unreachable.

The other night when the younger boy asked her about Manuel, my heart almost stopped beating. I waited, listening behind the kitchen door, knowing her ability to respond would be as crucial to her future as a baby's first steps. I was as excited as any proud parent when I heard her answer him.

As for me, I've never had a future. The painful weight of my past has allowed me to only live in the present. My burden is one that can never be lifted or lightened. It's not guilt that I live with but the horror of possibility.

By telling Manuel that his Candy was in the stands that night, I may have provided a fatal distraction. If I had used better judgment, my greatest friend might have lived.

Part II
Suerte de Capote

Chapter Ten: Kyle

We've been here at Miss Jack's house for a month now and I still wake up every morning not knowing where I am. I look around the big room at the old-fashioned furniture until I see my few possessions, looking pathetic and puny, sitting on the shelves of a huge antique cabinet decorated with brass curlicues where some duchess probably used to keep her silver tea sets. Then I remember what happened to us: how Mom and Aunt Jen showed up in our front yard a day earlier than expected and told us we were going to go live with Miss Jack, just like that, with no explanation; how Klint told her a hag and a slut weren't going to tell him how to live his life; how Mom swung at him and he stepped backward and Aunt Jen got between the two of them to break it up while Mr. B came around the corner of the house, took one look at the commotion, gave me a sideways glance out of his golden eyes, and left again; how I retreated inside myself searching for some

calm and couldn't find any.

This morning's no different from any other one. I open my eyes and look around the huge room at all the polished wood and gold lamps and the six-foot-tall windows with the heavy drapes pushed back so I can see the hills in the distance. The wallpaper is navy with a gold pinstripe, and the rug next to the bed is the same blue but patterned with white and dark red braiding.

After I'm done scanning the room, I always expect a butler to come through the door with a breakfast tray, saying, "Good morning, Mr. President."

When that doesn't happen, I take a second look around and this time I notice my Eiffel Tower sitting on a long, low dresser and I marvel at how small it looks here. In my old room, I was daily impressed with its size. It was so tall, I couldn't even fit it on my desk; it had to sit on the floor. Now it seems insignificant.

In my old room, I had my nature crap spread out on a shelf where I could see it, but now I keep it in a box in a drawer. I had it displayed on a shelf in the duchess's cabinet, but one day I came into my room while the head housekeeper was here and she was throwing it all away.

I shouted at her, and she whirled around with her fists raised and her eyes flashing. Her name is Marge Henry, but she told me I

can call her Hen when Miss Jack's not around. Miss Jack calls her Marjorie.

Hen is a big, bustling, breathless, pink woman with tight brassy red ringlets who wears a gray maid's uniform with a starched white collar every day and is constantly sneaking outside to have a cigarette break. The first time we met she told me gruffly that she'd stay out of my business if I stayed out of hers, then the next time I ran into her she asked me nicely how I was doing and basically told me her life story. By the time she was done dusting the paintings in the upstairs hallway, I knew everything about her, including her love for cinnamon, the fact that she used to be a size 6 (I nodded, pretending I understood the significance), and that her nickname used to be Little Red Hen because of her size and hair color.

She also told me her dad owned The Mine Shaft, a tough biker bar outside Centresburg with a reputation for knife fights and raccoons the size of Labrador retrievers living off the trash in their Dumpster.

She apologized for her reaction to my intrusion and said it was habit from growing up in her dad's bar. She laughed and said it was a good thing that there hadn't been a gun handy or she probably would've shot off my kneecaps. Then she apologized for trying to throw away my stuff but told me I should hide it because it looked like trash and it

would drive her crazy each time she'd see it.

I asked her how a woman with a passion for neatness and cleanliness could have grown up in a dirty bar with sticky scuffed linoleum floors and smoke-blackened windows surrounded by greasy-haired bikers who rarely bathed. She said, what doesn't kill you makes you stronger.

I even keep my sketches in a tidy pile now.

I get out of bed and walk over to the painting hanging across from the windows and take down the T-shirt I cover it with every night.

Just my luck that with all the interesting art in Miss Jack's house, I get a room with a painting of a boat and one of a plane, and an eerily realistic portrait of a grim, thin-lipped old guy in a black business suit with flat black eyes that glimmer like headlights hitting fresh asphalt in the rain. They follow me everywhere and stare holes through me while I'm in bed. If I had to title the painting, I'd call it *Satan's Banker.*

I tell him "hey" like I do every morning after I pull off the T-shirt. I don't know if politeness counts when dealing with the forces of hell, but I figure it can't hurt.

Life here isn't as bad as I thought it would be, but it also isn't as good. A part of me was hoping that living in a mansion with a rich old lady would mean enjoying all the perks of wealth I've fantasized about. I thought we

might have an indoor swimming pool and a hot tub, and one of those home theater rooms with a TV screen as big as the wall and cushioned stadium seating. I thought there might be a special bell I could ring at any time day or night and a maid or butler would appear to do my bidding. Maybe I'd be given my own bank account with limitless funds and I could buy whatever I wanted.

I also hoped that, considering Miss Jack's reputation for avoiding people, she'd avoid us, too.

It hasn't worked out that way. We're not suffering. Miss Jack provides us with all the basics. She even took over paying for our cell phones, and she got a computer for each of our rooms because Shelby told her we need them for school. But she hasn't showered us with any extravagances and as for leaving us alone, she asks more questions and has more rules than our own parents did.

We have to eat dinner with her every night and we're required to make conversation. This has been rough on Klint, who I've seen go for an entire day back home without saying anything more than "Where's the remote?" and "I'm taking the truck."

Even though Miss Jack has servants, we have to clean up after ourselves. If we eat bowls of cereal for breakfast, we have to wash the bowls. We're constantly reminded to put our dirty clothes in the hamper. We have a

curfew and a bedtime, and we're not allowed to sleep too late on weekends. Our TV viewing is restricted, and wearing ball caps in the house is forbidden.

The rules don't bother me as much as the feeling I get from her that she wants to better us. She's made comments about getting us new clothes, and she's always correcting our speech. I want to tell her that I know how to speak properly but if I talked that way in the world I live in, I'd be bruised and friendless. She used to be poor. She was a coal miner's kid. She should know better than anyone that the life she left behind was a different country complete with its own language and its own form of justice.

I've been getting through the weeks okay. At school I can almost pretend that everything's fine and normal. The phony people have forgotten all about me and Klint, and the people who genuinely cared have decided we're okay now and they go out of their way to act like nothing ever happened.

The weekends are harder to endure. I'm stranded out here. Miss Jack only has one car, a big silver Mercedes sedan, and no one drives it but Luis. Klint says he doesn't care that she won't let him drive it. He says he wouldn't be caught dead tooling around in an old lady car. (Although I know he'd love to get a look at its engine.)

Luis has been forced to drive us back and

forth to school — since there's no bus that comes out here — and Klint has had to hitch rides from friends to get home from his job at Hamilton's Dairy.

It's obvious Luis isn't happy with the situation. I feel bad about asking him to drive me anywhere besides school, but I also haven't felt like inviting any of my friends here yet. The situation is too new and still pretty weird, plus Klint gets pissed at me whenever I suggest we have anyone over. Even though everyone knows we're living here, Klint needs to pretend nobody knows about it because he doesn't want anyone thinking we've got it made or that we're charity cases.

My brother has become completely worthless. I would've thought going through the same tragedy together would have made us closer but instead he's been ignoring me. The past two weekends Bill came and picked him up and he went and stayed with him. I know he spent part of the time working out in the Y's weight room and using the batting cages at Community Field, but the rest of the time he spent sitting on Bill's porch like Dad's ghost. I could have gone, too, but staring at my old backyard is the last thing I want to do. It's funny how a place that causes me so much pain can bring my brother so much comfort.

When Klint is around, he lies on his bed tossing a ball up and down staring at the ceil-

ing or at Dad's mangled chrome antler grill sitting on his dresser, or he goes to the one room in the house with a TV and watches World Series highlight DVDs or reruns of *Full House.* (He likes the show because the Olsen twins remind him of Krystal when she was little and cute, but he'd never admit this and he'd kill me if I ever told anyone he watches it.)

If Dad hadn't died, Klint would probably still be traveling around playing in some national showcase tournaments until the final ones wrapped up in November, but he told Coach Hill he was taking the fall season off. I would've loved to have been there to see Coach try and digest that information without his head exploding. There was nothing he could do. Off-season play is strictly out of his control. He's only got a couple players who are even worth encouraging in that direction: Klint; his best friend, Tyler Mann, a crackerjack first baseman who's got loads of natural talent but no discipline (Tyler isn't even sure he'd like to play pro ball — for as long as I've known him, if anyone asks him what he wants to be when he grows up he says a stunt man or a bear); and Brent Richmond, who's got some talent, some discipline, but enough ambition and push from his dad to make the other two qualities unimportant. Our dad wanted Klint to be a pro while Brent's dad expects him to be a pro. Tyler's dad just wants

him to survive to adulthood.

The other person who's disappeared on me is Shelby. We've been texting like crazy — much more than we ever did before I started living with a member of her family — but I haven't seen her since the night we met Miss Jack. At first I thought she was mad at us for the way dinner ended, but she said that wasn't true and she'd just been very busy at school.

I've decided that the worst part of loneliness isn't being alone. It's being forgotten. I went through the same thing after Mom left. For a year, I followed Dad around like a shadow. The sight of him was assurance that I still existed, like glimpsing my reflection in a mirror.

In my old life, I may have been shut up in my room for hours doing my own thing, but I knew Dad was around if I needed him; and if I went looking for him, he'd make time for me even if all that meant was clearing a place next to him on the couch while he watched TV. Dad made me feel wanted. Now that feeling's gone and when I look in the mirror of my new life, the image is dark and blurry.

I walk over to the dresser and pick out a pair of jeans and a T-shirt. Even my clothes look small here. In my old dresser back home, I could barely get everything stuffed into four drawers. Now it doesn't even fill up one drawer, which is big enough to hold a person.

I should tell Tyler about this. It's the kind of thing he'd like to do: hide in a drawer.

I grab a sketch pad and my pencils and charcoals and slip Krystal's Barbie shoe into my pocket along with my knife. I've been carrying the shoe around ever since Dad's funeral. I don't know why exactly. I guess because I found it the night Dad died.

I head downstairs to grab some breakfast in Luis's immaculate blond wood and white kitchen with its walls covered in shiny silver pots and pans, knives of every size, ropes of colorful dried peppers and beards of garlic, and shelves holding rows of corked glass bottles filled with herbs and oils. I see a list sitting on one of the countertops. It's written in Spanish. I know enough food vocabulary now, since Luis announces every meal in Spanish, to recognize that it's a lengthy grocery list of some kind. At the top is next Saturday's date.

I take my cereal and a bowl of Cat Chow for Mr. B and go sit on the porch steps to eat. About halfway through my Corn Pops, Mr. B shows up. He rubs up against me, purring like mad, and gives me a few head butts. He knows the sound of a spoon hitting against a bowl means I'm eating cereal and there could be milk left when I'm done.

I don't disappoint him. When he's finished lapping up his treat, he cleans his face, sniffs his own food with disdain, and stretches out

on the step next to me.

I took a big risk bringing Mr. B with me, but I figured the worst that could happen would be Miss Jack telling me to get rid of him and then I'd just have Bill take him back to his place.

She was waiting on her front porch when Bill dropped us off a month ago. She wasn't dressed up this time, and she didn't look nearly as intimidating or rich. She was wearing a military green overcoat with big pockets, a scarf tied over her hair, and old hiking boots. I would find out soon enough that she went for a walk on her land every day, and this is what she always wore.

Bill didn't want to get out of the truck, but I told him he had to because staying in the truck would be rude and Miss Jack had a thing about people being rude. Klint said Miss Jack had a thing about everything, and the only reason I cared about what she thought was that I was a hypochondriac. I told him he meant I was a necrophiliac, a guy who had sex with dead people. A hypochondriac was a guy who always thought he had some rare disease he didn't have. He smacked the side of my head and called me a fucking geek. I jerked back when he did it, and the movement made Mr. B hiss inside the box sitting on my lap. Bill gave me a panicked look and told me he didn't know

what to say to Miss Jack. I told him just to say nice to meet you. Klint told him to ask her if she'd like to go to the Rayne Drop Inn for Hot Wing night. Bill looked even more panicked, and Klint and I cracked up when we realized he was taking Klint's suggestion seriously. Klint really, truly laughed like he was happy and for that moment, everything was good.

We all got out of the truck and trooped over single file to stand in front of Miss Jack like grunts waiting for a drill sergeant's inspection: Klint with his big, beat-up gray equipment duffel bag slung over his shoulder and his rolled-up Roberto Clemente poster held delicately in one hand; me in the middle grasping my mystery box to my chest, trying in vain to keep it from jostling around; Bill leaning on his cane staring intensely at the ground like eye contact with Miss Jack might turn him into stone.

Luis was standing behind Miss Jack back by the front door like he didn't want her to know he was there but he wouldn't miss this for the world. Even Jerry, the old handyman caretaker, came silently sauntering over from the barn, wiping his hands on an oil-stained rag.

"Good morning, gentlemen," Miss Jack greeted us.

"Good morning," we all muttered at various volumes and levels of clarity.

She stared at Bill, who didn't notice because he was busy staring at his feet. I nudged him with my elbow.

He took a step forward and stood nervously in front of her looking just like the Cowardly Lion asking the Wizard of Oz for some courage.

"Hi, there, Miss Jack. I'm Bill Fowler. I'm their next-door neighbor. I mean, I was their next-door neighbor. Well, I still live there but they don't anymore . . ." His voice trailed off as he noticed her glaring at his head.

He quickly pulled off his ball cap and she seemed to lighten up a little.

"You're a good friend, Mr. Fowler. The boys are lucky to have you."

He glanced at me, amazed, and a small embarrassed smile crept onto his face while he blushed noticeably.

"Well, you know, they're nice kids," he stammered.

"Kyle," she announced, cutting him off. "Your box is growling."

Mr. B had stopped moving around, which was probably a bad sign. He was lying heavily in the middle of the box now, crouched, poised to attack, and letting out a long, low, sinister warning wail.

"I have a cat," I blurted out.

Miss Jack drew back.

"There will be absolutely no animals in this house."

"He doesn't like to be inside," I quickly explained. "He lives outside. Even in winter. If you put him in your house, he'd run right to the door and cry to get out."

I set the box down.

Jerry walked over.

"Does he hunt?"

"He's a great hunter," I cried happily, realizing this could be the talent that saved him.

Jerry reached down and pulled open the top of the box.

Mr. B escaped with one graceful leap. He circled me several times, then sat down at the bottom of Miss Jack's wide porch steps and began indignantly cleaning his face with his paw while casting slit-eyed bored glances at each of us in turn that seemed to say, "Yes, yes, I'm here. I'm fabulous. Now back off."

"Good Lord," Miss Jack exclaimed. "He's huge."

"We could use a good mouser around here," Jerry told her. "We've got a chipmunk problem in the barn. They're destructive little buggers."

"Chipmunks don't stand a chance around him," I gushed. "If chipmunks had an FBI top ten most wanted list, he'd be number one on it."

"Would you shut up?" Klint said to me.

"It's true. You know he kills chipmunks like crazy."

"So what? You sound like an idiot. Chip-

munk FBI lists? How old are you?"

Miss Jack interrupted us.

"Shelby's mother has a Chihuahua, a horrible shivering bug-eyed thing. I think this cat is three times its size."

"He's killed full-grown squirrels," I told her. "He's even killed rabbits that are probably bigger than this Chihuahua you're talking about."

"Really?"

She seemed very intrigued by this last bit of information.

Mr. B finished washing himself. He stood up, surveyed his surroundings, and trotted off toward the nearest tree with the tip of his orange tail flicking behind him as if he'd lived here his whole life.

"What do you call him?" Jerry asked.

"Mr. B. The B stands for big."

He nodded his approval.

I looked at Miss Jack.

My Spanish was limited to what I've heard on TV cop show episodes involving drug cartels and learned from the Taco Bell menu, but it was enough for the simple translation I wanted to do.

"Or you could call him señor Grande."

Luis barked a one-note laugh, and Miss Jack shot him a look that made him laugh harder.

"I don't plan to call him anything," she said.

For the first five days we lived here, I didn't

see Mr. B at all. I started to worry about him, not about his safety or well-being but that he was pissed off at me for moving him and had decided to go live somewhere else. On the sixth day, I came home from school and found a trail of two dead voles and a chipmunk leading from the driveway to the front porch where Mr. B was stretched out on one of Miss Jack's little wicker sofas.

Jerry showed up with a shovel and disposed of the dead rodents without a sound but gave the sleeping cat a nod that I think was a sign of approval.

I return my bowl and spoon to the kitchen making sure to wash and dry them and put them away, then I go back outside and find a good spot away from the house where no one can find me and start to sketch.

Today I'm working on a picture of Miss Jack's house set against the autumn hillsides. The leaves are at their most colorful right now. In a couple more weeks they'll fade and fall off the trees and the mountains will become a cool smoky shade of lilac, but right now they are covered with patches of pumpkin orange and eggplant, coral and rain-slicker yellow, gingerbread brown and the deep burgundy of Krystal's velvet Christmas dress.

My plan is to eventually do a painting and make the colors of the leaves even more vivid

than what they are in real life. I want them to be neon and unnatural like the ones on the bullfight posters in Miss Jack's house. It turns out she has more than just the one we saw downstairs. I've found six altogether. All of them mention El Soltero and are from 1958.

The bullfighter's face is never clear. He's always dark-haired and wearing the crazy pink socks, but the colors of his gold-encrusted suit vary from emerald green and turquoise, to Valentine red, peach, and lavender.

The contrast of the carnival colors of the suits and capes next to the bulls barreling past is surreal to me.

I put aside the sketches I've been working on and start a new one of a solitary gigantic tree where the leaves are tiny bullfighters snapping their capotes and the trunk is a stack of bulls slick with blood fitted together like puzzle pieces.

I'm really into the idea and forget about the time. It's not until my hand starts to cramp and my butt starts to hurt from sitting on the hard ground that I decide to stop, but before I quit altogether, I do a quick sketch of Coach Hill dressed like a woman just for the fun of it. I give him long gray hair and an old-fashioned lady's hat with flowers on it. I put him in a lacy blouse and tight skirt. His bare hairy legs end in big feet stuffed into high-heeled shoes. He carries a pocketbook

in the crook of his arm. He's smiling and waving. Along the bottom I write the words: Mrs. Hill says, "Good luck, boys!"

I'll definitely show it to Klint if I can ever get him in a good mood again.

I've been drawing and painting since I was a little kid. Last year my painting of two Hamilton dairy cows grazing around a rusted, broken-down old red Chevy pickup with masses of goldenrod growing out from under its hood won second prize at the middle-school art fair. It was very traditional. Usually I'm more off the wall with my subject matter, but I knew it was what the judges wanted. First prize went to a painting of a puppy lying in a field of daisies. I'm not kidding.

I kept the ribbon and gave the picture to Mr. and Mrs. Hamilton as a gift. They bought a nice frame for it and hung it in their living room as if it were a real painting by a real artist.

Members of my own family have never been very enthusiastic about me wanting to be an artist.

My mom says artistic people think they're better than everyone else, that their art is a form of snobbery done only to make people who don't have any talent feel bad about themselves. My dad wasn't as hostile toward the subject as my mom was, but he made it clear that he thought it was a waste of time.

He had much more respect for a guy who could throw a horseshoe ringer than one who could paint a mural.

Klint thinks the fact that I'm artistic is just one more sign that I'm a fairy, yet I know deep down he likes my pictures. He still has a sketch I did for him at the beginning of last season. Coach Hill's screaming face takes up almost the entire piece of paper. His eyes are bulging, veins are popping out in his neck and forehead, spit's flying everywhere. In the background are three players in shadow: one's standing with his arms folded over his chest, cocky and defiant; another is sitting on the bench with his face in his hands, destroyed; the last one is walking away with his bat over his shoulder, ignoring everything. Klint knows which one is him. At home, he kept it in a desk drawer. Here I noticed it sitting on top of his dresser next to Dad's antlers.

The only person who openly liked my drawings was Krystal. I used to paint and sketch for her all the time. Usually the subjects were at her request. Draw me a flower. Draw me a castle. Draw me a horse. Draw me a Barbie swimming pool party. Draw me a birthday cake. Draw me, me, me!

She never threw away a single picture. She kept them in a folder I gave her that she decorated with glitter glue and sequins. I wonder if she took the folder with her when

she and Mom left us or if she threw it away. I never saw it in the trash after they left, and I went through the trash looking for signs of what we'd done to make them go. I didn't find any answers.

As I'm making my way across the gravel drive back to the house, Luis practically runs into me. He's striding toward the barn with an uncharacteristically stern look on his face, deep in his own thoughts, but when he notices me, he seems happy to see me and smiles.

Luis has been friendly and helpful ever since we arrived. He also seems to be the voice of reason with Miss Jack on certain topics. She's out of touch about a lot of things, not because she's stupid but because she lives in a different time period. Luis had to explain to her about iPods, cell phones, and video games. She knew about them, but she didn't realize they were necessities, not luxuries.

I also think Miss Jack might be the only person left in the world who doesn't have a computer. Luis has one. He has a big family back in Spain he visits once a year. He has over thirty nieces and nephews and they all have kids. He says he could never stay in touch with all of them if it wasn't for e-mail. Plus he also uses it to keep up on the news and politics in Spain, and he uses it to run the estate and Miss Jack's affairs, although he doesn't take care of her money. When I asked

him if he did, he had a good laugh and said no and laughed some more.

He asks how I am and what I've been doing. I try to hide my sketchbook, but I realize it's pointless. He asks to see what I've drawn, and I show him Coach Hill.

"This is very good," he says, nodding and laughing.

"It's okay," I reply with a shrug.

"No. You have a gift for caricatures. It's better than okay."

He hands the sketch back to me.

He puts his hands on his hips, and the serious look returns to his face. He blows out an exasperated puff of air from beneath his walrus mustache.

"Is something wrong?" I ask him.

"No, no, no." He holds up a hand and shakes it at me. "Everything is fine. Just Miss Jack is driving me crazy. She always does when she has people over, especially her nephew. They don't get along."

"You mean Shelby's dad?"

"Sí, sí. My God." He glances skyward like God might actually hear him. "It's never good. She doesn't get along with Shelby's mother, either, or her sisters."

"What are her sisters like?"

"Pretty. One is dumb and very spoiled. The other is smart and very bad. I think the bad one's coming."

"Did you say they're coming over? Shelby,

too?" I ask hopefully.

"Yes, but not today. Next week. For dinner. But it doesn't matter. She's already in my way. No, not just in my way. She's . . ." he pauses and stares into the sky again. "How do you say it? She's in my face. I'm going for a ride to try and relax."

He raises his eyebrows like a good idea has just occurred to him.

"Do you ride?" he asks me.

"Horses?" I wonder stupidly.

He nods.

"Yeah. Sure. We used to live close to the Hamiltons' dairy farm. They had horses they let people ride. They weren't really great horses. They were kind of old and broken down. It wasn't any kind of fancy riding," I'm quick to add as I take in his pair of tan trousers tucked into oiled brown leather riding boots and his red scarf tied inside the open neck of a crisp white shirt.

"We don't do fancy riding here, either. You want to come with me?"

"Sure. I didn't even know she had horses. I guess I've been kind of out of it."

"It's understandable."

He lets me take my stuff back up to my room and I change out of my gym shoes into the old harness boots I wore when I worked at the Hamiltons' farm this past summer.

I meet him in the barn. It's the first time I've been inside it. The barns I'm used to are

either abandoned and falling down or part of a working farm. They're dusky and musty, dirty and cluttered, full of the sounds and smells of machinery and livestock.

Miss Jack's barn is clean, bright, and airy. It's cleaner than our high school cafeteria. Sunlight pours through the open doors and makes a pool of white warmth on the swept floors. Dust motes twirl slowly above it like planets in a tiny lazy universe. I take a deep breath and smell new paint, and fresh, sweet hay.

Everything is neat and well organized. There's none of the haphazard junk that always makes its way into the corners and unused stalls of most barns. Bridles hang on shiny brass hooks. Bags of feed are stacked in a pyramid against one wall. A huge John Deere tractor mower that would have made my dad salivate is parked off to one side.

On the opposite wall from the tractor are three large framed photos of black bulls, each with a gold plaque at the bottom engraved with a name.

Luis sees me looking at them and joins me with two harnesses in his hands.

"Calladito, Viajero, Ventisco," he reads off the names.

Shelby already told me Calladito was her aunt's first bull and Ventisco is the one she has now. I ask Luis about the second name, trying to pronounce the "j" the way he does,

like I'm choking on an "h" in the back of my throat.

"The Traveler," he explains.

He gestures at each picture in turn.

"Grandfather, father, son. Miss Jack keeps a bull from each generation. The one she thinks is most like Calladito."

I study the pictures more closely. At first glance, they could all be different shots of the same bull. All three of them are massive coal-black monsters with sharply pointed up-turned white horns that look like they'd slide through a grown man's chest as easily as a power drill through butter.

They all have the same air about them. They're simple and noble: a combination of pure muscle and pure arrogance.

After staring at them for a minute, I see slight differences in their eyes and their stances, and I begin to wonder if bulls have personalities like people do.

Calladito seems sad and wise. His coat has a lot of brand marks on it so he's not as sleek and shiny as the other two. He's on the scruffy side but looks tougher than they do, a guy who's been through a lot and relies on his street smarts as much as his size and strength. The picture of him is very natural. He's standing in a field of tall grass. He's not trying to impress anyone.

Viajero has movie star good looks. He's young and healthy with blank eyes. He's

definitely posing, holding his head high and staring right at the camera. The muscles beneath his blue-black coat seem to shimmer in the sunlight. I can imagine him tossing his head and asking the photographer to be sure and shoot him from his good side.

Ventisco is staring at the camera, too, but there's no acceptance in his eyes. They glint with challenge. Even though it's a still photo, I can feel energy radiating from him. He's a cocked gun. A fastball ready to be launched. He wants to attack, but this desire isn't motivated by a wish to harm; it comes from a refusal to be dominated. He's not a bully. He's a badass bull.

"Why does she like bulls?" I ask Luis. "Most old ladies like cats."

He smiles.

"This is true, but Miss Jack is not like most old ladies. And Calladito was not just any bull. He is the bull who killed El Soltero."

"You mean the guy in all those bullfight posters?" I look back at the photo of the bull. "He killed him?"

"Yes."

"Killed him?" I repeat myself, but I don't know what else to say. "Killed him? In a bullfight? In front of hundreds of people?"

"In front of thousands of people. And me. And Miss Jack."

I instantly see Miss Jack in a different light. I try to imagine her young and can't, but

knowing she watched some guy get torn apart by a bull fills me with the same kind of morbid respect I felt for Aunt Jen when I found out one of her boyfriends in high school accidentally shot himself in the face while cleaning his rifle.

"Did he die instantly?" I blurt out and immediately regret it, but I can't help myself. This concept has been weighing heavily on my mind ever since Dad was killed.

Luis gives me a wary look out of the corner of his eye.

"Yes," he replies, stiffly. "I worked for Manuel Obrador. He was my best friend and one of Spain's greatest toreros. I was around your age when I first met him."

"I don't get it. Miss Jack kept the bull that killed your best friend and now you work for her?"

"It's complicated."

I want to ask him tons of questions. Exactly how was he killed? Where did the bull get him? Did he stick him with his horns a bunch of times or only once? Was there tons of blood? But I realize these kinds of questions would be in poor taste. I learned my lesson when I asked Aunt Jen if pieces of brain are really gray when you see them spattered on a wall and she started crying and Mom smacked me and sent me to bed.

"Was Miss Jack friends with him, too?" I ask, instead.

He considers my question. I get the feeling he's not sure if he should answer it. Finally he says, "They were in love."

I try again to picture Miss Jack young and even decide to make her pretty, but the image won't come. I try to see the setting in my mind, but this is equally difficult. The only bullfight I've ever seen was in a Bugs Bunny cartoon. Then I decide to try and duplicate her emotions. I take all the pain I felt when Mom left and all the sadness and betrayal I'm still feeling over Dad's death and mix it with the imagined horror of watching someone as beautiful as Shelby die in front of me, and I feel really bad for Miss Jack.

"That really sucks," I tell Luis.

"Yes," he says, nodding slowly; then he suddenly turns on his heel. "Vamos. I have lots of work to do later."

I follow him down a lane of stalls toward the sound of a horse nickering.

He disappears into one with a harness, then leads out a big, sleek, reddish-brown horse the color of a polished acorn.

"This is my beauty, Águila," he says, smiling and stroking the animal's silky neck. "Eagle," he clarifies for me.

"He is beautiful," I confirm. "I've never seen a horse this nice."

A smaller black horse but an equally attractive one sticks her head out of the stall next to Águila and snorts at us.

"That's Shelby's horse, Molinera," Luis says.

He makes big circles with both of his arms.

"Runs like a windmill," he explains the name. "She calls her Molly. She's a spoiled princess of a horse, and she's going to be jealous and throw a tantrum when we don't take her out. You're going to ride our other lady, Seta Loca."

"Seta Loca?"

"Crazy Mushroom."

"What kind of name is that?"

He hands me the reins to Águila and goes into another stall a little farther away. I can feel the power in the big horse just from standing next to him, and I'm relieved I'm not riding him, although I'm not exactly thrilled about being put on a horse with the word *crazy* in her name.

Luis leads her out, and I instantly understand at least half of her name. She's the same creamy gray-brown as the raw mushrooms in the Ponderosa salad bar that Klint and I never eat, but the color looks good on a horse.

"She's only crazy around women," Luis tells me. "Put a female on her back, and she'll do anything to try and throw her off, but she's a pussycat around men. See."

He rubs his cheek against hers.

I reach out and stroke her velvety nose. She has kind, calm eyes.

"I like her," I say.

"Good."

We get the horses saddled and leave through a back door.

I can tell immediately that Luis is an excellent rider by the way he sits in his saddle and guides his horse with seemingly no effort.

I'm a good rider if all that's required of riding is being able to stay seated on the horse. I can handle a canter, but I have a feeling I look like I'm always about to fall off. I know I feel that way. Luis, on the other hand, looks like he's part of the horse. The faster Águila goes, the more the difference between man and horse blurs.

Miss Jack has acres and acres of open fields. The summer green has faded from them and now they're streaked with yellows and browns. All around us are distant hills crowded with trees in their colorful party clothes. The sky is a soft blue with motionless popcorn-shaped clouds stuck to it. If Shelby was riding with us and my dad was still alive, it would be pretty close to a perfect day.

Luis pulls up next to me, and we bring our horses to a slow trot.

He calmly announces, "There's very little chance we'll see Ventisco but if it were to happen, you do exactly what I do."

"You mean we could run into the bull?"

"Probably not. I doubt he's this close to

the farm. Águila is acquainted with him. He would sense Ventisco before Ventisco would see us."

This doesn't comfort me much.

I realize Luis is wearing a red scarf. I mention it to him.

"Bulls respond to motion, not to color. The use of a red cape in bullfighting is a tradition. A bull would run at a blue cape just as happily."

"I remember Miss Jack telling us that."

"Ventisco would only charge if he felt threatened, and he would only feel threatened if we were to come upon him suddenly and aggressively."

"Is that why we're walking very slowly right now?"

"Yes."

"I thought you said he's probably not around."

"What is that expression? Better safe than sorry."

I look over at him. He's grinning. I see a line of small, perfect white teeth set in his dark face beneath the bushy gray mustache.

"He could kill us, though."

"Oh, yes. Very easily," he says, nodding his head vigorously and still smiling, "but so could a fish bone."

Again, his words don't comfort me very much. I think he might realize this because he changes the subject.

"I'm very impressed with your drawings. Do you think you could make a set of caricatures for me? I have a brother who is mad about them. I'd love to have pictures made of all of us — the eight siblings — and give them to him as a gift."

I don't know what to say. I've never drawn a picture at someone's request. I've always only drawn for myself and Krystal, but she was just a kid who used to love me.

"I'd pay you, of course."

"Pay me? That's a lot of pressure," I say. "What if they're bad?"

He laughs.

"If they're bad, I won't send them. Do you think you could work from photographs if I explained to you about each one's personality?"

"I've never tried but I suppose I could."

"Good," he says, happily.

He actually seems excited about this. A lot more excited than I am.

"Have you always been an artist?"

"Me? I'm not an artist."

"Of course you are," Luis says sharply.

"But I've never gone to art school or sold a painting or anything like that."

"Being an artist is not like being a lawyer or a dentist or even a baseball player like your brother," he tells me. "You have to earn the right to be called these things. You need society's permission. An artist simply is what

he is with or without anyone's approval."

He keeps staring at me like he's expecting a brilliant response from me. He goes on when he doesn't get one.

"An artist doesn't create in order to get money, or fame, or acceptance, or love. It's a force inside him, something he must do or his soul will shrivel up and die."

This part of his explanation I can relate to.

"Once when I was real little, my dad bought my mom this blown-glass fish for her birthday," I start to tell him. "My mom's always had a thing for blown-glass animals, I think because her dad bought her a couple before he ran out on them. This fish my dad got for her was the most beautiful thing I'd ever seen. It seemed to have every color in the world in it. They were all swirled together in ribbons with tiny frozen bubbles caught between them.

"I stared and stared at it and I knew I had to draw it. If I drew it, somehow I would make it mine. Dad was at work. Klint was at school. Mom was on the phone. I couldn't find any paper so I took my crayons and drew it on the kitchen wall. The whole time I was doing it I knew I was going to get smacked and sent to my room. I knew my mom wasn't even going to like it. It was going to make her hate me. But I couldn't stop myself. I had to draw it. Is that what you're talking about?"

Luis is watching me. He doesn't look so stern anymore.

"Yes, that's what I mean."

It's a strange feeling having someone want to know about me. I keep waiting for the conversation to turn into questions about Klint.

"When I paint and draw, I feel like I'm not part of the real world anymore. I sort of get lost but lost in a good way, like taking a long walk down the railroad tracks and you know where you are but no one else does. Not in a scary way like when you're a little kid and you can't find your mom in the grocery store. I guess it's escaping reality even though I need reality because I'm drawing what I see, but I'm making it look the way I want other people to see it. Does that make any sense?"

"It makes good sense," Luis says. "It reminds me of something Manuel once said to me about bullfighting.

"He began when he was a little boy, too. He was a farmer's only son and it was expected he would grow up to be a farmer, also, but from the moment he saw his first fiesta del toros he knew he was born for the ring. As he used to say, the bulls called to his soul. Just as you could say this glass fish called to your soul.

"One day when he was only eight years old and he knew his father was nearby, Manuel took one of his mother's aprons from the

clothesline and jumped into the corral where there was a very mean cow, one who kicked and bit and had even been known to charge. He began taunting her.

"He performed the poses he'd seen the toreros do. He threw off his shoes, made his face very commanding, and shuffled his feet in the sand calling, 'Hey, hey, Vaca,' mimicking the torero's call of, 'Hey, Toro.'

"His father came to the fence, shouting at him to stop. Then his mother and sister and a farmhand came running. Manuel ignored them all even though he knew he was going to get in trouble, even though he knew this cow could easily crush him if he made the wrong move.

"He waved the apron and kept shouting at her and what he calls the miracle of his life happened: this mean old cow charged him.

"That moment, as the cow was running toward him, when he knew if he turned and ran, he would be dead, or if he froze, he would be dead, that his only chance of survival was to control this animal with his cape and his will, he described that to me as the thrill of being lost."

"Wow," I say when Luis falls silent. "That's a much cooler story than one about drawing a fish on a wall."

"It's a good story," he agrees.

"But I thought bullfighting was a sport, not an art."

"A sport!?" he exclaims. "Forgive me, Manuel."

He looks at the sky yet again the same way he did when he mentioned God earlier and Miss Jack getting in his face. He must really believe in heaven.

"Americans and their sports. Everything is a sport. A competition. Even your relationships. Everything is about winning and losing," he says disgustedly.

"It took me so long to get used to that American expression, You win. You use it for everything. A simple conversation. 'Where shall we go for dinner?' 'I'd like to go here.' 'I'd like to go there.' 'Okay, you win.' Win what? What have I won? Was choosing a restaurant a contest between us? Have I now proven that I'm somehow better than you?"

He's starting to get really mad, but then he takes a deep breath and calms down.

"No, bullfighting is not a sport. It is an art."

"Like dancing?" I ask. "When I look at the bullfight posters in Miss Jack's house, the bullfighters kind of look like they're dancing with their capes."

"A dance? Yes, in some ways. Toreo requires athleticism, strength, and grace just like dancing does. But it is a dance with an unpredictable, deadly, wild animal."

"Yeah." I smile at the idea. "I guess if you threw a tiger onto the stage of America's Best

Dance Crew it would be a whole different show."

"Some people compare it to dance. Others compare it to theater. They say what unfolds in the corrida is a drama depicting the eternal struggle between man and beast where the civilized torero with his suave manners and lavish suit tames and then destroys Nature's champion, El Toro. But what most people forget is bullfighting requires a mental composure that no other art demands. It's something more. It's something unique. Something incomparable."

The passion in his voice and the zeal in his eyes remind me of an evangelist talking about the healing powers of God. His words soothe and arouse at the same time and make me want to know more about this strange religion of blood and beauty.

We ride a little farther before Luis suggests we turn back.

The whole time I can't stop thinking about an eight-year-old El Soltero taking on a pissed-off cow. I've been around plenty of cows and even the docile ones are intimidating just because of their size. To a kid, they seem as big as dinosaurs.

I picture him staring down the cow, his serious little face all scrunched up with concentration and determination the same way Krystal's face was the first time I put her on the tire swing over the Hamiltons' pond and

explained when and how she was supposed to jump.

His dad must have been proud of him.

I remember how Dad used to love to show off Klint's hitting. Back when Klint was still too young for Little League but he'd been banned from all the T-ball teams, Dad used to take him to parks in the summer where people were having family reunions or company picnics. He'd put him in a Pirates ball cap, pack his lower lip with bubblegum chew, and set him up in a field with the shiny blue aluminum L'il Slugger bat he bought with money Mom had saved to buy a new lawn chair and start throwing him pitches. Within ten minutes, a crowd would form around him, marveling at how far the pint-sized dynamo could hit a ball. Dad's head and chest would swell. He'd eventually pass off the ball to someone else who wanted to try pitching to Klint, and he'd stand nearby calling out already unneeded instructions to him to "choke up" to "drop your shoulders" to "watch the inside corner," while also making small talk with bystanders about how someday they'd be watching his boy on a major-league diamond and they could talk about the time they saw him as a little kid practicing with his dear old dad.

"What did Manuel's family do after his show with the cow?" I ask Luis. "Were they amazed? Were they excited? Did they go out

and buy him a real cape?"

"No," he replies, glancing skeptically at me from the corner of his eye. "He was sent to bed without supper for dirtying his mother's clean apron."

Chapter Eleven: Candace Jack

I've never regretted not having children. I've never mourned my barren womb. People don't believe me. People never believe that a single woman prefers to remain single. They never believe a childless woman is content to have no children.

This is one of the many reasons why I've chosen to live in relative isolation away from my fellow man. I have no tolerance for strangers who know nothing about me yet are constantly telling me what I should think and feel. This is one of the curses of the American people: our moral arrogance. We're well known for wielding it as a nation, but each individual also possesses it and beats everyone he or she encounters over the head with it.

No matter how many times I insisted that I didn't care to have children, I was informed that I didn't know what I was talking about. Sometimes this was conveyed to me bluntly and rudely, sometimes subtly and sympathetically, but always with great condescension.

I've been coolly lectured that it's my biological imperative to have children. I've had my hand patted kindly and been assured there was no need to worry: I was young, I was pretty, I still had time. I've been told whether or not I had children was in God's hands, not mine. I've been told whether or not I had children was in some random man's hands who I hadn't even met yet, not mine. I've been told a woman who doesn't have children isn't a real woman.

I never paid any attention to these sentiments.

For me the mere thought of having a child, of being solely responsible for the welfare of an innocent, unformed creature, of knowing that my own life would be forever controlled by concern for someone else, was overwhelming and terrifying to me.

I remembered too well what it felt like to be the child who depended on the parent. I loved my parents, and I lost them. I loved them in the way that only a child can love. It wasn't a feeling, it was a simple reality. They were the earth from which I grew. When I lost them, I lost not only a family and a home but I lost myself, the self I would have been if I had continued to be blessed with the love of a mother and a father.

When others would start to berate or console me on the absence of my own offspring, my thoughts would instantly turn to

my relationship with my own mother and I'd ask myself, Would I ever want to be that important to another human being?

Manuel and I never got around to discussing having children together. We talked about marriage, and it was disastrous. We were young, though, and even as we fought and accused each other of outrageous selfishness, we knew in the backs of our minds that we had plenty of time to resolve our differences and make a life together. We were so sure of this, and we were so wrong.

If we had married, I was well aware I would have been obligated to produce a litter of caramel-skinned, coffee-eyed replicas of their famous father. He was a Spaniard, after all, and incredibly yet selectively Catholic, which meant he was very devout but his religion never stopped him from doing whatever he wanted.

When we talked about marriage, we didn't argue about religion or children or money or any of the usual topics couples struggle with. We fought over the fact that he couldn't leave his country and I couldn't leave mine.

No one was more surprised by my insistence that I had to return to America than I was. When I had left home almost a year earlier, I left at a gallop with no intention of ever going back.

I left so abruptly and so recklessly that I didn't even know the woman I was traveling

with or where we were going. She was a friend of Bert's and that was good enough for me. Bert wanted to take me to Europe himself, but he had to stay behind and help my brother.

I ran away from Stan. It was the first and last time I would ever abandon him.

At the time I thought there was one specific reason for my going. The strike had become too ugly and gone on for too long. The miners and their families were starving. There had been too much violence and even a death. Stan had become irrationally obstinate. He had done exactly what he promised he would never do. He had become the enemy of the miner, the type of owner our father used to curse.

Stan and I were barely on speaking terms the day Randy Dawes walked into his office with a crowbar and attempted to beat the life out of him. He might have succeeded except he was weak not only from lack of food but from the advanced stages of black lung, and Stan was able to subdue him despite the blows he suffered to his head and shoulders.

When I received the news, I was filled with panic and concern but not with outrage. I didn't go so far as to let myself believe my brother deserved to be attacked, but I couldn't hate the man who did it.

Three days later that man would be dead in his jail cell. No one believed it was suicide,

but it was called that and no one dared to say otherwise.

I went to see Stan in the hospital right after I heard about the miner's death. He was already looking tremendously better than he had a few days earlier. His respirator and IV had been removed. His head was still bandaged, his left arm was in a sling, and he had two black eyes; but he was sitting propped up in bed, on the phone, with a sheaf of business papers in his lap.

He smiled when he saw me and called me his Dandy Candy.

I wanted to ask him outright if he had had Randy Dawes killed, just as I had wanted to ask him years earlier if he had pushed Joe Peppernack off that mountain.

Then as now I couldn't do it because I didn't want to know the truth.

The problem for me was I understood Stan, so I couldn't judge him. I knew why he did what he did and although I couldn't condone it, I couldn't condemn him either. We had been through the same trauma but had dealt with it in completely different ways and who was I to say my way was right and his was wrong. After the loss of our parents and our home, and our own close encounter with death, we had both been filled with a constant dread. I hid from it inside myself; he conquered it from outside himself. These would be our separate paths through life: I would

avoid the world while he would rule it.

What he felt compelled to do in order to stay on his path was none of my business, just as my actions were none of his. This isn't to say he didn't control me and tell me what to do to an extent, but he understood there were a few lines he couldn't cross. Joe represented one of those lines.

Stan wanted me to marry him. Joe wanted the same thing. I couldn't do it.

I had slept with Joe to get things for Stan, but I couldn't marry and promise to spend the rest of my life with a man I didn't love, I didn't care for, and I wasn't attracted to in order to cement certain business dealings for my brother. Stan said he respected those feelings.

A few months later, Joseph Peppernack, the single and childless heir to the Peppernack Steel fortune, whose father had passed away a decade earlier and whose mentally unbalanced mother was a resident of a picturesque asylum in upstate New York, was dead, having left his best friend and trusted business partner, Stanford C. Jack, the vast bulk of his wealth.

While I sat next to Stan's bedside making chitchat and avoiding the subject of the dead miner, all I could think about was Joe.

If he had killed Joe, Stan would have seen it as an act of love and generosity toward me: he killed him so he wouldn't have to make

me marry him.

As horrible and indefensible as that reasoning may seem to an outsider, as a longtime observer of the workings of my brother's mind and psyche, I understood how he could justify his actions to himself; but there could be no justification for the miner's death. It was blatant murder, an act of revenge and the sending of a message to those he considered his enemies.

He seemed so normal, so sane. He was my big brother, Stan, looking uncomfortable and silly in a hospital gown. We had been joined at the hip since we were children. He had always taken good care of me. He had given me everything I wanted as long as he approved. We could talk to each other about anything. We laughed together. We worked together. My admiration and devotion toward him was no different from what Kyle so obviously feels for Klint.

Stan was all I had.

I couldn't face the idea that he could be a monster, so I ran away across an ocean.

I don't think Cameron is a monster. He's a bully and bullies can do unpleasant things and cause grief, but they're not ruthless. They're motivated by a sense of inferiority. All their bluster and cruelty is a misguided and distorted attempt to find love and gain approval, whereas a man like my brother did what he did and took what he took because

he believed he was superior and entitled.

Cameron was the only child I've ever had any real exposure to during his formative years, and it was enough to convince me that there are other reasons not to have children besides a fear of the overwhelming responsibility of parenthood. What if you had a child who was an idiot? Were you still obliged to love him and care for him?

Cameron was obnoxious, but his personality wasn't entirely his fault. He was overindulged and ignored. He was a blank canvas surrounded by the finest brushes and a palette of the richest colors left alone in a dark room and expected to paint himself. It wasn't any surprise that when the door to the room was finally thrown open, he was still a big blank.

Yet I will admit that even he had his charming moments. I remember the way he used to slip his little hand into mine and lead me around the vast grounds of his parents' new mansion chatting all the while about cartoons and killing flies and the merits of sprinkles on ice cream. I remember his shrieks of delight whenever he'd start to run away from me into the woods near my house and he'd see me coming after him with my hands raised like claws threatening to eat him up when I caught him.

I still have the clumsy construction paper cards he made me for various birthdays and

Valentine's Days decorated with doilies and glitter and dozens of exclamation marks: TO THE WORLD'S PRETTYEST ANT!!!!!!!!!! TO MY FAVRIT ANT!!!!!!! TO ANT CANDIS FROM THE BEST BOY SHE NOSE!!!!!!!!!!!!!!! (To my dismay, his spelling never improved much past this point.)

There's something about the earnestness of little boys and their boundless joy and curiosity that has always tugged at my heart. Maybe it's the tragic knowledge that they will lose their spirit and zest for life when they become men as surely as they will lose their freckles and lopsided grins.

Men are cursed with the onerous task of finding a purpose. They need more than something to do; they need something to be. Women don't have this problem. Women are women. Our purpose is to be women. But to simply be a man is never enough.

I watch these two boys, Kyle and Klint, and I try to imagine what kind of men they will be and I can't. I can't imagine what kind of children they were, either. I don't think they were ever allowed to be children, even though one is a type of deified child, frozen in perennial boyhood, a man whose destiny is to play a game for most of his adult life. And the other exudes a street urchin sweetness and ruin that attracts and also repels. In him it's all too easy to see the cherub face barely alive beneath a layer of emotional grime. They've

come from a different world than mine, one strewn with empty beer cans and cigarette packs where a mother's bony embraces can be lost forever if she suspects you're not on her side. I can't begin to understand it.

My decision to offer them a home was a rash one, but I haven't regretted it. I'm treating them like any pet project and have busied myself making plans for them I haven't unveiled yet.

I'm also getting an education myself. I've already learned quite a bit about teenage boys. For one thing, they smell. I can't adequately describe the odor that comes from their rooms, but it's very distinctive: a combination of sweat, livestock musk, stale snack food, and bizarrely enough, motor oil.

They make an amazing amount of noise. The way they place a glass on a table, close a cupboard door, walk across a room, take a seat at a table, eat, drink, breathe; it's all done aggressively, even the manner in which they express their emotions. Happiness, affection, anger, and disappointment are all displayed the same way: by cursing, punching, and calling each other terrible names.

Marjorie has informed me that they're completely incapable of putting anything away in a drawer or a cabinet, of making a bed, or of lowering a toilet seat. And the amount of food they eat is incredible. Not good food, mind you, although I've been

extremely pleased to see Kyle's willingness to try everything Luis puts in front of him, and it's been wonderful to see how much he enjoys his meals. He's a budding gourmet while Klint picks at everything like Rae Ann when she's on one of her fad diets. But dinners aside, between the two of them they eat a loaf of white sandwich bread, two pounds of bologna, a dozen eggs, a gallon of milk, a pound of bacon, a quart of orange juice, a large box of cereal, a box of Little Debbie snack cakes, and two bags of spicy Doritos every day.

My attempts to get to know Klint haven't fared well. He arrived here rude, sullen, and uninvolved and has remained that way. However, I find I can't dislike him as much as I should. I think this is because I don't believe his behavior stems from conceit or animosity as much as from an inability to communicate.

Kyle is willing to talk, but he's much more comfortable asking questions than providing answers. He's naturally inquisitive and appears to have a sharp and imaginative mind, although he sometimes tries to hide it by using poor grammar or resorting to an uninspired vocabulary. I can tell he does this on purpose.

Klint, on the other hand, appears to have the mental enthusiasm of a garden toad. Yet I don't think the boy is dumb; I think he simply

chooses not to think. I've seen the way his features collapse into a wince of pain whenever someone speaks to him. He deals with questions as if they were punches to be dodged or absorbed without flinching.

I don't know if he's decided not to use his brain because no one has ever expected him to or as a form of self-defense against flatterers and users. People make a fuss over what this boy is, but I don't think anyone cares who he is. I don't think anyone has ever looked past his amazing ability with a ball in search of a personality.

Manuel had similar problems. People adored him but without knowing him. They thought since he was exceedingly good at one thing, he must be good at everything. He wasn't allowed to have problems and if he tried to claim that he did, people could be almost vicious in their insistence that he didn't.

What they failed to understand was not only did he have many of the same problems they did, but those problems affected him in a much more debilitating manner.

An accountant can be down in the dumps and still add up his daily figures. A teacher can be concerned about her sick mother and still assign chapters for her students to read. A truck driver can be angry at his spouse and still cover all the miles on his route. But an artist's self is his work. If something is wrong

with one, the other falls into decay. I imagine it's the same for an athlete and his performance.

Manuel didn't have to deal with this problem too often. For the most part, he avoided people outside the bullfighting world and those he did spend time with were either too tongue-tied or too much in love with him to say anything critical.

I think it will be harder for Klint. Americans have an obsessive need to tarnish their heroes while Spaniards have an equally obsessive need to keep theirs shiny. Both practices require a great deal of denial and unfairness toward the heroes, but at least Manuel never had to feel guilty about being good.

I've come up with an idea that can only improve my relationship with Klint and will also make life easier for Luis, thereby giving him less to complain about, which will make my life easier, too.

As things stand now, Luis has to drive the boys everywhere and I can tell he's had enough. It's been a very big imposition on his time and it was wrong of me to ask him to do it, but I came to realize after the fact that I wasn't fully prepared to care for two teenage boys. Transportation was a problem I never considered.

Luis never outwardly fumes to me at first whenever I've upset him. He rolls his eyes. He makes his disgusted put-upon snort. In

this case, if he has to leave in the middle of preparing a meal to drive the boys somewhere, he lays down his knife a little more forcefully than needed. He hasn't yet uttered a word of complaint, but I know he's accumulating the memory of each instance, stacking them inside himself like kindling, and one day some random word or action from me will provide the match and I'll be forced to spend the next week trying to put out his latest inferno of grudges.

It's occurred to me that if Klint had his own vehicle, Luis would be released from one of his many wretched bonds. It would also give the boys more freedom and independence. Not to mention, something of that magnitude would have to finally elicit a smile from Klint. I haven't seen him smile once, not even when talking about baseball, his supposed reason for living. This fact is beginning to haunt me.

I know he doesn't like the current transportation situation. I've heard him grumble to his brother about how embarrassing it is to get dropped off like a little kid, and he's also told me to my face that my Mercedes sedan is an "old lady car" and an "in your face car." I'm not absolutely certain about the meaning of the latter expression, but it made Luis grin from ear to ear. I sense it has something to do with showing off, which neither of these boys wants to do. They're both humble. They

don't seem impressed at all by wealth and what it can buy. This is one of the reasons why I've felt compelled to be generous to them.

Taking all this into consideration, I've decided to buy Klint a truck. I'm observant enough to realize he'd prefer a pickup truck to a car and one that isn't too flashy.

Both boys talk reverently about their father's truck and enviously about Bill's truck, a vehicle so covered in mud and rust, I've never been able to quite decide on its color. I've seen them standing with Jerry peering under the open hood of his old Dodge, saying nothing to each other, just staring contentedly with hands in pockets.

I discussed the idea with Bert yesterday, and he agreed it was a good one. He's going to take care of all the financial arrangements for me, but he doesn't feel comfortable picking out the truck since he knows nothing about them.

I'm certainly not going to do it, and the odds of Luis succeeding at picking out the appropriate vehicle for a teenage boy like Klint would be about the same as Starbucks-sucking Aunt Jen being able to pick out an appropriate hair color for her age.

There is only one sensible candidate for the job.

"Good morning, Jerry. How are you?"

He looks up from loading a roll of barbed

wire into the bed of his truck. A half-dozen fence posts are already waiting there.

"Can't complain, Miss Jack. You?"

"I'm fine, thank you. It's a beautiful day, isn't it?"

We both glance around at the vividly colored trees surrounding us. Their leaves of red, yellow, and tangerine pink look as though they've been painted onto the flat blue sky.

Jerry nods.

"Cold, though. Was almost cold enough to have a frost last night."

"Yes, I noticed. I haven't seen Kyle's cat around. You don't think last night was too cold for him?"

"I'm sure he was fine. You don't have to worry about a cat like that."

"I wasn't worried."

He nods again.

"You're sure this break in the fence wasn't caused by Ventisco?"

He pulls his cap off, folds it in two at the bill, and sticks it into his back pocket, his sign that he's prepared to give me his full attention. The cap on his head seems to act as a protective covering for his thoughts like a blanket thrown over a birdcage.

"There weren't no signs that anything hit it or tore at it," he answers me. "It's just an old fence falling down. Also too close to the road. I've never seen signs of Ventisco near a road."

He rubs at the white stubble on his jaw.

"I guess it's about time to let the cows loose into the upper pasture to help coax him back down closer to home."

"Soon," I say. "Luis will let you know. Jerry, I was wondering if you could assist me with something?"

"That's what I'm here for."

"This is not the type of thing you usually do for me."

He doesn't say anything. He waits for me to continue.

"I've decided to buy Klint a pickup truck."

He rubs his jaw again, sniffs, and looks past me toward the house, squinting.

"That's an awful extravagant gift," he says.

"It wouldn't be a gift."

"What would it be?"

"A necessity. Like buying the boy socks."

He nods.

"Uh-huh."

"I've provided both Kyle and Klint with a myriad of things since they moved here," I explain. "I replaced Kyle's iPod when it broke. I pay their cell phone bills. I bought them computers for their schoolwork. My grocery bill has tripled. But I don't consider any of this extravagant. I'm providing for their basic needs. I am acting as a de facto parent, after all."

He drops his gaze from the house to his hands and starts pulling off his work gloves. He sticks them in his coat pocket and pulls

out his keys.

"I'm not spoiling him," I go on. "I remember that car of Cameron's when he was Klint's age. The Thunderbird. I remember him driving it out here to show me. I remember how angry I was at Stan for giving it to him. He seemed determined to ruin that boy.

"This is different. I'm not trying to buy Klint's affection or make him beholden to me. I'm simply trying to make both our lives — all our lives — easier."

"Uh-huh."

"I was wondering if you would mind picking out the truck for him. Bert Shulman would accompany you. He'll take care of the actual purchase. But I thought you'd be the ideal person to make the selection. You know about trucks, plus you know what Klint would like. What would be appropriate for him. Since you come from similar backgrounds."

He abruptly takes his cap out of his pocket and sticks it back on his head, signaling the end of any meaningful exchange between the two of us.

"Okay," he tells me.

"Would you have time later today?"

"I can make time."

"Thank you, Jerry."

He climbs into his truck.

I tighten my scarf and set out on my daily walk.

"Oh, one more thing," I remember and call back to him. "I assume the make should be American."

He leans out of his window and nods at me a final time.

"Yes, ma'am. A boy like that would never want to drive a foreign truck. We'll get him something American made in China."

I fully expect the truck-procuring mission to take weeks. I'm amazed when Bert calls me a few hours later to tell me he and Jerry have found a suitable vehicle: a dark blue Chevrolet that's a few years old but in good condition.

He comes over later with some papers for me to sign, then he and Jerry leave again to pick it up.

Now it's sitting in the driveway in front of the house waiting for the boys to get home from school.

I have to admit, I'm excited. I'm looking forward to seeing the joy on Klint and Kyle's faces and knowing I put it there.

I'm not stingy with my money. I give quite a bit to various charities and community concerns but always without fanfare and public acknowledgment. However, I rarely give personal gifts because I rarely like anyone.

I suppose I'm going to have to accept that I like these boys. Even the one I don't like.

Luis has already left to pick them up with

instructions to bring Klint home directly after school at my request. Usually he drops Klint at his job. Today he'll be told there's something urgent at home and that he can go to his job a little late after the problem has been solved.

I'm settled here on my porch with a cup of strong tea in front of me, wrapped in my coat and scarf, reading a back copy of *El Mundo*. Luis reads all the Spanish newspapers daily on his computer but I could never do this. Even though it means getting the news late, I won't sacrifice the feel of shaking open the paper and the crackle of turning the pages.

I make a mental note that I should do something nice for Bert. He's always been a difficult man to thank for all the many kindnesses he does for me. He won't accept gifts or favors. The only thing he will accept is a dinner invitation. I try to have him over once a month.

Some people would probably consider me a heartless harpy or an unapologetic flirt in my dealings with Bert but I think it's safe to say that at this stage in our lives, I can no longer be accused of leading him on.

Bert proposed marriage to me before we slept together, while we were sleeping together, after we stopped sleeping together, after a substantial mourning period after Manuel's death, and then routinely after that, once a year, until I received my first Social

Security check, and I asked him to stop.

In hindsight, I'm sure I hurt Bert when after years of trying to get me into bed I suddenly jumped in, stayed for a little while, then permanently jumped out again without any seeming rhyme or reason or so much as a single "I love you" or "Thank you. I had a good time."

In my defense, I didn't know what to think about sex and love and how the two mixed or didn't. I had entered adolescence without a mother. I had never had any female friends. I lived in an orphanage for most of my teen years, and what I learned from watching the other girls was confusing at best.

There were the quiet, frightened good girls who escaped their daily lives through fairy-tale dreams of swooning in a prince's embrace while all along accepting the reality that their survival depended on giving themselves to men they didn't love who would probably abuse them.

Then there were the predatory, promiscuous bad girls who blatantly used sex to get food and presents, yet these were the same girls who fell in love the hardest and would cry for days over men who treated them horribly.

Except for vocabularies peppered with French phrases and an absence of head lice, the girls at my Ivy League college proved to

be no different when it came to dealing with men.

I remained a virgin until my midtwenties and when I finally decided to sleep with a man, it was purely out of curiosity. Despite Bert's well-known regard for me and his long-established pursuit of me, when I finally decided to "rock his world" as the youngsters say, it was simply a matter of him being at the right place at the right time in relation to my rather selfish whim.

Granted, I cared a great deal about Bert and I even found him attractive (unlike Joe Peppernack or that poor DuPont boy with the lisp), but these were not exceptional emotions. I was certainly not in love with him or hot for his bod.

I was disappointed in sex. I did my best to find it exciting and pleasurable. There were no obstacles in my way. I have no religious or moral objections to it, and I'm not shy about baring my body. I wasn't afraid of the physical act of penetration, regardless of the stories I'd been told. To hear some girls talk, the average man's member was the size of a rolling pin and just as hard. Even so, some of them seemed to find its insertion gratifying while others described it as an agonizing invasion of their bodies tantamount to being ripped in half.

I relaxed and gave myself over to Bert's kisses and caresses, waiting for a spark of

desire to ignite somewhere deep inside me and spread to all the nerve endings in my body. I waited to feel some wonderful physical assault on my forgotten country girl senses, something that made me salivate like the smell of fresh-baked homemade bread or the bright red sight of raspberries finally ripe amid their thorns.

Nothing happened.

Actual intercourse was even more frustrating in that it wasn't bad or good. I was expecting something extreme and what I received was something mundane: a monotonous moving of muscles with an eventual useful goal in mind not unlike the process of kneading dough for dumplings.

Bert, on the other hand, seemed to have quite a good time.

I couldn't understand how he could get so wound up about something that left me so unmoved. I wondered if there was something wrong with me as I continued to be unmoved by other men. Then I met Manuel and as much as my rational, sensible self fought against the illogical, romantic notion, I finally accepted that there is such a thing as chemistry.

I'm engrossed in an article about the exhumation of Spain's mass graves filled sixty years ago with thousands of Franco's victims when I hear a car coming.

I stand up from my chair and wait for the

Mercedes to appear. Luis parks it in front of the barn. Klint and Kyle get out and begin walking slowly across the driveway toward me, their heads bowed, ball caps pulled down over their eyes, hands deep in pockets, backpacks hanging from one shoulder, kicking at rocks.

Luis follows with a bag of groceries. I see a loaf of sandwich bread and a box of Little Debbie snack cakes sticking out of the top.

"Hello, boys," I call from the top of my front porch steps.

"Hi, Miss Jack," Kyle replies.

Klint nods his head. I hate this.

"You got company?" Kyle asks, glancing at the truck.

"No," I tell him as I join them. "This truck belongs to your brother."

I smile complacently, immensely pleased with myself, and wait for their reactions.

Kyle's mouth drops open, and he lets his backpack slip off his shoulder onto the ground

"What?" Klint says.

"The truck is for you, Klint."

"No way!" Kyle shouts.

He runs over to the truck and throws open one of the doors.

"I thought you could use it," I continue addressing Klint. "I know you and your brother don't like being dependent on Luis for rides to and from school."

Luis clears his throat.

"And Luis is also much too busy to drive you," I quickly add. "I know once your practices and games start you'll need your own transportation. Possibly you might want to go on a date someday."

"Klint, check it out!" Kyle shouts. "It's a Silverado! It's got camo seat covers!"

Klint ignores his brother's excitement, but his cries bring Jerry out from the barn. He pauses to spit a stream of chewing tobacco into the grass, then begins one of his long-legged strolls toward us.

"You're giving me this truck?" Klint asks me.

"Yes, I am."

"Why?"

"Because I want to."

"A truck?"

"Yes."

I pull the keys from my coat pocket and dangle them until he puts out his hand and takes them.

He stares at them for an exceedingly long time. When he finally looks up at me I expect to see joy on his face, but it's twisted with an emotion I can't define. I think it might be rage, but then I notice tears in his eyes.

"I don't want it," he blurts out.

"What?" Kyle cries. "Are you nuts?"

"I beg your pardon," I say.

He stops and searches desperately for the

right words and comes up empty-handed.

"It's wrong."

"What do you mean? It's a simple gift," I explain.

"It's not simple. There's nothing simple about a truck."

We all stare at the innocent vehicle.

Klint's gaze returns to the keys in his hand. He stares at them with a terrible longing, then turns and throws them with a relaxed, fluid stroke of his arm that seems to require very little effort but sends them over and well beyond the barn.

I gasp in outrage.

Jerry makes a low, complimentary whistle.

Klint takes off running down the driveway.

"Sorry, Miss Jack. I better go talk to him," Kyle says.

"You do more than talk to him," I reply, trying to control the quiver of anger in my voice. "You tell him to come see me. Immediately."

Luis sighs, sets down his bag of groceries on the porch, and begins walking in the direction of the thrown keys.

Jerry comes up beside me.

"Why does that boy dislike me?" I ask him. "I've done so much for him."

He works the plug in his mouth a few times.

"That would be the reason," he says.

I excuse myself and go back inside the house. I stop by the kitchen to get a glass of

ice water and gulp it down standing at the sink, a practice I abhor. My heart is racing from the shock of what just transpired.

What kind of teenage boy turns down a vehicle?

I fill my glass again, then go to a drawer where I keep a Spanish fan. I snap it open and wave it rapidly in front of my face. I know I must look flushed.

Luis enters the kitchen with his bag of groceries.

He nods and smiles.

"Go ahead," I sigh. "You obviously have something to say to me."

"Yes. I've decided to serve a potato and anchovy gratin with the veal tonight."

He begins humming as he puts the food away. I join him and take the milk jug to the refrigerator.

"You think I handled it wrong."

"Yes."

"How would you have handled it?"

"The right way."

I pick up the box of snack cakes and examine it.

"What are these?" I ask Luis.

"Butterscotch Krimpets. They're not bad."

I open the box and take out a little blond cake wrapped in cellophane.

"Maybe this has all been a big mistake. What made me think that I could be a mother this late in my life?"

Luis laughs.

"You're not exactly a mother. Why not think of yourself as a guardian angel?"

"That's very nice. I like that."

"These boys don't need a mother. From what you've told me, much of their grief and torment comes from the fact that they have one. They need someone to care about them."

"You mean like a zookeeper?"

"Not someone to take care of them. Someone to care about them. I think my English has become better than yours."

"But doesn't giving someone a truck show you care about him?"

"No. It shows you have a lot of money."

I tear open the cake. Luis does the same and devours his in two bites.

"You hurt his pride," he says, brushing crumbs off his hands into the sink.

"That's ridiculous. And even if it were true, there was a better way to handle it. He didn't have to be so horribly rude."

"You see rudeness. I see a boy who doesn't waste his words."

"When he does speak, the words are always offensive."

"Not always. Often they're just concise answers to questions that should have never been asked."

I bite into the cake, and I'm surprised by the softness of the spongecake. They're not bad at all.

"You think any answer that isn't the one you want to hear is a rude answer," Luis goes on. "I understand him. Don't you remember? When I worked for Manuel I hardly ever talked. It wasn't because I was rude or sulking or dumb. I was humble."

"Really?" I say, smiling.

"You shouldn't be so hard on him. What you saw today was a colossal act of integrity."

"Miss Jack?"

I turn around at the sound of Klint's voice and pop the remainder of the cake into my mouth. I cough and almost choke. Luis hands me my water.

"Kyle says you wanted to talk to me."

"Yes," I sputter.

Luis sets the keys on the counter and leaves us, humming.

My coughing fit passes.

I frown at Klint's hat, and he removes it.

"You owe me an apology," I state.

"I don't owe you an apology for not accepting a gift. There's nothing wrong with that."

"Actually, it is wrong not to accept a gift, but that's not why I'm upset. It was the way you did it."

"Sorry."

"Complete sentence, please."

"I'm sorry."

I glance at the keys.

"Can you throw a baseball that far?" I wonder.

I realize from the look on his face that I've asked a ridiculous question.

"Yeah," he says.

"I think I gave you the wrong impression. The truck isn't solely for you. I bought it thinking of Kyle, too."

"Kyle?"

"Yes. You saw how excited he was. I know how much he dislikes being driven to and from school by Luis. It makes him feel like a baby," I tell him, knowing that I'm voicing his own complaints. "Think how much Kyle would love to go places in that truck. Losing your father has been a terrible ordeal for him. This truck could help take his mind off his troubles."

"He did seem pretty excited."

The same torn expression I saw earlier plays over his face again. He twists his cap in his hands and looks up at me.

"I want to pay you for it. It will take me a while. I don't make that much at my job, but I have some saved up already."

"All right. If that's what you want."

I wait for the smile but don't get it.

I hand him the keys.

He takes them and walks sedately out of the kitchen. I stand perfectly silent listening at the door. When he gets far enough away that he thinks I can't see or hear him any-more, he starts to run. I let him go, enjoying

the slaps of his shoes on Marjorie's freshly waxed floors almost as much as a smile.

Chapter Twelve: Kyle

Capitalism is based on the concept that in order for someone to succeed, someone else has to suffer.

I just learned that in school yesterday from my history teacher, Mr. Pankowski. He's the only teacher in the whole school district with a Ph.D., so everyone calls him Doc.

He's a smart guy, but he doesn't dress like one or talk like one either. He uses regular words, and he wears old faded jeans, scuffed brown loafers, and the same two baggy sweaters over different-colored shirts with the collars sticking up crookedly every day. He's tall and thin, and his eyes have the permanent starved, weary look of a rescued POW or one of my aunt Jen's ex-boyfriends. I think he's only in his thirties, but he has a worn-out face. He's the opposite of Luis, who has a smooth, youthful face and happy eyes. (I still don't know what Luis's formal job title is. Klint calls him Miss Jack's "Taco Boy." I've been trying to explain to Klint that there's a

big difference between Mexico and Spain, but so far it's not getting through to him.)

I'm enjoying Doc's class not just because he knows a lot but because he doesn't sugar-coat anything. He tells it like it is and he doesn't take sides, even though you know he probably has a side and it's fairly easy to guess which one it is. He doesn't think the way to learn about a war is to memorize a bunch of dates and names of battles. He makes us study the people living in the opposing countries, their sameness and their differences and how some of those differences go back forever and can't ever be changed and maybe shouldn't be changed. He says going to war to protect yourself is okay, but doing it because you think you can change someone else is always going to turn into a never-ending disaster. People will only fight so hard to try and hold on to what they have, but they'll dig in and fight forever to protect who they are.

It's too bad President Bush didn't take Doc's class, but he probably would've slept through it anyway like Klint did.

According to Doc, usually the men who are succeeding at capitalism don't want to be anywhere near the men who are doing the suffering. That's why they go off and live in cities like New York or Paris or travel around on their yachts.

Stan Jack — Miss Jack's brother — was an

exception. He could've lived anywhere in the world, but he didn't even go as far as Harrisburg. He based his business in Centresburg and built his mansion in the middle of nowhere.

Some people say he did it because he loved the Pennsylvania countryside. He cared about the hills he ripped up and the rivers he polluted. He was devoted to the wildlife he hunted and killed. He valued the people and built his empire with an eye not solely toward making himself rich, but also toward bringing jobs and prosperity to the region.

But most people say he was a power-hungry sadistic SOB who got off on watching people grovel or, better yet, watching the suffering in their eyes and knowing they couldn't do anything about it.

(I've been wondering lately if Satan's Banker might be a picture of him, and since I've been thinking this I've been covering it with two T-shirts at night.)

There's always been a rumor that he killed his partner Joseph Peppernack, the P of J&P Coal, who was the heir to Peppernack Steel and the partner who put all the money into their company while Stan contributed the ambition and cunning. They were hunting up in Cameron County when Peppernack took a tumble off a cliff and broke his neck. The county coroner ruled it an accident; a year later when Stan Jack finished building his

hospital in Centresburg, he gave that same county coroner the job of head administrator.

To this day, if a guy gets royally screwed over in any way — from having his woman leave him to getting laid off from a job — the coal miners around here say he was "peppernacked."

Plus everyone knows the story of the miner who attacked Stan Jack during the strike of 1958. It was the first time a strike had turned violent here since the 1800s. Two supervisors were badly injured, and one miner was killed.

Another miner snuck into Stan Jack's office and beat him with a crowbar. Stan barely lived through it. The miner was arrested, and a couple days later hung himself with a belt in his jail cell while awaiting trial, which was kind of suspicious since the prison uniforms didn't have belts.

Miss Jack doesn't talk about her brother. I don't know how involved she was with her brother's shady dealings or if she got along with him, but obviously he liked her enough to leave her his mansion and a lot of his money.

I remember the first time I saw his house. It was a photo in a book called *Human Capital: An American History of Men Owning Men from the Age of Slavery Through the Establishment of Labor Unions.* I came across the book in a university library while Dad

and Klint were meeting with some athletic department bigwigs about scholarships.

There along with sketches of Africans in chains being dragged off slave boats and black-and-white press photos of workers with raised fists picketing in front of factories was a picture of the very house I'm living in now with a caption identifying it as "The former home of Stanford Jack."

On the next page was a gray, grainy photo taken of one of J&P Coal's old company towns. It showed about three dozen one-room shanties clinging to the stripped hill-side, stubborn and ugly, like a cluster of warts.

I know the place. It's not far from the railroad tracks and an abandoned tipple where a bunch of us kids used to play when we were little. The tin from the roofs was scavenged long ago, and the wood from the shacks has rotted away. People haven't lived there for fifty years, but Mother Nature doesn't seem to want it back. Nothing grows there. Not even weeds. During the summer when the mountains are covered in lush green, what's left of the town can be seen from the interstate as clearly as a scab on a knee.

Now I wish I'd taken the time to read about Stan Jack, but how could I have guessed that I'd ever be staying in his house? It's exciting in a creepy way to be here, sort of like living

with the sister of Darth Vader.

The other reason I like Doc is that his brother, Nate, is the baseball coach for Western Penn University. It's a college not far from here. It's not as big and well known as Penn State and not as prestigious as the Ivy League University of Pennsylvania in Philly, but it's a place where a guy could get a half-decent education and play for a fairly respectable ball team.

Klint's good enough that he might get some offers from a few of the major Division I schools in some of the best conferences, but the competition's fierce and scholarship money is scarce even at the schools with the most famous baseball programs.

Full scholarships are almost nonexistent, and when they do happen, they almost always go to pitchers. The little money that's left usually goes to up the middle positions. Klint plays one of them: second base; he's got that going for him.

He could maybe get 50 percent and still go to a big school in a pretty good conference, but he could get a full ride to a smaller school and that's what's most important because we've got no way of paying for college. Working a job, keeping up with classes, and playing ball sounds impossible to me, plus there's no job Klint could get that could pay for something as big as college. Taking out loans would be okay if there was any guarantee he'd

be able to pay them back someday, but one thing I know for sure is there are no guarantees in life about anything.

A smaller school wouldn't be so bad for Klint. He'd get a lot of attention and playing time. He'd still get noticed by pro scouts and could still be on the road to a great future. It's his pride that's going to screw up everything. He thinks if he doesn't go to a school with a nationally ranked team, it's the same thing as saying he's not good enough to be on a nationally ranked team, but it's not true. He's good enough to play ball for any school, but the program might not be good enough for him. I can't make him understand this any more than I can make him understand that Spain isn't a country filled with banditos in big sombreros drinking tequila and eating tacos all day.

I was in Doc's class for a couple weeks before he mentioned Klint to me. He asked me to stay for a minute after class one day to compliment me on my essay.

I already felt like I knew Doc before we talked privately because I was one of the few kids who talked to him in class. He told me he was sorry about what happened to my dad and used the topic of Dad as a way to ask about Klint, too. I guess I could've been offended, like the only reason he cared about my essay was because he wanted to find out something about Klint, but he seemed to read

my mind and told me this wasn't true.

It turns out Doc could care less about baseball, but he loves his brother and wants to help him. We have that in common.

He tried to talk to Klint about going to West Penn when he had Klint in class, but he said he rarely saw him awake.

I had a good laugh over that one.

Every time Doc's tried to pin him down in the halls since then, he always manages to escape. I told Doc not to take it personally. Klint has a fear of teachers because he has a fear of learning anything new that might make him have to change one of his opinions.

Doc laughed at that one even though I didn't mean it as a joke.

Nate has tried to talk to Klint, too, at games and tournaments, but Klint takes one look at the WPU on his ball cap and walks away.

While Dad was still around it didn't matter as much to me where Klint went to college. I knew our lives would go on the same, and Klint would come home and visit us on breaks. Now I don't know what will happen to me, and the idea of Klint going to college twenty miles down the road from here sounds like a good deal.

Today's the day Shelby and her family are coming for dinner.

I got up earlier than I wanted because I couldn't sleep. I ate my Corn Pops and

wandered around the house a little bit. When we moved in, Miss Jack told us we could go anywhere we wanted except for her room and Luis's room. We could even check out the basement and attic. Apparently she doesn't have a secret room where she keeps some crazy, drooling, axe-murderer relative locked up or one that's filled with the bones of the kids she supposedly ate after Ventisco killed them for her.

I was kind of disappointed to find this out.

I was hanging out near the main staircase looking at some paintings when I heard loud voices coming from another room. I followed them as far as the dining room and realized it was Miss Jack and Luis arguing in the kitchen. I couldn't understand any of it, but I knew it was probably about dinner. Whenever they disagree about food or wine, they always speak Spanish.

I went outside and I've been sitting here on the front porch steps for a while thinking about what I'm going to say to Shelby, and how good she's going to look, and if it would be a good thing if I can get her parents to like me or if she's one of those girls who only likes guys her parents hate when Jerry comes down the drive pushing a wheelbarrow full of mulch.

I wave at him. He nods. I figure he'll keep going, but he comes over to me, stops, takes off his ball cap, runs a plain white handker-

chief over his face, and puts his cap back on.

He gestures at the house with his head.

"Miss Jack and Luis going at it?" he asks me.

"Yeah."

"In Spanish?"

"Yeah."

He nods again.

"Want some help?" I ask him.

"Love some."

Working with Jerry turns out to be very relaxing. He doesn't say a word to me the whole time. When we finish, he walks away and comes back a few minutes later carrying a six-pack of beer.

He pops open a can and hands it to me.

We drink in silence except for one comment he makes about Mr. B's hunting skills and how he's been happily finding bodies all over the place. He says Mr. B reminds him of a cat he had when he was a kid growing up in Coal Run. I'm intrigued by this because Coal Run is a ghost town now. A mine fire went crazy and spread through miles of tunnels underneath it, poisoning the ground and burning all the way through to the top soil in some places. The air smells like sulfur and the ground steams. The government came in and put up barbed wire and warning signs and made all the people move. This was almost forty years ago, but nothing will ever change there. It's impossible to put out a

mine fire. The town will burn forever.

Coal Run was also the site of the Gertie explosion, one of the biggest mining disasters in Pennsylvania history. Ninety-seven men were killed.

I ask Jerry if he was living there when it happened.

"I'd just gone to bed after coming off the graveyard shift," he answers me, staring into the distance like he's talking to himself.

I study his face after he says this, looking for the telltale signs of a miner's life in his eyes that I've seen so many times in the eyes of Bill, and Tyler's uncle, and the other miners I've known. It's there: the stubborn loyalty and sadness of a dog who knows he's going to be fed and kicked by the same man.

I'm dying to ask him more, but I know I better not. He's the kind of guy who only talks when he wants to say something; no amount of questions will get anything out of him.

He finishes his first beer and opens another, then takes a seat on the ground and leans against a tree trunk, his long, thin legs bent at the knees making sharp triangles beneath the dirty gray fabric of his work pants. He picks up where he left off without any prodding from me.

"I woke up and thought we were having an earthquake. The whole house shook. The windows shattered. Pictures sprang off the

walls. The dresser drawers flew open before the whole thing fell over and crashed on the floor. Then I heard the siren and knew what had happened. What I'd felt was an underground explosion so powerful it could break glass and knock over furniture two miles away.

"I ran outside and there was the rest of the people in the town standing there staring dumbfounded in the direction of the mine."

He tells the story squinting intently at the empty space in front of him like he's watching his past life unfold before him on an invisible screen but the picture's blurry.

"What'd you do next?"

"Found my mother. That was the first thing I did. I knew my brother was working that shift. Then I spent the next three days digging for remains and survivors like everybody else."

"Were there any survivors?"

"Nope."

"Does that mean your brother . . . ?"

"Yep. All we got back was part of a leg and a foot still inside its work boot. We buried it in one of those coffins for babies."

He tells me this in a matter-of-fact way like he's explaining where he keeps the weed killer.

I imagine Klint being nothing but an arm and a hand in a baseball glove. I picture myself digging for him, praying that he's still

alive but hoping if he's dead he died instantly like Dad and El Soltero and didn't have to suffocate two miles beneath daylight blind and buried alive in a coal tomb.

While I'm thinking all this, I start to get a creepy sensation in the pit of my stomach that makes my hands feel clammy and the skin on the back of my neck crawl. I can see Klint all too clearly trapped in the darkness, but I can't tell what's pushing down on him. I can only sense it's the burden of his life filled with secret pain he won't ever reveal to me. He's not screaming to get out. He's not thrashing around or crying. He's lying very still, staring back at me. His blue eyes that all the girls love are black and terror-filled but resigned. He won't fight, he's silently telling me. He's given up. He wants to die.

I shake my head to get rid of the idea and take a big gulp of my beer.

Jerry hasn't noticed anything. He hasn't looked at me once during his entire story.

"Did you keep working in the mines after that?" I ask him, trying to distract my thoughts.

"For a while. Then word spread that Mr. Jack was looking for a full-time handyman and groundskeeper for his sister's mansion in the country after he moved his wife and kid to Centresburg. I'd worked for J&P Coal for twelve years by then, all of them in Gertie."

He pauses and adds, "You know that's the

mine he named after his mother."

"Sure," I say, even though I didn't know.

"I wasn't too anxious to keep working in the mines after the explosion. I met with Mr. Jack and got his approval. Then I came out here and once I saw Miss Jack, I took the job without even asking what it paid."

This last statement catches me off guard, and I turn and stare at him waiting for a smile that means he's joking, but nothing changes in his wooden expression.

Luis said Miss Jack had been El Soltero's girlfriend, and he doesn't strike me as the kind of guy who dated ugly girls. And now it turns out Jerry took a job working here based solely on how she looked. Could she have been beautiful? That would make her the human equivalent of a dried flower.

Jerry chugs the rest of his beer and stands up, and I know he's done talking, but there's one final question I can't resist asking him.

"What was Mr. Jack like?"

He takes a snuff tin out of his back pocket and puts a pinch of tobacco inside his lower lip. He works the chew around a bit, then spits in the grass behind him. When he picks up the empty wheelbarrow, I've decided he's not going to answer me, but he surprises me as he starts walking away.

"Ruthless bastard," he says. "That was the general consensus."

After Jerry and I split up, I take a long walk

down the road. I don't get passed by very many cars out here but when I do, I grin and wave, knowing it'll drive them crazy trying to figure out how they know me when they don't.

By the time I get back to the house, I've started feeling weird about Klint again. The image I had of him being crushed like a trapped coal miner keeps coming back to haunt me.

Something inside me panics and I'm overcome with a need to make sure he's okay.

I'm bounding up the porch steps when he comes walking out the front door.

He looks good, and the worrying I've been doing about him seems stupid. He's washed his hair and is wearing clean jeans, a shirt with a collar, and the new buttery suede Timberland hiking boots I got him for his last birthday because I'd seen him admiring them when we were at Shaw's Sporting Goods getting a new pair of cleats. He's only worn them twice, and both times he complained that he looked like a fag lumberjack.

"What are you all decked out for?" I ask him.

He makes a serious face while brushing at his shirt cuffs and tugging at his collar.

"Dinner, my good man," he says in a poor English accent. "I can't wait."

"Are you sick or something?"

"Tyler's coming."

"What? Tyler?" I cry in absolute astonishment. "You asked Miss Jack if you could invite Tyler to dinner?"

He grins at me.

"Yeah. Why not?"

"How did you do it? What did you say?"

"I said, 'Excuse me, Miss Jack, but would it be possible for me to invite one of my friends to dinner, too? I've told him a lot about you and how nice you've been to me and Kyle and he'd like to meet you.' "

"No way you said that."

"Yeah, I did."

"You think she bought it?"

"Yeah."

"You're wrong. She's not stupid."

"She said, yes. If she thought I was messing with her, she would've said no."

"Not necessarily. Not if she knows what you're doing and has plans of her own."

The smile leaves his face for a moment as he mulls over the idea.

I shake my head at him, as much out of respect for his daring as in disbelief.

"Jesus, Klint. You invited Tyler to dinner? I don't think I've ever seen him use a fork. He even eats Jell-O with his hands."

His smile returns.

"I know."

We both hear the rumble of a car coming up the drive. As it gets closer, I recognize the purr of Shelby's engine and see a flash of red

in the trees.

"Who's that?" Klint asks.

"Shelby."

"Shit," he says.

He goes inside, and I'm left standing on the porch like an overeager, loser idiot who's been waiting for her since the crack of dawn.

She parks and comes walking toward me, smiling, in a brown-and-red plaid miniskirt, a clingy red sweater, and flat brown shoes with sparkly copper buckles on the toes. All that red makes her chestnut hair glow and brings out the golden flecks in her tea-colored eyes.

I can picture her standing in front of her closet full of perfect outfits for every occasion picking out this one: autumn weekend wear for dinner with her parents and persnickety aunt. But I like to think she chose the miniskirt for me.

On her wrist is a chunky gold bracelet made of heart-shaped links. It jingles past my ear as she reaches around me to give me a hug. I hold her close and bury my nose in her hair.

She pulls away and gives me a funny look I've never seen before. For a moment I try and convince myself it's love I'm seeing, but then I realize it's surprised confusion. I guess I buried my nose too deeply.

"Hey," I tell her.

All week long I've been practicing what I was going to say to her. "Hey" wasn't it.

"Let me go say hi to Aunt Candace and

Luis and I'll be right back," she tells me, and I take some satisfaction in realizing she didn't ask about Klint.

I watch her run up the stairs and try to catch a glimpse of her panties. I can't help wondering what kind she's wearing. Silky ones. Lacy ones. Plain cotton ones. Maybe a thong. Probably a thong. Girls only wear thongs nowadays, according to Tyler, and he should know since he has three older sisters and two younger ones and sees their underwear piled on the dryer before they come and put it away. Thongs are impossible to fold, he's informed us, and equally impossible to sort out among all those girls, so his mom heaps them all together in what he says looks like a snarl of multicolored fishing line.

I'm always amazed at how calmly he can talk about girls' underwear. Not just their panties but their bras, too. I almost break out in a sweat just thinking about it.

Shelby comes back out, shaking her head over the chaos in the kitchen. She starts talking about nothing in particular and I nod and watch her. She has a very animated, breathless way of speaking. Everything sounds urgent and exciting coming out of her mouth, even bad stuff.

I remember one time when we were at one of Klint's ball games, a couple girls from my school kept staring at her and whispering to each other behind their hands and busting

out into shrieks of laughter. I figured they were making fun of me, but later I ran into them at the concession stand when I went to get Shelby a drink and one of them was doing a dead-on imitation of her.

They recognized me, but it didn't stop them.

I got Shelby a can of Sprite and as I was leaving one of the girls called out to me, "She's a total phony."

I didn't think much of it. I chalked it up to female jealousy. I know a lot about this particular topic.

Once when my mom and aunt Jen had just finished one of their big blowouts, and Aunt Jen had gone storming out of the house calling my mom a heartless bitch while my mom called her a worthless slut — when an hour earlier they'd been giddy to see each other and had been complimenting each other's hair and making plans to go shopping — I asked Dad why they did this.

He said it was because the most powerful emotion women feel is jealousy.

I said I thought it was love for their children, and he laughed and repeated, "Jealousy."

I asked him what was the most powerful emotion men feel, and he said hunger.

As Shelby talks, she starts to wander and I follow. Before I know it we're in the woods where the late afternoon sun is filtered

through the leaves, softly coating everything in gold. Beyond the trees is a sky the same Easter egg blue as my first school backpack, but it's slowly being filled up with mounds of threatening gray clouds.

Shelby talks about her classes, and how she's happy she's going to see her sister tonight even though she's in big trouble with their dad again, and about going shopping with her mom in New York next weekend.

I don't pay much attention to what she's saying; I just like the sound of her voice.

I want to ask her if she knows Calladito killed El Soltero and her aunt Candace was there and she was in love with him, but then I remember her surprise at our first dinner with Miss Jack when she found out her aunt even knew Manuel Obrador. She couldn't know anything about their story.

The real question for me is why? Why doesn't she know? She's been around her aunt her whole life, and I only met her a month ago and during that time I've been overcome with curiosity about the bulls, and El Soltero, and Luis, and her obsession with everything Spanish. How could Shelby not want to know?

It could be one of those family things where nobody cares. I had a friend in elementary school whose grandfather was one of the guys in World War II who first drove up to Auschwitz when they were liberating the prisoners.

He said no one in the army had any idea it was as bad as what they were going to see. It was a fence lined with living skeletons in rags shouting in strained, cracked voices in many different languages but then someone shouted "Freedom" in English because they realized the tanks were American. Soon they were all shouting "Freedom!" and "America!" He and the other war-hardened soldiers on top of the three tanks stared back in bewilderment, and tears streamed down their young faces.

Teachers loved to trot this guy out to talk to their history classes, but if you brought up the topic in front of his own family, they rolled their eyes and turned up the volume on the TV.

I remember how casually Shelby threw off my question about Ventisco and her aunt's love for Spanish things by saying that she spent some time in Spain when she was young and liked it. I thought her answer was on the weak side. A woman vacationing in a foreign country brings back trinkets; she doesn't bring back livestock and people.

"So everything's fine with Aunt Candace?" Shelby asks after she finishes filling me in on her own life.

"We're getting along."

"She can be tough sometimes. She has very definite ideas about how people should behave."

"Most people do. Even quiet guys like Bill.

You should see how he acts if you mow vertically instead of diagonally."

She smiles at me.

"Yeah, but her ideas are so old-fashioned."

"I don't know. She wants people to speak properly, and be polite to each other, and care about art and other cultures. None of that's bad stuff. It's basically what separates us from the animals."

"Wow, Kyle," she laughs. "That was deep. You're turning into a little Aunt Candace disciple. I never saw that coming."

She's making fun of me. I don't understand why. Shelby's got money and class, and I know she cares about education. She freaks out if she gets less than an A – on a test, and she expects to go to an Ivy League college. Yet she's crazy about a guy like Klint who barely squeaks by with a C average and thinks a bus trip to Pittsburgh for a Pirates game qualifies as traveling abroad. This isn't the first time she's reacted to one of my intelligent observations with the patronizing tone of someone praising a little kid for telling a dumb "knock knock" joke.

"How's Klint?" she asks, which only makes me feel worse, but I realize she doesn't know she hurt my feelings.

"He's okay. The move's been harder for him."

"Does he still hate Aunt Candace?"

"He doesn't hate her. He never did. He

hates change. Dad was the same way."

"That's great about the truck."

"Yeah," I say, brightening. "The truck is awesome."

"My dad went through the roof when he found out."

"What do you mean?"

She blushes deeply.

"I mean . . . ," she begins to explain, obviously embarrassed. "My dad was just concerned. He doesn't want Aunt Candace to get carried away and spend too much money."

"Klint didn't ask for that truck," I reply, trying to keep the anger out of my voice. "It was all your aunt's idea. And he's paying it off. I told you that."

"I know, Kyle, and that's very noble of him, but do you know how long it will take to pay for a truck with the salary from a part-time job at a dairy? Let's be real. Aunt Candace paid for the truck."

She smiles at me again.

"Do you think he'd take me for a ride?"

"He'd take Bigfoot for a ride," I grumble.

She bursts into giggles. She laughs so hard she falls against me and grabs my arm for support. I wasn't trying to be funny, but I'm pleased with the results.

By the time we turn back, we realize we've gone farther than we thought. The sun has already begun to set and the air has become

cold. Neither one of us has a coat, plus we both fear the wrath of Miss Jack if we're late for dinner.

We give each other half-panicked glances as we finally approach the house. Two other cars are parked by Shelby's and people are sitting on the porch. Miss Jack loves candles and there are colorful blazes of light everywhere.

We're a little late, but I don't care. I almost laugh out loud when I see Klint sitting stiffly in a chair at the mercy of Miss Jack and her family without any assistance from me.

One of the cars is a big, black Cadillac with a vanity license plate that reads: JPCOAL1. I don't have much trouble figuring out it belongs to Shelby's dad. The other car is a little silver Mercedes I assume belongs to the little silver man Miss Jack introduces as Bert Shulman, "a dear friend of mine and a very dear friend of my late brother's."

Bert Shulman has silvery hair and a silvery mustache and in this light his eyes even look silver. They twinkle behind his glasses like polished nickels. He's wearing a gray suit with a kind of pewter sheen to it and a pink shirt and purple bow tie. He gives me a friendly smile and shakes hands briskly while saying he's very happy to meet me.

Cam Jack is not happy to meet me. He looks me up and down like I might be the kid he saw throwing eggs at his front door last night. He has a flabby, sweaty handshake.

"So you're the other kid," he says to me.

"Yes," I reply, uncertainly. "I'm Kyle. It's nice to meet you."

He sits down without saying anything else.

Shelby's mom is a much nicer and tanner person with a toothpaste commercial smile and lots of frosty hair.

She doesn't stand up to greet me. She just holds out her hand, and I'm forced to look down at her and her boobs bursting out of her sherbet orange dress that's also showing a lot of leg. I'm never comfortable looking at a mother's breasts, even when they're good ones, so I concentrate hard on staring at her face.

She's pretty from a distance, but I realize up close her face has cracks and creases just like my aunt Jen's. They're not the natural kind of wrinkles like Miss Jack has that come from being old. They're the kind that come from being varnished and baked.

She tells me she feels like she already knows me since Shelby's told her so much about me. That makes me feel pretty good. Then she introduces me to her dog, Baby.

I didn't even notice him. He was huddled between her hip and the side of the chair she's sitting on. At the sound of his name he tries to hop up onto her lap but slips twice and falls back onto the cushion. He yips a couple times and makes a final effort and

meets with squeals of approval from his mistress.

She picks him up in both hands and holds him out to me. I don't know what I'm supposed to do. I reach out my forefinger and tap him lightly on the head.

"Nice doggie," I say.

Miss Jack was right. Mr. B's at least three times as big as Baby. I wonder what Mr. B would think of him. I doubt he'd think he was a dog. Maybe some kind of hairless, uncoordinated rodent.

Shelby's sister Starr is the last one to be introduced to me. She's sitting the farthest away, with her long legs in a pair of tight jeans and black leather high-heeled boots swinging over one side of a blue wicker chair.

She's smoking and each time she leans down to tap ashes into the ashtray on the floor, her hair covers her face like a blond silk handkerchief, and I get a good shot of her breasts, too. I don't have a problem with this. I've imposed no personal restrictions on myself regarding the viewing of sisters' breasts.

Hers aren't pushed up like her mother's. They're soft and free beneath a gray and blue blouse. I don't think she's wearing a bra. I wish Klint was the kind of brother I could share this information with.

I know about her. Shelby's told me some of her checkered past. Her parents caught her

in their bed having sex with her boyfriend when she was only fifteen. She's been arrested for underage drinking and got kicked out of one of her boarding schools for spray painting FAT ASSES UNITE on the cafeteria wall. She ran away to Australia for three months with some old guy in his thirties and came back alone with a broken arm and two Campbell's Soup thermoses filled with hundreds of the most beautiful opals Shelby'd ever seen. She's wrecked two cars, shaved her head once, and can use chopsticks with her toes.

Standing in front of her, I feel like I'm presenting myself to some mythical warrior princess who's probably going to torture and enslave me, but I don't really care if she does.

She looks me up and down like her dad did but without any hostility, only a bored curiosity. Her smoking is slow and sensual, nothing like the frantic, gulping way my mom and aunt Jen smoke. She smiles slightly and doesn't say anything.

I sit down next to Klint, who gives me such a look of gratitude that I completely forget being mad at him for being such a distant jerk to me lately.

Everyone has a drink. Miss Jack tells Shelby to run inside and get sodas for us. Miss Jack and her nephew are drinking whisky. Shelby's mom is slurping at something pink and frozen. Bert has a martini. Klint has a Coke.

Starr's drinking a bottled beer. I think she's only nineteen, but what's the point in telling a girl like that she's not old enough to do something?

Mr. Jack starts talking to Bert about tax shelters and other business-related stuff. His wife chatters about a shopping trip she wants to make with her girls next weekend and how she's thinking of remodeling two of the bathrooms in their house in Florida.

Miss Jack watches her with a pained expression on her face and occasionally glances at a large vase full of yellow roses sitting on a small table next to her.

Starr smokes in silence, stretched out on her chair, watching everyone in a detached yet intent manner like a beautiful, deadly, honey-wheat-colored panther.

Shelby returns with our Cokes. She scoops up Baby and plunks him down in her lap where he curls up in a trembling ball no bigger than a fist. Every once in a while he raises his tiny head and yips at me. I can't help smiling at this. I'd give anything for Mr. B to come by right now, but he'd never come near all these people.

The unmistakable roar and rattle of Tyler's pickup truck suddenly drowns out the voices.

Miss Jack looks momentarily startled, then stands up and walks to her usual greeting place at the top of the steps. She looks very regal tonight in a long skirt and deep purple

velvet jacket over a high-necked lace blouse.

Klint glances at me, smiling.

Tyler's truck is his pride and joy. It's a 1990 sky blue Chevy he bought for $600 and fixed up himself. He did a good job, but the engine's not exactly fine-tuned.

He parks and jumps out seemingly before the truck's even come to a complete stop.

Aside from my dad's funeral and the All-Star banquet last year, I've never seen him as dressed up as he is now. He's wearing polished black shoes, brown corduroys with a belt, and a dark green sweater over a shirt with a collar.

He comes sauntering toward the porch with something in one of his hands. It takes me a second to realize he's carrying flowers: a grocery store bouquet of carnations and mums.

He's always had a buzz cut as long as I've known him. He says he can't be bothered with hair. The combination of the clothes, the haircut, and the flowers make him look like a guy from the 1950s on his way to pick up his date at her parents' house.

He walks right up to Miss Jack and holds the bouquet out to her.

"Miss Jack, this is a true pleasure," he tells her. "I'm Tyler Mann. You may call me Tyler, even though I'm known far and wide to high school baseball fans everywhere simply as The Man. Thank you for inviting me to your

beautiful home."

Miss Jack takes the flowers and says, "Thank you, Tyler."

The smile falls off Klint's face, and his mouth hangs partially open in shock.

"You know Tyler's a wild card," I whisper to him. "You can't ever count on him acting the way you want him to. He only acts the way he wants to."

"It's still early," he whispers back.

"I feel we have a kind of bond, Miss Jack," Tyler continues, "because quite a few members of my family have worked for J&P Coal. My grandfather and his brother were both miners in Lorelei, and I have an uncle who used to work in Marvella and another uncle who currently runs one of your continuous mines in Beverly. My own father would've gone into the mines except for an unfortunate fear of small, dark places that he developed as a child when a couple of his cousins locked him in the trunk of a car overnight."

He stops and laughs at the memory of the story like it's the funniest thing he's ever heard.

"I applaud your family for their long-standing affiliation with J&P Coal," Miss Jack tells him after he's calmed down, "but I have nothing to do with the hands-on running of the company."

She gestures at Shelby's dad.

"My nephew, Cameron Jack, is the CEO."

Tyler bounds across the porch to where Cam Jack is getting up from his chair. He takes his doughy hand and pumps it.

"Mr. Jack, this is an honor, sir."

"Thank you," Mr. Jack replies, looking a little stunned.

Miss Jack introduces him to Bert Shulman next, then to Shelby's mom and sister.

"I must apologize," Tyler says, grinning and glancing from female to female. "If I had known there were going to be so many beautiful ladies here tonight, I would've brought flowers for all of them. Mrs. Jack, it's certainly easy to see where Shelby gets her good looks."

Shelby's mom giggles and gets all flustered. Even Starr and Miss Jack are smiling at him. It takes some nerve to be able to throw around clichés the way Tyler does it, but he gets away with it because he sincerely means what he's saying. It also doesn't hurt that women love praise, any praise, even the empty kind.

"It never occurred to you he might like coming here?" I whisper to Klint.

"No. Did it occur to you?"

"No."

"Tyler, may I offer you a drink?" Miss Jack asks him.

He takes a seat after flashing a smile at Klint and me and crosses one ankle over his knee like a junior executive.

"A Jack Daniels on ice, please."

Shelby busts out laughing.

"For now I'm afraid I can only offer you something nonalcoholic," Miss Jack says, without showing any surprise or amusement at his request, "but you may certainly have wine with dinner."

"Sweet," he says.

He grins at Shelby, then suddenly gets up from his chair, returns to the bottom of the porch steps, and looks back at the house with his hands on his hips.

"Anyone ever jump off this roof?" he asks.

"You mean on purpose?" Miss Jack replies.

"Yeah."

"Not that I know of."

He shakes his head sadly and walks off around the side of the house.

"Where's he going?" I hear Cam Jack ask.

"He has a hard time sitting still," I explain. "But he'll be right back. He never misses dinner."

Miss Jack's formal dining room is a lot like her regular dining room where we usually eat except it's bigger and has a chandelier made entirely of blue glass that looks like a frozen shower of tears hanging over the table. The floor is made of more hand-painted ceramic tiles — these are decorated with brilliantly colored birds — and the walls are covered with the impressionist-style paintings she likes so much. Just like in the other rooms,

it's a collection of images that doesn't seem to go together: small white houses near a teal sea, a crowd of people in a smoky bar, a girl in a pink gown sitting stiffly in a chair, a dark battle scene with piles of corpses and pools of scarlet blood, a hunter and his dog carrying a dead rabbit, a fat man dancing. I notice right away there are no bulls or toreros in this room.

The table is set with so many different plates, glasses, and pieces of silverware, it looks like we're going to eat ten meals.

We all take our seats and instantly two serving women appear, one with a pitcher of water and the other with a bottle of wine she presents to Miss Jack who approves it with a nod.

Luis comes walking out of the kitchen looking very serious and dressed in a white collarless shirt buttoned up to his throat and black trousers. He's holding a corkscrew and practically rips the bottle of wine out of the maid's hand without saying a word to anyone. He opens it and pours a small amount for Miss Jack. She lifts her glass, smells the wine, then tastes it. Luis watches her intently.

She purses her lips and nods slightly while looking away from Luis.

He doesn't smile, but a look of triumph lights up his eyes.

He opens a second bottle and pours wine for everyone, including us kids. He has a mut-

tered word with the two maids hired for tonight, who scurry back into the kitchen. He's about to follow but stops short when Bert Shulman stands up with his wineglass held toward Miss Jack.

"I'd like to propose a toast if I may," he says. "To our lovely hostess and the fabulous dinner she's invited us to share with her. And to Kyle and Klint. Welcome to the elite inner circle of those people privileged to know Candace Jack."

Tyler jumps out of his chair with his own glass extended.

"And me, too. I'm privileged now, too."

"And Tyler, too," Bert adds. "Welcome."

Miss Jack smiles up at Bert.

Luis glares and leaves. The hard soles of his shoes make fast, angry, echoing clacks on the tile floor as he heads back to the kitchen.

He returns with the women a few minutes later, each carrying plates of what looks like black rice. They set them down in front of each of us.

"Chipirones con morcilla de arroz negro," Luis announces formally once we've all been served.

"What the hell is that?" Mr. Jack asks.

"Cuttlefish with black rice sausage," Miss Jack translates.

"What the hell kind of fish is a cuddle fish?"

"Cuttlefish, honey," his wife explains. "It's not really a fish at all. It's related to squids

and octopus."

She empties her glass immediately and smiles prettily at Luis.

"May I have some more wine?" she asks him.

He refills her glass by emptying the second bottle.

I'm momentarily surprised by Mrs. Jack's knowledge, but then I remember Shelby told me once that along with being a beauty pageant junkie her mom was into marine biology and had hopes of working at Sea World before she met Cam Jack and decided to become a rich guy's wife instead.

"The rice is black from its ink," she also informs us.

"Cool," Tyler comments. "Squid ink. Does it have any special powers?" he asks no one in particular.

I look over at Klint to get his reaction to Tyler's excitement over the food, but he's too busy staring, white-faced, at his own plate to notice his buddy's latest betrayal. Even covered in bacon and melted cheddar or slathered in gravy, there's no way Klint would ever try this.

"There's no way I'm eating this," Mr. Jack says.

Klint's eyes flicker in his direction.

"Cam, don't be rude," his wife scolds him.

"What'd you say to me?"

"I'm sorry. It's just . . ."

"You know what rude is? Rude is serving food to people you know is going to make them sick. Rude is talking in a language nobody understands just to make other people feel stupid."

Luis watches Miss Jack. As soon as she tries the rice, he steps up to her and bends down to speak into her ear.

"May I ask what you think of the first course?"

"Bueno."

This response seems to enrage him, and he grabs the already empty first wine bottle and stalks out of the room.

I'm a little scared at first to try the cuttle-fish. I can't get the image of tentacles and the concept of squishiness out of my mind, but I've loved everything else Luis has ever cooked for us so I close my eyes and pop a bite into my mouth.

The taste is smooth, slightly salty, and even though I've never been anywhere near an ocean, I realize I'm tasting the sea.

Klint doesn't try it. He fills up on Luis's ciabatta bread and butter, but I notice Mr. Jack cleans his plate.

While we're waiting for the next course Shelby's mom suddenly announces, "Aunt Candy, Shelby has some exciting news for you."

"Mom, I thought I'd tell her after dinner," Shelby protests. "I didn't want to make a big

deal about it."

"But it *is* a big deal," her mom says delightedly, and then before Shelby can tell us anything, her mom tells us everything.

"Shel's best friend, Whitney, is moving to Paris with her family and they've invited Shel along to help ease the transition. She's going to be there for at least a couple months, maybe more if she likes it. She might even want to go to school there. In the meantime, everything's arranged with her school here so she can do her work online and not fall behind."

She finishes and reaches across the table to give her daughter's hand a squeeze.

"It's so exciting," she gushes.

"That's wonderful, Shelby," Miss Jack says with a pleased smile on her face. "I've always encouraged you to see other countries."

Shelby's sitting beside me. She looks at me guiltily.

"I wanted to tell you earlier but I couldn't," she says under her breath.

"Why not?"

"Because I knew you'd be upset."

"It's not like I would've thrown a fit or begged you not to go. It would be pointless to beg you not to go, right?"

"It's only for a couple months."

I look at the floor expecting to see a gigantic crack rip open beneath me and my chair teetering on the edge ready to topple into a

bottomless pit of loneliness. I can't lose someone else right now, but I can't tell Shelby this. She wouldn't understand. She thinks we're just friends and we are for now, but how am I supposed to change that if she's gone? Plus she's not going just anywhere. A few months in Paris aren't the same thing as a few months in a Pennsylvania coal town. She's going to live life faster and more intensely. It's like the difference between dog years and people years.

Starr watches us from across the table and seems to read my thoughts.

"Even just a couple months in Paris can change you forever. The food. The wine. The men. You can drink. Go to clubs. Make out on the banks of the Seine."

Miss Jack casts an irritated look at Starr.

"Yeah, I've heard it's really romantic over there," Tyler volunteers. "They sell flowers in the streets and everyone speaks French."

"There's also the beauty and excitement of the city," Miss Jack joins in. "And the fashion and culture. Theater and opera and museums and exhibitions."

Her eyes shine as she makes her list. If she loves it so much, I don't understand why she doesn't go to Paris or to one of her beloved Spanish cities, but Shelby says she never travels.

The rich, beefy smell from the next course greets us before the maids even come back

through the doorway with the next set of plates.

"Rabo de toro guisado con ruibarbo, mostaza, y miel," Luis announces again to oohs and aahs from Bert and Mrs. Jack.

"Bull tail in a stew with rhubarb, mustard, and honey," Miss Jack translates again.

"Bull tail?" Tyler exclaims. "No way. It's really his tail?"

"Along with the cheek, the tail is the most tender, most flavorful part of the bull," Miss Jack tells him.

She takes a bite. I do, too. It's way past delicious.

"Riquísimo, Luis," she says.

He remains expressionless and turns and leaves, but his footsteps going back to the kitchen are silent this time.

Everyone eats, even Klint.

There's not a lot of conversation after Shelby's announcement. Most of it is initiated by Mrs. Jack, and most of it is ended by Mr. Jack making fun of her or saying something mean to her.

It's uncomfortable to witness. I want to stick up for her, but I realize it's their family dynamic, and I should stay out of it. We had a similar routine, only with us, Mom was the mean one and Dad was the one who always tried to calm her down and appease her.

Shelby's mom reminds me a lot of my dad as I watch her deal with Cam Jack. She tries

to make a joke out of his abuse and she drinks to make herself feel better, but the same confused, wounded look comes into her eyes every now and then that I used to see in my dad's eyes. They don't understand where the hate comes from.

I don't pay much attention to anything. I can't stop envisioning Shelby sitting at some beautiful café in Paris drinking wine with a good-looking French guy who will take her to an art museum afterward and will know all the right things to say about every painting. He doesn't even exist yet, but I'd give anything to be him.

Starr finishes each course quickly, then contents herself with sipping wine while staring at Klint.

I figure she must have the hots for him like most girls do. The idea makes me feel disappointed in her. Klint's much too tame for someone like her.

"So I hear you're a big baseball star," she says to him.

"I'm not bad," he tells her.

Tyler kicks me under the table. Klint's false modesty always kills him.

"Good enough to play in the pros?"

"Maybe."

"Pro baseball teams draft kids right out of high school, don't they?"

"Klint wants to go to college," I answer for him.

Starr smiles at me for the first time. It's not much of a smile, nothing like a hundred-watt Shelby smile, but somehow it means more because I sense it's much harder to get a smile out of her.

"Really?" she says and turns her attention back to Klint. "What schools are looking at you?"

Klint rattles off a few. All of them are hundreds, some even thousands, of miles away. The nearest one is West Virginia and it's still a good six-hour drive from here.

"Western Penn had a good season," I throw in.

"Western Penn?" Klint scoffs at me. "Who cares about Western Penn?"

"Hey, Ben Varner plays for them," Tyler points out.

"Ben Varner? Hum Vee? Give me a break."

"Yeah, Hum Vee," Tyler cries out, defensively. "How quickly we forget. Fourth game of districts last year. An oh-and-two pitch in the bottom of the eighth, two men on, losing by two." His breathless narrative brings him to his feet. "Pitch looked like a curveball that didn't curve. Inside and low but it didn't really break. We thought it was all over and wham!"

He brings his hands together and swings at an imaginary ball.

"A drive to left field. It's hooking. Ah no. Ah yes. Could it be? It's outta here, folks."

He does a little victory dance, then takes his seat again and goes back to eating.

Klint shrugs.

"One great hit his entire high school career. Big deal."

"He was a worker bee, man," Tyler explains. "A steady, dependable guy doing his job without anyone noticing him, and that's what he did. He didn't need big hits. Not everyone can be a flashy diva like you, Sparkles."

He turns to me.

"He's doing great at Western Penn. His stats are way up. He loves the coach."

"You know I used to play ball in high school," Mr. Jack joins our conversation as our plates are being collected and taken away.

Klint, Tyler, and I all look at him. It's the first time he's said anything to one of us since Tyler shook his hand.

"It was football. Not baseball. I was damn good. My sophomore year I was already starting varsity. I wanted to go on and play in college. My dad never came to a single game. He didn't like sports. He was a sportsman, mind you — he loved to hunt and fish and he could beat the crap out of you if he wanted to — but he never cared for team sports.

"Not long after my sixteenth birthday, at the end of my sophomore season he came to me and gave me the keys to a Thunderbird convertible, the slickest car I've ever seen to this day. Cost almost seven grand. That was a

small fortune back then. He said to me, 'You can stay a boy and distract yourself with games or you can be a man and concentrate on making money.' I knew what he meant. I took the keys and I stopped playing ball. He didn't make me. It was my own decision."

"Perdiz roja en dos vinos," Luis suddenly announces the next course.

"Red partridge in two services, one with red wine sauce, the other with white wine sauce," Miss Jack supplies.

Mrs. Jack sways a little and puts an elbow on the table where she rests her chin on one hand. She and her breasts lean toward her husband.

"That's sad, honey," she says to him.

He frowns at her angrily.

"Why is it sad?"

"Because there are other ways to be a man besides making money."

"Name one."

She looks around her at the maids setting down plates of glistening, juicy birds.

"Making partridges."

"You're drunk," he sneers at her in disgust.

"I'm not drunk."

"You're always drunk."

"Why is that, Cameron?" Miss Jack asks him.

"Mr. Jack, I heard an interesting theory the other day." I interrupt the same way I used to break in on my mom and dad's fights to try

and distract them. "Capitalism is based on the concept that in order for someone to succeed, someone else has to suffer."

The room becomes completely silent. Everyone stares at me with different degrees of surprise, pity, and hostility showing on their faces. Even the maids pause in their duties and glance at me out of the corners of their eyes like I might be crazy.

"So is marriage, honey," Mrs. Jack says, reaching across the table to pat my hand.

I try my best not to look at her boobs, but I can't help myself. They're simply too noticeable and too fascinating. It's like trying not to look at a river while you're driving over the bridge.

When I raise my gaze to meet her eyes, she bursts into tears.

I guess my comment was bad timing, but I didn't mean any harm. I'd waited all night to bounce Doc's idea off Cam Jack. I thought it would be an interesting topic to discuss with a captain of industry.

CHAPTER THIRTEEN

"Don't sweat it. I had a great time," Tyler tells me as he strips a leaf off one of Miss Jack's rhododendrons and starts picking at his teeth with the pointed tip. "I love watching other people's families fall apart. 'Sides, did you see that sister?"

"I think Shelby's prettier."

"Hey, who cares? I know what I'm dreaming about tonight."

He puts his hands together palm against palm and even in the darkness, I can see his Cheshire Cat grin.

"Sister sandwich."

He bends down and scoops up a handful of gravel and starts picking through it looking for a rock worth throwing.

"So what's up with your brother?" he asks me.

Klint ignored him all night, and when all hell broke loose at the dinner table after Mrs. Jack started crying and Mr. Jack went stomping off, Klint got up and left, too.

"I think you kind of pissed him off," I reply. "I think he only invited you 'cause he thought you'd get under Miss Jack's skin and he could have a good laugh. I know he thought there was no way you'd eat the food."

He takes a stone about the size of a marble and whips it sidearm out into the night. It seems to take forever before we hear the click of it hitting the barn.

"You kidding me? I got to eat squid ink. Killer whales eat squid. I swear I feel pumped."

He pauses to do some shadowboxing.

"I'm not making this up. I might start eating it all the time. You think this Luis guy could tell me where to get it?"

"He special orders a lot of stuff that gets delivered to the house, and I think it probably costs a lot of money."

"Figures. You wanna drink squid ink or take a trip on the space shuttle, you gotta be rich. Doesn't seem right, does it? Seems like those should be activities available to the common man."

We walk on toward his truck.

The sky above us is a solid mass of sooty nighttime clouds. The moon and stars don't have a chance of shining through.

"But seriously. What's up with Klint? I'm not just talking about tonight," Tyler starts up again. "I'm talking in general. Something's wrong with him."

"What do you mean?" I ask, uneasily, remembering the image I had of him being crushed and suffocated by his own life.

"He's different. That's all. It's like he doesn't care about anything. I mean, I know how hard it was when your dad died and I know you don't get over something like that right away. Maybe you don't ever get over it. But you have to keep on living. You know what I mean?"

He looks at me for a moment like he expects me to confirm his theory. I nod and he goes on.

"The way I figure it is when something bad like that happens to you, you get over it by going through the motions even though you don't feel anything inside, and eventually after you've gone through the motions long enough, they start to have meaning again."

That's what I did when my mom left. Now I'm doing it again. All this going through the motions leaves me feeling seasick sometimes. I always thought grief was solely an emotion. I never knew it could mess with your gut and your equilibrium.

"You owe it to the person who died. I mean, think about it. Imagine how upset your dad would be if he knew Klint stopped playing ball because he got killed."

"No, it's not possible," I say forcefully, shaking my head. "Klint would never stop playing ball. It's his whole life. It's his dream.

He hasn't said anything to me about quitting. He talks about the upcoming season like everything's okay."

We arrive at Tyler's truck. He looks worried. It's an expression that doesn't sit well on his open, good-humored face.

"He hasn't said anything about quitting to me, either. It's just . . . I don't know. For one thing, I think it's kind of creepy that he still goes over to Bill's and sits and stares at your old house. I've met him over there a couple times. What's that about?"

"He's going to be okay," I assure him, trying to keep any doubt out of my voice.

He claps my shoulder and gives me a smile before hopping into his truck.

"Hey, let's hope so. For my sake," he says out his open window over the cough and roar of his engine struggling to life. "Once he's in the pros, I fully intend to be the screw-up friend who borrows money from him and hangs out at his parties and bangs all the girls he doesn't have time for. I don't want to see all my hopes for the future go down in flames."

"I thought you wanted to be a bear when you grew up."

"Man, if only I could," he tells me, wistfully. "If only I could."

I watch him drive away, thinking about how much I'd like to be going with him. Mr. Jack's car is gone. Much to Miss Jack's horror, he

left without his wife.

Miss Jack did everything in her power to convince her hysterical, drunken niece-in-law that she should let Shelby or Bert drive her home. Mrs. Jack refused, saying she planned on never going home again; Miss Jack pursed her lips so tight they turned the same purple color as her skirt.

Starr didn't seem fazed at all by the scene, but Shelby was obviously upset. When her mom went stumbling off to find Baby who'd been left outside on the porch in his fur-lined, crystal-accented carrier since Miss Jack refused to let him in the house, Shelby went after her. Then Miss Jack excused herself and followed. Then Bert followed her. Then Klint got up without saying a word. I looked up at him standing next to me and for the first time since we came to live with Miss Jack, I noticed the dark circles under his eyes and a slight tremble to his lips. I opened my mouth to say something but before I could figure out what it should be, he walked away.

Tyler and I ate our partridges alone while Starr went into another room and came back with a square-cut glass bottle filled with amber liquor. She poured some in her wine-glass and sipped at it until Shelby came back with tears streaking her cheeks and told us Baby was missing.

Starr reluctantly stood up with her drink and said she'd help look.

Tyler and I volunteered to go look for Baby, too, but Shelby insisted that we stay and eat and we didn't need much convincing.

When Luis reappeared to check on everything and only found me and Tyler devouring his partridges, I thought he'd lose it, but he behaved as if he'd been cooking just for the two of us all along and didn't even glance at the six other plates of untouched birds.

He even personally brought us dessert: almond cake with pear ice cream drizzled in caramel. Tyler and I both agreed no amount of family fireworks would have ever kept us from finishing such a great meal and we told him so.

He made a formal little bow and said, "Me alegro."

The night certainly didn't turn out the way I wanted it to. Luis and I have that in common. I had entertained visions of impressing Shelby's parents and Shelby finally beginning to look at me as potential boyfriend material.

Instead, her dad hated me, and I turned out to be responsible for the comment that started her mom blubbering and sent the whole dinner to hell.

I don't even know where anybody is right now. I'm almost tempted to walk down to Jerry's place. He has a little house that's not much bigger than a shed about a mile down a path through the trees behind Miss Jack's mansion.

I came upon it the other day when I was out walking around on my own. I never asked him about it, but I knew it must be his because his favorite flannel shirt was draped over a rocking chair sitting on the front porch, and his rifle was leaning against a wall next to the front door.

I assumed he was inside if he left his gun sitting there that way, but I didn't bother him for the same reason I know I won't bother him now. Jerry's the kind of guy who wants to be left alone. I wish I could be like that.

"Baby! Here, Baby!"

Shelby's voice rings out, startling me with its nearness.

I turn toward the sound and see the white sweep of a flashlight and the red wink of a cigarette coming up the driveway.

I'm about to head toward the two female shadows when I clearly hear Starr say, "Like I said, screwing a professor is fun because it's a power trip but unless you're into the whole daddy thing, the sex is never good. They're old men. They smell like old men. Plus if they're screwing you, it means they're usually screwing other students or they're planning on it."

Hearing this, I instantly decide there might be more advantages to overhearing the sisters' private conversation than trying to be part of it. I quickly duck down behind Bert's Mercedes and peer out from under his bumper at

the girls as they come to a stop in front of the house.

I've always thought of Shelby as pretty innocent, so I'm expecting her to be shocked by her sister's comments but she seems to ignore them.

"What's Dad going to do with you?" she asks.

"Nothing. Like he always does. Throw some money at me. Tell me to go away."

"What are you going to do?"

"I don't know, but I'm definitely dropping out of college for good."

"You only went for a year."

"What's the point? It's not like I'm ever going to need to get a job."

Starr takes a drag off her cigarette, tilts up her head, and blows a soft stream of smoke into the air.

"But don't you want to do something with your life?" Shelby continues prodding her. "Won't you get bored?"

"Partying with Dad's money is going to get boring but sitting in an office somewhere isn't? It's all boring."

"Sky did it and she's not half as smart as you."

"You don't have to be smart to go to college," Starr laughs. "Where'd you get that idea? Sky went to college because she saw it as one more big social event. She joined her little sorority and took the easiest classes she

could find and accomplished her goal, which was to snag a rich husband. She'll graduate this summer with a degree in wasting time and spend the next two years planning her wedding with Mom."

The two of them take a seat at the bottom of the front porch staircase. The outdoor lights shine behind them, causing everything about them to be shadowed in black except for their hair, which throws off glints of copper and gold each time one of them moves her head.

Tyler may see them as slices of human bread to be slapped on either side of him. I see them as treasure to be discovered then spent.

"Not everyone's cut out for college. That's all," Starr continues. "You'll love it, though. It's right up your alley."

"What's that supposed to mean? You make it sound like an insult."

"It's not an insult. Maybe you can follow your sweetie. Go to the University of Fast Balls."

My heart starts beating quicker. I know they have to be talking about Klint, and Starr called him Shelby's sweetie.

"You never told me what you think of him," Shelby says.

"He's good-looking but that's it."

"You don't understand him."

"What's to understand? He's dumb as a brick."

"You're one to talk."

"Hey, I'm the first to admit I've been with some real dim bulbs, but I knew what I was doing. It's fine to screw a guy just for fun and know the whole time you're doing it that he's a moron and completely self-centered but you don't care because he's got a bod to die for and he's a great lay, but not every girl can handle that. You're not like that, Shel, and I don't want you to be. You're going to have to fall in love before you do the deed. Your problem right now is you're physically attracted to this Klint kid, but instead of accepting that he's a self-absorbed, dumb jock, you try to make him into a deep, misunderstood guy so you can convince yourself you're in love with him when you're not. You just think he's hot."

They fall silent for a moment, and I use the time to crawl completely under Bert's car. I'm as close as I can get without them seeing me.

"What about his brother?" Starr asks.

"Kyle? He's sweet."

"And cute."

"And cute, I guess. But he's a kid."

"I thought he was your age."

"He'll be fifteen next month."

"So what? You just turned sixteen. That's one year."

"Klint's a man."

"He's not a man. Trust me."

Starr stands up and tosses her cigarette into the grass.

"None of this matters anyway, Shel. Some hot Frenchman's going to whisk you off your feet."

Shelby laughs.

"Even if you don't hook up with anyone seriously, after a couple months in France, the guys here are going to seem so immature and pointless to you. You'll be dying to get back to Europe. Come on. Let's go back inside."

"But what about Baby? What if he's really lost? What if he makes it down to the road and gets hit by a car or something eats him in the woods?"

"Mom will mourn him for a day, then replace him with a Pekingese. Come on."

Starr reaches out a hand for her sister and helps her to her feet.

"I'm going to get Bert to take me back into town. I've had enough quality family time for one night. You have to stay with Mom and convince her to let you take her home. We can't leave her here. We can't do that to Aunt Candace."

I stay under the car even after they've gone inside and the door has closed behind them. My head is whirling from everything I just heard.

I try and separate the good from the bad.

Shelby and Starr both think I'm cute. This is good. Very good. Shelby doesn't think I'm a man. This is bad. Starr doesn't think Klint is a man. I don't like to hear my brother insulted, but this could work in my favor. Shelby likes Klint a lot more than I thought, enough that she's been discussing him with her sister. This is bad. Shelby thinks I'm sweet. This could be good or bad now that her sister's informed her that it's fine to have sex with jerks as long as you know they're jerks.

I don't know how long I've been lying here with my face smashed against the driveway staring at the world from an ant's-eye view when someone kicks my foot.

"Hey!"

I jerk up my head and smack it on the underside of Bert's car.

"Ow!" I cry.

A hand grabs me by the ankle and starts pulling me out. I'm relieved to see it's Klint, then I'm pissed to see it's Klint.

I sit up, brushing dirt off the front of my clothes, and start picking gravel out of my cheek.

He's no longer wearing his nice clothes. He's changed into old ripped jeans and a gray Flames hoodie sweatshirt. Peeking out of the front pocket pouch is Baby.

"You found him!"

"I took him," he says.
"What do you mean?"
"I mean, I took him. When everybody went running off and I realized the whole night was ruined for you, I got the idea to take the dog. I knew Shelby and her mom would freak out. Then later I figured I'd give him to you and you could be the big hero who found him and make major points with them."
I don't know what to say. I don't know if I'm more stunned by the thoughtfulness behind the act or by the brilliance of the plan.
"Thanks."
"I know you like her."
He sits down next to me and we both lean against the car. Baby's head disappears inside the sweatshirt at the sight of me.
"Yeah, well. A lot of good it does me," I tell him while gingerly fingering the bump on my head. "She likes you."
"Not really. She just thinks she does."
"I guess none of it matters now that she's going to Paris."
"She'll be back."
He reaches in his pocket and takes out the tiny dog. He holds him against his chest with one hand and strokes the top of his head with one finger. Baby closes his eyes.
"Tonight didn't turn out good for any of us," I say.
"Except for Tyler."
I smile.

"Yeah. I think he's hooked on cuttlefish."

Klint's expression sours.

"Probably has something to do with him wanting to be a bear," I quickly add, trying to keep him from falling back into a bad mood. "Bears love fish, you know."

He doesn't say anything.

"Remember when you guys were kids? You used to always dress up for Halloween as a baseball player and he used to wear that old bear costume that was way too big for him," I laugh. "All these years later you guys still have the same dreams."

"Being a baseball player's not my dream; it's what I'm good at."

I laugh again.

"Right. Then what is your dream?"

"I don't have a dream."

"You have to have a dream."

"Says who?"

I rack my brain trying to come up with some famous person who said we should all have dreams. All I come up with is Martin Luther King Jr., but he said he had a dream not that everybody else should have one.

"You know what Coach Hill says," Klint reminds me, "winners win; losers dream."

"Then to be a professional ballplayer is your goal."

"I don't have any goals," he says roughly. "Being a ballplayer is what I am. Period. It's

what I do instead of being a drunk or a janitor."

He gets to his feet, cupping Baby in his right hand like he might use him to throw someone out at third.

"People make a fuss over me because I'm a good ballplayer, but that doesn't make me better than anyone else. I'm not a knight in shining armor. And I'm sure as hell not some character in one of those fruity novels you love to read about a boy with a dream.

"I could've gone down any road. Any road. But I got lucky. Dad put a bat in my hand when I was a little kid and encouraged me and when I was able to do what he wanted me to do with that bat, I could tell I made him happy. And I wanted to make him happy. Then somewhere along the way I realized that playing ball made me happy because it was something I was good at. Then somewhere further along the way when it wasn't making me happy anymore, I realized it didn't matter because playing ball is all I know."

It's the most Klint has said to me at one time since Dad died. Probably even since Mom left.

I want to keep him talking, but I choose probably the worst question to ask him.

"What do you mean it doesn't make you happy anymore?"

He sighs in frustration, turns his back to

me, and starts to walk away.

I scramble up from the ground and go after him.

"You haven't played a game since Dad died. Just wait until this spring," I assure him. "Everything's gonna be okay."

"It doesn't matter. Nothing matters."

"That's not true."

He comes to a sudden stop and whirls around on me.

"What about you? Do you have a dream?"

"I have goals."

"Goals. Dreams. Whatever you want to call them. It's all bullshit. Everything's random. Don't you see? We got no control over anything.

"He could've put a cigarette in my hand, or a can of beer, or a remote control and everything would have been different. But it was a baseball bat."

He stares at me without seeing me, yet he still manages to know my fears and he tries to make me feel better.

"Don't worry about me," he says. "I'll play ball. I'll always play ball. I don't have a choice. Same way that damn cat of yours has to kill everything that runs across its path."

He hands me Baby.

"Here. Take him."

I reach for the shivering little beast. I almost feel reluctance in Klint's grip to let him go.

"Where are you going?"

"Bed. I'm tired. I'm tired all the time."

He walks off, his shoulders slumped, his feet dragging.

I think of Cam Jack and his dad putting a set of keys to a tricked-out T-bird in his hand. I think of El Soltero standing in a sunbaked corral with his mother's apron in his hand pretending it was a torero's cape and how no one put it there; he picked it up himself.

I don't know if I should envy or pity my brother.

The only thing Dad ever put in my hand was his own.

Chapter Fourteen: Candace Jack

I left Rae Ann in a guest room upstairs sobbing anew after her daughters returned from searching for Baby and informed her they had no luck. She insists she won't leave without her dog. I insist she will. Between Bert and Shelby, someone is driving her home.

I don't know how long I've been standing here behind my house. I didn't even bother to grab my coat before I came outside, I was in such a hurry to leave. I can't tolerate cold the way I used to, but I find I crave it more. I want to feel the chill on my face and hands. It makes me feel alive. Warmth and comfort seem too much like death.

A movement in the grass catches my eye. Kyle's cat comes padding across the yard with a good-sized, limp body dangling from his mouth.

I sigh when he gets close enough for me to see the creature's identity. It's a small rabbit. I'd been hoping it was that damned

Chihuahua.

He drops it in front of me, purring loudly.

I reach down to pet him. He immediately grabs up the rabbit, thinking I want to take it from him. I scratch him behind the ears, and he narrows his golden eyes above the furry carcass. I don't really want to see what he's going to do with it next and besides, I can't put it off any longer: I have to talk to Luis.

I find him in the kitchen with a glass of red wine in his hand and Joaquín Sabina singing in the background. He's staring intently at a saucer of anchovies marinating in vinegar. The help has been sent home. Two dishwashers are quietly humming. Everything is spic and span except for the plates of leftovers still sitting on the counters.

He glances at me, then turns his back on me. He takes a sip of his wine, sets the glass down, and crosses his arms over his chest in a huff.

I don't have to say anything. I know his silent treatment rarely lasts more than thirty seconds.

"Look at this," he says suddenly, whipping around and nodding at the plates of uneaten partridge. "What would Manuel say?"

"Manuel's not here."

"Manuel is everywhere. That's the problem. And he's definitely anywhere a partridge is going to waste."

"You know you won't waste these. You'll do

something fantastic with them. What about empanadas?"

"Easy for you to say. Are you the one who's going to pull the meat from their tiny bones?"

"You love it."

"Don't tell me what I love. You don't know."

He turns his back on me again.

I take down a wineglass from one of the racks and pour myself some of the wine he's drinking.

I see him watch me from the corner of his eye. It's killing him that he's not pouring it for me. Luis is a consummate gentleman.

"I'm sorry about dinner, Luis. It was beyond my control."

"You knew exactly what was going to happen."

"How can you say that?"

He takes a step toward me, and the hands begin to fly.

"What a combination," he exclaims, gesturing first at the door leading to the dining room, then at the heavens, then in the direction of Sabina's gravelly voice singing about forgiving a woman he wronged for making him wrong her. "No one in their right mind would bring together such a group.

"I know why you did it," he adds. "You were showing off. You wanted Cameron to see you with the boys. You wanted to rub his face in it."

"And what about him? The only reason he

came here tonight was because he was curious and wanted to see the boys. And then his only intention was to be rude and put them in their place. Beside all that, since when have you become so concerned about Cameron?"

"Since you ruined my dinner."

"*I* ruined your dinner?"

"Bueno, bueno," he mimicks me. "You know this was one of the best meals you've ever had in your life and all you can say is, bueno."

"I said, riquísimo."

"Bah. Riquísimo. You should have said, fabuloso. And you know I was right about the wine."

I don't say anything. He was right about the wine. This one isn't bad, either. I take another sip and desirously eye the partridges. I didn't get to eat much tonight.

"Haven't you heard?" he asks me. "No, of course not because you were hiding."

"I wasn't hiding. I've been dealing with Rae Ann for the past hour. I stepped outside to get some fresh air."

"Kyle found the dog. Aha!" He claps and smiles triumphantly. "I see your face. You were hoping he was dead. You are a mean, old lady."

"You hate that dog as much as I do."

"Don't tell me what I hate."

"Never mind."

I wave a hand at him and reach for a plate,

but he yanks it away from me.

"This is pointless," I continue, my voice rising with anger. "I tried to apologize. I tried to take the high road. You are being unreasonable. You are being Spanish."

He pulls back like he's been slapped.

"You are being a redneck."

I laugh.

He points a tyrannical finger out the door I came in.

"You take your high road, Pennsylvania coal miner redneck. You take it right out of my kitchen."

I laugh again, then pick up the bottle of wine and my glass and oblige him.

I walk through my house with the intention of going upstairs to my room when I notice the front door is wide open and there's a commotion going on outside it.

I don't want anyone to see me if I can avoid it. I creep as close as possible and flatten myself against a wall.

It appears that everyone I've been unable to rid myself of is standing on my porch. Shelby, Starr, and their mother are casting adoring glances at Kyle while cooing over bug-eyed Baby who's wrapped in a little pink blanket and has all but disappeared inside Rae Ann's cleavage where she's pressing him tightly.

Bert stands nearby, impeccably and elegantly groomed, holding the dog's gaudy

neon pink, fur-lined, jewel-encrusted carrier coolly at his side, looking like some homophobic screenwriter's idea of a gay doctor who makes house calls.

"But we have to say good night to Aunt Candy," Rae Ann whines between hiccupping giggles and a few last remaining sobs at the thought of losing her precious rat dog.

Her makeup is a mess. Someone really needs to explain waterproof mascara to this woman. It should be handed out to her with her first drink instead of a bowl of peanuts.

"Oh, no, no," Bert tells her, putting a hand on her shoulder and shaking his head with concern. "I'm sure Candace has gone to bed. It's been a very long night for her."

Bless you, Bert.

"Bert's right, Mom," Shelby adds. "We should just concentrate on getting you and Baby home."

"I don't want to see your father," Rae Ann sniffs indignantly, trying to bring some self-respect back into her tearstained, alcohol-puffed face.

"You won't have to," Starr tells her. "He'll be passed out in front of the TV in his den."

"I guess that's true." Rae Ann brightens up. "I hope he remembered to take his shoes off."

They depart. All except for Kyle, who stands at the top of the steps and waves like he's the man of the house.

I can't help smiling at this. I know he's very

fond of Shelby, but apparently his feelings aren't strong enough to make him follow the weepy, stumbling Rae Ann and her cloying entourage any farther. The object of his affections will have to see herself into her own car.

I wait until the taillights have winked out of sight, swallowed up by the midnight black cavern of trees lining my driveway, then I set the wine bottle on a table in the foyer and step outside.

"Hello, Kyle," I say.

He looks over his shoulder at me, surprised.

"Oh, hi, Miss Jack. I thought you went to bed."

"No. I was hiding, for lack of a better word. And eavesdropping."

"My dad always said you can't eavesdrop in your own house. You have a right to hear anything anybody says if it's said under your roof."

"I think your father was absolutely right."

I step up beside him and we both stare out at the night.

"I owe you a debt of gratitude," I tell him.

"What for?"

"You found the dog."

"Yeah." He offers me a flicker of a smile. "I guess Mrs. Jack was pretty upset."

"You don't know the half of it."

"I was glad to help."

"But I'm sure you would have liked for

Shelby to spend the night."

"I don't know. I guess it would be nice to see her more but, you know . . ."

"What about girls at your own school?"

"What about them?"

"Are you," I pause to carefully pick my words, "friends with any of them?"

"I don't know. Some of them are okay, I guess."

Another thing I've learned about teenaged boys: whenever asked a question, they either "don't know" or assume "you know."

If I were to rule a country, all my spies would be teenage boys. No enemy would ever be able to get any information out of them: Would you like a drink? I don't know. Have you seen any good movies lately? I don't know. What would you like for your birthday? I don't know. Where are the plans to the new military installation? You know.

"I must apologize for my family's behavior tonight."

"They didn't bother me. They seemed pretty much like any other family."

"Aside from Luis's wonderful meal, which I didn't get to enjoy, I think your brother's friend proved to be the highlight of the whole evening."

"Tyler?"

"Yes. The Man."

His smile returns and settles happily onto his face. He has an engaging smile. It takes

some of the emotional weariness out of his eyes and makes him look his age.

"Yeah. Tyler's an interesting guy."

"He's living proof that consideration for others and being open to new experiences has little to do with socioeconomic class. Tyler, though a bit crude and overly boisterous, has very nice manners and proved to be an amusing conversationalist. I wish I could say either of those things about your brother."

"Klint's still adjusting."

"I think you make too many excuses for him. I think he's always been this way."

"Maybe. But that doesn't make him a bad person. There are worse things to be than a guy who's awkward at dinner parties."

I smile at this.

"I suppose you're right."

I motion for Kyle to follow me inside.

I pause to lock the door, fully expecting him to say good night and head up to his room, but he lingers beside me. I get the feeling he has something more to say to me.

"You need to see Klint play ball," he finally informs me. "Then you can forgive him just about anything."

"And why would that be?"

"Because he has a gift. You know how people don't care if a great writer is a drunk or a great musician is a drug addict? They make excuses for them because they're good at other things nobody else can do."

"I don't agree with that way of thinking."

"What about El Soltero? Was he a great guy or was he kind of a jerk sometimes? And if he was a jerk, did people forgive him because he was a great torero?"

I'm taken aback by his question. Not only because it's a gross invasion of my privacy but also because it's very insightful. Manuel was a handful, to say the least. He could definitely be a bit of a jerk, as it were, and people always forgave him. Even the insanely furious fathers of daughters with ruined reputations would eventually return to his flock of admirers.

Ironically it was this crazed aspect of his — a self-destructive, almost desperate, burning inside him that made him stand in front of charging bulls — that attracted me most to him.

He was so different from Stan, who did everything in a calculated manner and never seemed to be guided by emotion of any kind. Both men refused to obey rules, but Manuel at least acknowledged their existence and sometimes made a pretense of feeling sorry for breaking one. Stan believed there were no rules.

Kyle must see the shock and disapproval in my face because he quickly apologizes.

"I'm sorry. I know it's none of my business. Luis told me you were in love with him and how you saw him get killed.

"He didn't volunteer it or anything like that," he quickly goes on. "We were in the barn and I saw the pictures of your bulls and I started asking him questions. You know. He didn't want to tell me. I could tell."

"It's all right," I assure him.

"I'm sorry that had to happen to you."

Again, I'm startled by this boy's words and forwardness, but this time I'm not upset by either. I'm touched by the genuine compassion in his voice. Also, I've just noticed he's covered with gravel dust and has a leaf in his hair.

"My aunt Jen had a similar experience and I think it really messed her up. When she was in high school, her boyfriend accidentally shot himself."

"Accidentally?"

"Yeah. In the head. I don't think she ever got over it. I mean, you know, she went out with lots of other guys after that but she never got married. Well, she got married once but they split up so quickly, my mom said it didn't count."

I can't tell if Kyle's waiting for me to comment on Aunt Jen's travails or not. He plunges his hands into his pants pockets and his eyes roam agitatedly around the entrance hall and up and down the winding staircase.

"What I don't understand is why you wanted to keep the bull," he asks with so much force, I get the feeling this question

has been eating at him for some time. "Wouldn't you hate the bull? I mean, the bull *killed* your boyfriend."

I clear my throat. I don't really want to have this conversation. I've gone out of my way my entire life to avoid having it.

"Let me ask you something, Kyle. Do you blame the truck your father drove or the alcohol he drank for his death? Or do you accept them as part of the risks he took with his life every day?"

I didn't mean for the question to be painful for the boy but obviously it is. His face falls.

"You knew he was drunk," he mutters.

"I'm sorry. I thought it was common knowledge."

"Yeah, I guess it is."

"What I'm trying to say is Calladito, your father's truck: they were the means of their deaths but not the reasons behind them. You see, Manuel and Calladito weren't enemies. Or even competitors. They were two equal parts of a beautiful whole."

He meets my eyes.

"Bullfighting, you mean. Luis tried to explain it to me. How it's an art and not a sport."

He becomes quiet for a moment.

"I think I get it. So you had to convince yourself it was okay. The way he died. Why he died. You had to make yourself defend the bull. It's like a kid I know whose brother got

killed in Iraq last year. His parents have to keep supporting the war 'cause if they admit the war is wrong, then they're saying their kid died for nothing."

I reach out and pull the leaf from his hair. I hold it out to him. He takes it and looks embarrassed.

"It's something like that, but not exactly. Come sit with me for a moment, and I'll try to explain."

I lead him into the front parlor. On our way there, I glimpse the bottle of wine and my glass still sitting on a table near the front door, and I bring it with me.

He takes a seat on a burnt orange velvet settee and stares at the mantel at the large, helmet-shaped clock crowned by a pawing diamond-eyed bull with a golden torero beside him who swings his capote left and right whenever the hour strikes.

I pour myself some wine and take my own seat in a crimson rattan wingback chair with gold chenille cushions that Shelby calls my Fantasy Island throne.

"A corrida usually consists of three different bullfighters fighting two bulls each," I begin to explain. "The day Manuel died he was performing in a special one-man corrida held in his hometown on the eve of his thirtieth birthday.

"Under normal circumstances, if one torero is badly injured or killed by a bull, one of

the other toreros takes over and continues fighting the bull. But this time there wasn't another torero. Calladito would have been taken out back behind the ring and put to death in obscurity by a nobody with a butcher's knife. He would have died in shame. Calladito had been an excellent bull. A toro bravo. Manuel would have wanted him to die with honor."

Kyle mulls this over.

"I don't get it. How can a bull die in shame or die with honor? He's just an animal."

"It's true that honor is one of the qualities that separates man from the lower animals," I concede to him. "Everything a dumb animal does is guided by instinct. He must eat. He must sleep. He must procreate. Honor is not about what you want to do or what you need to do; it's about doing what you should do. And only people are capable of this. And very few, at that.

"Spaniards don't view the toro as one of the lower animals. He's regarded in some ways as equal to man. Therefore, he can have honor."

I think I've explained myself perfectly, but the boy still looks unconvinced.

"It may sound improbable," I begin again. "I used to think so myself until I became acquainted with bullfighting, but once you know what you're looking for, you can recognize the bad bulls instantly. Bulls who are

distracted. Who are afraid. Who are crazy. Who are mean. The Spanish have an expression for it: *Este toro no tiene casta.* 'This bull has no race.' In English you'd say, this bull has no class.

"When a bull is absolutely terrible in the ring, he gets sent back to the farm. It's the ultimate shame for the bull and the breeder."

Kyle shakes his head, but he's smiling.

"So the reward for a being a great bull — a toro bravo — is death, and the punishment for being a crappy bull is getting to live?"

"That's one way of looking at it. But again, it's not about rewards and punishments. It's not a game. For Spaniards, the bullfight is an encapsulation of life, and like life, the end is death. An American, on the other hand, regarding the bullfight as a competition would see the end when the bull is about to die as the torero's triumph: I am the victor; I get to kill you. A Spaniard sees it as: Destiny is the victor; it's time for you to die."

I sit back in my chair and close my eyes.

"What about the really crappy bull who gets to go back to the farm?" Kyle asks. "Why isn't it time for him to die?"

Luis steps into the room bearing a tray.

"Because destiny doesn't care about him," he announces gravely. "Destiny doesn't care about the weak and the foolish."

"Have some milk and cookies," he says kindly to Kyle and sets down a plate of his

homemade almond cookies sprinkled with crystals of pink pastry sugar.

He hands him the glass of milk.

"Drink it. It's good for your bones."

He glances darkly in my direction.

"You should drink it, too, but your bones are beyond help."

"I have perfectly fine bones."

He snorts.

"I asked Luis to come back to America with me to assist me," I say. "He knew I wouldn't have any idea how to take care of a bull."

I reach for a cookie. Luis doesn't stop me which means they're meant as a peace offering. Kyle gulps at his milk and stops short at wiping his mouth with his sleeve. He uses one of the napkins from the tray, then pops a third cookie into his mouth.

"That was pretty nice of you," he says to Luis between crunches.

"Yes, it was. It was very nice of me."

"You were paid," I remind him.

"I shouldn't be paid?" Luis cries. "I should give away my skills and knowledge for nothing?"

"I didn't say that."

"It sounds like bullfighting is great," Kyle interrupts us, getting to his feet, "but it also sounds kind of terrible."

"Yes," Luis agrees ardently. "It's this combination of the beautiful and the terrible that makes it so powerful. We call it el duende:

the demon who makes the passions flow. Duende is not brought into being by talent or skill but by the artist's ability to give himself over to the moment. When possessed, he is capable of producing incredible art but sometimes at a terrible cost to himself."

"I think there's duende in baseball, too," Kyle says.

"I don't think so," Luis sniffs. "You only find it in toreo, flamenco, and poetry."

"Sure, there is. You should see Klint when he's in the zone. It's like he's possessed. Sometimes there's this concentration on his face that's almost scary. You feel like he's seeing things you can't see. Like he's in another world."

"But where is the beauty in baseball?"

"Have you ever seen a three-base line drive off a low inside corner pitch?"

"I've never been to a baseball game in my life," I tell them both.

"Really?" Kyle exclaims. "Never? Not even when you were a kid?"

"No."

"You need to see one, Miss Jack. All this talk about Spanish people and their bullfights. You can't be an American and never go to a baseball game. You should come to one of Klint's games with me in the spring. I could take care of you."

Luis raises an eyebrow at me.

I can't help being affected by the boy's

enthusiasm.

"That sounds very nice, Kyle. We'll talk about it more when the time comes."

"Thanks for the cookies, Luis."

"De nada."

"Good night."

"How long were you standing there?" I ask Luis the minute Kyle has gone upstairs.

"Long enough."

He walks over to the sideboard and comes back with a highball and pours himself a healthy dose of wine.

"What was I thinking, Luis? Asking you to come with me back to America. You were so young. You were only a few years older than these boys. I took you away from your family. From your country."

"You didn't take me away from anything. I came willingly. It was my choice. I wanted to leave Spain after Manuel's death. And as for my family, I love them dearly but I'm content to love from a distance."

"Yes, but you're intelligent and talented."

He acknowledges my compliment with a nod.

"You could have done other things once you were here. You could have been a great success."

"A successful man is the man doing what he loves."

"Confucius?"

"No. Luis."

"Excuse me, Miss Jack."

I look toward the doorway where Marjorie is standing.

"Oh, hello, Luis," she adds quickly.

"Hello, Miss Henry."

"Miss Jack, I'm done for the night, but I wanted to remind you that you said I could take tomorrow off to go to my nephew's birthday party."

"Yes, of course. Have a good time."

Luis extends the plate of cookies to her.

"Please," he says.

"Maybe just one."

She takes one happily, bites into it, and smiles at Luis with sugary pink lips.

"All right. Enough," I say with exasperation and wave Marjorie out the door. "Good night."

"You damaged that girl," I tell Luis after she's gone. "You are solely responsible for her weight problem."

"It was fifteen years ago, and I didn't damage her," he protests. "I gave her some of the best months of her life."

"When you stopped giving her love, you replaced it with tarta de whisky and crema catalana."

"No one forces her to eat it."

"Do you know that's how I can always tell when you're about to break up with one of your lady friends? You start taking them desserts."

"It eases the pain."

"It eases your conscience."

He smiles grandly at me.

"When you take away something sweet, you must replace it with something sweet."

Chapter Fifteen

Since attending my final bullfight well over forty years ago I've lost the ability to subject myself to large groups of people. I can no longer stand public events. I avoid them at all costs. I don't attend graduations, weddings, funerals, or church. No one around here has ever seen me at a parade, a Presidents' Day sale, a demolition derby, or swap meet.

I won't admit to having a phobia. I prefer to believe my feelings stem from a combination of being a mature woman with good taste (I rarely feel the need to demolish or swap) and having outgrown the desire to share intimate emotions with a milling pack of strangers. Love, grief, faith, triumph, a yen to purchase linens at a reduced price are all sensations I prefer to celebrate on my own.

Kyle's suggestion last month that I attend one of Klint's baseball games in the spring has left me feeling uneasy. I know spring is a long way off. His first game isn't for five months and one week. (I had Bert call the

high school's athletic office and ask for me.) Kyle might not have been serious about the invitation. He could forget about the offer or change his mind, but ever since he made it that night of uneaten partridge and Baby's disappearance, I can't stop thinking about it.

I suppose I would be obligated to go. I have no idea what I'd wear. I have no idea what I could possibly say to someone sitting next to me if he were to start talking about curving balls or popping flies. Would it be expected of me to eat a hot dog, and if so, would it be in bad taste for me to ask the vendor if it was all-beef? Would it be expected of me to cheer?

I once stumbled upon a few minutes of a professional baseball game on TV and the audience performed a maneuver called "The Wave." It was interesting to watch but frankly, the thought of having to take part in one is somewhat unsettling. What if I remained seated?

I know I'm worrying too much, but the fact is I'd like to go to a game and not just because I feel I should but because I'm curious.

The other day as I was coming back from my walk I came upon Jerry, who had joined Marjorie for one of her countless cigarette breaks outside the back door to the kitchen, and I overheard them discussing Klint's upcoming season with great zeal and intensity.

I don't know anything about baseball or any team sport for that matter and I'm always baffled by the amount of passion and devotion these mindless games inspire in grown men and women, so I was surprised to find myself suddenly intrigued by the topic. Here were two levelheaded adults well past their high school years avidly talking about a teenage boy's ability to hit a ball across a field and how this will impact the morale of an entire county.

They seemed to know everything about how he played last year, and that was before any of us knew him personally. They spoke with profound respect not only for his skills but for his strength and composure. I couldn't believe they were talking about the same uncommunicative, somewhat dull, young man I dine with every evening who inspires very little in me aside from frustration and concern.

My relationship with Klint has improved, but it's still far from friendly. He's polite and has cleaned up his vocabulary. He responds when I talk to him, and he appears in my study each Saturday morning to give me fifty dollars to put toward the cost of his truck (I know this is the bulk of his part-time, minimum-wage paycheck and the rest he uses for gas money), but it's clear that he has no intention of letting me into his heart or his confidence.

Ironically, these moments when he's paying me for the gift I gave him are when he seems happiest to see me. He's at his most relaxed then and we have our best chats. He can only be comfortable with me when he's proving that he doesn't need me.

I put aside my thoughts of Klint for the moment and turn to Rafael's latest letter. He's also cursed with a terrible pride — all toreros are — but unlike his great-uncle, he doesn't have the fully developed ego to support it. His is plagued by self-reflection and second guessing, two modes of thinking Manuel never entertained. Neither did my brother. I can't tell yet what goes on inside Klint.

I'm sitting in my yellow sunroom filled with fresh flowers and old books where I have my breakfast once it becomes too cold for me to eat outside. We had our first serious frost last night. This morning the valley behind the house was filled with a heavy mist as thick and white as milk. When it cleared, the grass on the back lawn was covered with an opalescent gleam.

Ventisco will be full of fire on a brisk day like today. His breath will come in frosty snorts and he will charge for no reason. I haven't seen him for two months, not since the day Shelby first asked me if Kyle and Klint could come here to live with me. I remember the absurdity of the idea at the

time. Sometimes I still question what I've done. I wonder if I'm helping them at all.

Rafael's enclosed several clippings. True to his fair-minded nature and typical of his career, one is complimentary and one is not.

After his remarkable performance at the autumn feria in Madrid, *6 Toros 6,* the most influential bullfighting magazine in Spain, put him on its cover with the quote: *Lo lleva en la sangre.* Literally translated: He carries it in his blood. The photo captures a perfectly executed *derechazo* pass as he drags the charging bull behind his back with his cape.

The photo accompanying the other article was taken at the important Feria de San Miguel in Sevilla, where he failed to kill even one of his bulls on the first two attempts. This one shows a dejected Rafael, spatters of blood on his face and his suit, holding his great-uncle's sword in front of him, his dark eyes filled with troubled exhaustion.

One more clipping falls out of the envelope. It's from *la prensa rosa* — the pink press — the name gossip-mad Spaniards have given to their tabloid magazines and TV shows.

It's a picture of Rafael walking down a city street holding hands with his American actress, a skinny blonde with enormous sunglasses.

Dear Aunt Candy,

My season is over. I performed 65 times

in these past six months. I killed 130 bulls and cut 58 ears. For my trouble I was ranked number 8 on the leader board in 6 Toros 6. The lukewarm zone. That's what it's called, and that's what I am.

I'm not feeling sorry for myself. I was pleased with my season. I had moments of greatness, but I also had many disappointing times. I am becoming frustrated. I'm 27 years old. I'm at a crucial point in my career. Am I to continue on and overcome my inconsistency and finally become the figura máxima de toreo I know I can be, or am I to sink into oblivion? Am I to end up on some young hotshot's cuadrilla? Or should I leave the life altogether? Should I be like Lucio Sandín, the great torero of the 70s who lost an eye in the Sevilla arena and started an optical company!

I've given much thought to this and what I keep returning to is the magic. In bullfighting, as in all the arts, the difference between mere greatness and brilliance lies in the magic that no one can explain. An artist either has it or he doesn't. I have it, Aunt Candy. I know I do, yet I have no control over it. I can never be sure when it will or won't appear.

Uncle Manuel didn't have this problem. Of course he had his share of bad bull-

fights. He was human, after all, but the magic was always with him.

I've listened to stories from the old-timers, the true taurinos with their white caps and big, scarred hands, who talk about some of El Soltero's worst corridas with the same awe they use when talking about his best. Even when faced with a terrible bull, or a terrible crowd, or terrible weather, or whatever mortal problems were plaguing his heart and mind, his style never suffered or his intent.

Enough about bullfighting. I can find other things to tell you about.

The movie is done. I don't think they will dare to release it in Spain. It is full of clichés and stereotypes about the Spanish people and many misconceptions.

There is a scene where the torero is sitting at dinner with his cuadrilla and he launches into a speech about why it's okay to kill the bull and how they love the bull. He compared his death to a soldier giving his life for his country.

I watched them film this with amazement. I was certain it was a comedy scene. I pictured me delivering the same speech to my own men and when I finished, all of them sobbing with laughter.

It was a serious scene!

I tried to make them understand that a torero would never say these words. He

would never think them. A torero never gives a thought to his relationship with the bull because it is not negotiable. It simply is. In the same way he has a relationship with his mother or his child.

My actress and I argued a lot about this. She called me everything from a murderer to a barbarian. One night when she had been drinking, she burst into tears and started crying about how scared the bull must be before he dies. I told her there isn't a single moment in the ring when the bull is scared. I'm the one who's scared. As Antonio Ordoñez once said, "For me the bull is a friend, a great friend, who I am mortally afraid of in the ring."

I tried explaining to her that one of the biggest differences between animal and man is animals don't fear death the way man does. They have no concept of what it means for life to end. They sense danger and react, but they don't fear death. This is hard for people to believe since we as a species are obsessed with death.

People who feel bad for the bull are putting human qualities on him. They are making him a cartoon. These are the same people who refer to their dogs as their children and put costumes on their cats. These are pet lovers; they are <u>not</u> animal lovers.

I could never make her see reason. Eventually she went back to America, and I finished my season. Now I'm visiting my grandmother, who sends her best wishes to you and Luis as well. She's looking forward to seeing him in December when he comes home to see his family.

I was very interested in what you wrote about the boys who lost their father, and I'm flattered you asked for my advice. Their story is tragic yet it is their story. It is what it is supposed to be. You need to decide if you are meant to be part of it. I'm sure something will speak to your heart, and you'll find the answer. My personal opinion is that these boys would be very lucky to have you in their lives, not just as a benefactress, but as a woman with much wisdom and love to share.

Aunt Candy, please no more talk about La Vieja Compañera! You are worrying me. You say you've learned not to fear her but please don't get too comfortable with her! Death is my old friend — the torero's friend — not yours.

I will write again soon.

Many kisses,
Rafi

I put Rafael's letter and clippings back in the envelope.

I must remember to write something to him about Manuel's crazed magic. It was true he had it, but it was all he had.

Rafael has more of a struggle not because he isn't as talented but because he is a complex individual. His duende demon has not been allowed to grow overwhelmingly large and powerful within his soul because it must share its home with human emotions and concerns.

Manuel's demon had the whole place to itself.

Along with Rafael's letter I also received a postcard from Shelby. She sounds happy and busy and promised to write more soon.

I finish my breakfast and wait for Luis to appear. Ten minutes pass. Then another ten. I decide to seek him out to show him the postcard and letter.

Luis has a suite of spacious rooms next to the kitchen consisting of a living room, bedroom, and bath. They're tasteful and uncluttered, furnished in dark wood and leather with simple white walls but with a Spaniard's love of color evident in the red cushions on the couch, the bright green and yellow of a ceramic pitcher, and the rich peacock shades of a rug.

He's a stickler for privacy and would be livid if he found me in his home without an invitation, but his door is wide open, his computer is on, and a steaming cup of coffee

sits next to it along with a half-eaten Napolitana.

I venture inside.

"Luis," I call out. "Luis, estás aquí?"

He knows I don't approve of smoking but he has an occasional cigar here. The smell of tobacco mingles with the light lemony scent of a wood polish. I believe what first brought Luis and Marjorie together all those years ago was their shared love of cleaning products. They used to put their heads together in the kitchen and discuss the merits of Comet versus Ajax and Pledge versus Endust while Luis would eye Marjorie's long legs and she would giggle each time he'd refer to Mr. Clean as Don Limpio. I didn't particularly want to see any part of this courtship, but I occasionally stumbled into it quite by accident.

One entire wall is taken up by shelves filled with pictures of his large extended family ranging in age from his mother, who is well into her nineties, to his newest grandniece, who is only four months old.

In the midst of all of it is a framed black-and-white photo of Manuel after a corrida offering the crowd a dazzling smile while holding his hat out to them in his upturned hand in the traditional torero's salute. Next to the picture is the glass he drank from on the day Luis first met him fifty years ago in his father's bar.

People knowing my history with Luis would be surprised to know that we weren't friends when he originally came to America with me. We were acquaintances in love with the same man whose individual worlds had been destroyed with one unlucky thrust of a bull's horn. Afterward, we were both lost and searching for a way to go on.

I had done my best not to cause problems between myself and Manuel's men, and for the most part I succeeded. They respected me because I respected them. I stayed out of their way and tried not to distract Manuel. I traveled on my own, near them but not with them. (I knew that a woman traveling with a cuadrilla was considered extreme *mala suerte.* Bad luck.) I made Manuel happy but not content, because a contented Manuel would have lost his fire.

Still, none of this was enough to win over Luis.

It would greatly simplify the situation to say that he and I were in competition for the same man and that was why we didn't get along, but there was some truth to this. Luis's feelings for Manuel were obviously different from mine. Manuel was my lover, and my desire for him was rooted in poetic passion and physical longing. He had changed my life by suddenly becoming my life.

To Luis, he was an idol, friend, mentor, and savior. He not only offered Luis an

escape from the confines of a large family and small town but he provided him with a new philosophy to live by. He changed his life by allowing him into his own.

"Qué te pasa?" I hear Luis behind me. "Snooping? Looking for cigarettes and pornography?"

"Oh, please," I tell him. "I came by to show you Shelby's postcard and Rafael's letter, and your door was wide open."

I hand them to him.

"Where were you?" I ask.

"Outside. I was haggling with that new man over his price for rabbits."

"And?"

"And I see conejo con ciruelas in our future."

I smile and take a seat in an easy chair.

"Shelby seems to be having a wonderful time in Paris. She made me start thinking about Kyle and Klint. I feel like I'm not doing enough for them. I should be expanding their horizons, not just feeding them. I thought that maybe we should give them Spanish lessons."

Luis puts down Rafael's newspaper clippings, throws up his hands, and rolls his eyes.

"Te has vuelto loca o qué?"

"There's no need to be so dramatic. No, I'm not crazy. What's wrong with wanting them to learn a second language?"

"You can want it but unless they want it,

it's not going to happen."

"Then how about a trip to Pittsburgh? I could take them to a museum or to see some live theater. Or maybe something historical? An outing to Gettysburg?"

"Oh, yes, yes, that would be good," he replies with exaggerated eagerness. "That's what they want. To drive two hours so they can stand freezing in an empty field while you tell them about cannonballs and slavery. At least it will be an interesting account coming from someone who lived through that time period."

"You're very funny."

"I think you are doing enough for them."

I get up from the chair with the intention of leaving, but as I'm crossing the room, I catch sight of a sketch lying next to Luis's computer.

"What's this?" I ask.

"Oh, no," Luis rushes over and tries to take it from me.

"It looks just like your brother Javier except it's obviously a caricature. It's very good. Where did you get it?"

Some inner turmoil plays across Luis's face. I can't imagine why he'd want to hide the identity of the artist. I'm about to ask him again when he replies defeatedly, "From Kyle."

"Kyle?"

"Yes, Kyle. He's doing one of each of my

siblings. It's going to be a Christmas gift for Miguel."

I examine the sketch closer.

"I had no idea he could draw."

"He can paint, too."

"Paint? You've seen paintings?"

"Yes."

"Why hasn't he told me about this? He sees the paintings hanging in my house. He must understand how much I love art."

"I found out about it only because I ran into him one day when he had his sketch pad with him and he was forced to explain. He's shy about his talent. I'd say he's almost embarrassed by it. He has no confidence yet."

"Then he needs to get some."

Luis takes the sketch from me and puts it in a drawer.

"He's not going to get any if you come down on him like a pound of bricks."

"A ton of bricks," I correct him.

"It doesn't matter. Even one brick is a lot if someone throws it at your head. You'll scare him away," he scolds me. "You have to be subtle."

"I can be subtle."

"No, you can't."

My head is instantly whirling with plans.

"He probably needs some quality supplies. I could let him turn Stan's upstairs study into a studio. It has wonderful light. He should take art lessons."

Luis stops me with a glare.

"Great artists find their own way. They aren't coached like baseball players."

"I don't want to coach him. I want to encourage him. He should be nurtured."

"He should be left alone."

I reach past Luis, open the drawer, and retrieve Kyle's picture.

"I can't ignore this," I say.

Luis sighs.

"I know."

I spend the next few days trying to decide how I should broach the subject of art with Kyle. Luis did have a good point about the need for subtlety. Every scenario I concoct seems too deliberate, and I finally accept that I'm going to have to be spontaneous.

An opportunity presents itself on a Sunday afternoon when I happen to run into Kyle in the upstairs hallway, which is an extremely rare occurrence. He's without his brother, and he doesn't seem to be in any particular hurry.

He greets me and I motion him toward me.

"What do you think of this painting?" I ask as he comes to stand in front of a reproduction of *Los Borrachos.*

"Almost all of the paintings here in my home are originals," I explain to him, "but I have a few copies of some of my favorites that are out of my league, so to speak. This one is a reproduction of a very famous paint-

ing by one of Spain's most famous artists. Have you ever heard of Velázquez?"

"No."

"No? Well, certainly you've heard of Goya."

"No."

"No?! What do they teach you in school?"

"I don't know. A bunch of stuff, I guess, but not much about Spanish artists."

"Have you heard of Picasso?"

"Sure. Everyone's heard of Picasso. Even the guys on Klint's team know who he is."

"Really?" I say, pleasantly surprised. "You mean to tell me these baseball players discuss Picasso's artwork with you?"

"Not exactly. One time one of them came up on me while I was drawing a picture waiting for Klint to finish practice. He took it and showed it to everyone, and they all made fun of me. Then after that every time I'd come around one of them would say, "Hey, look. It's Klint's brother. He thinks he's friggin' Picasso."

My brief hopes are dashed.

"Sorry about the language," he quickly adds.

"That's terrible."

"It's nothing."

He shrugs off the memory.

"Yeah. I like this painting. I've noticed it before. The expressions on their faces are very realistic and . . ."

He pauses to search for a word and comes

up with the correct one.

". . . and modern. They look like guys I know. They could be my dad's bowling buddies. They're drunk, right?"

"Yes. It's called *Los Borrachos.* The Drunkards. This figure over here is Bacchus, the god of wine."

"When was it painted?"

"In the early sixteen hundreds."

"It's kind of cool to think that four hundred years ago people were still pretty much the same."

"I've always thought it's a shame they haven't changed."

He smiles at this, and I'm seized by an urge to show him my most cherished painting.

"Come this way, Kyle. I want to show you something else."

I lead him to my room. It's large and airy with a high ceiling, two walls of windows, and a soothing pale green color scheme. I can't stand clutter in the place where I sleep. For this reason I have few furnishings and none of the bric-a-brac — the jewelry boxes, perfume bottles, and framed photos — that most women display on dresser tops and bedside tables.

I have only one painting here.

"This is my pride and joy," I tell Kyle. "It's an original Joaquín Sorolla. It was given to Manuel by a wealthy fan who was an art collector. Manuel gave it to me because I loved

it so much."

Kyle studies the beach scene. A girl and boy, holding hands, stand in front of a spangled sea. The shirtless, barefoot boy stares down at his younger sister in a billowing pink dress who's tugging him toward the water. He watches her with touching patience.

"It's beautiful," Kyle states simply.

He continues staring at it, and his expression turns sad.

"What is it?" I ask him.

"The girl. Her face. She looks a lot like my sister."

"You don't talk much about your sister."

"There's not much to talk about. I don't get to see her."

"Would you like to see her?"

"Sure."

"Why don't you tell your mother this?"

"I don't know. It's kind of hard to talk to her about stuff like that."

"Surely you can ask to see your own sister," I say, trying to control my temper against this woman who I've only met once but feel a lifetime of hostility toward.

"She'd take it the wrong way and get mad."

"How could she possibly . . . ," I start to ask him but he looks so uncomfortable, I decide it's a topic I should drop.

"Kyle, I wanted to talk to you about your own art."

The panic in his eyes should be enough

warning to me that I should drop this topic, too, but I forge ahead.

"I've discovered that you're quite talented. I'd like to help you. I could arrange for art lessons."

He shakes his head vigorously.

"No. I don't want any help. It's not like that. It's just something I do."

"But don't you want to improve?"

"I don't know. I guess. But I don't want to make a big deal out of it."

"Art lessons wouldn't be a big deal."

He continues shaking his head while he blushes deeply.

"No. No lessons."

"Are you embarrassed?"

"I entered an art contest once. I wouldn't have done that if I was embarrassed."

"How did you do?"

"I took second place."

"That's wonderful," I cry as a startling burst of irrationally extreme pride surges through me.

"No. See. That's what I mean. It's nothing great."

"It is great."

"No, no, it's not."

Watching the torment on his face, I suddenly recall Luis's words. If Kyle was actually dodging real bricks, he couldn't look more frantic and distressed than he does now.

"I'm sorry. I've made you uncomfortable.

I'll drop the subject."

"Thank you."

"But could I at least see some of your work?"

He turns back to the painting, which seems to calm him. I see a level of comprehension in his eyes that I know I don't possess.

"Okay," he says.

It will be his first act of faith in me and my first true test as a guardian angel.

Chapter Sixteen: Kyle

Everyone assumes if you're going to paint a picture, the reason behind it is so other people can look at it. I guess that makes sense, but that's not why I do it. I don't like to show people my artwork. I'd rather stand in front of someone naked than show them one of my paintings, and believe me, I'm not exactly thrilled about my body.

My mom used to say I was obsessed with drawing when I was a little kid. There was no pride in this observation. She made it sound like I had a disease. My dad was a little more forgiving. He'd take the time to look at what I handed to him, and, for a moment, I'd see a glimmer of wonderment in his eyes before they'd fill with confusion. He didn't understand what I was doing or why I was doing it or how I was able to do it. My talent was an attack on his sensibilities and on my mom's ego. In their minds, it was something I did on purpose to make myself different from them. If I had to pick one quality in my mom

and dad that harmed their parenting skills the most, it would be that they took everything personally.

Maybe I was different from them but not because I tried to be. I look at the world in a different way. I see shadows and angles instead of objects. I see light and color instead of situations. What I see I need to put on paper.

Once I'm finished with a project, it feels like a violation of my privacy to show it to someone else. (Except for the drawings I used to do for Krystal and now the ones I'm doing for Luis. It's not the same when you make something especially for someone.) This isn't because I'm embarrassed. I don't care if someone hates my work, and I'm definitely not searching for compliments. The only thing worse than people who make fun of an artist is the people who make too much of him. The reason I don't like anyone looking at it is because I feel like no one has the right to have any opinion at all.

Miss Jack liked what I showed her. She knows what she's talking about when it comes to art — and she's not a bullshitter — so hers was one opinion that meant something to me for a change. She also didn't do any phony raving about how great I am. She talked mostly about my promise and potential. I liked the fact that she assumed I'm not going to stop.

She was true to her word and didn't bring up art lessons again. She brought me a couple art books instead: one about the Prado in Madrid and the other about Joaquín Sorolla. She told me I should copy some of the pictures in them, and I told her I thought it was wrong to copy. She said not in the case of painters. It was very important to copy the masters in order to learn technique and form. Hadn't I ever seen people in art museums doing sketches of the paintings? What did I think they were doing? she asked me. When I told her I've never been to an art museum, she got the same outraged look on her face that she did when I told her I didn't know Goya. At first I regretted the confession because I saw a forced trip to an art museum looming on my horizon, but the more I thought about it, I realized I wouldn't mind going.

I've had the books for about two weeks now, and I'm having a hard time concentrating on anything else. All I want to do is look at the paintings. After I'm done, the images seem seared onto my brain, and I can see them clearly even while I'm falling asleep at night. Sometimes I'll remember something specific about a particular painting and I feel like I'm going to go crazy if I can't get back to the book to check it out.

I even started taking the Sorolla book to school with me. (The Prado book is too big.)

Not only is it a book filled with paintings of children frolicking in the sea and women with parasols strolling through gardens but the cover is pink with bright purple lettering. I keep it well hidden in my locker and only take it out when I'm sure no one's going to see it. Once I even took it to the john with me.

I know I'm taking a big risk but I can't stop myself. I feel the same way I did when I had to draw the blown-glass fish on my mom's kitchen wall. My personal safety has become a secondary consideration.

I finally chose two pictures to try copying. One is a dark, intricate battle scene by Goya. The other is a sunny impressionist seashore scene by Sorolla similar to the one Miss Jack owns. This time the roles are reversed and the sister is older and is trying to lead her baby brother into the surf.

Klint's begun winter workouts with the team, and I took over his job at Hamilton Dairy so we could still keep paying for the truck. The truck is one of the best things that ever happened to me — even though Klint's the only one who gets to drive it — so I'm okay with the arrangement.

In warm months, people come from all over the place to sample the Hamiltons' famous homemade slow-churned ice cream, and the dairy is always busy. Winter is a different story. We have our regular customers who get

their farm fresh eggs, milk, and butter here, but most of them come in the morning. During the hours I work, there's a flurry of activity between four and six when people stop by on their way home from work, but by the time I'm closing up around eight, the place is pretty dead and I'm working alone.

I've been bringing the Sorolla book and a sketch pad with me and drawing when I'm bored. I know I'll always have time to put it away since I can see the headlights of anyone pulling into the parking lot.

Tonight is worse than usual. Winter's finally kicked in, and people aren't used to the cold yet. No one wants to go out if they don't have to.

I've been able to spend most of the night working on my sketch at the front counter, and I've become so engrossed that I don't notice anyone approaching until I hear the tinkle of the bell over the front door.

I look up and see Chad and Danny Hopper walk in along with their ever-present sidekick, North Campbell.

The Hopper boys live out by our old house with their grandma in a double-wide trailer that receives frequent visits from Social Services and stray dogs drawn by the smell of the hundreds of old pizza boxes stacked around the perimeter of their yard like a fortress wall. They're both in Klint's grade. Chad should've graduated last year, but he's

been held back twice. Even though he hasn't been able to earn a diploma with his brains, I think he should be awarded one based on his size and facial hair. Danny's claim to fame is that he was sent to juvie for beating up his own mother when he was ten. She forgave him but shot his father, saying he was the one who taught him to be violent. She's been in jail for as long as I can remember.

No one knows what grade North's in.

"Hey, fuck face," Danny calls out when he sees me, which means he recognizes me.

"Hey," I reply.

I close my notepad and book and shove them under the counter, but I haven't been quick enough. Chad saw me. I'm dead.

"I need some eggs," Danny tells me.

"You know eggs are cheaper at Bi-Lo," I inform him, foolishly hoping I can get them to leave before Chad's brain finally computes what he just saw and he'll want to know what I hid from them.

"You have a problem with me buying eggs here?" Danny asks menacingly.

"No."

"You think I can't afford your eggs?"

"No. Nothing like that."

"Bi-Lo's not on my way home tonight so I'm going to get my eggs here. Got it?"

"Sure. Okay."

He leans across the counter, and I can smell chewing tobacco and hot sauce on his breath.

I see his whole life summed up in his stained, crooked teeth, the lazy eye he was born with, and the shiny pink jagged scar on his cheek where no stubble grows.

Chad and North join him, and I'm faced with the dumb brute mentality of a trio of bears in ball caps.

"So get my fucking eggs," Danny says.

I rush off to the freezer. Out of the corner of my eye I see Chad heft his bulk over the counter and pull out my book and sketches.

"Why are you even working here? We thought you were rich now," Danny asks while Chad starts paging through the book with North looking over his shoulder already snickering.

"The person we're living with is rich," I explain, returning with a carton of eggs. "Not us. We don't get any of the money."

"What about your brother's truck? Did he have to fuck the old lady to get that?"

Danny bursts into laughter at his own joke, then realizes the other two stooges aren't joining in.

"What are you doing?" he asks them.

"Look at this shit," Chad says gleefully.

"What is it?"

"I don't know."

He grabs the book, rifles through it, then looks over at me.

"Are you a fucking fairy?"

"You gotta ask?" North comments.

Chad flips over the cover of my sketch pad. "Look at the shit he's drawing. Hey, this kid is naked."

"He's a baby," I explain.

"Christ, he's a fairy and he's one of those . . . what do you call those guys who fuck kids?"

"A pedophile," I provide without thinking.

"Yeah," Danny and Chad say together.

I step around the counter realizing the futility of what I'm about to do, but I can't stand by and watch them destroy my work and Miss Jack's beautiful book.

"It's just some stuff I was drawing for art class. You know. Can I have it back?"

"It's just some stuff I was drawing for art class," Danny mimics me in a high-pitched lisp.

"Come on, you guys," I plead.

I reach for the book and Chad holds it over my head while North gives me a shove in the chest.

I'm still considering my next course of action when the bell over the door tinkles again and in walks Klint.

"Hey, Klint," I call out, maybe a bit too enthusiastically.

If I had been cornered by anyone else, Klint's presence would have immediately diffused the situation. Just about everyone at our school knows who he is and has some level of respect for him. Unfortunately for

both of us, the very qualities that make most people admire Klint are the same ones that make these three hate him.

Klint sizes up the situation and puts on his most inscrutable game face.

"Hey," he greets them with a nod. "What's going on?"

"We're looking at your fag brother's artwork," Chad announces.

Klint flashes me a look full of exasperation that I was dumb enough to get caught, but he doesn't look angry at me for being who I am.

"Give him his stuff back so we can close up and go home," Klint tells them.

"Or what?" Danny says, stepping up to Klint. "What are you going to do if we don't?"

"You don't want me to do anything. Give him his stuff."

I try reaching for the book in North's hands, and he tosses it to Danny. Chad tears out one of my sketches and rips it down the middle.

"Don't!" I cry and dive at him.

He pushes me away and I fly into one of the freezers.

"Leave him alone," Klint yells at him.

He hauls off and smacks Chad in the face. Blood gushes from his nose.

Danny's all over Klint instantly. I watch his fist connect with Klint's face and his head jerk back. I throw myself on Danny's back.

Someone tries to drag me off. I see Chad get in a solid punch to Klint's gut while North pins back his arms. Klint doubles over for a moment, then stands up and runs backward as fast as he can, smashing North into shelves of empty glass milk bottles that rain down on his head as he collapses to the floor.

Chad charges at Klint. I don't see what happens next because Danny flips me over his shoulder. I hit the floor hard, and he kicks me in the ribs. All the air rushes out of me. I can't move because I can't breathe.

"You're a dead fairy," he promises me.

He pulls me up by the front of my shirt and hits me in the face. I spin around and see the edge of the counter come rushing toward me.

Surprisingly, I don't feel anything. I just hear a dull thud and crunch that seems to come from inside my head before I fall to the floor.

A sound like rushing water fills my ears until it's cleared away by the crash of the front door being thrown open.

Through my blurred vision, I'm able to make out the figure of a large, angry woman.

"What the hell's taking so long in here?" she shouts. "Where are my goddamned eggs?"

We are saved by Grandma Hopper, who got tired of waiting in the car.

■ ■ ■ ■

We put the store back in order and assess the damage to ourselves. I have a gash on my forehead and a black eye. Klint has a torn lip that won't stop bleeding. His right hand is swollen and his knuckles are skinned. We both know we can't let Miss Jack see our faces in their current condition.

We need someone who knows how to deal with fight injuries, someone who isn't squeamish and can keep a secret. I think I know the perfect person.

Hen is the only member of Miss Jack's house staff who lives on her estate besides Luis and Jerry. She has an apartment over the garage, which doesn't sound like much but since the garage is bigger than most people's houses, it's not too shabby.

Sometimes she works late and sometimes she helps Luis clean up after dinner, but usually she's done for the day by early evening. We see a light in her window and slowly head up the outside stairs clutching the railing and wincing in pain. Our internal injuries are probably worse than the ones we can see.

She reacts exactly how I thought she would. She's not shocked, flustered, or appalled by our appearance. She invites us in and eyes us clinically.

"How many were there?"

"Three," I answer.
"Weapons?"
"No."
"Ambush?"
"No. They came right at us."
"What was it about? A girl? Money?"
"Destruction of personal property," Klint provides.
"Sit down," she motions at an immaculate room where everything glows with cleanliness.
She leaves and returns with a first aid kit, an ice pack, a steaming bowl of water, a couple washcloths, and a plate of Luis's *marquesitas.*
It's weird to see her in regular clothes, although she still looks as neat and tidy as she does in her uniform. She's wearing a long tan corduroy skirt, a pink sweater, and white satin slippers embroidered with pink roses.
She looks me over first while telling Klint he better ice his throwing hand.
"This cut on your forehead could probably use a stitch or two but don't worry. I'm a wiz with butterfly bandages. It won't even leave a scar. But who cares if it does? Right? You're a boy. Chicks dig scars."
"Not the kind of chicks he's interested in," Klint chimes in. "The kind he likes are interested in trips to Paris and little Beemer sports cars."
"You mean Shelby?" Hen asks.

"Shut up, Klint."

"She's nice and pretty, but I think she's too immature for you."

"She's too immature for *me?"*

"I don't know her all that well, but she's obviously spoiled and sheltered," Hen comments while dabbing some kind of cream on my cut that burns like crazy. "You're very worldly."

"I'm worldly? What do you mean? She's the one in France."

"Some of the worldliest people you'll ever meet are sitting over at my dad's bar right now, and a lot of them have never been any farther than Centresburg. I'm not talking about knowing how to travel around the world; I'm talking about knowing how the world works."

She applies the first bandage to my forehead using so much concentration that the tip of her tongue pops out the corner of her mouth. She steps back to appraise her work. Satisfied, she puts on one more.

"You're going to have to tell Miss Jack what happened," she informs us. "You can't hide from her, and she's going to know right away you were in a fight."

"No way," I tell her. "She'd probably call the cops or even worse, she'd go to the Hopper house and give them a lecture about their barbaric use of violence."

Klint laughs at this. I'm surprised. I wasn't

expecting to even get a smile out of him for the next six months.

"Nah," he says. "There's no way she'd set foot in a trailer park."

"I wouldn't be so sure of that," Hen says, smiling slyly like she knows a juicy secret. "Do you want to hear a great story?"

Before we can answer her, she plops down on the couch beside us, and we're all squeezed together as she begins her breathless narrative.

"Miss Jack advertised for a maid, and I applied for the job. I didn't come from the best background and I didn't have any experience, but I told her the only thing I was good at was cleaning and she gave me a chance. Things were going great until one day my dad showed up here. I was twenty. I was old enough to be on my own, but he didn't see it that way. He thought I should take care of him and work at the bar for the rest of my life whether I wanted to or not. He waited for me outside the house in his truck, and when I went out to talk to him, he kidnapped me. He had a gun!"

"Holy crap!" I exclaim.

She nods excitedly at us. Her normally rosy complexion has grown even pinker, and her blue eyes are sparkling.

She lowers her voice.

"I don't know how she found out what happened, but later that night Miss Jack showed

up at the bar."

"Miss Jack went into The Mine Shaft?" Klint marvels.

Hen grins.

"She walked right in. Everyone went dead quiet. I'd never seen anything like it. She went straight to the bar and said to my dad, 'I'm looking for the owner of this establishment.' "

Hen does an excellent impression of Miss Jack.

"My dad stared at her like she'd just got off a spaceship and he said, 'That's me.' Then she said, 'Mr. Henry, in the future I would like to ask you to please refrain from trespassing on my property and interfering with my employees. If it happens again, I will have to contact the local authorities.' "

She pauses and claps her hands together in delight.

"Then she looked right at me and said, 'Marjorie.' At first I didn't know who she was talking to. I'd been Hen since I was a little kid. I'm not even sure my dad knew Marjorie was my name. I followed Miss Jack out the door, and the rest is history. My dad never bothered me again, and no one else has ever called me Marjorie."

Her story ends as abruptly as it began. She jumps up from the couch, dips a cloth in the bowl of hot water, and starts cleaning Klint's lip.

We thank Hen and leave the moment she's done fixing our faces. We're late for dinner and we have to explain what happened. We want to get it over with.

We stop at the truck to get our backpacks and Klint's team bag. I left my sketchbook on the seat, and Klint gets to it before me. My instinct is to grab it from him but after what happened tonight, I don't feel like I have the right to do that. I'm still not sure if he was defending me or my drawings. I wonder if he understands it's the same thing.

He gets to the front door before me and stands beneath the light looking through my sketches. He hasn't said anything to me yet about the cause of tonight's fight. I brace myself for his verbal attack.

He's staring at a drawing I did of some kids in my earth science class. I wait for his smart-ass remark.

"When you do this, does it keep you from thinking about anything else?" he asks me.

"Yeah."

He closes the book and hands it back to me without saying anything more. I wonder if he's suddenly realized that I've had to find a way to escape from our lives, too.

Chapter Seventeen

I've never been too big on Christmas. I don't mean I don't like it. I enjoy getting presents and eating turkey and having family togetherness just as much as the next guy. The problem is all those good things came along with a few bad things in my family.

I can't remember a single year of my life when my mom wasn't in a crappy mood from November through January. She complained about all the decorating, baking, and cleaning she had to do, which I always found a little hard to swallow considering Dad and us kids put up the tree and the lights, her idea of holiday baking was slapping red frosting and green sprinkles on a box of store-bought sugar cookies, and the house was as big a mess on Christmas as any other day of the year.

My dad was always stressed out, too, not just because he had to deal with Mom but because of all the money we were spending that we didn't have. He'd drink more than

usual and get really sentimental.

He'd talk about the sled he got from Santa when he was six years old and how he smashed it into a tree and got fifteen stitches in his head. He'd reminisce about the year the ruffled collar on Grandma Bev's dress caught on fire when she leaned into some candles and how she got a third degree burn on her neck. He'd recall with a tearful smile the year he and his best friend were crawling around their snow fort late on Christmas night and a drunk uncle came out with his rifle thinking they were raccoons getting in the garbage cans and shot his friend in the butt.

All my dad's fondest Christmas memories involved bodily harm.

Mom, on the other hand, had no Christmas memories or at least not any she chose to share with us. Aunt Jen was the same. Even when I'd ask them straight out what Christmas was like when they were kids, all I'd get in response were blank stares and a reach for the nearest bottle.

Despite all this, the big day itself usually started out well. We'd get up and open our presents while a disheveled, bleary-eyed Mom and Dad in his-and-hers plush red bathrobes covered in cartoon reindeer quietly nursed their Christmas Eve hangovers with big steaming mugs of coffee and a half-dozen cigarettes.

By midday, Mom would be feeling much better and would have changed out of her robe into one of her painfully glittery holiday sweaters, a black velvet miniskirt, and a pair of high-heeled red patent leather boots Dad called her Naughty Elf boots. For a few hours they'd be in love, flirting, and kissing, and drinking toasts to each other.

They'd love us, too. That was back when Mom and Klint weren't always fighting or avoiding each other, back when she used to give him hugs after his games and stroke his hair while he wolfed down his breakfast and gave him a kiss before bed every night.

We'd be one big happy family for a while. Aunt Jen would arrive down in the dumps because she didn't have a date or because she had a date she didn't want, and Bill would come over wearing a white beard and a Santa hat toting a case of beer and a bag of presents. Mom would set about cheering up Aunt Jen, and Bill would crack open a beer and take a seat next to Dad where he'd listen to him talk wistfully about his mom catching on fire for the hundredth time. We'd have dinner and everything would seem okay, but then about halfway through the meal something would set off Mom. Dad would try to appease her, but when Mom decided she was going to be pissed, nothing could change her mind.

Eventually when the shouting, door slam-

ming, and dish throwing got to be too much for us, Klint, Krystal, and I would get our new toys and sneak into one of our rooms where we'd barricade the door with a dresser and have our own celebration. I always liked this part. It was cozy and quiet, and it calmed down Krystal, who tended to get pale and twitchy when Mom and Dad started to fight.

I've been relieved to find out that Miss Jack doesn't make a big deal out of Christmas. Jerry puts up a tree for her and Luis sets up a Nativity scene, but that's about it.

I think her lack of interest in the holiday comes from the fact that Luis isn't here. He spends almost the whole month of December in Spain with his family.

He went off a couple weeks ago, dressed to the nines in a charcoal gray suit and a fur-trimmed black overcoat, smiling and humming "Deck the Halls with Boughs of Holly" while lugging four big suitcases filled almost entirely with presents.

He must be a star when he returns to his small hometown in Spain: the exotic American uncle laden with gifts who works for a wealthy heiress and who once worked for El Soltero.

I finished the caricatures on time. It wasn't easy. I worked on them every day for a month, but it was worth it. He loved them and paid me thirty bucks apiece, which came to $240!

He said he would've spent more than thirty dollars on each of his siblings to get them some impersonal gift they probably didn't need. The caricatures were something unique and thoughtful.

I was pumped up at first and started to think maybe I could make a decent living at being an artist until I realized I'd just been paid $240 for an entire month's work and then it didn't seem like so much. I'm still happy about it, though, and excited to think some of my work with my signature at the bottom will be hanging in houses in a different country an ocean away from here being appreciated by people who don't care at all about baseball.

Before he left for the airport, Luis gave Klint and me a few instructions about Miss Jack. They weren't really commands about what we were expected to do for her as much as they were reminders of her deficiencies due to her extreme age and her dependence on him.

We both knew Miss Jack was within hearing distance. Luis probably knew it, too.

"Remember Miss Jack is very old," he told us as he slipped into his coat and gloves. "You must make sure she doesn't fall down and break her bones.

"And remember Miss Jack is getting senile," he added. "You must check on her time to time and make sure she hasn't done some-

thing stupid.

"And remember Miss Jack is used to me doing everything for her. No one expects you to take my place. God knows no one ever could," he said, making one of his customary glances toward heaven, "but you must not get upset with her if she starts ordering you about like a slave the way she does with me. Just remind her you're not a slave. Tell her the slave is having a good time without her."

He also made a ton of meals and froze them for us. We've discovered over time that he can cook anything, not just Spanish food but all the best American food, too: lasagna, pizza, gravy, tacos, fried chicken, mac and cheese, stuffed pork chops, and the best french fries I've ever had. He doesn't even mind doing it. At first I thought he might be insulted, but he said it's Miss Jack who wants Spanish food all the time. He loves cooking all kinds of food as long as he can add his own personal touch.

Miss Jack has been gloomy, and I feel kind of bad for her. I know I should feel bad for myself. This is my first Christmas without Dad. It's a mental health milestone. I should be buried beneath a pile of poignant memories. The grief counselor at school would be disappointed in me if I didn't cry my eyes out at least three times today. But I don't miss Dad any more today than I do any other day.

Maybe it's because Christmas ceased to be a big emotional deal for us once Mom and Krystal left. All the fun seemed to go out of it, not to mention Mom took all our decorations with her.

Fortunately for us, we discovered purely by chance that the tractor supply store has a seasonal section stocked with a selective line of ornaments, so from then on our tree was decorated with John Deere tractor mowers and rifletoting snowmen dressed in camouflage hunting gear.

What depresses me most about today is the absence of Shelby. This was going to be my first opportunity to spend a major holiday with her, but she decided to stay in France.

She texts me now and then with brief, bubbly messages about how great Paris is, and she continues to thank me for saving Baby. But other than that, she's one more person who's disappeared from my life.

Miss Jack told me that under normal circumstances we would have spent the entire day with her nephew and his family, but since Shelby's parents decided to join her in Paris and Skylar is spending the holidays with her fiancé, it will be impossible this year. She didn't seem too broken up over the situation.

Starr chose to stay home by herself. She's supposed to come over later today, and this is the one thing I'm looking forward to. I don't know why I'm excited about seeing her

again, other than the obvious fact that she's sexy. But she also scares me. I've been picturing her in my mind as a sleek tawny wild cat pacing agitatedly around Cam Jack's empty mansion looking for prey, and even though I know I'm not meaty enough for her to want to eat, there's always the possibility she might pounce on me out of boredom.

Miss Jack is sitting, fully dressed, in a stiff-backed, satin, striped chair near the tree. Jerry started a fire for her this morning, and the dancing flames in the huge, open fireplace are cheerful and warm.

This is the first time Klint and I have been in this room other than checking it out when we first moved in looking for a TV or a ghost. It's a beautiful room but about as inviting as a museum display. The only things missing are red velvet ropes and a low-voiced tour guide explaining the history of the pictures on the walls, which period the furniture is from, and the names of the famed sculptor who carved the twilight-blue marble mantelpiece and the artist who painted the mural of a hunting party on the high scrolled ceiling.

Most of the other rooms in the house are colorful and interesting and reflect Miss Jack's taste, but this one only reflects her money.

Just looking at the furniture here makes our butts hurt, so Klint and I have chosen to sprawl out on the floor next to the tree in our

pajama bottoms and T-shirts while Miss Jack sits primly wearing a high-necked green silk dress and big square-cut emerald earrings.

She told us one night at dinner that she doesn't believe in making a big fuss over Christmas and she especially dislikes the practice of buying ridiculous amounts of gifts for people. She said that one humble, thoughtful gift meant more than twenty expensive gifts bought solely for the purpose of showing how much money one could spend and how little effort. Gift-giving, like everything else in America, had become a competition.

Klint and I had looked glumly at each other. We had been hoping for lots of thoughtless presents, but we agreed with her that one would be plenty.

Now looking at the meager heap of gifts sitting under the huge tree dripping with gold and silver, I'm having second thoughts.

"Well," Miss Jack says, getting up from her chair and smiling at us. "Let's get started."

She reaches under the tree and hands us each a box from our mom.

"I think you should open these first."

Klint and I exchange skeptical, defeated looks with each other. The orange wrapping paper is covered with smiling chili peppers wearing Santa hats. Arizona even gets Christmas wrong.

I let myself get a little excited as I begin to

wonder if Krystal made me anything this year.

She used to make me things all the time. She was a creative kid. She had tons of those arts and crafts kits that made everything from jewelry to candles, but she also liked to make up stuff on her own. One time she took an old mayonnaise jar and made this little farm under glass. She decorated the inside with cutout trees and a barn she drew on construction paper and glued some plastic toy animals and a silver foil pond into it. It was one of the best things I've ever seen.

Another time she made Mr. B a muscle shirt by taking a sleeve off one of Dad's old T-shirts and cutting two little holes for the cat's front legs to go through. She sewed a bunch of hearts and "Mr. B" onto it using red sequins and beads.

He almost scratched my face off while we tried to get him into it, but it was worth it. He tried everything to get rid of it and then when he figured out he couldn't, he did the classic cat thing where he sat down and licked himself and acted like nothing had ever happened, like he wanted to wear it. Even Klint broke down laughing.

The first Christmas after she left with Mom, Krystal made me a needlepoint pillow with the Pirates' logo on it, but last year she sent a pair of gloves and a hat I know Mom probably picked out for her.

Every year I wonder what Krystal's Christ-

mas is like. Does she think about what it used to be like when we were a family? Does she remember how beautiful our tree was and her favorite decorations? Does she remember Mom singing along to her endless supply of pop Christmas CDs, and Dad and Bill in his Santa hat sitting on the couch holding tinsel-trimmed beer cozies and cheerfully recounting how much Dad bled after he hit that old maple on his new sled? Does she remember going outside and playing in the snow, how I dragged her around for hours on our sled, how we licked icicles, how we made snowmen and snow angels and did all the dopey stuff kids are supposed to do never thinking for one minute one day it would all be taken away from us?

Is she sad or does she like it better out there? Does she do weird stuff like go swimming or play tennis on Christmas Day? Do they have a fake tree? Do they have a tree at all or do they decorate a cactus? Do they eat turkey and gravy or do they have a cookout and eat Christmas burgers and red and green macaroni salad? Does Jeff have his own set of memories from his childhood that he tells while he's drinking a margarita with a little paper umbrella in it?

Klint and I realize what's in the boxes and give each other stunned stares.

We take out the Arizona Diamondbacks sweatshirts and ball caps and hold them

gingerly in our hands like they might be contaminated with a flesh-eating disease.

If we were countries, this would be considered an overt act of war.

"She really hates me," Klint says under his breath.

He puts the offending items back in their box and pushes it as far away from him as possible.

I dig around in my box to see if there's anything else. All I find is a store-bought card signed, Love, Krystal.

"Is there a problem?" Miss Jack asks, peering at the contents of my box. "You wear sweatshirts and baseball caps all the time. I thought you liked baseball."

"We do like baseball," I explain, "but not this team."

"And that makes a difference?"

Klint continues shaking his head in dejection and disbelief. The tips of his ears have turned red.

"Yeah," I say. "A big difference."

"Here, Miss Jack," I say to her and hand her a box.

"What's this?"

"It's a present from me."

"This is entirely unnecessary," she says, sounding flustered, but she can't hide the pleasure in her eyes.

She takes the wrapping paper off very carefully like she might save it and use it again,

then pulls out the piece of pink, green, and yellow watercolored silk from the tissue paper.

She holds up the material and rubs it between her fingers.

"Kyle, I'm deeply touched. This is beautiful,"

"I know you like scarves."

She puts it over her head and laughs like a little girl playing dress up. For a brief moment, I see the woman she might have been if she had been able to spend her life with Manuel and maybe have children of her own. She's not an unhappy woman or a cold one. She's incomplete.

She takes off the scarf, folds it, and puts it back in the box.

"I promise I'll wear it very soon. And now, it's your turn."

Her eyes dart toward the biggest package. It's flat and rectangular.

I pull it toward me and tear off the wrapping paper. It's a wooden case with a gold clasp and leather handle. Inside it is a collection of paints, pencils, charcoals, and every size of brush.

"This is great," I gush. "I've never had a kit like this. I usually steal my art supplies from school."

Miss Jack smiles broadly and seems even more excited than I am.

"I'm glad you like it. I know you're going

to get a lot of use out of it. And now, Klint. That one is for you."

Klint's been off in his own world since opening Mom's gift. He hasn't been paying any attention to us, which is okay by me because I already know exactly what he thinks about scarves and art supplies.

Miss Jack points at a present that's obviously book shaped, but I'm not sure if Klint realizes this since he spends so little time around them.

I'm thinking it might be a classic novel like *Moby-Dick* or maybe *Table Manners for Dummies,* but it turns out to be *Clemente: The Passion and Grace of Baseball's Last Hero.*

Klint looks like he might cry when he opens it and sees Roberto's face on the cover, but I can't tell if it's because he's touched or because he knows he's going to have to read.

"Thanks," he tells her, sounding a little confused but also respectful.

He realizes she's managed to find a way to get him to undertake a task entirely against his will by giving him something he can't resist.

There's one small box left beneath the tree along with our gifts for each other, and we know they're computer video games because we picked them out and bought them together.

Klint reaches for it and hands it to Miss Jack.

"From me," he tells her.

"Thank you, Klint."

She opens the box and takes out a blown-glass horse the same bright pink color as El Soltero's socks.

I recognize it immediately.

"It was my mom's," Klint states flatly, his tone making it sound like Mom's been dead for years.

"Well, Klint. I don't know what to say," Miss Jack replies. "Shouldn't it still belong to your mother?"

"No. Kyle and I bought it for her when we were little. Remember, Kyle?"

I'm instantly stabbed by the unwelcome memory of the love I felt for Mom at the moment I spied the fragile treasure glimmering among tons of junk in the dusty front window of the Goodwill store in Centresburg, and how I understood in a flash of childish instinct that the only thing I wanted to do in my life was please her.

I nod.

"When she came back to get the rest of her stuff, she left it behind," Klint explains to Miss Jack.

"It was a mistake to give it to her. I know that now," he goes on, his words having a harsh, hollow sound to them. "But it's not my fault I didn't know it then. She was my mom. I trusted her."

He finishes his strange declaration.

Miss Jack looks to me for some kind of guidance as to how she should respond, but I can't offer her any. I'm not sure what he was talking about, but I don't think it had anything to do with a little glass horse.

"I didn't want to throw it away," he adds. "You like pretty things. I thought you might appreciate it."

She holds it up in front of her face and turns it from side to side to catch the light coming from the Christmas tree and admires the delicacy in the details of the mare's flowing mane and tail, the slenderness of her prancing legs, and the sparkle of her tiny fake gemstone blue eyes.

"I certainly do appreciate it," Miss Jack says solemnly and places it on an end table next to her chair where we all stare at it.

The richness of the room and its contents should overwhelm the little knickknack and make it look as cheap and common as it is, but it has its own stunning value.

Starr was supposed to eat dinner with us but she called and said she couldn't make it and would be over later.

We had a traditional Christmas turkey dinner with all the trimmings. Luis wasn't able to prepare a meal like this ahead of time, so Miss Jack had it catered because she insisted no one else on her staff — including the versatile Hen — can cook.

Later I find Miss Jack warming herself by the fire and then drifting off to stand in front of a painting in the room that I didn't notice earlier. I walk over and find another portrait of the same man, same suit, same cold penetrating black stare I've been forced to share my nights with.

"Is this your brother?" I ask her.

"Yes."

It's official, I tell myself: Satan's Banker is the Ruthless Bastard.

"What was he like?"

She purses her lips and taps them with the end of one of her index fingers while she considers the question.

"He was very ambitious. Very focused."

I nod. Ambitious, focused: the polite way of saying ruthless.

"Very self-assured," she goes on. "Very assertive."

I nod again. The polite way of saying bastard.

"Did he die instantly?"

"What a strange question," she exclaims, looking at me curiously.

She drops her hand away from her face and studies her brother again.

"I suppose he did. He had a massive heart attack while relaxing at home one night."

"Luis said El Soltero died instantly."

"Yes," she agrees haltingly. "That's what the newspapers said."

"The cop said my dad died instantly. I'm not so sure about it."

"Is it important to you?"

"Yeah, I guess. I don't like to think of him being scared and alone."

"I'm afraid there's no way to avoid being alone when we die. We're even alone when we're alive. We can surround ourselves with other people, with noise, with glory and possessions, but it doesn't change the fact that ultimately we must face everything by ourselves."

She continues staring at the portrait, and I'm sure she's talking to it and not me.

The tinkle of bells suddenly comes from somewhere outside the room. The sound gets louder, and Baby appears running at full speed wearing red booties, a red sweater, and a red elf hat, all of it adorned with white fur and jingle bells.

"Oh, good God," Miss Jack exclaims.

The dog runs past both of us and leaps onto the same chair where Miss Jack sat earlier.

All the color drains from her face.

Before she can do anything, Starr strolls into the room. She's dressed entirely in black. Her jeans are leather, her boots are sky high, and her sweater is scattered with tiny glittery stones that give the impression of stars against a night sky.

She's definitely not chasing after Baby. She

moves slowly but without seeming lethargic or lazy; she just seems like someone genetically incapable of hurrying.

"Merry Christmas, Aunt Candace."

"Get this animal out of here."

"I promised Mom I wouldn't leave him alone on Christmas Day."

We all look at the shivering Baby, who fixes us with eyes bulging from his small head like black marbles.

"He can't be in this house," Miss Jack insists.

"Oh, come on. It's just for a few hours.

"Hello, Kyle," Starr says on her way past me to grab up Baby.

A brief surge of excitement rips through me as I realize she remembered my name. I try to think of anything I can say that might interest her.

I wish she'd seen me a month ago when I still had my black eye and the gash on my forehead. Starr's exactly the kind of girl who could appreciate the merits of a man who can take a punch or two in the face.

I didn't receive as much notoriety from the fight at the dairy as I would've liked. I thought maybe I'd get a little credit for trying to fight back, and I also thought the black eye made me look tough. But the Hoppers and North didn't waste any time telling everyone that I was a fag who was carrying around an art book and a bunch of dirty

pictures of naked kids. By the time they got through talking about me, everyone thought I deserved to be beat up. Klint came out as the hero, as usual, because he defended me.

I expected further trouble. I kept waiting to be ambushed in the halls or dragged off behind the parking lot after school, but the Hoppers left me alone. This hasn't been much comfort for me, though. I'm still in a constant state of uneasiness. I've come to think of them the same way I think of the gigantic meteors that are supposedly circling the earth and will eventually destroy the planet: I know they're out there but by the time I realize they're coming at me it will be too late.

"Hey," is my brilliant response.

She doesn't smile at me, but there's amusement in her eyes.

"Where's Slugger?"

"He's around."

"Here."

She hands me Baby.

"You saved him. You can watch him."

She takes Miss Jack's arm.

"I'm going to visit with Aunt Candace."

Miss Jack casts a terrible look at the dog, then a pleading one at me.

I join Klint in his room, and we play one of our new computer games while keeping Baby occupied. About an hour passes before Starr shows up and tells us Miss Jack wants us to

join her for her traditional Christmas viewing of *It's a Wonderful Life.*

Klint tells her she's got to be kidding.

"No, I'm afraid not. We do it every year. But if you want, we can send your little brother to keep her company and you and I can have a beer."

Klint tears his eyes away from the screen.

"There's no beer here."

"I brought some. It's out in my car. What do you say, Slugger?"

"No way," I whine. "Don't make me watch a sappy Christmas movie with her by myself."

Starr ignores me and walks over and expertly exits the game for Klint.

"Come on," she urges.

He gets up and follows her.

I do the right thing and watch the movie with Miss Jack. I don't know where Starr and Klint went to or what they're doing until about halfway through the movie we hear the front door open and slam shut. Then Starr appears a few minutes later in her coat holding the trembling dog.

"I'm leaving now," is all she says.

She gives her aunt a kiss and tells me to hang in there.

After the movie is over I look everywhere for Klint but can't find him in the house. I begin to wonder if the slamming door was the sound of him leaving, but where would he be going and why?

I throw on my coat and go outside and take a seat on the top porch step. The night sky is hidden behind a blanket of winter clouds as white as the snow-covered ground. The world is without definition, without light or darkness, without sound, without shadows; a cold muffled place void of all color and life but somehow it's not uninviting. Sitting here I can almost believe I've stumbled through a tear in the fabric of reality and ended up in a parallel universe where everything begins as a blank and stays that way.

A flicker of movement breaks the pale stillness. I'm not fast enough to see what caused it, but I don't have to be because the cat shoots out from under a bush and dashes up the steps toward me.

I hardly see Mr. B in winter. He's been spending his nights in the barn since it turned cold, and during the day he leaves little evidence of his presence except for an occasional set of paw prints in the snow.

He stops and stares at me, trying to figure out if I'm an animal he can trust. His eyes are black and unforgiving against the white night; ruthless bastard eyes, the chipmunks would call them.

He comes closer, recognizes me, and begins to purr. I scoop him up and slip him inside my coat. The warmth of his body and the vibrations from his purring are starting to make me sleepy and I'm about to go back

inside when I see Klint walking up the driveway with his head bowed and his hands deep in his pockets.

He doesn't say anything — he won't even look at me — when I ask him where he's been.

I release Mr. B and go inside, too. Klint is nowhere to be seen.

On my way up to my room, I stop by the Nativity scene for a final reminder of the real reason for this holiday. All of the figurines gaze adoringly at the swaddled baby in the manger except for one shepherd holding a lamb in his arms looking toward the stars. His face is twisted with something that's probably supposed to be ecstasy but looks like terror to me.

Jesus: Now there's a guy no one ever tells you died instantly.

Chapter Eighteen: Luis

Ah, *mi familia.*

I can stand to be around them for two days.

One of the great mysteries of life is that of family ties. How is it that we can love people who drive us crazy? How is it that we can desperately miss people and then want to leave them again after only one paella and a few puffs of a Cuban cigar?

I have a wonderful family and they treat me like royalty each time I visit them. There are endless feasts, toasts to my health, blessings from my mother, presentations of new babies, and introductions to future spouses of my grandnieces and nephews. I'm not allowed to lift a finger, to wash a dish or make my bed or drive myself. I'm consulted about every topic under the sun from stock market investments to rap music. I'm asked how Bush was elected twice and if Angelina Jolie's relationship with Brad Pitt will survive.

However, along with this flattering faith in my foreign-bred wisdom comes the belief that

I should also be able to solve everyone's problems. I'm dragged into every family squabble and dispute no matter how big or small. I'm asked if I think Miguel's eldest son, Jose, who now runs our family hotel and restaurant, has made the right decision to add a swimming pool and lounge bar. I'm asked if it's right for my sister, Sofia, to continue snubbing my sister-in-law, Maria, for allowing one of her children to miss the christening of one of Sofia's grandchildren. I'm asked if Jaime should buy a Peugeot or Ford, if Ana's daughter should take a job in Colombia, if Javier (still the spoiled one) deserves Papa's humidor, and if five-year-old Leticia should get her ears pierced.

It's more than I can stand.

I've become a solitary man, or maybe more accurately I've always been one, but I came from a culture and a family that allowed for very little isolation. Manuel was the same. I think he sensed in me a kindred spirit, someone who needed to be left alone from time to time and allowed to be still and contemplative.

This quality also helped me to adjust to my adopted country.

America is a big sprawling place and historically, the people have always liked their space. It was forged by individuals who willingly faced immense virgin forests and the inescapable emptiness of the western prairies to

continue expanding an already vast nation.

A family might have traveled for months in a wagon train, but once they settled down, they didn't live in communities. All self-respecting families lived apart in their own little cabins facing an endless expanse of nothingness.

This way of life is inconceivable to a Spaniard. I won't go so far as to say we fear space; but it makes us very uncomfortable.

Even when we live rurally, we are an urban people choosing to reside huddled together with our neighbors in a tightly packed village of stone houses. Everyone is in everyone's business, and noise is a constant, much-needed presence to keep our thoughts away from the unfriendly wilderness surrounding us on all sides.

Today the narrow streets of Villarica reverberate with commotion and noise every night: people argue loudly on the streets, children run wild and mothers shout for them, little dogs wander without leashes yapping incessantly, motor scooters scream by like gigantic angry insects, the squawk of TV voices spills out from open windows, horns honk and teens whistle shrilly for their friends, old people bring their lawn chairs outside and sit by their front doors where they play cards and talk to every passer-by.

Compare this to the silent hum of an American town with everyone behind their

doors in their huge houses with their huge yards. Even within the houses the inhabitants rarely interact with one another. When I first arrived in America, I found this sad and unnerving.

Now I'm used to the wide open spaces and I crave the quiet. When I go back to Spain, the towns make me feel claustrophobic, and the din is unbearable (except for the bliss of siesta). I spend half my time shouting, "Callate!" at dogs and children, only to have them stare back at me without any comprehension as to why I'm upset.

My nieces and nephews call me Tio Puro Nervio. *An uncle who is made purely of nerves.* They find my impatience endearing.

I used to invite Candace to come along with me on these trips, but she always refused and eventually I stopped asking her. Since she has chosen to never reveal her relationship with Manuel to her own family and friends and never to discuss the trauma of his death, she has never been able to reduce the intensity of those memories. They've been trapped inside her for more than forty-five years, where she's been forced to face the full weight of them daily. If she had let them escape, they'd be nothing but harmless vapors by now that might still drift by her occasionally but that she could easily disperse with a wave of her hand.

She has never discussed Manuel with

anyone except me and her brother and now Kyle. I never realized until she began to open up to Kyle that all anyone ever needed to do to get her to tell her story was to ask.

I think it's been very good for her to have this boy to talk to; even though she hasn't revealed much, I've noticed a difference in her. A valve has been loosened.

The members of her own family are too self-absorbed to wonder about her past. Even Shelby, who is the kindest and most inquisitive of them all, has never had a desire to dig into her aunt's youth or tried to find an explanation for her unreasonable attachment to Spain.

The opposite is true in my family. The story of Manuel and Candace is a legend of mythic proportions. Each time I return I'm forced to tell the tale over, and it must always begin with the day they met.

Manuel Obrador spent all of his time out of the ring chasing after women who weren't running from him. He was caught in a perpetual child's game of tag where everyone lays down for the boy who is It. This can get boring after a while.

I was in awe of his conquests, but as a boy with many opinionated sisters and a strong, vibrant mother who was very much my father's equal, I was also troubled by them. He was sweet and kind to these women

before the act, then became cold and dismissive. Most of his dalliances were for one night only, and the few that continued longer rarely lasted more than a handful of torrid meetings.

He broke many hearts, and I don't think it's an exaggeration to say he destroyed some lives. This is what troubled me.

When I first started traveling with him, I was barely sixteen. Sex was on my mind frequently but unfortunately, never in my lap.

I would lie awake in bed at night in the hotel room I shared with Paco — the head banderillero and the oldest, most respected member of the cuadrilla — knowing very well what was going on in Manuel's room next door.

Earlier it would have been my job to approach the woman he had picked out from among the groupies crowding around the bus as he left the ring or hanging around the hotel where the bullfighters always stayed. Or if no one had appealed to him, sometimes I'd be sent out to find some professional talent.

Prostitution wasn't illegal — even if the brothels were banned in 1956 — and didn't have the same stigma attached to it in Spain that it did (and still does) in America. Considering the strict control Spanish society had always placed on its women, especially in matters of sex, it could have been argued that prostitutes provided a necessary and valuable

service. Most of the men I knew back then had lost their virginity to one.

I was looking forward to this happening to me. I was at an age where my physical longings far outweighed my emotional sensibilities and any romantic notions I might have had about falling in love yet I wasn't able to completely separate women as people from women as body parts, so in my fantasies I would imagine a conversation where I found the woman fascinating before I helped her to undress.

I was certain this would be easily possible in real life. Each time I'd bring a woman to Manuel's room I'd stand next to her staring at the curves of flesh beneath her tight dress and drinking in the smell of her perfumed hair, and she'd inevitably say something to me, whether it was to ask nervously if Manuel had a lot of girlfriends, or to restate her price, or to glance at me and growl, "Qué está mirando, chico?" *What are you looking at, kid?* I found every word out of their mouths to be charming.

Manuel would open his door, wearing a robe, in his bare feet, with his hair dripping from the shower. He'd give the girl one of his irresistible smiles and hand me his heavily beaded and bejeweled *traje de luces* that I'd take next door to my room and scrub in the bathtub.

Did he realize what had been placed in his

hands? I'd wonder as I walked away burdened by the weight of the suit and the knowledge of his callousness. Did he understand the magnitude of what he was about to be given?

Along with his one-night conquests he also had respectable relationships. He dated daughters of moguls and royals, but these women bored him because they required attention he didn't want to give and they did not surrender sex so easily.

He was nearing thirty and I thought his habits would never change, but then he met Candace.

We were in Madrid as we had been dozens of times before. Manuel had a corrida that night. It was a stiflingly hot day. The sky was intensely blue, and everything seemed to be covered in a thick syrup of heat.

We had just stepped out of our hotel, the Reina Victoria, on our way to meet the rest of the cuadrilla for lunch.

People were beginning to noisily fill up the tables and chairs outside the restaurants surrounding the square. Men were taking off their hats and suit jackets and opening their ties. Women were pulling their fans and cigarettes from their pocketbooks. Waiters weaved among the tightly packed patrons, their trays heavy with pitchers of ruby sangria and cold glasses of gold beer that would be warm before the first sip.

We began crossing Plaza de Santa Ana

when a woman passed before our eyes who made both of us slow our steps and come to a stop without realizing we'd done so.

She was lost in her thoughts, strolling, with a guidebook held loosely in one hand. She wore the colors of the day: a dress of blue one shade lighter than the sky cinched at the waist with a wide sun-yellow belt that matched her high-heeled shoes. Her hat was yellow, too, broad-brimmed, trimmed in blue ribbon, and from beneath it fell a mane of copper hair as silky and touchable as a show pony's.

We couldn't see her face, but we both instinctively knew it wasn't possible for a woman with that body, in those clothes, with that hair, and those legs to be anything less than heavenly.

Manuel came out of his spell and quickened his step after her.

I hurried to keep up.

I knew he was intrigued. Despite advances in relationships between males and females in our country, Spanish men still persisted in thinking of women as either Madonnas or whores. One who could be both was the most amazing creature on earth.

This woman was too well dressed to be thought of as a whore yet she was extremely sexy; she looked too independent and New World to be a Madonna yet she seemed somehow innocent.

"I want you to go talk to her," he whispered to me.

"Why don't you go talk to her?" I whispered back.

"I want to watch her from afar. You can tell much about a woman's character by the way she reacts to a stranger."

"Since when do you care about a woman's character?"

She stopped in front of the statue of Calderón de la Barca and he stopped, too.

She turned in our direction. Her eyes raked the crowds of people as though she was looking for someone.

Her face was beautiful.

"I know," he said excitedly. "I will come to her rescue. You can pretend to steal her purse."

"I will not!" I insisted.

"Then go talk to her. Ask her for directions."

"She should be asking me for directions. She doesn't look Spanish. She has a guidebook."

"So?"

"I only speak Spanish," I explained, my exasperation rising along with my fear that he was going to make me do something truly stupid. "Why would I try to ask for help from a woman who doesn't speak my language when I'm surrounded by thousands of people who do?"

"You think too much."

"I don't want to look like a fool."

"Go ahead."

He gave me a little push.

"Do it. I'll be right behind you."

I approached her reluctantly, constantly glancing back at Manuel, giving him many opportunities to call me away, but he didn't.

He stood beneath the awning of a café, smoking a cigarette, looking nonchalant in his gray suit and white shirt, attracting plenty of attention himself not only because he was famous but because, like her, he was also beautiful and commanded the eyes of everyone who saw him.

I had no idea what I was going to say to her.

I hoped with all my heart that she would suddenly see the person she'd been looking for and hurry off to greet him or that she'd just walk quickly away for no particular reason.

She didn't do either of these things. On the contrary, after scanning the crowd, she'd begun reading her guidebook with great intensity and showed no signs of moving.

"¿Con permiso, señorita, tiene fuego?" I asked her, then wanted to smack myself for my stupidity.

I had just asked her for a light and I didn't have a cigarette.

"I don't know," she told me with an embar-

rassed smile, then broke into a bit of very basic Spanish. "No sé. No hablo español. Lo siento."

Up close she was even lovelier, with skin like a peach-colored pearl and teal-green eyes the color of deep water in a motionless cove.

"Excuse me."

Manuel came up beside us.

"May I assist you?" he went on in English while casting a doubting look at me. "You can never be too careful. He might have been trying to steal your purse."

I opened my mouth to protest, but he grabbed my shoulder and squeezed.

"I don't think so," the woman replied and smiled at me again. At me. Not at Manuel. "He looks honest to me."

I puffed out my chest with pride. Not only was she standing up for me, she was standing up for me to Manuel. No one ever did that — not even his manager, one of the most powerful *apoderados* in the business.

"As I said, you can never be too sure," Manuel went on. "You're obviously a visitor to our city."

"Yes. I'm American."

"Ah, of course. American."

He fixed her with his bedroom eyes and gave her a slow, sensual smile that turned most women into giggling jelly or she-wolves with their tongues out.

She smiled back, but her gaze flicked play-

fully in my direction as if she thought — she knew — it was all a game and I was in on it, too, but on her side.

"Have you been to the Prado? To El Retiro?" he asked her.

"Yes."

"Have you seen a bullfight?"

"Yes."

"And what did you think?"

"It was very interesting."

This response seemed to puzzle him.

"Interesting? Do you remember which toreros you saw?"

"No, but I remember the bulls."

Without any encouragement, she began talking about each of the six bulls she had watched. She didn't know their names or even the breeder, but she remembered their appearances — everything from whether the tips of their horns turned up or down to the amount of branding on their hides — and she remembered their performances. Eager, confused, reluctant, aggressive, magnificent, mean: she described them all.

Manuel listened. It was the first time I could ever recall a woman's words holding his attention.

"Did it bother you that the bulls were killed?"

"No. Should it have?"

"I'm curious because you seem so fond of them."

"All bulls and cows are eventually killed for meat. It's their lot in life."

"And what is your lot in life?"

"To eat the meat."

Manuel smiled.

"Are you going to the bullfight tonight?" he asked.

"No, I'm afraid not. I just got back to Madrid this morning and there are no tickets left."

"I could get you one."

"How is that?"

"I have connections."

"I see."

"Where are you staying?"

"The Reina Victoria."

His smile became a grin.

"Did you know this is where all the bull-fighters stay when they come to Madrid?"

"Yes, I gathered that from all the photos on the walls of bullfighters and the mounted bulls' heads."

She gave me another one of her knowing glances.

"If you'll excuse me, I really must go."

"Your name? For when I leave the tickets."

"Candace. Candace Jack."

She turned her back to him and walked away. What I remember most vividly about that moment besides the sway of her hips and the shine of her hair was the fact that she didn't ask him for his name.

She went to the bullfight that night, and Manuel was brilliant. I didn't see her. I was too busy taking care of the capes and swords.

He knew exactly where she was sitting and as he took his victory stroll around the ring with a pasodoble playing and the applause swelling from the adoring crowd while flowers, shawls, and wine flasks were thrown at his feet, I'm certain he paused in front of her and made sure she knew who he was.

Yet afterward, she was nowhere to be found in the throng of fans waiting outside the toreros entrance hoping to catch a glimpse of their idols as they left.

He was certain then that she'd be waiting at the hotel bar for him.

She wasn't.

We went up to his room where I helped him undress. He immediately sent me back down to the lobby to wait for her while he took his shower.

She never showed up.

He declined eating dinner and celebrating with the cuadrilla, choosing to have tapas sent to his room while I continued to wait for her.

He had me ask the front desk manager if she had come in, and he told me she'd gone out earlier and hadn't returned.

Eventually Manuel came down to the bar where he took a seat and spent the rest of the evening with a cigar and a bottle of his favorite scotch, accepting congratulations and

brushing off advances. He was so agitated, he didn't take any woman to bed that night.

The next morning we were due to leave early. We had another corrida many miles away.

Manuel paced the lobby while we loaded the van, and finally in a fit of frustration demanded her room number from the front desk. The man working there had no choice but to give it to him. El Soltero was one of the princes the hotel had been built to serve.

He went racing upstairs while we threw up our hands, checked the clock in the church tower across the square, and shook our heads.

It's a cliché but it's true for this kind of man: when he finds a woman who isn't interested in him, he must have her.

I don't know what he said to her or what she said to him. I only know she was at the bullfight in Valencia that night. And afterward, he had dinner with her alone.

It's the end of a long Christmas Day that's been an endless cycle of eating, drinking, gift-giving, arguing, laughing, attending mass, and abusing Javier for still being Mama's favorite.

Kyle's caricatures were a big hit, especially the one of Javier who was drawn wearing a baby's bonnet, drinking a bottle, and sitting on Mama's knee who was depicted as a tenth of his size.

I'll be excited to tell Kyle he can have countless more commissions from my family if he'd be interested in the work.

I've stepped outside to get some air. This year was Teresa's turn to host the holiday. She and her husband have a beautiful finca not far from town, one of the many rewards for owning all of the olive orchards for as far as the eye can see.

Tomorrow I will pay a quiet visit to Manuel's sister, Maria Antonia. Rafael will be there as well, and we will talk about toreo and I will feel the old familiar pain and also the joy.

The sky is clear tonight, a deep indigo salted with white stars and dominated by a full moon that seems to swirl like a jostled saucer of milk if you stare at it for too long.

Candace will be sleeping under the same moon tonight four thousand miles away. I hope she had a nice day with Kyle and Klint. I hope she didn't try to buy them clothes for their Christmas gifts.

I've enjoyed my trip as I always do, but I'll be glad to go home. I've lived in America twice as long as I lived in Spain. Even so, to this day, I feel Spanish when I'm there yet when I come back to Spain, I feel utterly American.

People ask me which country I prefer and would I ever return permanently to my native one. I try to make them understand that

there is no competition between the two. It's not a question of advantages and disadvantages. I'm equally bound to both. The struggle lies in the difference between a lover choosing you or you choosing a lover. I belong to Spain but America belongs to me.

Part III
El Duende

Chapter Nineteen: Kyle

My dad spent a lifetime playing baseball, watching baseball, and talking and dreaming about baseball; yet somehow he managed to know nothing about the game except the most important thing and that was how it made him feel.

He was hopeless with numbers. He could never remember statistics or figures. RBIs and ERAs, the clocked speed of a fast ball, the eight thousand pounds of force when the bat meets the ball: all of this was lost on him. Half the time he couldn't remember the ball count from one player to the next.

He hated the men behind these numbers, the analysts sitting at their computers looking for hidden patterns in the games, the sports medicine doctors and scientists conducting tests and studies to find out how much force and rotation is needed for a pitcher to send a ball across a plate at more than a hundred miles an hour.

He hated the philosophers, too, the scholars

and writers, the guys who didn't play but sat around spouting romantic notions about the sport offering a peek into the American psyche or symbolizing man's eternal struggle to get to home.

As far as my dad was concerned, all these people missed the point. Baseball was a game. Nothing more, nothing less. But it was a helluva good game, one full of unpredictability, of mind-numbing boredom that could suddenly turn into lightning-quick displays of athletic prowess and mental magnificence, one that had moments of luck in the clutch — a ball missed, a ball caught, a double stretched into a triple, a stolen base, a soft fly dropped into the only spot in the park where no fielder could get to it — that were so unbelievable, watching them unfold before him made him feel like he was part of something bigger than his own shitty little existence, that he'd been let in on a great cosmic secret.

He'd take that knowledge and joy to work with him the next day. We're all the same. No one is better or worse. We're all just banking on the hope that at any moment something astonishing can happen.

But I think the thing my dad liked most about baseball was that it was a game where errors determined the outcome. One team's superior abilities didn't matter nearly as much as how many mistakes the other team

could get them to make.

What was most important wasn't a man excelling but a man getting the other guy to screw up. Dad could relate to that.

I don't think Klint has ever played a game without my dad watching him. I don't know how many people sitting here on the bleachers know this.

I know Bill does, but he's so busy thinking about the fact that he's never watched Klint play a game without my dad watching that I know he's not concerned about Klint.

I'm pretty sure Coach Hill does, but it's impossible to tell with Coach. This isn't because he keeps his feelings hidden. (At every game he displays a wide array of emotions ranging from mad to angry to really pissed off.) It's because he doesn't allow himself to ever think about other people's feelings. His players aren't even supposed to have feelings. They have positive mental zones where they visualize everything they're going to do correctly in the upcoming game and the pizza they'll get afterward.

I doubt he's worried about Klint, especially since he's been playing better than ever during this past month of practice. All Coach cares about is that his physical talent is still there. What's going on in his head and heart isn't his concern. He doesn't see him at home. He doesn't hear him wandering around in the middle of the night when he

should be asleep. He doesn't realize that he never jokes around anymore. He doesn't know he's struggling more than usual in all his classes. He doesn't understand that he's lost his love of Doritos and Little Debbie Oatmeal Cream Pies.

I worry about Klint, but I don't know what I'm worried about and that makes it hard to do anything.

Sometimes I think I'm the one with the problem, and he's fine. For instance, I worried like crazy he was going to fall apart and not be able to play ball this season. He's been playing better than ever, but instead of me feeling relieved, I feel a kind of dread.

Each time I've watched him in a scrimmage step up to the plate and I hear the crack when the ball hits the bat and gets drilled over the shortstop's head, instead of jumping out of my seat screaming and shouting with joy, my throat closes up and my stomach crunches into a knot.

Today is his first official game. I have no doubts he'll play fine, and I can already tell this is going to bother me.

The turnout's not too bad for a cold, crappy day. There's the usual hard-core parents who show up no matter what the weather's like, and since the school we're playing isn't too far away, some of those parents have driven over.

A couple dozen students have shown up,

too. It's the first of April and spring definitely hasn't sprung yet, but everyone's already gotten rid of their coats and boots and are only wearing sweatshirts and gym shoes. Their shoes are soaked and covered with mud from the earlier rain. They're sitting in knots, hunched over their knees, their hoods pulled up over their heads, stamping their feet and rubbing their hands together for warmth. Sitting on these bleachers when they're cold is like sitting on a slab of ice.

The Flames also get their share of regular fans since they're a top-twenty team. Only sixteen teams per division make it to the state championships and we were one of them last year, but we got knocked out in the first elimination round by one run. It was Brent Richmond's error.

His dad freaked out so much, we all felt bad for him even though he's a total jerk. School was out by then and their whole family immediately left town for a two-week vacation. They came back without Brent.

A lot of rumors flew around. Some people said his dad killed him in the Virgin Islands where they have a time-share and dumped his body off a yacht into the Caribbean. Some said they sent him to a baseball camp in Cuba. Others said a church camp in Mississippi. Still others said they brought him back home and his dad killed him here and buried him under the foundation of one of the new

houses he was building in his latest Sunny Valley subdivision.

(Mr. Richmond was so upset about Brent's screwup that he even gave the new streets in this section sort of disturbing names. That was almost a year ago, and there are still people who won't buy a house on Whimpering Dog Lane.)

It turned out Brent spent the summer in a kind of boot camp where people send their misbehaving or poorly performing athlete kids to get a taste of what army life was going to be like if they didn't shape up and snag college scholarships in their respective sports.

Brent's folks could pay for his college, but his dad insisted his kid wasn't going to have his life handed to him on a silver platter — and then he would hand him a hundred dollars to fill the gas tank in his new SUV and let him keep the change.

Mr. Richmond's here today standing off to one side in a tan trench coat under a big black umbrella even though it's not raining anymore. He's frowning and talking to someone on his cell phone.

His wife's not here. She never comes out in bad weather.

"Looks like it's starting to clear off," Bill tells me.

I look above me at the sky. Not even the smallest patch of blue is showing through the clouds, but they've begun to lighten from a

soot gray to a dirty sock gray.

"Yeah," I reply.

Bill's already opened one of the bags of chips he brings to every game. He holds it out to me, and I take a handful. He also always brings a twenty-two-ounce Big Gulp cup filled with beer. He takes a few slurps through the red straw and looks innocently around him.

He hasn't said anything to me about how weird it is to be sitting here without Dad. He hasn't even asked about Klint except for his usual questions about how life is with Miss Jack.

I tell him what I always tell him: it's okay. And I'm not lying. It's not as good as living with parents who love you, but Miss Jack's not that bad. I see why people think she's mean and call her a snob, but I think she's just very private. She's not a touchy-feely person. She has very strong opinions, but she'll seriously listen to yours, too, before telling you you're wrong. I think I could go to her with pretty much any problem, and she would do her best to help. I'd like to talk to her about Klint, but I don't know what I'd say.

"There's Klint," Bill tells me and gives my arm a nudge.

He's stepped out of the dugout for a minute. His red jersey with the number 8 emblazoned on the back is still clean for the

time being, but his white pants and socks are already spattered with mud from warming up. His white batting glove hangs limply from a back pocket. He has his arms crossed over his chest and is staring out at the fence at the far end of the field where he hopes to send a few balls this afternoon.

"Hey, Klint!" Bill shouts through cupped hands.

Klint has always refused to look at anyone yelling for him in the stands, even Dad, but he raises one hand in acknowledgment.

Bill grins happily. One ritual successfully completed.

I'm watching Klint when I notice Doc and his brother, Nate, the baseball coach at Western Penn, walking over to the diamond. Coach Hill joins them and exchanges a few words with Nate, then goes back to his clipboard while they continue on their way over here to the bleachers.

College coaches don't usually show up to scope out the talent during the regular school season because they're busy with their own seasons, but Western Penn is nearby and I know they don't have a game tonight. Coach Pankowski probably ducked out of practice to come have a look.

I'd never say hi to a teacher, even one I like, so I start looking around everywhere except where Doc's standing; eventually, though, my eyes sweep by him and he sees

me and waves at me then gestures for me to join them.

I get up as reluctantly as I can, put a little scowl on my face, and clump down the metal steps doing my best to look like I have no choice.

"Hi, Kyle," Doc greets me.

"Hey, Mr. Pankowski."

"Kyle, this is my brother, Nate. He's the head coach at Western Penn."

"Yeah, I know."

He holds out his hand, smiling. I take it and he shakes my hand vigorously.

"Nice to finally meet you, Kyle. I've met your brother and your dad. I'm very sorry about what happened."

"Yeah. It's okay. Thanks."

At first glance, Doc and his brother don't appear to resemble each other at all, but the more you watch them, the more you realize they look almost exactly alike except Doc is long and stretched out, thoughtful and weary, and looks older than his years, while Nate is cheerful and compact, full of pep with the face Doc might have had when he was ten. He also talks with his hands while Doc keeps his buried deep in the pockets of his baggy corduroy blazer.

"Kyle's one of my top students," Doc tells him. "He's got a bright future ahead of him."

"Yeah, if my future's taking true or false tests about ancient Rome," I say.

They both laugh. I'm feeling pretty good.

"And what about your brother's future?" Nate asks.

I frown and shrug.

"It's no secret how poorly he's doing in school right now," Doc provides.

"You know even with his talent, he's not going to be able to get scholarships with bad grades," Nate adds.

"I know."

"Who's he looking at? He leaning toward any one school?" Nate asks me.

"I don't know. Not really anyone in particular. He already had a lot of schools sniffing around him at the end of last summer: South Carolina, Florida State, Wichita, Virginia."

Nate nods and smiles.

"Big names. Big teams."

"Yeah. That's what he wants. He's got it in his head if he doesn't go to a school with one of the top nationally ranked programs, he'd be a failure."

"That's a shame," Nate says. "You know a lot of kids think that way, but what they don't realize is the school or the program might not be right for them, no matter how good it looks on paper. They're not baseball machines, after all. They're human beings with different personalities and backgrounds and plans for their futures. They also usually can't get the same amount of scholarship money from a big school as they can from a smaller

one. I'd like to talk to Klint about all this."

"Yeah, well, good luck."

He laughs.

"You don't sound like you have much confidence in my recruiting techniques."

He leans forward confidentially.

"Haven't you heard I got a shot at Shane Donner?"

"Yeah, I did hear that. I wondered if it was true. Wasn't his fastball clocked at ninety-five miles per hour?"

"Sure was. Everyone was amazed when he didn't sign a letter of intent this past fall. He's going to graduate in two months and everyone's circling. He'll probably get drafted in the third or fourth round and could pull in a half-million-dollar professional contract, but his parents are insisting on college and they love Western Penn. Both his brother and sister went there."

He pauses.

"Klint's never hit off him, has he?"

"He would've," I tell him, "if we would have made it to the semifinals last year."

We all automatically look over at Mr. Richmond who's still on the phone.

"I'd sure love to see that," Nate says wistfully. "Hopefully it'll happen this year."

"And what about you, Kyle?" Doc breaks in. "Where would you like to see your brother play? Would you be okay with him all the way down south in Florida or across the country

in Kansas?"

"Well, you know, I'd miss him but it's his life."

"Would you continue living with Candace Jack?"

"I guess. I don't know. I haven't really talked to her or my mom about it."

"What do you think about Western Penn?"

"I don't know. It's a good school, I guess. If Klint went there, I could live with him."

"In his dorm room?" Nate asks. "Where would you sleep?"

"I could hang upside down from the ceiling like a bat."

They both laugh again.

"I can tell you've given it a lot of thought," Nate says. "Hey, I'd like to have you and Klint come over to the school some time. Check out a practice. Meet the team. You could even check out a dorm room." He winks at me. "Take some measurements."

He hands me a business card.

"E-mail me or give me a call any time."

"Okay, sure."

"We'll let you get back to your seat. They're starting to announce the lineup," Doc says. "See you in school tomorrow."

I hear Klint's name called over the loudspeaker. I don't bother to watch him trot out to second base, but I do stop and turn around when Tyler's announced and the crowd erupts into wild applause.

He jogs backward to first base, a huge grin on his face, his arms held in the air in a victory sign.

He has a big family, plus he's a popular guy with the fans. All his siblings are here, and they've all brought friends. His parents will show up later when they get off work.

I cheer for him like everyone else. His pack of sisters wave at me, and I wave back before taking my seat.

Two seconds later one of his sisters sits down next to me. She's a beauty with long, blond curls and big, blue eyes who wears little lace-trimmed denim miniskirts all the time and this great-smelling peppermint perfume. She's also madly in love with me.

She's six. This is my luck.

"Hi, Britney."

"Hi, Kyle," she smiles at me and snuggles up next to my arm. "I made you something."

Her words, the candy smell of her, the small, warm, soft weight of her all mix together and send an unexpected stab of pain into my heart. She reminds me too much of Krystal at that age.

"No kidding? What is it?"

Britney produces the picture she'd been holding behind her back.

It's the usual little kid subject matter: an apple tree and a house with a family standing in front of it. In Britney's case, a very large family. She's also added a dog they don't have

that's bigger than any of the people and a couple of pink cats that look a lot like piglets. It's very cheerful and colorful except for the black clouds in the sky spitting out black raindrops.

On the back she's written: Roses are red, violets are blue, today is yucky, I love you.

"Did you write this poem all by yourself?" I ask her.

She nods.

"Nikki helped me spell."

"This is really nice."

"Are you going to hang it in your bedroom?"

"Sure."

"Tyler says you live in a mansion now."

"Yeah, it's kind of a mansion, I guess."

"Do you got a swimming pool?"

"No."

"Do you got a movie theater?"

"No."

Soft creases of confusion appear on her smooth little forehead as she tries to figure out what kind of stupid mansion I'm living in.

Bill gets to his feet.

"What the hell?" he shouts. "Come on! What was that? What're you thinking, Martelli? What're you, blind? Get your head out of your ass!"

"Did Tyler do something wrong?" Britney asks me.

"No. The left fielder did."

Bill's not the only one expressing his displeasure at the error, but the commotion quickly dies down.

No one is bothered by the name-calling and the occasional curse word. It's considered a good healthy display of the crowd's love for its team, which translates into a desire for the team to win and therefore a need to tell certain players they suck.

I definitely prefer our more colorfully expressive parents over some of the types I've encountered at other schools.

The two types that bother me the most are the well-off, social-time moms who don't spend any time actually watching their sons play because they're too busy loudly bragging to each other about how drunk they got on their last Club Med vacations and how much the new marble countertops in their kitchens cost.

And then there's the self-esteem moms who have mindless smiles pasted on their faces throughout the entire game no matter how badly their team is losing, who bring healthy snacks no one wants to eat, who call out ridiculous lies every time someone screws up like, "Nobody cares. It's okay," or "You'll do better next time," or the worst one of all, "Everyone's a winner."

Everyone's not a winner, I want to explain to them, and telling people who are losers

that they're winners isn't good for anybody. How are kids who suck ever going to get better if people tell them they're good when they're not?

I'm not saying our parents are perfect. Sometimes they go a little too far, like the time Cody Brockway's dad took his belt off and chased Cody around the field during a Little League game after he fumbled a groundball.

But for the most part, they're just being honest with us. They aren't worried about hurting our feelings or treading on our self-worth. This isn't because they don't love us. It's because they understand we come from a place where we need to hear the truth about what we are, not a lie about what we're never going to be.

"A double. A damn double," Bill grumbles as he sits down again.

"Look at this, Shel. I think we've got some competition."

My head turns at the sound of Starr's voice. I can't believe what I'm seeing. Shelby told me she didn't think she'd be able to come to the game, and I didn't even know Starr was still around. The last I heard about her from Miss Jack, she had run away to India.

"Hi," Shelby says as she smiles prettily at Britney. "I'm Shelby. What's your name?"

"Britney."

"Are you Kyle's girlfriend?" she asks, wink-

ing at me.

"No," Britney giggles.

"She's one of Tyler's sisters," I explain.

"Oh."

"You better get back to your family, Brit," I tell her.

She goes scampering off with the agility of a kid who spends a lot of her time on baseball bleachers.

I'm so happy to see Shelby, I can almost make myself forget that she's not here to see me; she's here to watch Klint.

I'm glad to see Starr, too. I've never been able to get Klint to tell me what happened between the two of them on Christmas Day. It's a closed subject like so many subjects with him.

Starr's got on the kind of plaid cap old Irish guys are always wearing in movies about old Irish guys and a bulky cream-colored sweater over her usual skintight jeans tucked into high-heeled boots. She's completely covered up, but her presence feels so naked to me, I can't look at her directly.

Shelby sits down next to me, taking over the spot where Britney had been. Again I feel a warm soft weight against me and smell a sweet girl smell, but this combination has a different effect on me than the first one. It's not emotional pain I feel coming from loss. It's physical pain I feel coming from desire.

I want to put my arm around her. She's

rubbing her own arms because of the cold. It should be easy. I even have a reason to do it. But I can't.

Before Shelby left for France, I was too intimidated by the differences in our backgrounds to try and make a move. Now that she's returned, I'm too intimidated by the difference in her. She ended up spending six months in Paris and came back serenely sophisticated. She talks passionately about politics, surrealists, and cheese. She drops French phrases into every conversation. Her color-coordinated, perfectly put together outfits have become a careless wardrobe of textured tights, patterned miniskirts, and slouchy tops in black and other neutrals. She always wears a scarf wrapped around her neck — even when it's not cold — and she gives everyone air kisses on both cheeks.

She's been out to Miss Jack's house twice since she's been back and spent both times talking to her aunt. I was invited to sit in on the conversations but after a few minutes, I felt like an outsider.

I remembered Hen telling me the night of the fight with the Hopper brothers that she thought Shelby was sheltered and I was worldly, and I wanted to laugh out loud.

"Where's your hotshot brother?" Starr asks me.

"Second base," I tell her.

The words are hardly out of my mouth

when a groundball is hit between second and third. Klint snags it on the first bounce, tags the runner who hit the double only moments earlier, and throws out the hitter on first.

It was a play he could do in his sleep and one that wouldn't receive any excessive praise from Coach Hill but the smoothness and beauty of that one fluid motion — snag, tag, throw to Tyler — has everybody on their feet.

"A bee-yooooo-tee-ful double play by Klint Hayes," the announcer booms.

Shelby bursts into shrieks and squeals that sound like something I'd expect from Britney. She claps, whistles, and jumps up and down.

Starr has stood up, too, but only because she had to in order to see what was going on. She doesn't clap or scream, but she smiles at me as she rolls her eyes at Shelby before sitting down and taking a pack of cigarettes out of her purse.

She leans forward to light her cigarette, and her hair falls over her face like a veil. She parts it with her fingers and sees me watching her. I turn back to the game.

Shelby squeezes my arm.

"He's going to be okay," she whispers.

"Yeah, he's good."

The next batter hits a fly ball to Matt Martelli, and he's able to redeem himself.

Klint and his teammates jog into the dugout.

"Excuse me, Miss."

The woman sitting in front of us cranes her head around and glares at Starr.

"There's no smoking allowed here."

Starr slowly takes her cigarette out of her mouth and blows a long stream of smoke in the woman's direction.

"Says who?"

"It's a public place," the woman says indignantly.

"So?"

"There are children here."

"So?"

"Smoking can kill you."

Starr leans forward over her bent knees.

"Don't worry, lady. You have a much better chance of dropping dead from a heart attack caused by those fifty extra pounds you're lugging around than by being exposed to a couple minutes of outdoor secondhand smoke."

She sits back, smiling, and blows another cloud of smoke at her.

Everyone around us falls silent. The woman picks up her purse and leaves along with another fat woman sitting beside her.

Shelby's face has turned pink with embarrassment.

I'm pretty embarrassed, too.

People wonder why jerks rule the world. It's because everyone gets up and goes and

sits somewhere else instead of dealing with them.

Starr was being a jerk, but I forgive her almost immediately. It's hard for me to hold anything against a girl this good-looking, but Shelby obviously doesn't feel the same way. I can tell that she's genuinely upset with her sister, another sign of her newfound maturity. The old Shelby looked up to Starr, went to her for advice, and admired her wild behavior even thought she didn't approve of it, but right now she looks almost disgusted by her.

Cody Brockway, long since recovered from his days of fleeing from his father, is our leadoff man. He hits a two-bouncer into near left field and makes it safely to first in part due to his superior speed. The next two batters strike out, then Klint steps up to the plate.

The fielders adjust their positions. It's more subtle than it used to be when he was a kid and everybody just moved as far back as they could go. Now it's about infielders and outfielders alike trying to fill in the holes while knowing if he gets a piece of something good, it's all a waste of time.

The first two pitches are balls. The third is a strike, an inside pitch he misjudged, and I can tell as he moves away from the plate that he's pissed at himself.

Coach Hill yells something at him. He

doesn't turn around. He goes back into the box.

Klint swings faster than most high school hitters, so he can take more time to commit himself. The ball is one-third of the way to the plate and he hasn't begun to swing yet but I can tell he's decided to do it by the way he moves his weight to his back leg and cocks his fists back.

At this point his eyes have left the pitcher and are focused on a zone right in front of the plate. He lets loose with a roundhouse swing and the ball scorches into right center field, taking two bounces before coming to rest in front of the home-run fence. He's already running to first base as he completes his swing.

The right fielder goes after the ball. By the time he gets his throw to the cutoff man, Klint has rounded second with no intention of taking the easy double and Cody is already at home.

All the fans are on their feet again, the cold and wet forgotten.

Klint slides. The third baseman takes the throw high. He slaps down the tag, but Klint's beaten it.

Bill's cheering so hard, he's almost crying.

He grabs my arm the same way Shelby did and says the same thing, "He's going to be okay."

I watch my brother get up from the field.

For a moment I think he's covered in blood but it's only mud.

Chapter Twenty

Starr disappeared right after the game, but Shelby waited around long enough to say hi to Klint. I watched them standing next to his truck, her in Parisian black and a pink scarf and him in a mud-stained baseball uniform. He didn't say anything just nodded now and then. She chattered away giving him adoring smiles.

Even six months in France hasn't changed her opinion about Klint. It's unbelievable. She's stopped liking cheddar but not him.

Klint has a truck. Klint has a beautiful, rich girl in love with him. Klint has the potential to be a famous professional athlete. Klint has everybody in the world worried about him.

He's lucky he's my brother or I'd hate his guts.

No one's worried about me. Maybe a few people were for a little while, but it was over pretty quickly. They didn't follow me around holding their breath to see what my grades would be like after Dad died. When they saw

I got an A on my first geometry test, they didn't grab each other's arms and cry, "He's going to be okay!"

No one asked about my drawings, or my eating habits, or if I'm still able to masturbate effectively.

The really funny thing is, the only person in the world who ever seemed to care more about me than about Klint was Mom; but I don't know what that's worth since she woke up one day and decided she didn't care about me at all.

The game on Thursday was good. The Flames won 4–1. But the game today had been great. A 12–2 blowout called in the fifth inning. Klint hit a triple and two singles, had two RBIs, and scored twice himself. Brent Richmond hit a home run with two men on. Cody Brockway loaded the bases with a bunt and a blazing sprint to first, and then Tyler hit the double that brought two of them home.

It's a Saturday and since the game ended earlier than expected, a bunch of the guys were planning to go over to Lucky Lanes and bowl a few games then head to Quaker Steak & Lube for some hot wings.

They invited me to come along, too. This year they're a lot nicer to me. Maybe it's because they feel sorry for me after Dad died or because I grew four inches in one year or because I'm in high school now and I'm not

a puny middle-school kid anymore. Whatever the reasons, I don't care. I plan to take full advantage of any opportunity to improve my social life. Not to mention, baseball players attract some of the best-looking girls.

I walk into Klint's room just as he's finished his shower. He's got on his jeans and he's going through his drawer full of T-shirts even though there's only three he ever wears. He finds one of them and pulls it on over his head.

"Do you know how much money Miss Jack makes off Ventisco's jizz?"

"What?"

"I'm serious. They sell his stuff. Twenty grand a pop for prize bull semen."

"Are you shitting me?"

"No. Luis and Jerry were talking in the barn just now. They're getting ready to bring Ventisco in to hook him up to this machine that basically jerks him off . . ."

Klint makes a face at me.

"Enough. Thanks."

"I can't wait to finally see him."

"Yeah, great. Have a good time. Maybe the two of you can wank off together."

He takes a seat on the corner of his bed and starts pulling on his socks.

"I would if somebody'd pay me twenty grand."

"Nobody'd even pay you twenty cents."

"Nobody'd even take it off my hands for free."

Klint looks up from tying a shoe, and he's actually smiling.

I look past him at the blankets bunched up on the unmade bed and notice something moving.

I walk over and see a stretched-out Mr. B rolling over onto his back. He opens one eye and looks up at me.

"What the hell? Mr. B? What's he doing here?" I ask, completely stunned. "He's not allowed in the house."

"She doesn't know."

I sit down next to my cat and scratch him between the ears. He starts purring. For once the sound doesn't make me feel good. Shelby's bad enough because she never belonged to me, but this is a serious betrayal.

Mr. B and Klint have always mutually hated each other, but then I remembered the way Baby took to him and how Klint seemed reluctant to give him back.

"I thought you hated him," I say, angrily.

"I was walking around outside one night when I couldn't sleep. He followed me in. I think he was cold. He's an old cat."

"No, he's not."

"Yeah, he is. Look at him. You don't have any idea how old he was when you found him."

I keep petting him, but his purring slacks

off quicker than it used to. He's in a sound sleep already.

Great. Someone else to lose. My cat's going to die. Suddenly, I don't want him around at all. I want him to be gone already. I don't want to wait for it.

"Are you gonna take him to college with you?" I ask.

"Are you nuts? The cat's just lying on my bed. Big deal. He's your cat. I don't want him."

Just as quickly as I was overcome with anger, now I'm overcome with grief. I feel like I'm going to start crying for Mr. B because Klint doesn't want him.

"You know you're gonna have to start getting serious about college soon."

"It's only spring of my junior year. A lot of guys don't decide where they're going 'til they graduate."

"Not if you're serious," I start riding him. "Not if you're serious about big schools and big scholarship money. You're going to have to sign a letter of intent in the fall."

"Lay off," Klint shouts at me.

"How about going over to Western Penn next week and checking out the team? Coach would let you miss a practice."

I've really gotten under his skin. The tips of his ears are turning red.

"What the fuck's the matter with you? You're the one who's obsessed with my future

and now you want me to go to a crappy college?"

"Western Penn's not crappy. It's just smaller than the other schools you're looking at. You know, they've got a shot at Shane Donner."

"Shane Donner," he scoffs. "Give me a break. He's going pro."

"Why do you always think the worst of everybody?"

"How is making shitloads of money being a pro pitcher thinking the worst of somebody?"

"I don't know."

"Why do you have such a bug up your ass about college?"

I don't answer right away.

"You don't think I can hack it in the majors, do you?" he spits at me.

"That's not it. It's just . . . what if something goes wrong? There's all kinds of things that can happen even to the world's greatest players."

"And you think a college degree will save me?"

"At least it's something. I don't want you to be one of those broken-down guys playing on some farm team going out drinking every night."

Like Dad, we both silently finish the sentence.

"No, I'll be one of those broken-down guys with a useless college degree working in a cubicle going out drinking every night. You

think too much about the future."

"You never think about it."

"Maybe I don't care. Maybe I don't want a future."

"What do you mean? You're going to have a future whether you want it or not. You might as well try and make it a good one."

"I don't have to have a future. That's my choice. That's the one fucking choice in this world no one can take away from me."

"What are you talking about?"

He gets up and strides toward the door.

"Wait up for me," I call after him.

"No way. You stay here. I don't need you hanging around me worried about me all the time like some fucking faggot."

I follow him out into the hall.

"Come on," I beg.

He keeps going, never looking back, his way of dealing with everything: don't deal with it.

I feel tears burning my eyes. I wanted to go do something. I'm tired of never having fun.

I look in Klint's room. Mr. B yawns at me.

"Traitor," I yell and pull Klint's door shut, then go to my own room and slam the door behind me.

I throw myself on my bed.

I really miss my dad right now. My dad never solved a problem in his life, but he could always make me not care about the problems I had.

If he were here right now, the last thing he'd

do is let me talk about my feelings. He'd never sit around and listen to me call Klint a selfish jerk. (He'd never let me say anything bad about Klint.) He'd have no interest in hearing about Shelby, about how she thinks I'm a cute, nice guy — which is the kiss of death when it comes to the possibility of ever getting laid — or how Mr. B's affection for me turns out to be meaningless because he'll hang out with any asshole with a warm bed, or how much it bothers me that Krystal hates me now, or how much I miss my mom every day.

He wouldn't want to hear about these things because he couldn't change any of them and that would make him feel bad, but he wouldn't want me to feel bad either because he loved me, so what he'd do instead is take me with him to Wal-Mart to pick up some new long underwear for our next hunting trip, or take me over to the Go-Kart track and let me beat him every time, or let me drive the truck once we turned off the main road, or have me come sit with him and watch TV and let me drink a beer.

Dad wasn't a fixer; he was a distracter. But when none of your problems are fixable, a distracter can be your best friend.

There's a knock on my door.

I know it's Miss Jack. She probably heard me slam the door.

"I'm doing my homework," I call out.

"Are you kidding me? On a Saturday afternoon? You can't possibly be that boring."

It's Starr. I didn't even get to say good-bye to her after Thursday's game. She disappeared into thin air like she has a habit of doing. Sometimes I'm convinced she's not entirely real.

I go open the door.

"I thought you were Miss Jack," I explain immediately, trying to appear as cool as any guy can be who's spending his Saturday alone and doesn't even have a TV or an Xbox in his room.

"Obviously," she says, peering over my shoulder. "Can I come in?"

"Sure."

She walks past me, and I stand in the doorway and watch her.

It's the first time I've seen her bare legs. She's wearing a black miniskirt and a pair of high-heeled shoes. Her white shirt looks like a businessman's. She has the cuffs rolled up, the collar open, and a lot of the buttons undone. She's carrying a purse, a leather jacket, and the cap she wore to Klint's ball game. She throws it all on my bed and turns around to face me.

"I was visiting my aunt and thought I'd come say hi. Thought it would be the polite thing to do."

I'm trying hard not to stare at her legs, but their length and nakedness make it almost

impossible. When I try and look up, I'm staring at her boobs in a black bra peeking out of her shirt. Making eye contact with her is the worst thing of all because I feel like she can see into my brain.

I'm spending so much effort trying to figure out where I can look, I'm incapable of making conversation.

"I saw your brother rushing out of here with his usual scowl on his face. Does he ever lighten up?"

"He's got a lot on his mind."

"I bet," she says.

She picks up her purse and takes a flask out of it. She opens it, takes a drink, and extends it to me.

"How old are you, Kyle?" she asks while I take a swallow.

It's whiskey. I'm not used to drinking it, but I do my best to seem nonchalant.

"Fifteen," I cough out.

She starts strolling around my room, touching things. She stops in front of Stan Jack's portrait, and I realize with a sinking heart that I never took down the T-shirt this morning.

She yanks it off and laughs when she sees it's her grandfather in the picture.

"Scary SOB, isn't he?"

"Kind of," I reply.

She covers him back up and continues checking out my stuff.

"I remember fifteen," she says. "I lost my virginity when I was fifteen. A friend of my dad's. He got me really drunk. I threw up afterward."

She laughs.

"Don't worry. You should see the look on your face. I wasn't raped or anything like that. I was willing. As a matter of fact, I'd been a terrible flirt with him."

She takes another slug from the flask.

"I thought I wanted to do it, then when it came down to the moment, I didn't but it was too late."

"Kind of like committing to a pitch," I suggest, not quite sure what's appropriate small talk for this particular subject.

"Once you start your swing, you gotta follow through even if you know you're going to strike out," I further explain.

"Something like that," she says, smiling. "You know a lot about baseball."

"Sure."

"But you don't play? It's all from watching your brother?"

"I guess."

"Why don't you play?"

"Sports aren't my thing."

"What is your thing?"

"I don't know."

She stops in front of the art kit Miss Jack got me for Christmas and picks up one of the brushes. I have it opened up next to the

painting I'm working on now.

"I'd say art's your thing. Interesting subject matter for a fifteen-year-old boy."

"It's for my sister."

"I didn't know you have a sister. Where is she?"

I join her where she's standing in front of my desktop easel looking at the painting of the four fairies representing earth, sky, sea, and fire. Sky is an ethereal blonde draped in silvery white and pale blue. Fire is a redhead in scarlet with wings that look like flames. Sea has lavender curls tangled with green seaweed and is covered in glistening multicolored scales like a rainbow trout. Earth is a brunette wearing a bikini made of leaves and nothing else. She looks a lot like Shelby. I hope Starr doesn't see the resemblance.

"She's in Arizona with my mom."

"So your mom just took your sister and left? Was your dad okay with it?"

"No, but he didn't really have a choice."

"What do you mean? Of course he had a choice. One parent can't just run away with one of the kids. He could've hired a lawyer."

I shake my head.

She hands me the flask, and I take another drink.

"We couldn't have afforded anything like that. Plus I don't think my dad saw the point in trying to drag back someone who didn't want to be with him. He didn't want to fight

with her. He couldn't make himself hate her no matter how much people told him he should."

"Your dad sounds like a decent guy. What did he do?"

"He was a miner when he was young, then he got laid off."

"Good old J&P Coal." Starr toasts me with her flask and drinks again. "What a bunch of bastards we are."

"The last job he had was being a janitor," I add quietly.

"Then you should be really proud of yourself. And your brother, too. You're both going places. Moving up in the world."

I know what she's implying. I don't say anything because I could never explain how I feel about my dad to someone like Starr.

I might end up being more than him but not better.

"It's a beautiful painting," she says.

"It's not done yet. I still have a lot of work to do. And I want to add some glitter. She used to love glitter. I don't know if she does anymore."

Starr walks over and sits down on the end of my bed. I watch her, not caring at all anymore where I'm looking. I've only had two slugs of whiskey, but I already feel a little weird. Not bad. Just different.

"Maybe you could paint something for me someday."

"Maybe."

"Maybe I could pose for you. Do you think I'd make a good fairy?"

"I see you more as a sorceress."

She smiles her slow, sexy, disturbing smile at me.

"I like that."

She pats the bed beside her, and I go sit down next to her.

"Skylar's more the fairy in our family. You haven't met her yet. She's beautiful but stupid. Don't get me wrong. I love her. I love her like a sister. But she has trouble connecting the dots even when there's only two of them."

Before I know what's happening, Starr is sitting in my lap with her miniskirt bunched up around her hips and her thighs clamping my thighs. Her breasts are directly in front of my face.

I brace myself by digging my hands into the mattress.

She sits back on my knees.

"What do you think of Shelby?"

"Huh?"

She puts her finger on my lips like she's trying to keep me from saying it.

"You don't have to answer. I know you're crazy about her. What do you think about me?"

"You're hot."

She takes her finger away and runs it down

my throat.

"That's easy. What do you think about my personality?"

"You seem very nice."

She laughs.

"You're so full of shit."

She slides off onto the floor and kneels between my legs. She starts unbuttoning her shirt.

"Do I scare you?"

I shake my head no.

She takes off her shirt, and I'm left staring at real live human girl breasts covered by only two tiny scraps of see-through black material.

The nerve endings in my fingertips start to burn and the muscles in my arms start to tremble. I'd give anything to put my hands on them, but I'm still not sure I'm allowed.

"Not even a little bit?"

I shake my head again.

"You're breathing like you're scared."

She reaches up her hand and places it on my boner. For a second, I'm pretty sure I've swallowed my tongue, and I get panicked thinking about how embarrassing it would be to go into seizures and suffocate to death on one of my own body parts.

She fingers my dick and rubs it through the material of my jeans.

"But I guess you wouldn't have that if you were scared," she says and stands up.

"Have you ever done it, Kyle?"

I try to answer but no words come out. I shake my head no.

"Would you like to do it?"

"I guess. I mean. Yeah. I think most guys would."

"Not all guys. Not your brother."

"What do you mean?"

She kicks off her shoes and slides her skirt down over her legs.

While I'm looking at her, I realize I'd do anything to have her. Promise anything. Give away anything. Forsake people I love. Break laws. Humiliate myself.

It's a desire that's stronger than anything intellectual or emotional or even physical. I feel joyously enlightened. I think I even understand how religion works now. If gods can get people to feel about them the way I feel about this girl, it's no wonder they can convince their followers to sacrifice their sheep, and senses of humor, and firstborn sons.

She crawls on top of me, straddling me again, and pushes me back on the bed. Her hands start pulling at my zipper while she licks my ear and whispers in it, "He couldn't get it up."

I finally reach for her. She unhooks her bra for me.

"Don't worry," she says. "I'm on the pill. And I'm clean. I get tested all the time."

I laugh out loud. I can't help myself.

Fatherhood, disease, and death are the furthest things from my mind yet they're all risks I'm willing to take.

She takes me in her hand and starts to guide me inside her. I can't look. I don't want to look.

I close my eyes.

I'm expecting something spongy or fleshy. Something similar to my hand but hopefully moister and kinder. But it feels like nothing I've ever been able to imagine, like a warm, thick, exquisite oil.

She slips her hand between her legs and starts rubbing while rocking back and forth on me.

"I'm going to help myself out," she says. "I don't think you're going to last long."

She's right.

Chapter Twenty-One: Candace Jack

During the winter months, the weather prevents me from having my breakfast outside. I don't approve of breakfast in bed. I think if one is awake enough to dine, one is awake enough to get dressed and sit at a table. Therefore, when I've been forced indoors, I have traditionally eaten my breakfast in the sunroom, where I have a lovely view of the grounds extending off into the tree line and the hills beyond.

My increasing inability to get a good night's sleep has led to my getting up ever earlier, which meant, eventually, that I was awake at the same hour as Kyle and Klint while they were getting ready for school.

They ate in the kitchen and even though their passage through that room rarely lasted for more than fifteen minutes, it was filled with enough banging, crashing, slamming, and foul-mouthed verbal exchanges to lead an uninitiated guest to believe there was a prison cafeteria somewhere in my house.

I decided to start taking my breakfasts with them in the hopes that I could tame them. They've improved, but they still have to be constantly reminded, and certain acts — such as shutting the refrigerator door and opening new boxes of cereal — they simply can't do quietly. I think it may be beyond their control. It may be a question of genetics. Asking them to chew softly is as futile as asking an elephant to tread lightly.

Today is the first morning I've attempted to eat outside since November. It's the end of April and still brisk in the mornings, but the past few days have been mild and the fresh smell of spring is in the air. The trees are covered in bright green buds. Crocuses are scattered all over the lawn in patches of white and purple bullets.

We could still have snow next week. Western Pennsylvania weather is unreliable at best. We're usually teased with a gorgeous week or two in May, then handed a dismal rainy June before summer truly arrives in July. But I've seen many, many springs and my bones have become adept at knowing when the worst of the cold has passed and I'm sure it has for this year.

I'm wrapped in my coat and the scarf Kyle gave me for Christmas, sipping at my tea and reading the newspaper, when the front door opens and slams shut and what sounds like a small herd of bison thunders across my porch

toward the steps.

"Boys!" I shout.

They come to a skidding halt.

Klint is loaded down with what they call his "team bag." I tried picking it up once and couldn't budge it. Both of them carry backpacks. Kyle's is heavier than his brother's because his contains books.

"Quiet, please."

They walk toward me.

Luis, having followed the commotion, sticks his head out of the front door. He has my plate of toast.

Kyle is carrying a stack of three bagged bologna sandwiches in each hand. He makes his brother close to a dozen every morning.

"Hey, Miss Jack. We wondered where you were," he says.

"I decided to eat outside this morning."

"It's still pretty cold."

"The cold air is good for me. Don't you have somewhere to put those?" I ask about the sandwiches.

"Yeah, sure."

He sets them down on my table and makes his brother turn around so he can unzip his backpack.

"Come on," Klint says. "We're gonna be late."

Luis gives me my toast and fusses around in order to have an excuse to stay and watch me interact with the boys so later he can tell

me how I failed to do it correctly.

"Hey, look at this," Kyle exclaims and pulls a book from his brother's backpack. "Are you finally reading it?"

It's the biography of Roberto Clemente I bought Klint for Christmas.

"Put it back. I gotta read a book for my gov class on a famous politician or humanitarian."

"I thought he was a baseball player," I comment.

"He was also a great humanitarian," Kyle informs me. "He had el duende."

"Possibly," I say, solely to rankle Luis. "He was Hispanic, wasn't he?"

"Yeah. He was Puerto Rican. So what are you saying? Are you saying gringos can't have it?"

"Gringos," Luis repeats with a sharp laugh.

"What's wrong with saying gringos?"

"It's not used in Spain except as a joke. It's a Mexican word."

"What do Spaniards call people who aren't Spanish?"

"Unfortunate."

I try not to smile. He shouldn't be encouraged.

Kyle returns the book and finishes stuffing the sandwiches into his brother's backpack.

"Are you going to the game?" he asks me.

I look over at Luis, who widens his eyes at me.

"I don't think so. Not today. I'm feeling tired."

"But you just got up," Luis points out.

"Yes, thank you, Luis, I know. I've been feeling tired in general."

"Well, you gotta come someday," Kyle says. "You gotta see Klint play. He's on fire."

I study the boy. It's hard to imagine him "on fire." I see him more as the smoldering remains of a house that's been burned to the ground.

"Come on," Klint says again and they head off.

"You should go," Luis says once they've departed. "We have a baseball star living in our house. Don't you read the papers?"

I pick up the paper again in lieu of an answer and hold it up between my face and his.

"You know I don't like to go out."

"You went out a few days ago."

"To see Bert."

"That's different, I know. Nothing would keep you from seeing Bert. Not any kind of phobia."

"I don't have a phobia."

"You have a people phobia."

"I am not afraid of people. I went to see Bert on a business matter."

"And that's why he sends you two dozen yellow roses the next day?"

I put the paper down on the table.

"Oh, please. What do you think went on? We made wild passionate love on his desk?"

"I doubt it could be very wild. Dusty, perhaps."

"That's enough," I snap.

He holds up his hands like he's surrendering himself to a Wild West sheriff.

"Your love life is none of my business," he says.

"I don't have a love life."

"Speaking of Satan."

"The expression is, 'speak of the Devil.' I've told you that thousands of times."

I turn around in my chair to see what he can possibly be referring to.

Jerry has come out of the barn and is walking toward the Jeep.

"Luis, you are the most infuriating, unfair, resentful, malicious . . ."

"Ah, see," he interrupts me, smiling. "There's some passion. So maybe it's for Jerry not for Bert."

"It's for you," I cry, heatedly.

Our eyes meet, but only for a moment before we quickly avert our stares out of embarrassment. I'm certain I'm blushing.

"Mornin', Miss Jack," Jerry calls across the drive.

"Good morning, Jerry," I return the greeting, cheerfully. "How are you?"

"Can't complain. Mornin', Luis."

"Good morning, Jerry," Luis says lightly,

clearing away my toast before I have a chance to eat any.

I sigh.

There was a time in the not so distant past when I would have demanded Luis bring back my breakfast. I might have even ordered him into the kitchen to scramble some eggs for me even though I wasn't hungry.

I don't have the energy for it anymore. Arguing seems like such a waste of time to me now.

Luis, on the other hand, still actively looks for reasons to fight with me. I don't hold it against him. He's at a different stage of life than I am. I celebrated my seventy-seventh birthday several months ago. Eighty is looming on the horizon. Luis is ten years my junior, and I know to young people like Kyle and Klint and Shelby and Starr those years don't matter at all. To them, we're just two old people, but to me, those years matter very much.

In the middle of life a decade isn't as important. A thirty-year-old is very much like a forty-year-old (although you don't realize this until you're almost an eighty-year-old). It's in childhood and old age that the years seem to stretch out endlessly. A twenty-year-old to a ten-year-old is impossibly ancient and a sixty-year-old to a seventy-year-old is enviably young.

This is because time passes more slowly at

the beginnings and ends of our lives. As children time is thick and sweet like syrup yet we can't wait to get older. We enter adulthood and time escapes like water through an open hand. Then it slows again in the twilight years, becoming the congealed consistency of fat skimmed off a stewed chicken, and we have nothing left but to wait for death. It's not morbid to feel this way. It's the reality of life. Life ends.

In his latest letter, Rafael wrote about how all people fear death while animals don't know what it is. I used to fear death, but I don't anymore. Fear comes from the unknown, but before there can be the unknown there must be the known. Animals never face this dilemma. They're blessed with the ignorance that comes from living solely by instinct without consciousness.

Lately I feel as though I'm subsiding into a sort of animal clarity. My consciousness has been saturated. I've seen the world change too much. I *know* too much.

I find myself not caring at all about the life I've led. I'm neither satisfied nor disappointed by it. I'm neither impressed by my accomplishments nor hampered by regrets. I don't sit around wishing I had taken that trip to Bali or learned to play the piano or returned Ted Kennedy's call.

My thoughts seem to center almost entirely on my body, on the animal me: I'm tired; I

ache; my eyesight is failing; my sense of taste is fading; my hair is falling out; my bladder has spasms and my intestines barely move at all.

In the midst of all this, a wonderful thing has happened; I've realized I've lived as much as I want to.

Toreros refer to death as *la vieja compañera,* the old friend, because he's always with them. I've come to think of death the same way.

I'm not ready to embrace him yet, but it's somehow comforting to know he's waiting for me, especially during moments when I'm not feeling at all well and some morally superior Spaniard has decided to tease me about something that happened forty years ago.

I don't know exactly what Luis expected of me. That I should have never given myself to anyone ever again since I once belonged to Manuel? That I should have lived trapped forever in some perverse kind of chastity where I was forced to remain faithful to a ghost?

I wonder what he would have done if I'd been a typical woman, one who would have wanted to marry and have children or with my looks and money, one who wanted to be an unapologetic slut? How would he have dealt with me throwing slews of parties and indulging in countless affairs rather than whiling away one afternoon with a handyman

in the barn?

It was a summer day. I wandered into the barn as I had done countless times before. Jerry was pitching hay. He had his shirt off. He was slim but very muscular and slick with sweat.

I was thirty-five. Manuel had been dead for six years, and I still had more than half my life to live. On the surface I was young and beautiful, but my soul was old and my heart was ugly.

I'd been lonely. I'd had sexual longings. I craved companionship. I wanted to be adored and cared for. I wanted to make love again but with only one man. A dead man. I tried but I could never make myself feel any other way.

Jerry and I greeted each other. I commented that he looked hot and asked if I could bring him something cold to drink. He said he had a cooler full of beer. I asked him if I could have one. He looked surprised and a little uncomfortable but he complied with my request.

A beer in a barn on a hot summer day with a stoic, hardworking, sweaty, muscular man who never even graduated from high school and as far as I could tell wasn't the least bit interested in money and power, or artistic perfection and fulfilling a destiny: what could be less complicated?

It was this simplicity that led to the sex, my

realization that for a brief moment in time, I might be able to shut down my thoughts. I might be able to slip outside my emotions and back into my body and only feel with my skin.

I was the one who stood too close to him. I was the one who kissed him. He dropped and spilled his beer. There was a moment where I thought he might be afraid of me or my brother but whatever caused him to hesitate, he quickly pushed it aside.

I wanted to be filled by him. I wanted to be grabbed and hammered. He complied and it felt good, but it didn't stop me from thinking.

To this day I don't know how Luis found out. I know Jerry would have never told him. He must have been spying. He probably came looking for me when I didn't return to the house. We did do it twice.

Afterward, it never crossed my mind that it might happen again. It may have crossed Jerry's mind. I don't know. He does spend a lot of time in that barn.

I get up from the table, tighten my scarf around my head, and start off on my walk without telling Luis where I'm going.

Today I begin by heading down the driveway. I don't feel up to tramping across fields or walking in the woods alone. There are too many things to trip over.

I've been meaning to have Luis take me in

the Jeep on a search for Ventisco. I haven't seen him since the day Shelby and I were taking this same walk last September. I think that might have been the day she first asked me about taking in Klint and Kyle.

The bull's become increasingly adept at hiding and even more resistant to human contact than usual. It took the men five days to find him several weeks ago when it was time for his annual checkup, and he gave them such trouble they didn't even try to bring him in.

This is also when we usually take sperm to sell to breeders. I've never cared much for this practice, but it has made me a tremendous amount of money. This year it's not going to happen. Maybe it won't ever happen again.

Ventisco has been the wildest of my bulls. He has no tolerance or use for people. I've often wondered how he'd perform in the ring, but then my thoughts always drift to a favorite fantasy where Manuel and Ventisco meet here, alone, in these chilly quiet fields far away from the cheering crowds and blistering sun of a Spanish bullring. In my mind I watch Manuel stride across the green grass, unadorned, with a practice cape draped over his arm. Without crystals, without a cuadrilla, without a sword, he plants his feet and makes a magnificent sweep of the fabric while singing out, "Hey, Toro!" I see Ventisco

charge and the two of them dance against the backdrop of the ravaged, smoky hills and I finally know the marriage of my two great loves: a spectacular, doomed Spaniard and my beautiful, poisoned Pennsylvania.

Ventisco's father, Viajero, was a more sociable bull. I believe this came from the fact that he was such a remarkable physical specimen and, like all extremely attractive creatures, had a compulsion to be admired. I kid you not. I truly believe this animal knew how to pose. I have more photos of Viajero than of my other two bulls put together. I have more photos of Viajero than I do of Cameron's wedding.

I suppose there's great irony in the fact that my favorite bull was Calladito, the one who took Manuel's life, or maybe it makes perfect sense since he was the only one of the three that Manuel knew. From the moment he fell, I was consumed by a desperate desire to save this animal that he admired tremendously, but I was only able to do so because of extraordinary extenuating circumstances.

The breeder, Carmen del Pozo, was in the audience that evening. She had become a friend of mine during the year I'd spent with Manuel and had been a dear friend of Manuel's for most of his life.

She was a striking, alternately charming and terrifying woman who had gone as far in life as was possible for her sex in Franco's

Spain. Her family had bred bulls for generations, and her older brother, Bonifacio, was the obvious heir to the *ganaderia,* but he had no head for business, was affected and lazy, and had little fondness for the animals that had made his family one of the wealthiest and most respected in all of Spain.

He had tried to be a torero himself, having been attracted to the glamour of the profession as a boy without giving any thought to the hard work and danger involved, and he failed miserably. His capework was clumsy, his movements hesitant, his stiff practiced stance comical.

Even the bulls didn't seem to take him seriously. They would make a few runs at the skittish jerks of his capote, then plant their hooves solidly in the ground and glance around at the faces in the crowd as if to say, "Are you kidding?"

Bullfight aficionados particularly hated him. They had no tolerance for seeing their precious art sullied by the spoiled son of a breeder who had no grace or scruples.

El Gato de Circo, they called him. The Circus Cat. The only animal in the circus who doesn't work.

Carmen was the complete opposite of her brother. While he spent money on gambling and women and dabbled in bullfighting solely because of a love for attention, she stayed at home with her father and made herself indis-

pensable.

She was an early riser, went late to bed, and rushed around the ranch all day long from the barns and outbuildings to the corrals and back again to the main house, with her skirts tucked up, a pencil sticking out of her long dark braid, and a bunch of keys jangling at her hip.

Her mother had died when she was a baby and her father never remarried. She was very close to him and only she had the ability to cheer him. Whatever she did or said, it warmed his stern widower's heart, and his black eyes would sparkle as he watched her give orders to the household staff or jump into a Jeep with one of the hands to drive out to a pasture to inspect a new bull.

His son, however, was an embarrassment to the family, and his daughter never lost an opportunity to point out this fact to him.

By the time their father passed away, he was completely estranged from El Gato. He left Bonifacio a living but left the family business, the estate, and all the land to Carmen.

She was in her fifties when I met her and as energetic and controlling as she'd ever been. She was still attractive: a handsome woman, though never pretty, who tried to distract from her mannish features by painting them in garish makeup and dressing in a flamboyantly feminine manner. Her party gowns were extravagant, tightly corseted affairs made of

sequin-spangled taffetas in the same garish palette of colors that her beloved toreros wore. Her business wear was equally colorful but in the form of pencil skirts and fitted suit jackets adorned with some type of beading, embroidery, or lace at the lapels and cuffs.

The night of Manuel's death she greeted me before the corrida wearing a scarlet suit lavishly trimmed in jet bugle beads. She was the only person in Manuel's circle besides Luis who knew I was there. In her typical fashion, she was delighted to see me and extended a warm invitation to me to sit with her in the president's box, but she didn't inquire about where I'd been or what I'd been doing or anything at all about my personal life.

She somehow managed to embody both sides of all coins to me: she was a man and a woman; the new world and the old Spain; generous and small; stunning and frightening.

My affair with Manuel was well known in the bullfighting world before it ended. People knew El Soltero was not so solitary anymore. The former lothario who each year had cut a path through Spain's new crop of beauties as cleanly and determinedly as a farmer wielding a scythe was now content to sit and watch a single American rose bloom in the sun.

Carmen had no choice but to take an interest in me since she adored Manuel. At first

she regarded me as merely another conquest and barely tolerated me. Then, as time passed and she saw Manuel's uncharacteristic devotion to me, she began to befriend me.

The turning point, I believe, was the day he took me to her ranch to look at bulls. Apparently, he'd never done this with a woman before. We saw Calladito that day. He was a magnificent animal — a solid mass of muscle the color of a clear midnight with brilliant white horns, as thick as a sapling's trunk, elegantly curved skyward into lethal points of bone. Manuel watched him intently, breathlessly, his dark eyes glimmering with a passion I'd only seen when we'd been in bed together. He was in love.

When we returned to the house, for the first time ever Carmen slipped her arm through mine, not Manuel's, and led me off to one of her terraces where a gorgeous lunch was waiting for us, all the while chatting confidentially to me about frivolous female matters that we'd never discussed before as if we were long-lost sorority sisters.

Eventually she went so far as to decide I was the one for him. It was time for him to settle down. It would be good for him to have a lifelong companion, a real home, children and stability. She mentioned marriage to me before Manuel did, and later on when Manuel and I had argued publicly about my hesitancy to leave America for good, she took

it upon herself to try and convince me my concerns were trivial.

"A country is just a place; a man can be a world," she told me once after pulling me aside at one of her dinner parties.

I didn't pay much attention to her at the time. She was prone to dramatic, metaphor-ridden proclamations and always delivered them in a hushed, hurried voice while grabbing my wrist and staring deeply into my eyes before someone else caught her eye and she rushed off suddenly with her taffeta rustling and a dazzling smile parting her painted lips.

In hindsight, I've thought of those words often over the years and I've realized the wisdom behind them. Carmen had been right. I had made the wrong choice because I didn't understand the all-important difference between a place and a world and why one is so much more precious than the other: you can find a new place but a lost world is gone forever.

Carmen, of all people, understood why I needed to spare Calladito the shame of dying outside the ring. She knew Manuel would not only want it; he would demand it. But she was first and foremost a businesswoman and wasn't going to let one of her prize bulls trot away for a peseta less than he was worth.

I paid dearly for Calladito, but there was no way around it. Carmen wasn't the only one who required money. Even with the as-

sistance of one of the most powerful breeders in Spain along with her agreement to sell, I still wouldn't have been able to bypass the laws and superstitions governing bullfighting if the corrida had been in Madrid or Sevilla or any other major town or city. I wouldn't have even been given a chance to plead my case. The officials were much more important there, public men with much more at stake and many more eyes watching them.

This had been a one-man corrida in the torero's small, insignificant hometown. The president of the bullfighting organization was a grasping mill owner I'd met once before who was easily corrupted. His only involvement in bullfights consisted of showing up for them, where he sat on his mock throne in his lofty box listening to the roar of the crowd and watching the sea of white handkerchiefs before deciding whether or not to grant the torero an ear. He had no great love or commitment to the art; he was only interested in the local prestige and the free drinks he received afterward if he had abided by the crowd's wishes, which he always did.

I was also overwhelmingly pitiful and ghastly standing with Carmen in one of the poorly lit stone corridors beneath the ring, trembling in my chic, slim, pale green summer suit covered in Manuel's blood. My nylons were ripped, my shoes and hat lost, my knees and the palms of my hands bloody

and encrusted with sand, my hair hanging loose around my dust-covered, tearstained face.

Outside and above us, people moaned and wailed. Inside and down the hall from us Manuel's body lay on a cold, metal infirmary bed while his family stood around him sobbing and praying. They were rarely able to see him perform because the travel was difficult and expensive, but tonight he had come home and they had all been in the audience: his mother, his father, his sister, her husband, and her three-year-old son, Juan Manuel, who would grow up to be Rafael's father.

I was able to bribe the president.

In 1959, there were about sixty pesetas to a dollar. I paid six million pesetas for Calladito. Roughly $100,000. That would be the equivalent of paying almost $1 million for him now.

At the time I remember thinking about the men who had been on strike back home and one dead man in particular who had originally sent me fleeing to Spain. Calladito had cost fifty times more than one of them earned at a year's hard labor. He had cost a generation of miners.

It seemed appropriate to me that I was buying him with Stan's money.

According to Spanish history, the bull who killed Manuel Obrador was put to death that same evening at the plaza de toros in Vil-

larica. It's a necessary part of his legend.

The reality was Calladito was spirited off under cover of night to the nearest port city like a wanted fugitive along with a stubborn, imperious, grief-stricken twenty-year-old Spanish youth whose devotion to Manuel was so great, it even extended to the woman he had loved.

The sound of a car coming in my direction shakes me out of my reverie.

To my great surprise, I see Cameron's Cadillac coming up the drive. He never stops by unannounced, and even scheduled visits are rare.

He slows as he approaches and rolls down the window. I continue walking and he's forced to drive slowly in reverse in order to stay with me.

"Hi, Aunt Candace."

"Hello, Cameron."

"Where are you going?"

"For a walk."

"Why don't you come with me back up to the house? I'd like to talk to you for a minute."

"Why don't you park the car and come with me?"

"I don't think so. I'm not dressed for it. Come on. Get in."

"I want to finish my walk first."

"Why? Why can't you finish it later? You

have the whole day to take a walk."

"I've already started it."

"For Christ's sake, why do you have to be so difficult?"

"Why do you have to be so lazy?"

"I'm not lazy. I'm wearing a suit and good shoes, and I don't want to go walking down some goddamned country road."

"Then I'll see you at the house when I get back."

He puts on his brakes so forcefully, gravel flies out from under his tires.

My heart leaps into my throat, but I refuse to show that I am startled. I quicken my pace.

I hear his car door slam and the sound of him muttering under his breath as he comes up behind me.

"Are you happy now?" he asks me, already sounding out of breath.

"No," I reply.

"Why not?"

"Because you're walking with me."

"You invited me."

"I never thought you'd accept."

"Aunt Candace," he practically shouts at me. "Would you stop for a minute?"

I do.

"What do you want, Cameron?"

He thinks for a moment about what his response should be. I watch the exertion in his face as his brain begins to grapple with ideas.

"I want to talk to you about your will," he blurts out.

"Ha," I laugh.

I continue laughing as I turn and hurry on my way.

He catches up with me.

"I know you were at Bert's office on Monday. I know you changed your will."

I stop and gasp.

"How dare you?"

"How dare I what?"

"Pry into my affairs. How did you hear about this? Do you have a spy in his office? Surely, Bert couldn't have told you."

"Of course not. Bert would never tell me anything. He'd have his tongue ripped out before he'd talk about your so-called affairs. It doesn't matter how I found out. You're not giving those kids any of our money."

"Our money? There is no 'our money.' There's your money and my money, and I'll do whatever I please with mine."

"You didn't do something stupid, did you?"

"I want you to leave me alone."

"Aunt Candace, what did you do? Did you make those two janitor's boys your heirs?"

I'm so furious, I'm struck speechless.

"I'll fight it," he goes on. "Whatever you've done. After you're dead in the ground, I'll take them to court and I'll fight it. They'll have to spend half the money you left them on legal fees before they find out they're not

getting any of it."

It's difficult to gather my thoughts. I look down at my hands and notice they're actually trembling with rage.

"I have been very disappointed in you over the years," I tell him, picking my words precisely and delivering them very slowly so there can be no misunderstanding between us. "You have depressed, and angered, and occasionally even disgusted me but never before have you repulsed me. Now go back to your car and get off my property."

We stand toe to toe with our eyes locked for what seems an eternity. A wealth of emotions play over his face, most of them awful, but for one bittersweet second I think I see the same loss in his eyes that I've sometimes felt for him.

He turns and storms back to his car.

I start walking again and try to ignore him. I hope he'll drive past at some ridiculous speed but once again, he slows down as he approaches me. He has to lean across the front seat to yell at me this time.

"I knew it," he shouts over the sound of the engine. "I knew you were going to get suckered in by those two boys. You're easy prey. Childless old lady. She can finally pretend she has kids."

I continue walking, with my head held high, but with tears stinging my eyes.

"Do they tell you they love you? Do they

give you good-night kisses?”

I do something I’ve never done to anyone in my life.

I give him the finger.

Chapter Twenty-Two

My confrontation with Cameron leaves me rankled for days. His visits always upset me, but I'm usually able to forget about them in a matter of hours. This one, however, won't stop plaguing me.

I don't know what upset me more: his belief that he could tell me what to do, his assumption that I could be "taken in" by someone, his audacity in snooping into my private legal affairs, or the fact that I haven't received the affection he assumed I'm getting even though he assumed it would only be given to me as part of a grand scheme to get my money.

Is it possible to feel bad because someone *hasn't* tried to take advantage of you?

When I took in Kyle and Klint eight months ago, I was convinced I was mounting a rescue mission. After meeting their mother, I believed keeping them away from her was a noble cause tantamount to stepping between two baby seals and a club-wielding Canadian. I also wanted to spite Cameron after he told

me I wasn't allowed to do it. And I suppose, in some small way, I wanted to please Shelby.

I never really stopped and thought about the boys as human beings and that a relationship could or should develop between us. I tended to see them more as a project to be undertaken or large lumps of clay to be molded. I never thought about what they might need from me outside of large amounts of food and a constant supply of new socks.

I thought they could reside here in my home as if it were a sort of very large bed-and-breakfast but one in which the owner had no interest in interacting with the guests.

I never thought I would become attached to them or, worse yet, want them to become attached to me.

I don't think they dislike me. This is something in my favor. Even Klint has thawed slightly, although it's difficult to tell. The boy has still never smiled in my presence, yet I believe progress has been made. He makes eye contact with me now, and he answers all straightforward questions without being prodded, although I tend to think he does both because he's finally surrendered to my training like a weary dog to a stubborn master.

I also sense a tiny bit of regard coming from him when there was absolutely none at first. The night we met, I'm fairly certain if I had collapsed on the floor in front of him, he

would have stepped over me and left. Now I think he'd call 911 before leaving.

All this aside, I have to accept that I've failed to make them fond of me.

It sounds so silly. I didn't even realize I wanted this until my encounter with Cameron.

I suppose I haven't tried very hard. I haven't spent much time with them. I haven't tried to engage them aside from my attempt to encourage Kyle's art and that didn't go very well. I haven't shared much of myself.

I also haven't given them much in the material sense, either. I definitely haven't been extravagant with them.

Cameron accused me of making them my heirs! Two teenage boys I barely know? I'm going to hand over a fortune to them and the house my brother built?

Although when I think about leaving it all to Cameron or dividing it among my three nieces, giving it to Kyle and Klint doesn't strike me as such a bad idea.

I'm fond of Shelby and have high hopes for her, but for all her newfound worldliness and maturity she's brought back with her from Paris, she's still very much a spoiled little girl with too many romantic ideals and a selfish streak I see in her from time to time that I don't like at all. During the two times she's been here to see me since she's been back, she made several comments to Kyle in my

presence that I found condescending and bordered on rude.

Skylar is already engaged to a fabulously wealthy, dim-witted young man. They'll have an extravagant wedding and live an extravagant life with several dim-witted children, climaxing in an extravagant divorce.

Starr at nineteen is dangerously unstable, self-destructive, and uncontrollable. She's run off again this past week — no one is quite sure where this time — after inciting a near riot at a local eatery by gyrating topless on the bar at the culmination of something called Wing Night, then being arrested for drunk driving. If she lives to see thirty, I'll be amazed.

More wealth will only provide them with more opportunities to destroy the family, yet they are my only living blood relatives. Isn't it my duty as the matriarch to make sure they continue to have the means to eventually degrade and humiliate themselves to the point where they warrant their own reality TV show and clothing line? Isn't this the new American dream?

Whatever it is, it's not something I wish on Kyle and Klint. Money isn't what these boys need, or at least it's not the only thing they need.

Money can make life easier, but it doesn't make life livable.

In the midst of being distracted by these

thoughts, I received a most disturbing phone call from Bert who had received an equally disturbing phone call from Chip Edgars: the boys' mother had returned and wanted to pay them a visit and see where they're living.

This request bothered me on many levels. I knew a meeting between the three of them couldn't possibly result in anything positive. To my knowledge she hasn't had any contact with Kyle and Klint since they started living here other than the gifts she sent at Christmas that upset them both so much. I don't think they've made any effort to contact her, either. They've never once referred to her in my presence except for Klint's painful explanation of the glass horse he gave to me.

She's aware of my wealth and has already managed to extort a large sum of money from me. Her desire to see my home and to see the boys could only be part of an even more elaborate scam, and it was this knowledge that led me to agree to her request. Frankly, I can't wait to hear the latest scheme she and her sister have concocted.

They were due to arrive fifteen minutes ago. Their tardiness doesn't surprise me in the least. Selfish people are never on time.

I'm not nervous about seeing the two chinless wonders, but I am nervous about the boys' reaction. I never told them she was coming. I'm aware this is an act of betrayal on my part, but I was afraid if I told them

and gave them advance notice, they would run off and refuse to see her.

As much as I dislike this woman, she is their mother, and regardless of the repulsive manner in which she abandoned them and now is using them to make money, she is their mother.

This is not a relationship that can be ignored. The boys may not live with her, they may not like her, they may choose to have no contact with her in the future, but they can't pretend she doesn't exist.

I'm not presuming to play social worker or family therapist, but anyone with common sense can see that they're too young to simply sever all ties with her without first resolving a few issues. They need to understand that she can be avoided for the rest of their lives, but she can't be erased.

Bert wanted to be present at our little get-together, but I decided against it. I think Ronnie and I should finally meet one on one (her sisterly appendage aside).

I've asked Luis to provide refreshments, and I put on a lovely, dove-colored georgette dress with beaded pewter lace at the neck and cuffs.

My initial reaction was to meet them in the front hall, show them the boys' bedrooms, and then have them sit in their car until the boys got home, but Luis and I discussed it and we decided I shouldn't lower my own

standards for entertaining just because I happen to be entertaining someone of low standards. Everything should be approached in a civilized manner.

When they finally do arrive, Luis and I both hurry to the front door and peer out the side windowpanes. Luis has been dying to see what they look like.

They emerge from Aunt Jen's car in almost identical ensembles. They're both wearing extremely tight jeans with studded, thick leather belts, clunky platform sandals, tight black T-shirts (Aunt Jen's has the name of a bar emblazoned across the front of it and Rhonda's has the words TOO HOT TO HANDLE written on it in red foil letters shaped like flames), and dozens of bracelets that clink and jangle when they walk.

I'm sure they picked out their outfits together. It probably took them several hours, a bag of barbecued corn chips, and a two-liter bottle of Mountain Dew to arrive at this particular decision.

They come lurching toward the porch on their spindly legs and heavy hooves, their long necks craning in all directions like hungover giraffes.

"Which one is the mother?" Luis whispers to me.

"The one who's too hot to handle."

"Oh," he says and then words fail him.

I retire to the front parlor where I usually

receive guests.

I hear voices in the hall, then Luis walks into the room with an amused light in his eyes followed by the sisters.

"Your guests, Miss Jack," he announces.

"Hello, ladies," I say.

They mumble something I can't decipher.

"Please sit down."

They glance all around them, searching for an overstuffed sofa with a Steelers blanket thrown across the back of it.

They settle for a leather settee with hand-carved mahogany feet.

"May I offer you a drink?"

"A beer," Aunt Jen replies, assertively.

Rhonda nods.

"Yeah, a beer would be good."

"Luis, do we have any beer?" I ask him.

"I think I might be able to find some."

"So," I say in attempt to break the ice. "I'm sorry but I've forgotten your last name. May I call you Rhonda?"

"I don't care."

"So, Rhonda, what brings you back to Pennsylvania?"

"I'm visiting my sister."

"Is your daughter with you?"

"No. She has school. She's staying with friends."

"And your . . . ," I seem to recall she's not married to the man she lives with. I search

for the proper word for him, ". . . man friend?"

She doesn't reply.

"Things kind of fell apart with Jeff," Aunt Jen explains.

"I'm stunned," I say.

"Yeah, Ronnie's thinking about moving back here."

Rhonda shoots her sister a scathing look. Apparently, this information wasn't supposed to be revealed so early on in our discussion.

"Really?" I ask.

"Yeah, and that would mean she'd want her kids back."

I try not to show any surprise or concern. When trying to envision how this meeting would go and what we'd talk about, I never once imagined this.

"Is that true?" I ask her.

"Well, it would be kind of stupid for me to be living here in the same town as my kids and not have them living with me."

"Whereas running off with another man and leaving them behind with their father and then, after their father died, selling them to a stranger wasn't stupid?" I ask.

"My private life is none of your business."

"Believe me, I can't think of anything that I'd like to know less about than your so-called private life. I'm just trying to understand how your mind works, which I'm afraid is going to prove as futile as trying to apply a moral

compass to a badger."

Luis reappears with a tray carrying two frosted glass mugs filled with beer, an iced tea for me, and an assortment of tapas.

"Toasted almonds tossed in sea salt," he says as he sets down the first bowl. "Dates stuffed with guindilla chilies, wrapped in jamón iberico, then baked."

"Wonderful, Luis," I tell him, smiling. "I had no idea you were making these. I love them."

"You know those things," Jen whispers to her sister, who's wearing the same look of fearful disgust I've seen on her eldest son's face so many times. "We had them one time. When they wrap bacon around stuff."

"Croquetas de pollo and of course, aceitunas."

"What did you call these?" Jen asks, pointing to the croquetas.

Luis repeats himself.

"They look kind of like chicken nuggets," she observes.

"Yes," Luis replies, cordially, smiling grandly. "Consider them a sophisticated nugget. I think you will enjoy them."

He gestures for the women to help themselves.

"Por favor."

The adventurous Rhonda pops an olive into her mouth while the hungrier Jen tries a croqueta.

"Mmm," she says. "These are really good. Try these, Ronnie."

Her sister scowls at her while working an olive around in her mouth.

"These have seeds."

"Pits," I correct her.

"Be careful," she tells Jen, ominously.

"Yes," I concur. "We wouldn't want you to hurt yourself on an olive."

"What do I do with the pit?" she asks me.

"What would you do with a watermelon seed?"

She looks around the room.

"Spit it in my hand."

"There you go."

She puckers her lips and deposits a slimy stone into her palm.

I hold out a plate.

"And then place it here," I instruct her.

Luis leaves after making a dramatically low, poker-faced bow.

Jen picks up her own plate and begins loading it with food.

Rhonda gulps at her beer.

"Now where were we?" I ask. "What were we talking about?"

Jen looks up from licking salt off her fingers.

"You just called Ronnie a badger."

"Oh, yes. I remember now. Even if you do move back here, what would make you want to have the boys live with you again?"

"They're my kids," she tells me with her

endearing sneer.

"Yes, no one has ever disputed that, but tell me, other than feeling the need to constantly point out this fact to people, what exactly do you think motherhood entails? You've shown no interest in your sons the entire time they've lived here."

"I thought it would be better for them if we didn't talk too much. That way they wouldn't be distracted by thinking about me."

"I see. It was a selfless act on your part. You were doing them a favor. And before that? What favor did you think you were doing them when you left them three years ago?"

Her hackles begin to rise again.

"I told you before I had lots of good reasons for leaving."

"There are plenty of good reasons for a woman to leave her husband, but there are no good reasons for a mother to leave her children," I say, then take a toothpick and spear one of Luis's fabulous dates.

"What do you know about being a mother?" Rhonda counters and snorts a laugh. "Or about having a husband?"

I finish chewing and ask, "Do you know who the secretary of state is?"

"Huh?"

"Do you?"

"No."

"And see? You're still allowed to vote."

"What does that have to do with anything?"

Jen drains half her beer and laughs.

"I think I get it."

"Go to hell, Jen," Rhonda says icily. "One beer and you'll roll over for anyone."

She turns back to me.

"Anyway, I've given it a lot of thought and I'm taking my boys back as soon as I get settled."

I don't respond.

"You don't have a problem with that?"

"It doesn't matter if I have a problem with that. As you just reminded me, they're your children. I'm happy I've been able to assist them, but I have no say in their futures."

"So you're dumping them just like that?"

"What do you mean?"

"I guess you really are a nasty, old bitch like everyone says. You got two kids living with you all this time and you don't even get attached to them at all? You don't care if I take them back?"

Relief floods through me as I suddenly realize why she's really here. Bert's original warning comes back to me: these kinds of people never go away. She wants more money.

However, my relief quickly turns to indignation and then to an overwhelming sadness as I understand in a flash of self-preservation and pride that I won't pay her a cent more than I've already given her.

"No," I lie to her. "I don't care at all."

Chapter Twenty-Three: Kyle

I used to think guys who screwed around a lot were wrong and kind of disgusting. Now I understand them. I want to have sex as much as possible. It's my new and only goal.

And it doesn't matter if I love the girl. I don't think I even have to like her very much. I actually think it might be better if I didn't care at all. If I experienced that much physical pleasure with someone I loved like Shelby, I think the combination of the two forces would make my heart explode inside me, and if it didn't, I'd still be a dead man anyway because afterward she could control everything about me. I'd never be able to say no to her. She could tell me to wear pink shirts and aftershave and never let me go to a baseball game or watch pro wrestling and I'd say, "Yes, dear. That's fine, dear. Whatever you say, dear. Now let's have sex."

I'm not saying that I don't care about Starr, although I have to admit I cared a lot more about her while we were having sex than

before and after it. Deep down I think she might be a warm, caring human being, but I only got this feeling while I was inside her and she was doing this amazing thing with her hips and her fingers. When I was touching her breasts, I wasn't afraid of her anymore and while I was holding her perfect ass while she rode me, I didn't think she was selfish and spoiled and heartless.

It was weird, though, how quickly those feelings went away as soon as we were done and she was putting her clothes on. I watched her and instead of feeling freaked out with joy, I felt kind of sad and cheated.

When I used to fantasize about doing it with Shelby, I never thought too much about putting it in her or giving her the hard one or all the stuff Klint's buddies talk about. I wanted to experience her. I wanted to see her body and touch the pale softness of her, all the curves and hollows I don't have. I wanted to smell her hair and skin and kiss her everywhere. Then afterward if she'd let me give her the hard one, I wouldn't object.

I didn't get to do any of that with Starr. I'm not complaining about sex with her but days afterward when I was reliving it in my mind as I've been doing every minute for the past couple weeks since it happened, it seemed like I didn't even get the kind of time and enthusiasm from her that she puts into lighting her cigarettes.

She didn't even say anything to me while she was getting dressed, although I didn't say anything to her either. I wanted to. I tried to come up with something good, but everything I considered sounded too sentimental or desperate to me.

I thought I'd see her again. I knew she was older than me and rich and beautiful and had an exciting life. I didn't expect her to hang around and be my girlfriend or anything like that, but I didn't think she'd completely blow me off. It didn't make sense. She was the one who started everything, not me.

While I've been waiting to hear from her I've been giving a lot of thought to the male condition and applying my newfound knowledge to it.

My big question about men and sex is: Why do we ever do anything else? Why do we fight wars? Why do we waste our time playing video games and sports? Why do we have jobs? Why do we have a society? Why don't we just have sex and then get something to eat when we're hungry?

And why aren't guys with wives the happiest guys in the world? A married guy has a woman living with him all the time. He doesn't have to try and find her. She's in his bed every night. He can see her naked any time he wants. He has constant access to sex.

Then one day when I was sitting in school, staring out the windows thinking about

Starr's breasts and how I'd do anything to see them again, the answer suddenly came to me: in order for guys to have sex all the time, they have to find women who want to have sex all the time.

Apparently, women don't want to have sex all the time. This is the big shocker. Why not?

I'm way too inexperienced to even try and begin to answer that one, but this realization did help me figure out one of my other questions: What happens when there's a world full of men who want to have sex all the time but can't?

Sports. Video games. Wars.

These aren't just words to me. This has become my life. For the first time ever, I want to play baseball, not just watch it. I want to get out there with them and swing a bat with all my might, sprint the bases as fast as I can, and slide into the mud. I want to run deep into center field, snag a fly ball, and throw it as hard as I can to get somebody out and ruin his dream.

But when I'm at home, all I want to do is zone out in front of a computer game and numb my mind.

I've also been feeling bad about a lot of things that I would've been able to shrug off in the past. Shelby's stopped answering my texts and I'm worried she found out about Starr and me and now she hates my guts. She has no right to be mad at me because I had

sex with her sister instead of her since she didn't want to have sex with me and her sister did, but I don't think Shelby would buy into my argument.

I feel bad about Klint. I can't get Starr's comment out of my head. She said he couldn't get it up. Does that mean she did the same thing to him that she did to me but nothing happened? Does that mean he'll never be able to do it with anyone? Or has he already done it with someone and I don't know about it? If he did it with someone, why didn't he brag to me about it? I feel bad about that. If he hasn't ever done it and Starr humiliated him, I feel really bad about that.

I feel bad about the new tacoburgers that have replaced the regular cheeseburgers in the school cafeteria.

I feel bad I'm not getting laid every day.

Having sex has turned out to be the best and worst thing I've ever done.

On the way home, I'm leaning out the truck window like a bored dog, deep into thoughts about Starr and fantasizing that when we get home she'll be visiting her aunt Candace and I'll get to have sex with her again when I notice there's an unfamiliar car parked in front of Miss Jack's house.

My heart starts beating faster. I overheard Luis and Miss Jack talking one night about Starr. Her mom had called Miss Jack in hysterics because she'd left the country and

no one knew where she was. Maybe it wasn't true. Or maybe she's come back.

As we get closer, I realize the car isn't nice enough to belong to one of the Jack sisters.

It looks familiar but I can't place it until I glance over at Klint and see the agitated look on his face. It's Aunt Jen's car.

"What's Aunt Jen doing here?" I wonder.

I've seen Aunt Jen a few times since we moved in with Miss Jack.

Once she picked me up after school and we went to Eat N' Park for some pie, and she took Klint and me out for dinner around Christmas and gave us gift cards to Best Buy. And she came to one of Klint's first games this season.

Klint doesn't get along that great with Aunt Jen but he doesn't hate her the way he hates Mom unless she starts to talk about Mom, but she's learned not to do that around him.

Right now he looks more irritated and disgusted than upset.

"I invited her to come visit us," I tell him, "but she said she'd never do it. She said Miss Jack wouldn't want her to and I asked her how she'd know that and she said she and Mom met her once when Mom was deciding if we could stay here . . ."

"I know," Klint shouts at me. "You told me that a hundred times."

"So what's she doing here now?"

"How the hell would I know? Would you

shut up?"

"Lay off!" I shout back.

He gives me a strange look.

"I mean it. Leave me alone."

We don't say anything else to each other.

He parks and we get out and head for the front door.

I'm the first one in the house. As I'm walking past Miss Jack's parlor I notice her sitting in her favorite chair wearing a nice dress and eating something off a toothpick.

Our eyes meet and I'm about to say hi when hers flick back in front of her and I follow them and find Aunt Jen and Mom sitting across from her chugging down beers.

I stop so suddenly, Klint runs into me.

"Mom!"

She sets down her mug and jumps up. Aunt Jen does the same.

"Hey, baby," she calls out to me, smiling.

She throws open her arms.

"Come give me a hug."

I look behind me at Klint expecting to see the usual rage and loathing burning in his eyes, but this is the first time he's ever been ambushed by Mom and hasn't been able to prepare himself to see her. His face is a white mask of fear.

I walk over to Mom and give her a hug.

It's like taking a bag of sticks in my arms. She's even skinnier than she was before, and her hair is even blonder. It's almost as white

as Miss Jack's.

"Look how big you're getting," she tells me and ruffles my hair.

"How about you, Klint?"

She holds her arms open a second time.

He stares at her like he's looking into one of those haunted house mirrors where he sees his own reflection at first, then watches it slowly rot away into a hideous ghoul.

He doesn't move.

Mom lowers her arms and looks over at Miss Jack.

"He's my shy one. He's never been affectionate."

I don't know what Mom's talking about, then I realize she's putting on an act for Miss Jack, but I don't know why.

"What are you doing here, Mom?"

"I was in town visiting Jen and thought I'd stop by and see how you're doing."

"She might be moving back here," Aunt Jen provides.

Mom shoots her a look that would freeze blood.

"What's your problem, Jen?" she hisses at her. "Can't you let me tell anybody anything?"

"Sorry," Aunt Jen says.

"What do you mean?" Klint asks.

His voice sounds like it's coming from the bottom of a well.

"Just what she said. I might be moving back here."

"With Jeff?" I ask.

Aunt Jen starts to open her mouth, and Mom silences her with another terrible look.

"No," Mom says.

"Did you break up?" I ask, hopefully.

"Something like that," she sighs irritably and collapses back onto the couch.

The performance is over. Pretending to care and be cheerful has worn her out. She tosses a few nuts in her mouth and starts crunching loudly.

"Where's Krystal?"

"She's staying at a friend's house."

"Is she going to move back with you?"

"Of course. What do you think? I'm just going to leave her on the side of the road somewhere in Arizona? Although I have to tell you sometimes I think about it," she laughs. "She can be a little bitch sometimes. Can I have another beer?" she asks, turning to Miss Jack.

"I'm afraid we're out of beer," Miss Jack says.

"Well, that would be great, I guess," I say, glancing around nervously at everybody. "Klint and me could come visit you."

"You won't be visiting. You'll be living with us," Mom explains.

I look behind me at Klint, who's standing perfectly still and unblinking and doesn't

even seem to be breathing. For a panicked moment, I think he might have been turned into stone, and I look back at Mom half-expecting to see a bunch of Medusa snakes writhing beneath her cloud of hair.

"The only reason I agreed to this setup was so the two of you wouldn't have to move and leave your school and leave your team."

She says the words *school* and *team* in a sneering voice like they're the two stupidest things in the world.

"Besides, Miss Jack said she's sick of having you around."

Miss Jack opens her eyes wide and pulls her head back like she's just smelled something bad.

"I never said anything of the sort."

"I told her even if I moved back, the two of you could keep living here since you're all settled in, but she doesn't want you. She said it's better if you go live with your mother."

"I never said . . ."

"You're a liar," Klint shouts.

The hate and anger I'm used to seeing in his eyes whenever Mom's around finally appears. His face turns a dark shade of red and his eyes begin to bulge.

"No, I'm not!" Mom shouts right back at him. "She said she wanted to get rid of you. She said . . ."

He backs out of the room. Luis happens to be standing there between him and the front

door. I think it's the only thing that prevents him from tearing out to his truck and driving west until he hits the ocean. He looks confused when he sees Luis and turns around and runs up the stairs to his room instead.

Everyone looks stunned except Mom.

"I used to think he was just dumb and mean like his father," she says, "but now I'm beginning to think he's crazy."

I go after Klint.

I'm halfway up the stairs when I hear Miss Jack calling after me.

I don't want to see her. I don't want to talk to her, but there's something I have to know.

I stop and look down at her.

"Did you know she was coming?" I ask.

"Yes."

"How could you do that to us?"

She seems very small standing at the bottom of all those stairs. She folds her hands together in front of her and clears her throat.

"I thought if you knew she was coming, you might have refused to see her. I thought it was important that you talk to her."

"You should've told us," I say.

She calls my name one more time, but I don't turn around again.

I run up the stairs to Klint's room.

He's inside. The door's locked and I can hear him moving furniture up against it.

"Come on, Klint," I plead. "Let me in. This is stupid."

I wait for him to call me a name. I want him to call me a name. He doesn't say anything.

I pound on his door.

"Come on! Open up!"

Nothing.

I give up and go to my own room. There's no way I'm going back downstairs. I don't care if Mom gets mad at me for not saying good-bye.

I think about moving furniture up against my door, but I know no one's going to come looking for me.

My bed reminds me of Starr. My whole room reminds me of Starr.

I go sit at my desk in the fading light and look outside my window. A fiery copper sun wrapped in plum-colored clouds is setting behind the distant hills. Our mountains aren't spectacular or intimidating like the pictures I've seen of mountains out west in places like Arizona. They remind me of a bunch of sleeping old giants lying on their sides wrapped in gray blankets.

Krystal's fairy painting is almost done. I've added the glitter paint. All that's left are a few fine details.

The way Mom talked about her made me nervous. I've never really worried about her because I figured she must be fine. She's the one Mom chose to take along. She wasn't left behind.

Today's the first time it occurred to me that Mom wanting you around might be worse than Mom not wanting you around.

I get up from my desk, walk over to my bed, and flop back on it where I lie and stare at the ceiling while the room slowly grows completely dark.

The next thing I know, I'm waking up and my alarm clock says it's after 10 P.M.

No one came up and tried to wake me for dinner. That must mean Miss Jack realizes I'm genuinely upset with her.

We have a very exact dinnertime here and no one is ever allowed to be late. The first few times Klint and I missed it, Miss Jack came up here herself, rapping sharply on our doors and giving us lectures about punctuality and consideration for others.

Once after that, Luis snuck up here to try and save us from her wrath, but Miss Jack heard him and gave him as big a scolding as she gave us.

After that if I was ever late, I'd get a note slipped under my door that read, "Anda ya!" I'm pretty sure that's Spanish for move your ass.

I open my door as quietly as possible and tiptoe down the hall.

I stop at Klint's door and tap lightly.

"Klint," I whisper.

I try the knob and it opens without a problem.

His room's totally dark. He even has the curtains pulled shut so no moonlight can get in.

I let my eyes adjust. I can make out his shape stretched out on the bed on top of the covers. He's still wearing his dirty clothes from practice, including his ball cap.

"Hey, you asleep?"

He doesn't respond, and I walk over to him.

"We missed dinner. I'm gonna go get something to eat. You want something?"

"No."

"You sure?"

"Yeah."

"You okay?" I ask a little uneasily.

He doesn't say anything this time.

Normally, I say good night to Miss Jack at ten. She's usually sitting in the sunroom or her parlor where she gets Luis to light a fire and she reads a book, although more and more often she's asleep when I come into the room. She says it's hard for her to read as much now because her eyes give out.

Now that the weather's getting warmer, some nights I find her sitting on her porch wearing her funny old coat and the scarf I gave her with her hands folded in her lap staring straight ahead like she's waiting for a bus.

She has a huge house but hardly uses any of the rooms. She's got millions of dollars but never spends any of it. She's got brains and wisdom but hardly ever shares any of her

knowledge because she doesn't like being with anyone.

Sometimes I think she's the loneliest person in the world. Even lonelier than me.

I don't want to talk to her tonight. It's not because I'm mad at her for not telling us Mom was coming. I'm over that. She shouldn't have done it, but she didn't know any better.

I'm avoiding her because I'm not good at asking for favors and I need to ask her for a big one.

I get to the bottom of the staircase and I'm about to take the back way to the kitchen so I don't have to go anywhere near the parlor or the sunroom when I happen to look toward the front door and see colorful lights dancing outside the glass like bits of fire made from rainbows.

I have to check it out.

Every single candle is lit on the porch. It seems like hundreds of them. They sit inside mosaic glass holders of all different shapes and sizes and as they burn, brilliant colors flash everywhere. It's like standing inside a kaleidoscope.

Miss Jack is sitting in the middle of it wearing her coat and scarf and staring off into the velvety black night searching for her bus.

Mr. B is with her, sitting upright in one of the wicker chairs, his eyes big and yellow, his head jerking from side to side as he follows

the flickering lights.

"Hey, Miss Jack," I greet her. "The candles are cool."

"Yes, they are," she says.

"It must've taken a while to light them all."

She keeps looking ahead and not at me.

"I'm sorry, Kyle. I shouldn't have interfered. You and your brother are old enough to decide if you want to see your mother or not."

"It's okay."

"I'm not so sure that it is. How is your brother?"

"He won't come out of his room but I talked to him. He's okay."

"I had met your mother once before but I'd never seen her with the two of you. I have to say the effect she has on your brother is very disturbing."

"Yeah."

"Have they always been like that?"

"No. Things got weird between them, I don't know, maybe a year or two before she left."

"Weird in what sense?"

"I don't know. They just sort of stopped liking each other. Then after she left, he started hating her."

I walk over to Mr. B. I've stopped being sore at him, but he's still sore at me for having the nerve to be sore at him. He looks up at me like I must be kidding if I think he's

going to share his chair.

I pick him up, sit down, and plunk him on my lap. He starts to purr instead of trying to break free and run off. He is getting old.

"I don't like to be wrong," Miss Jack tells me.

"Who does?"

I pet Mr. B until he gets tired of it and jumps down off my lap.

This is the perfect opportunity to talk to her and as much as I'd like to just say good night and go grab some food, I know I'll regret it if I don't take care of this now.

"I know we've had our ups and downs, and I know Klint and I haven't really been the most grateful people in the world." I start talking before I'm sure what I'm going to say. "Especially Klint," I add smiling.

She doesn't smile.

"But we've really appreciated you letting us stay here. More than we could tell you even if we tried."

I take a deep breath, close my eyes, and let everything come out in a rush.

"Can we keep living with you? Just for another year. I mean, I can go live with my mom but Klint won't do it.

"He's going to graduate next year and go to college. His grades aren't great right now but his game is on. Something's gonna happen for him. Something has to happen.

"Please," I finish.

"Por favor," I think to add.

She doesn't say anything for a long time. She doesn't look at me, either. I'm beginning to wonder how long I'm obligated to sit there. What is the required time period in polite society for enduring rejection before one may go to his room and curse?

"As long as I have a home, you and your brother will have a home," she says.

"Thanks, Miss Jack."

I jump up from my seat. For the first time ever, I'm tempted to hug her but even though she's a mentally powerful woman, her physical self always strikes me as frail, like a hug or a hearty handshake might break all her bones.

I walk over and give her a kiss on the cheek instead.

She smells like lilac and baby powder, and her skin against my lips feels soft like tissue paper.

"Luis left your dinner in the kitchen," she tells me. "You'll need to heat it up."

"Thanks."

I rush back inside but turn around at the door to see the candles once more.

Miss Jack takes a handkerchief out of her coat pocket and raises it to her eyes.

Chapter Twenty-Four

A couple weeks go by and we don't hear anything else from Mom. I don't hear anything from Starr or Shelby, either.

Miss Jack gave me an update about Starr, though. She's really in India this time, and no one knows when she's coming back. This information should have been enough to make me abandon all hopes of having sex with her again, but instead I've started fantasizing about doing it with her in front of the Taj Mahal.

Miss Jack also told me that Shelby's very busy with school, which I know is bull because Shelby coasts through school because she's smart, and the teachers like her, and she's Cam Jack's daughter. Talk about having all the odds in your favor.

Even if she was busy, she could still find time to answer my texts. She's obviously mad at me and the only reason I can come up with is Starr told her about us, but I don't know why that should make her mad.

I'd be her boyfriend in a minute. She has to know that. If I made it any more obvious I'd be stalking her.

All I can figure is even though she's not interested in me, that doesn't mean she wants me to stop being interested in her.

From what I've seen of girls, they want to be wanted but they don't want to be taken. They're like delicious pastries in a display case that would rather stay behind glass and be admired than be taken out and gratefully devoured by someone starved for sweets.

Shelby can be mad at me, even if it's for a stupid reason, but she can't hide from me. One thing I hate is people who get mad at you and won't tell you why. It's what my mom did.

Since Shelby's not playing fair with me, I decide to do the same thing to her. I know it's wrong and it's mean, but I sent her a text last night telling her Klint wanted her to come to his game today.

She didn't write back. Now I'm waiting to see if she shows up.

Today's a big game because the Flames are playing Laurel Falls, one of the only teams that have a chance of spoiling their undefeated season.

Like a lot of towns around here that have scenic names, Laurel Falls is misleading. Hearing it conjures up images of a picturesque village nestled in a valley full of flower-

ing trees and a babbling brook ending in a silvery waterfall. The reality is a sooty gray shuttered town that's been dying for forty years. The only color comes from the red and yellow McDonald's and the bright orange rust streaks on the water tower.

There's still enough people there to have a small high school, but I have no idea what they do to make a living. Considering the poverty and bleakness of the place, I expected the residents to be frail and skinny like prisoners of war, but they were meant to be farmers and miners — strong, robust men who did hard physical labor — and instead of their bodies surrendering to disuse and shriveling up to nothing, they've mutated into something even bigger than before from the amount of junk food they consume and the amount of bitterness they swallow.

Their baseball team is made up of kids who spent countless hours standing in their backyards looking at the abandoned mining complex on the hillside that no longer employed their fathers and hitting rocks with their chipped, hand-me-down L'il Slugger bats before they were even old enough to go to school.

Their star pitcher is a guy whose dad used to make him throw golf balls through a Campbell's soup can, with the top and bottom cut off, hung on its side from a tree, until his arm needed to be iced and then he was

allowed to go inside and watch cartoons.

The other thing they've got going for them is everyone on their high school team has been playing together since they were little kids. No one ever leaves Laurel Falls, and no one ever moves in.

Big schools like Centresburg that have a lot of different middle schools feeding into them pick their varsity squads from guys who might have been playing against one another up until a few years earlier.

They can't read each other's minds. They don't know exactly how each one of them is going to react to a ball in play. And they're also usually plagued with hotshots only concerned about their own stats, trying to be stars.

Not Laurel Falls. Their team is a well-oiled machine, and each man is a perfectly functioning and strategically placed cog or gear, but even so they're not best known for finesse plays or outsmarting the offense. They're known for hitting the cover off the ball.

The stands are crowded. It's a perfect day for a baseball game. Everyone's in short sleeves and enjoying the sun. A lot of fair-weather fans have showed up along with our usuals: Coach Hill's daughters but no Mrs. Hill; the Mann clan; Cody Brockway's dad who can only come to games when Cody's mom's not here because of the restraining order; Mr. and Mrs. Richmond, arriving

separately and leaving separately but sitting together and talking to other people.

Mrs. Richmond is wearing the cotton-candy pink tracksuit she always breaks out near the end of the season along with her matching pink visor and her huge sunglasses. In the past I've looked forward to this moment — Brent's mom is pretty hot — but today I'm too distracted thinking about seeing Shelby again and worrying about Klint.

I'm not worried about Klint playing. He's having the season of his life and for Klint, that's saying a lot since he's never had a bad one.

Serious college recruiting doesn't usually start until summer but scouts have already been contacting him, and a few have even showed up at some of his games from as far away as Texas. They all say they're concerned about his grades, but no one has ever mentioned that he has to bring them up.

Considering all this I was amazed when he accepted Coach Pankowski's invitation last week and agreed to go check out the team at Western Penn.

I had a great time. Everyone was nice, and there were a lot of cute girls walking around. Even the dorm rooms weren't bad. They weren't any smaller than the one Klint and I used to share before Mom left with Krystal and we each got our own.

But the best part was listening to Coach

Pankowski explain his baseball philosophy. He's trying to build a winning team just like every other coach, but he's not recruiting based solely on talent. He uses a criteria he calls the 3Ps: potential, personality, physical conditioning.

When he said this, I told him Klint would fail the personality part. Klint just glared at me.

Coach laughed and said it didn't mean he was looking for someone with loads of personality, it meant he took each player's individual personality into consideration when designing his team. Would a guy fit in well with the other players and more important, was he decent, smart, and motivated? Where did he come from? What was his family like? What kind of goals did he have?

I didn't comment on any of that.

Coach was very proud of the potential part of his 3Ps. He showed us statistics on some of his players. He had about a half dozen who'd only had average records in high school but were top guns now. He said the key was being able to see what a guy was capable of doing if given the right motivation and the right training, and then given the freedom to use his knowledge to become the kind of player he wanted to be. He didn't believe in cookie-cutter coaches who tried to mold a team of identical baseball drones using a single unbendable, one-dimensional

coaching style.

I glanced over at Klint when Coach Pankowski mentioned this. I knew we were both thinking of Coach Hill and his coaching style: instilling fear. But I was thinking Coach Hill was wrong while Klint was thinking he was right.

On the way home he told me Coach Pankowski's philosophy was fruity and that he was probably a fag, which is why I liked him so much since I was one, too.

I didn't like hearing him talk that way about the coach, but considering how weird he'd been lately, I was more relieved than pissed off.

He hardly eats and he never seems to sleep. He never hangs out with his friends. He never kids around with me or fights with me. He won't have anything to do with Miss Jack even after I told him she never told Mom any of those things and said we could keep living with her.

The only thing he still does is go visit Bill, but even Bill is starting to get freaked out by him. He still just wants to sit on Bill's porch and stare at our backyard.

He's losing weight and he has permanent dark shadows under his eyes, but he's unstoppable at the plate. It's as if some kind of energy-sucking baseball microbe is devouring him from the inside, taking away his desire to do anything else and putting it into his swing.

Tyler's noticed and asked me what I thought was going on and I told him I didn't know. Coach Hill hasn't talked to me but Tyler said at an away game last week, he took Klint out during the fourth inning and made him eat a sandwich.

I take a final look around the stands for Shelby before I sit down next to Bill.

I don't see her.

"He doesn't look good," Bill says and takes a long drag from the straw stuck into his beer Slurpee.

The announcer has just called Klint's name and he's jogging onto the field while the fans hoot and holler.

"Your hot streak's over, Hayes!" someone yells at him. "No one can hit Tussey's curveball!"

Reid Tussey is the Laurel Falls pitcher who probably still has bad dreams involving the clang of a golf ball hitting the side of a soup can.

There are a lot of Laurel Falls fans here. It's going to be a rowdy game.

Our own pitcher, Joe Farnsworth, takes to the mound. He throws one of the best fastballs in the state, but he's got his work cut out for him.

The team he's facing today isn't hampered by stress. When they step up to the plate, they're not thinking about possible college scholarships or multimillion-dollar pro con-

tracts in their futures. They're playing for bragging rights in the present.

I reach for a handful of Bill's chips and when I do, I see a flash of coppery-brown down on the ground not far from the fence behind the dugout. I'd recognize Shelby's hair anywhere.

She's peering up into the stands. I'm stupid enough to hope she's looking for me and when her glance comes around my way, I wave at her.

She doesn't smile. She stares back at me with an expression I can't define, but I know it's not happiness over seeing me.

As long as I've known Shelby, she's always greeted me with one of her great smiles. I never realized until this moment how much I counted on it.

I get up and start down the bleacher stairs. She turns and starts heading back to the parking lot. She was looking for me but only so she could avoid me.

"Hey, Shelby," I call to her.

She doesn't stop walking.

"Hey."

I jog to catch up to her and reach out and grab her by the arm.

"Shelby, come on."

She stops and faces me. I've never seen her angry before. Her pale skin is tinged pink with passion, and her brown eyes have a feline greenish glow to them. Her long, loose,

dark hair full of red-gold glints falls messily around her face. I can't help thinking that this is what she'd look like if we were in the middle of having sex.

"On top of everything else, you're a liar, too," she spits at me.

"What do you mean?"

"Does Klint really want me here? Or was that just a lie to get me to come to the game?"

She puts her hands on her hips and stares me down. I thought since I'm a man now with some sexual experience, I'd have more confidence around her but I'm as intimidated as ever.

"Yeah, I lied. Klint could care less if you're here or anybody else. But what about how you've been treating me? You've been blowing me off for almost a month. And now today you're only going to show up because you think Klint wants to see you. What about that?"

She doesn't answer me.

"This was the only way I could think of to get to see you," I explain.

"I don't want to see you."

"Why? What did I do?"

"You know exactly what you did."

She takes off again.

"If this is about Starr," I call after her departing back, "I don't love her. I love you."

The minute these words are out of my mouth, I know they're a mistake. I didn't

think. I spontaneously put forth the only thoughts in my head that mattered as far as I was concerned. They were true, heartfelt words that explained and justified everything and should've been enough to smooth things out between the two of us.

But Shelby is a girl. If I thought girls were confusing before I had sex with one, it's nothing compared to what I think about them now. I don't understand anything about them except for one thing I've figured out for certain: anything a guy thinks about love and sex, a girl thinks exactly the opposite.

She stops dead in her tracks and gives me a furious look.

"You love me?" she shouts at me. "You're going to tell me you love me? After you had sex with my sister?"

"I would've rather had sex with you but you're not interested."

Again, I've said something that makes perfect sense to me, but her face turns practically purple with rage.

"Okay, are you interested?" I plead with her. "Do you love me? Do you want to do it with me?"

"No!" she screams at me. "And no!"

"I don't get it. Your sister comes on to me and then she tells you about it, knowing it will make you feel bad and you get mad at *me?*"

"She did it to show me that all guys are

pigs. Even the ones you think are nice."

"Why am I a pig?"

"Because you had sex with my sister!" she screams again.

"Is it because she's your sister? Would you be just as mad at me if I'd done it with someone you're not related to?"

She takes off again.

I go after her.

"So let me see if I get this straight," I say, panting as I jog alongside her. "I'm supposed to never have sex with anyone ever in my life because I had the bad luck to fall in love with a girl who doesn't love me back?"

She slows down and then stops.

The crowd erupts into cheers and applause. We both look back at the stands filled with happy people.

"Do you love Starr?" she asks me.

"No. I already told you that. I'm afraid of Starr."

"But you had sex with her."

I shrug.

"You don't have to be in love with someone to have sex with them."

"I do."

"Why?"

"Because sex is the most intimate, spiritual, beautiful act possible between two people."

Spoken like a girl who's never had sex, I think to myself.

"I guess that's true and I hope someday I'll

get to have sex with someone I love, but in the meantime I'm not going to turn down having sex with someone I think is hot."

"That's so disgusting."

"What's with you, Shelby? Did you find religion or something?"

She's joined the church of the fairy-tale love story. Why not? After all, religion is just blind faith in something that common sense says can't be true. There's no reason why Shelby can't be worshipping at the altar of "love and sex without pain and suffering."

"You don't have to be religious to think it's wrong to have sex with someone you're not in love with," she tells me in a snooty tone. "It's a moral question."

"Would you have sex with Klint?"

She doesn't answer my question. Instead she says, "I love him."

"You don't love him. You don't know anything about him. You've probably never exchanged more than three complete sentences with him. You think he's good-looking the same way I thought Starr was good-looking. That's all."

I wonder what she'd think if she knew Starr tried to do it with her precious Klint, too.

She starts walking again. We're almost to her shiny little red sports car. It's easy to spot parked in the midst of all the beat-up pickups and SUVs, most of them badly in need of a wash.

"You want to compare morals?" I go on. "You think it's okay for you to sleep with my brother but it's not okay for me to sleep with your sister?

"The moral difference isn't that you love Klint so it's okay and I don't love Starr so it's not okay. The moral difference is you don't love me, you don't care about me at all, so how does it hurt you if I screw your sister or anybody else? But I do love you so it would really hurt me if you screwed my brother. But you don't care about that."

She takes her keys out of her purse and presses the button to unlock her car from a distance. I hear a muted beep and its headlights flash once.

I realize this is it. I'm probably never going to see her again. Watching her open the door to her $60,000 car that she didn't pay for and flipping open her frosted ice blue BlackBerry that no sixteen-year-old on the planet needs to have, I've never felt more alienated from her.

In her mind, she'll be able to tell herself that I betrayed her and that's why the friendship ended. Being able to justify her actions and still come out seeming like a nice, decent person is all that matters to her.

I suddenly understand that what's happening between Shelby and me doesn't have anything to do with Starr and me fooling around. It just provided Shelby with a conve-

nient excuse to get rid of me.

She puts her BlackBerry away, opens the door to her car, and starts to get in.

The old me, the scared kid, would've let her drive away without saying anything else, but the new me, the disillusioned man, needs to further explain himself.

"I always thought you were kind and caring," I tell her. "Now I realize you're just as selfish as everybody else. You're only kind and caring when it's easy."

She looks startled but not hurt, another sign that she doesn't care about me or what I think.

"Look at everything I did for you," she replies, turning bitchy. "If it wasn't for me, you'd be living with that horrible witch mother of yours and her awful boyfriend in Arizona somewhere."

"You did it for Klint. Not me. I was stupid enough to think it was for me, too, but now I know better."

She slams the door on me and peels out.

"Este toro no tiene casta," I yell after her.

I'm not in the best of moods by the time I return to my seat next to Bill.

We're at bat.

"No score," he informs me as he holds out the bag of chips.

I wave it away.

I zone out. I'm not paying any attention to the game when Bill nudges me with his elbow.

"Klint's up," he tells me. "What's with you?"

"Nothing," I say.

The applause dies down and Klint steps into the box.

He gets into his stance.

Reid Tussey bends over with the ball clasped behind his back to read the catcher's signs.

He nods, stands up, winds up, and Klint steps out of the box.

Players and fans alike start yelling at him.

He drops the bat to the ground. He takes off his hat and wipes his face off in the crook of his arm like he's sweating a lot. I notice the back of his jersey is drenched. It shouldn't be. The day isn't that hot, and the game's just started.

He puts his hat back on and stands there, not moving, and not picking up the bat.

The crowd grows louder. A few of his teammates come out of the dugout but don't get too close to him.

The home plate ump starts walking toward him from one direction, and Coach Hill comes at him from the other direction, shouting and waving his arms.

He looks from one to the other and then takes off running.

"Holy shit!" Bill cries, jumping to his feet. "What the hell is he doing?"

I don't stop to ask myself the same question. I react. I scramble down the bleachers

and start running after him.

He has a head start on me, plus Klint's wicked fast when he wants to be. He's pumping his arms and legs like he's the winning run trying to outrun a throw to home.

The baseball field isn't near the high school. It's in a park in the middle of town. He's left the park and now he's running past houses, his cleats clicking on the sidewalk.

I do my best to catch him but it's impossible. I'm ready to quit when he suddenly collapses in somebody's front yard.

I pick up my pace and finally reach him.

He's kneeling on the grass, his face covered with his hands, his body shuddering with ugly, wrenching sobs.

I fall to the ground next to him breathing so hard I feel like I'm going to pass out.

"Klint. What is it? What's happened?"

He keeps crying. I'm afraid to touch him.

"Tell me what's wrong."

"I, I, I," he stutters. "I can't live with her."

I know immediately who he must be talking about.

"We don't have to," I assure him. "Remember? Miss Jack said we could keep living with her."

"Screw Miss Jack. We, we don't know. We can't trust her."

"Sure we can."

"I can't live with her," he tells me again.

This time he looks at me, and his eyes are

filled with terror.

"We don't have to live with her. I promise."

"I, I, I don't . . ." His words dissolve into more sobs. "I don't want her here. I don't want to see her."

"You don't have to see her."

"She touched me," he says in a whisper so low I have to lean forward until our heads are almost together in order to hear him.

"What?"

"She used to touch me."

"Who? Mom?"

He nods.

"She's your mom. Moms touch their kids."

"No!" he screams at me.

I jerk back.

He starts sobbing again.

A clammy fear begins in my stomach and spreads to all my nerve endings, making my skin feel cold and alive with something damp and sticky crawling all over it. My mouth fills with a sour metallic taste.

"Where did she touch you?" I ask slowly.

He starts breathing wildly, panting like a whipped dog.

"You know," he says.

"You were little. Maybe you made a mistake."

"No. No. I wasn't little."

I look away from my brother to the house sitting behind him. I wonder about the family living there. Do they have terrible secrets,

too? Or are we the only ones?

Can everyone see the damage? Does it show up on our surface? How many times can the shattered pieces of me be patched back together before the glue stops working? What happens when I can't hold on to anything good anymore, when it always leaks out through the cracks?

I stare at the house and imagine it on fire, but what I'm really seeing is my life engulfed in flames. I hear the roar of the inferno devouring everything inside. I watch the blackened frame begin to crumble. I feel my skin blister and burn from the heat. I should run, but I can't leave. Everything I am is trapped in that house and soon it will be devoured and it will be as though I never existed.

Klint falls on his side, curls up in a ball, and cries.

I lay down behind him and put my hands on his shoulders, absorbing his shudders and facing the fact that the person I love the most is someone I don't know at all.

Chapter Twenty-Five: Candace Jack

For the next four days Luis is gone on one of his periodic jaunts to New York.

He needs to escape the country and indulge in a city from time to time, plus he loves to visit shops specializing in culinary products and gourmet foodstuffs. He always brings home wonderful treats and all kinds of new gadgets for the kitchen.

Whenever Luis leaves me for any period of time, whether it be for a few days or the trips he takes to visit his family in Spain, he always cooks in advance and freezes meals for me.

I haven't decided yet what we shall eat tonight. Klint's appetite has decreased dramatically in the past few weeks, which has bothered me but getting any information from him is as futile as talking to a brick.

Eating has always been one of the great joys of my life, but I'm beginning to lose my sense of taste. Flavors don't stimulate and thrill me the way they used to. I'm also losing my appetite, but this isn't as troublesome at my age

as it is at Klint's.

My plumbing, as I've heard Jerry refer to the inner workings of his body, isn't what it used to be. Digesting a rich, five-course meal is quite impossible for me now. I practically nibble at my food.

At first, not surprisingly, Luis took this behavior on my part as an insult. He thought after decades of praising his cooking to the heavens that I no longer cared for it.

Once I convinced him this wasn't the case, he became concerned about me and after weeks of constant harassment finally persuaded me to see my doctor. After much poking and prodding and invasive whatnot on his part, a diagnosis was made: I'm old.

The boys are late tonight. I know Klint has a game but even so, they're usually home by now.

I haven't been able to bring myself to go to one of his games yet, although I still have plans to eventually do so. I'd never admit my misgivings to anyone, and especially not to Luis, but I do harbor a rather strong fear of people — not as individuals but in large cheering groups.

A screaming crowd takes me back to the day of Manuel's death. I'll never forget how beautiful the day was. The palpable love and excitement in the air of the humble town welcoming home their glorious native son, their prince, their star, on the eve of his birth.

They were magnificent when they met in the ring that day, Manuel and Calladito, the graceful, urbane man in his civilized suit of wealth and light, and the powerful, feral bull anxious to prove his strength; two very different beasts who seemed each in his own way to be completely in command, yet their meeting would end with one or both of them dead and bathed in each other's blood.

I was changed so profoundly that day that I never recovered. Observers would say naturally this occurred because I lost the love of my life and I watched him die in a horrific manner, but there was more to it than this.

That day I realized God or no God, Fate or no Fate, it didn't matter. All the centuries of man looking for answers with his philosophy and politics, his science and his arts; all of it was meaningless because none of it could help us cope with our most devastating enemy: the randomness of life.

This is why I dislike a cheering crowd. It will always symbolize for me the terror of knowing that we ultimately know nothing.

It's getting dark, and I'm growing concerned.

I make myself a cup of tea and take it out onto the porch.

I hope nothing's wrong. Klint has been acting even more withdrawn than usual. The change happened after he saw his mother, and I can't help placing some of the blame

on myself.

I'm afraid I didn't handle that situation very well. I know now in hindsight that I should have told them their mother was coming to see them. She's not the type of woman who should ever be sprung on someone.

I'm still negotiating with her. I certainly don't plan to send the boys packing, but she's demanding an absurd amount of money.

If I don't pay her, she'll take the boys and tell them I'm the one who decided they can't live here anymore. They'll believe her because she's already announced, with all of us present, that she doesn't mind if they continue to stay with me; therefore, if they don't get to stay, it will look as though it was my decision to get rid of them.

She's banking on the belief that I won't hurt the boys by telling them their mother is a monster who's using them to extort money from me.

It's ingenious in its way.

I've taken a seat with my tea when I hear the sound of a vehicle coming up my driveway. A few moments pass and I realize the racket can only be coming from Tyler Mann's truck.

My guess proves right.

The old truck rattles and roars to a stop in front of me. Tyler and Kyle get out.

"Hello, Kyle. Hello, Tyler."

"Hi, Miss Jack," Tyler responds to me but I

notice not with his usual vigor.

"To what do I owe the pleasure of your visit?"

"I don't know if it's gonna be a pleasure," he replies.

"Kyle, what's wrong? You look very upset. Where's your brother?"

"We don't know."

"What do you mean?"

Kyle looks at Tyler.

"What's happened?" I ask.

"He kind of had a breakdown at the game," Kyle tells me.

"What do you mean?" I ask again.

"He . . . ," he starts to explain. "He left. He was up at bat, and he ran away."

"And where is he now?"

"I told you. We don't know. I went after him and I caught up to him and talked to him."

His voice trails off and he stares at the ground while he continues his story.

"I got him to go back to the game, but he went straight to his truck and drove away. We haven't seen him since."

He won't look up. He's obviously not telling me everything.

"We've been looking for him," Tyler jumps in to assist Kyle. "We went everywhere he likes to hang out. We've been calling people. We drove all around town."

"He's not answering his cell," Kyle adds.

"What do you think, Kyle? Should I call the police?"

"No, no," he says vehemently, shaking his head. "No. No police. It's nothing like that. I'm sure he'll come home."

Tyler claps Kyle on the shoulder.

"Don't worry. He's just blowing off some steam."

Kyle nods. Neither one of them seems to put much faith in his words.

"Would you like to stay for dinner?" I ask Tyler.

"No thank you, ma'am. I appreciate the invitation, but I have to get home."

Kyle goes straight up to his room. He doesn't want to talk to me.

I manage to convince him to have some dinner but the meal is a dismal affair. He picks at his food and I pick at mine.

He refuses to make any eye contact with me. I think he looks ill.

After dinner I ask him again what he thinks we should do about his brother and again he says we should do nothing.

Time passes and Klint doesn't come home. Kyle continues to try him on his cell phone, and he doesn't answer.

I finally decide to go to bed, even though I know there's no chance I'll be able to sleep. I change out of my clothes into my nightgown, brush out my hair, and get into bed with a book that I open on my lap and stare at but

find impossible to read.

This is one of those situations where I'm hampered by the fact that I'm not a relative of any kind. I'm not even a legal guardian. I also don't have the instincts of a mother since I've never been one, but I'm fairly certain if Klint was my son, I would have already called the police.

But only if he were my son. Even if he were my grandson, I doubt I would be as equally presumptuous. If a similar scenario was unfolding involving Shelby, I wouldn't take it upon myself to involve the authorities. I'd leave that up to her parents, but this boy has no parents or at least, no functioning ones. But what if I were caring for Shelby because her parents were unavailable? Say they were out of the country? What would I do right now? Would I call the police? Yes, I'm fairly certain I would, but Shelby's a girl. There are so many more terrible things that can happen to a girl than can happen to a seventeen-year-old boy. But are those the kinds of things I'm worrying about? Am I supposed to be concerned that something terrible has befallen Klint at the hands of someone else? No, I think what Kyle is worried about is that Klint may harm himself. By design or by accident.

Despite my worry and my racing mind, apparently I do doze off because I practically jump out of my skin when there's a knock at

my door.

I hurry toward it without even stopping to put on a robe.

It's Kyle. He's visibly shaking.

"I just got a call from Klint. I think something's wrong."

"Why? What did he say?"

"Well, he was crying a lot."

"Klint was crying? What did he say? Where is he?"

"He wouldn't tell me anything. He just kept saying don't tell anybody what I told you. He told me something before. He wants to keep it a secret."

"What is it?"

"I can't tell you."

"Kyle . . . ," I begin to prod him but he interrupts by bursting into tears.

"He told me I'm a good brother," he sobs. "He'd never tell me that unless something was really wrong."

Before I have a chance to calm him or try to think clearly, the phone rings and this time we both jump.

I rush back into my room with my heart in my throat to answer it.

"Hello."

"What the hell's going on over there?" an unmistakable voice shouts at me.

"Excuse me? Rhonda, is that you? What are you talking about?"

"I just got a call from my kid and he was

blubbering like crazy."

"I still don't understand what you mean?"

"What is wrong with you? Go put your hearing aid in. I said Klint just called me. What did you do to him?"

"Did he tell you where he is?"

"What do you mean where he is? I figured he was with you and you'd done something awful to him. Maybe you told him he couldn't live in your palace anymore. That's a big mistake. They're gonna hate you . . ."

"What did he say to you?" I interrupt her.

"He didn't say anything. That's what I'm trying to tell you. He didn't say a goddamned word. He just cried and cried and hung up."

I hang up on her, too.

"Kyle," I call out.

He comes running into my bedroom.

"That was your mother. Klint just called her."

"What? Klint called Mom? Why? What did he say?"

"Apparently all he did was cry, then he hung up."

All the color drains from Kyle's face, and he sits down helplessly on my bed. His body begins shaking again.

"Kyle," I say to him. "You have to tell me everything. I can't help unless I know exactly what's going on."

It only takes him a few minutes to tell me what his brother revealed to him earlier, but

as he's doing it I feel as though time has come to a complete stop and by the time he finishes, I feel as if we've both aged twenty years.

I try to keep both my rage and my fear in check. I try to remain calm.

"What place means the most to Klint?" I ask Kyle. "In a good or bad sense. Where would he go to make a stand? The baseball field?"

"Home," he says.

"Of course. Can you call Bill?"

"He's not there."

"How do you know?"

He gives me an exasperated look.

"It's Wing Night."

"Oh, I see. Then let's go."

We both start toward the stairs. It doesn't even cross my mind to get dressed.

"Luis isn't here," Kyle says.

"I can drive."

"Ah, yeah, I know you said you could before but can you really?"

"Of course."

"When's the last time you drove somewhere?"

"It doesn't matter. It's like riding a bicycle. You don't forget how to do it."

We arrive downstairs. I pull on my walking boots.

"I can drive," Kyle suggests, anxiously.

"You certainly cannot."

"I know how. My dad used to let me drive out in the country when there was no one around."

"You don't have a license."

"So? This is an emergency like your wife having a baby."

"Fifteen-year-olds aren't supposed to have wives who have babies. I should take my purse. Where is my purse?"

"Come on!"

Kyle grabs me by the arm.

"We don't have time."

I refuse to be daunted by this task. I've been in this car countless times. I do know how to drive. It's been close to thirty years since I've done so, but all that's required is turning a key in the ignition, shifting into drive, pushing down a gas pedal, and steering. I remember how to do all that.

I insist that Kyle put on his seat belt.

He's breathing heavily and bouncing around in his seat like a cooped-up puppy. Apparently I'm not moving quickly enough for him.

We start on our way.

It all comes back to me. Driving is easy. I'm doing fine.

I remember to check my mirrors, to keep my speed under control, to hold the steering wheel securely. I'm feeling confident and capable, but then we get to the end of the driveway.

"Miss Jack!" Kyle cries out. "We've got to go faster. Come on!"

"Yes, yes, you're right."

I turn onto the road and I floor it. At least I feel like I'm flooring it. I watch the speedometer needle creep up to 40.

"Oh, God," Kyle groans. "Please let me drive. Please. Please."

I've never seen anyone so desperately upset in all my life. It goes entirely against my better judgment, but we are in a hurry.

"All right," I tell him.

I pull over to the side of the road and get out of the car. It isn't until I'm walking around to the passenger side that I realize I'm wearing nothing but a long white nightgown and a pair of old muddy hiking boots. My hair is down, not even caught up in a ponytail. I must look frightful.

Kyle pulls out at an alarming speed.

"Kyle, slow down. Watch where you're going."

"I know what I'm doing."

"I don't think you do. There's a curve up here."

"I see it."

"You better slow down."

"Miss Jack! Shut up! Please!"

I'm about to scold him, then I see the tears streaming down his cheeks and the determination in his eyes, and I don't say anything. I try to keep my comments to a minimum for

the rest of the drive. I'm not sure how successful I am at this, but Kyle doesn't feel the need to shout again, only to occasionally remind me that he knows what he's doing.

I've never been to their house so I have no idea where we're going. We drive through town, then head into empty countryside. We pass a few homes, a few farms, then turn off down a broken asphalt road.

I can barely make out anything in the distance but Kyle suddenly shouts, "There's his truck. I can see it. It's parked in front of our house."

I fully expect him to speed up but instead he begins to slow down.

"What the hell? What's going on?" he wonders then groans, "No way. I can't believe it. We're out of gas."

"We can't be," I say automatically but without any proof to back me up.

The car rolls to a complete stop.

"This is Luis's fault," I say, but Kyle doesn't hear me.

He's already out of the car.

The door slams and I'm left sitting alone in the dark.

CHAPTER TWENTY-SIX: KYLE

I run.

I glance behind me once and see this apparition following me. I think it's a ghost at first: a white billowing thing with white hair streaming out behind it. Then I realize it's Miss Jack. She's running, too.

I tear into our backyard, not thinking at all where I'm going or why, just letting my instincts carry me.

"Klint!" I call out. "Where are you?"

My eyes dart from the back porch to the sandbox to the swing set to Bill's porch.

Suddenly, I see him and relief rushes through me until I realize what I'm seeing.

He's sitting in the fork of the tree where our hideout used to be, holding a rope in his hands. One end is tied to a thick branch about ten feet off the ground and the other end is tied around his neck.

I run toward him, looking at him, trying to get him to look at me. I tell myself if he'll only make eye contact with me, everything

will be fine.

I'm wrong. He does look at me, but there's no recognition in his gaze. There's no life in his eyes at all.

He calmly swings down off the branch the way I've seen him do it so many times in the past. Effortlessly, fearlessly, with a born athlete's grace. Only this time his feet don't hit the ground. His body jerks at the end of the rope.

I know I scream. I know I make some inhuman howl, but I don't hear it.

My knees give out on me and I collapse to the ground but I'm up again instantly, pulling my knife from my pocket.

He's not dead. He's flopping around like a hooked fish. His legs are pedaling. His hands are clawing at the rope around his neck. But he can be saved. For now.

I grab him around the legs and try to hold him up.

He continues to convulse. A hideous hollow choking noise is coming from his throat. His eyes are wide open but not seeing. I can't do anything for him. I try to get beneath him and shift his weight onto my shoulder so he can sit on me, but he keeps kicking me in the head. He's jerking too much, and he weighs too much, more than he usually does. Dead weight, I think to myself and I start to scream.

Miss Jack is suddenly by my side, the expression of terror on her ashen face and

the moans as she tries to catch her breath making her seem even more like a ghost than before.

"Hold him," I beg her.

She tries to take my place. It's not easy. She's an old woman trying to do something a young man couldn't do. She reaches up and grabs him around his hips and gets under him while he continues to kick and flail.

I scramble up the boards nailed into the trunk that used to be the stairs to our tree house, crawl out onto the branch, and start cutting through the rope.

I don't know how long it takes. It seems like forever. It seems like I will never know a time where I won't be sawing through a rope pulled taut from the sickening weight of my dying brother, listening to the sounds of him gagging for breath and Miss Jack whimpering in pain.

But even forever doesn't really last forever.

The rope breaks, and Klint falls to the ground on top of Miss Jack.

I jump down and try to loosen the noose around his neck.

He's seizing and choking. I don't know how to help him. I take his hand, but he doesn't squeeze back. I say his name over and over again. His eyes stay open and stare straight ahead. I don't want to know what he's seeing.

Miss Jack is lying on the ground, and she isn't moving at all.

Chapter Twenty-Seven: Candace Jack

The first thing I see is two dozen yellow roses.

The second is a large smiling woman with short, bouncy brown curls in a neon pink smock covered in tiny blue cats.

I'd heard that modern-day nurses had dispensed with traditional white and now wore bright colors and busy patterns. I couldn't understand why this would be true, but now I see that it must be part of a plan to make patients even more eager to recover and leave.

She walks over to me, beaming. Her name pin reads: SANDI.

"Well, look who's decided to wake up. How are you feeling?"

"I'm not sure," I answer her and try shifting in my bed, only to be stabbed by pain in seemingly every part of my body.

"You better take it easy," she tells me. "We're going to need to get you some pain medication. You're pretty beat up.

"You've got a broken arm, a broken col-

larbone, and two bruised ribs," she tells me cheerfully as she busies herself around my bed. "And look at this."

She takes a hand mirror out of a drawer and holds it up to my face.

I gasp.

"Two beautiful shiners," she gushes. "You look like you've been in a bar fight. My teenage sons would love to look like that."

I don't know what she's talking about. I don't know why I'm here. I can't remember anything, then suddenly I do.

It must show in my face because her own expression changes from perky to concerned, and she quickly takes my hand that isn't in a cast.

"Don't you worry. He's fine."

"Who?"

"Your grandson."

"My grandson?"

"The boy you came in with. Is that why you looked so upset?"

"Yes," I tell her and feel tears spring to my eyes. "He's alive?"

"Very much so, honey."

She pats my hand.

"He's in his own room downstairs. Oh, here."

She hands me a box of tissues.

"I know," she says sympathetically. "It was a close call."

"Can I see him?"

"I don't see why not, but let's check with your doctor first. I don't know if he wants you up so soon."

"I don't care what my doctor says. I want to see him."

"And you'll find it pointless to argue with her," Bert says as he comes walking into the room with more flowers. "She always gets her way."

"Well, I'll see what I can do," Sandi says on her way out. "You'll need a wheelchair."

"Candace," he sighs.

He lays the flowers on a table and pulls up a chair next to me.

"Words fail me. Of all the problems I envisioned you might encounter by taking in these boys, ending up battered in a hospital bed certainly wasn't one of them."

"Does the entire world know?"

"No one knows. Kyle called me last night, and I haven't told anyone else yet. I assumed you'd want it that way."

"My family?"

"No. I was going to call Cam today if you weren't up to it."

"Luis?"

"He's been here by your side all night. I called him in New York, and he drove here straight from the airport. I finally convinced him this morning to go home and take a shower and change."

"What are you smiling at?"

"The fact that he wasn't here when you woke up, but I was," he laughs. "He's going to think I sent him away on purpose."

I smile at the thought.

"Yes, I suppose he will. And what about Kyle? Where is he?"

"He spent the night with Klint."

"Oh my God, Bert."

The horror of last night descends upon me in a rush. Poor Kyle. Does a boy ever recover from witnessing something like that? And Klint? What is to become of him?

Bert pats my arm.

"Everything's going to be fine," he tells me.

"Did Kyle tell you any of the details?" I ask him.

"No. Just that Klint tried to . . . ," he finds it hard to say the words, "to hang himself and you found him in time."

"It's too soon to talk about it now, but I'm going to need your professional help." I feel some of my old energy returning and I try to sit up, but the pain is too much.

"I want to become their legal guardian while they're still minors," I continue, "and I want to make sure their mother isn't allowed to have any contact with them."

"That won't be easy."

"Believe me. We can make it happen."

Sandi returns with a wheelchair and a syringe.

"Don't worry. I'm going to put this in your

IV, not your arm."

She gives me the shot, then stands back with her hands on her ample hips and eyes me skeptically.

"Are you sure you want to try this already?"

"Yes," I say.

"Okay, but you're going to hurt."

"I know."

I say the words cavalierly but only because I'm not prepared for exactly how much I'm going to hurt.

Trying to get out of bed and into the wheelchair is by far the most physically painful thing I've ever done in my life, but I try not to let it show.

Once I'm securely in my seat, Sandi steps back from me, grinning.

"I hope you won't take offense at this, Miss Jack, but I just gotta say it. You're one tough old bird."

I laugh.

"I'm not offended at all," I say.

Bert stays behind, and Sandi wheels me to the elevator and then to the wing where Klint is staying.

I'm surprised at first when we push through the doors into the corridor and the walls are painted with rainbows and papered with posters of puppies and dinosaurs. The waiting room is filled with toys, and the TV is playing an animated Disney film.

It slipped my mind entirely that he'd be in

the pediatric ward.

Sandi leaves me outside the door while she taps and sticks her head in his room.

"Hello, hon," she chirps. "Do you feel up to a visitor?" I hear her ask him.

She comes back out smiling, props open the door, and wheels me in.

"I'll leave you two alone," she whispers to me as she departs.

Klint is sitting up in bed wearing blue pajamas. He's drinking from a cup with a straw and looks heart-wrenchingly young.

His neck is an angry, raw mass of dark red and purple bruising, and the circles under his eyes make him look like he hasn't slept in months, but otherwise, he appears to be a normal, living boy and that's all I dared to hope for.

Kyle is fast asleep in a chair.

Klint's eyes dart in my direction. They're very blue against the pale skin of his careworn face.

"Hello, Klint."

He stares back at me and then something so odd happens to his face, I almost can't identify it at first.

The boy smiles.

"Hey, Miss Jack," he says in a soft, cracked voice.

The smile grows bigger.

"I'm sorry. I know it's not funny, but you're really beat up."

I smile back at him.

"I hear I look like I've been in a bar fight."

"Yeah," he says, nodding.

"I also hear it suits me."

"Yeah. Maybe."

I glance at Kyle.

"How long has he been like that?"

"A while. Since I woke up."

Kyle is slumped down in a hard plastic chair. His head has fallen forward on his chest. He reminds me of a wilting daisy when the flower becomes too heavy for the stem.

"It looks uncomfortable."

"Yeah."

"Did the two of you get to talk?"

"Yeah. I was conscious in the ambulance. You're the one everybody thought was dead."

We sit in silence for a few minutes. The only sound in the room is the sound of Kyle snoring. I'm not sure what the proper etiquette is for visiting with someone who less than twelve hours earlier had been trying to take his own life. What are the appropriate topics of conversation? Every idea I come up with I quickly discard. Everything seems either too frivolous or too serious.

I finally settle on asking him if he needs anything from home. Would he like Bert to bring him a favorite T-shirt or some of his *Sports Illustrated* magazines or a bologna sandwich?

I'm about to open my mouth to speak when

I notice tears are silently rolling down his cheeks.

He notices me watching him.

"I made a mistake," he says. "I don't want to die."

"I'm very glad to hear you say that, Klint."

I reach out my hand to him, and he takes it.

"You're a strong person," I tell him, "and one of the problems with being a strong person is that other people think because you can handle most things, you can handle everything. And after a while, you start to believe it, too."

He rubs his tears away by screwing his fists against his eyes, a gesture that makes him look younger still.

"Do you think you can handle everything?" he asks me.

"There was a time, yes, but I realized I was wrong."

"When did you find out?"

I consider his question.

"When you and your brother came to stay with me."

His smile returns. The expression suits him. I could easily get used to seeing him like this.

"We're really that bad, huh?"

"No, no, not at all," I protest. "I'm not referring to problems. I'm talking about the emotional commitment. I'm afraid I've kept very much to myself for most of my life. I'm

wondering now if this was a mistake. Here I am, approaching the end of my life, and I realize I don't have any friends."

"Luis and Bert are your friends."

"Yes, that's true, but they also work for me."

"We're your friends, Miss Jack. Me and Kyle."

"Kyle and I."

"Kyle and I," he repeats.

I was so concerned with correcting the grammar of his sentence, I didn't listen to the content. This time I do.

"Kyle and I are your friends."

"Well, thank you, Klint," I reply, unsure of the feelings welling up inside me.

I'm going to cry. I must be overmedicated.

I take out the tissue tucked into the sleeve of my robe.

"Thank you. That's very kind of you."

"You don't have to thank someone for being your friend," he starts to tell me, but his voice breaks into a rasping cough.

He winces and takes a sip from his cup.

"And I'm not being kind," he adds in barely a whisper.

"That's enough. You shouldn't strain your voice."

He reaches for a small pad of paper sitting on his tray and a pencil with Stanford Jack Memorial Hospital stamped on its side.

He writes something, rips the page free, and hands it to me.

The note says: It's my pleasure.

"There you are!"

Luis cries out from behind me.

"I leave for twenty minutes and everything falls to pieces. You shouldn't be out of bed. What are you thinking? Where is your doctor? Do you know how many broken bones you have?"

His voice is full of exasperation, but his eyes are soft and he looks refreshed and capable in a pair of tan trousers and a chocolate brown sweater with a mandarin orange shirt collar peeking out at his neckline.

Amazingly, his outburst doesn't wake Kyle, who continues to snore.

He nods at Klint.

"Cómo está, caballero?"

"He's not allowed to talk right now," I explain.

"It's okay. We talked last night and this morning while you were being Sleeping Beauty."

"I'm just lucky that when I did wake up, I had a prince waiting by my side to take care of me."

"Oh, yes, your prince," Luis says, rolling his eyes. "Of course, Bert was with you when you woke up. I knew he was up to something when he convinced me to go home. I knew he didn't really care if I looked rumpled."

He disappears behind me and I feel my wheelchair begin to move.

"I'm taking Miss Jack back to her room," Luis tells Klint. "You can see each other later."

Unfortunately, Luis navigates a wheelchair in much the same way he drives a car. I'm feeling rather jostled by the time we reach my room, and I'm happy to get back into my bed.

No sooner am I situated than he begins to unpack a small suitcase filled with breakfast foods.

He narrates as he lays everything out on my tray.

"We have some fresh fruit, homemade bread, quince marmalade, fresh-squeezed orange juice, your favorite tea, some cheese and hard-boiled eggs."

He ends by bringing out a single purple iris and a crystal bud vase. He fills the vase from a pitcher of water on my bedside table and sets the flower in front of one of Bert's many yellow arrangements.

"Luis, this is wonderful," I tell him, "but I'm really not hungry. You were right. I shouldn't have got out of bed. But I had to see him with my own eyes."

He studies the food, then my face, and begins repacking.

"You don't look so good. Maybe I should call a nurse."

"No, I'm fine. Could I have some water, please?"

"This is all my fault," he says, pouring me some water. "If I had been here last night . . ."

"It wouldn't have changed anything," I interrupt him. "The only difference would be that you'd be the one lying in the hospital bed."

"I would switch places with you gladly."

"Not gladly. Trust me."

I grimace at the pain and take a sip of the lukewarm water.

More worry shows on his face.

He reaches back into the bag and brings out a long string of beads that he hands to me.

"For you," he says.

"This is a rosary."

"I know what it is."

"I'm not religious, and I'm certainly not Catholic."

Next he brings out a small crucifix.

"Oh, dear Jesus," I sigh.

"Exactly right."

"Really, Luis."

"As a favor to me?"

"Fine," I concede.

As I watch him try to find the best location for his holy relics, I think about my talk with Klint and what's written on the scrap of paper I slipped into my robe pocket.

"Luis, have you stayed with me all these years solely because I've provided you with a marvelous job?"

"Marvelous job?" he sputters.

I can tell he's about to launch into one of his tirades where he compares his lot in life to that of an Egyptian slave toting great blocks of marble for his pharaoh, but he catches himself and turns contemplative instead.

"No, I have not stayed for the job," he tells me quietly. "You and I have never shared a bank account or a child or a bed. But you are my wife."

Chapter Twenty-Eight: Kyle

I think the biggest change in Klint since he's been seeing his shrink is that he doesn't call me a faggot anymore.

Other than that, he's pretty much his old self. He talks a little more than he used to and he seems more relaxed, but these are good things.

I always knew my brother had a personality. I knew he was smart and considerate and had a good sense of humor, but he did everything in his power not to let any of this show. He wanted to come across as a tough guy who didn't need anybody or like anybody and who thought he was better than everybody else.

I never understood where this came from. He certainly didn't get it from our father.

Dad was a friendly outgoing guy who loved to talk people's ears off and who spent half his time laughing at funny things and the other half laughing at life's tragedies. He bitched and moaned in private about his

circumstances, but these were only words he thought he was supposed to say. Deep down he was proud that he had a family and he was able to support it, even if he didn't have the most glamorous, high-paying job in the world. He didn't care what other people thought about him. I don't think the word *embarrassing* was in his vocabulary.

Klint seemed to be his opposite, but I knew better. I saw them together all the time and sometimes Klint would let his guard down with Dad and they'd joke around and talk about stuff and seem almost identical. I was the only person who could make Klint laugh, but Dad was the only one who could make him happy.

I never knew why Klint always seemed to be hiding, but now I do. He had been buried beneath a mountain of shame, and he believed if he dug even a small hole to show any part of himself, even a good part, there was a chance the bad part would show through, too.

Since his confession to me we haven't talked about Mom or any of the stuff he told me. Maybe we never will, and I'm okay with that. He definitely needs to talk to someone about it and that's what his doctor's for, but as far as how things stand with me, what matters the most is that he knows I know.

The burden of his secret has been lifted, and he can breathe again. When I think back

to his deterioration during the weeks before he tried to kill himself and even the way he tried to do it, I believe he was choking to death, suffocating on shame. Tying that noose around his neck was the only way he knew how to end it.

Besides me, only Miss Jack and Bert know what Mom did. Miss Jack said she had to tell Bert for legal reasons and didn't explain more than that and I didn't want her to. She took care of telling Mom and Aunt Jen what happened. It's been two weeks and we haven't heard from either of them.

We've been able to keep that part quiet, but it was impossible to hide the truth about Klint's suicide attempt. His breakdown was too public. It's a small town. He's a local hero, and the people here feel invested in his future and entitled to know about his present. And Tyler Mann is his best friend and if Tyler Mann knows something, all the Manns know it and exponentially speaking, within one hour of phone time, six hundred other people know it, too.

I don't blame them for this. It's not the kind of thing that could be kept secret. One of the cops who responded to my 911 call turned out to be married to our second-grade teacher. He would've had to tell her, and she'd go to school the next day and tell the other teachers. One of the ER nurses went to high school with my mom and dad, and the

cashier at the hospital cafeteria was the mom of a kid in my geometry class who always falls asleep.

I'm sure that even Bill spilled the beans the next night sitting in a bar having everyone ask him if it's true what they heard about the Hayes kid, the one who plays baseball.

When something dramatic and gut-wrenching happens to someone, everybody wants to talk about it. That's human nature. I just wish all the dramatic, gut-wrenching stuff could stop happening to me.

For the most part, everyone's been nice about it. I suppose that's not easy for some people. Coming face-to-face with a guy who tried to end his life, who actually put the rope around his neck and let go, can bring out all kinds of uncomfortable feelings from pity to fear and disgust. Some people think it's a sin. Some think it's a sign of insanity. Some people can't allow themselves to feel sympathy for him because he did it to himself. Others feel too much sympathy and treat him too cautiously, like he might get up and throw himself through a window at any moment.

Bill's been coming by almost every day. He's even started having tea with Miss Jack, which I thought would be one of the funniest things I'd ever see in my life but instead in some weird way seems totally normal. He even stayed for dinner once and had some paella.

Tyler comes a lot, too, always loaded down with cards and homemade gifts from his pack of creative sisters who all have crushes on Klint, except for Britney who has one on me.

She's the only one who's thought of me in all this. She made me a Get Well card. At first when I read it, I thought maybe she got confused and thought I'd been in the hospital, too, but the more I looked at the rainbow with birds flying around it and a smiling sun above it and read the simple sentiment, the more I was convinced she's just one very insightful kid.

"Dear Kyle," she wrote. "I hope you're feeling better."

Two people have been noticeably absent from visiting Klint.

The first is Shelby. I thought for sure she'd be racing over here to tend to her one true love, but she hasn't even sent him a text.

I know she visited Miss Jack in the hospital after Klint was already back home. (Miss Jack had to stay longer than Klint did.) I thought she'd come to visit her aunt once she got home, too, but so far she hasn't been here.

I'm not mad at her anymore. I regret a lot of the things I said in that parking lot. I wish she'd feel the same way.

The other missing person is Coach Hill.

A bunch of Klint's teammates have come out to visit from time to time along with Tyler. They go up to the TV room and at first

it's quiet, but then they start to joke around and it gets pretty rowdy.

Klint hasn't said anything to me about the team. I don't know if he even thinks he's still on it or if he wants to still be on it. I don't know if he's upset that Coach hasn't checked up on him. He hasn't talked about baseball at all.

He hasn't missed that much. The past two weeks have been nothing but practices leading up to the first game of the first round of the state championship in four days.

Counting the Laurel Falls game, he only missed the last three of their season. They ended up losing to Laurel Falls by one run. They were 1-1 their last two games.

They hadn't lost a single game this year while Klint was playing. A superstitious man might place some importance in this fact and do everything possible to get Klint back, but Coach Hill doesn't believe in luck of any kind. He believes a team that wants to win will win.

But if his logic is followed to its illogical end and it's assumed that the reason the team didn't win was because it didn't want to, then it might also follow that the reason they didn't want to win was because Klint was missing.

I don't know if this has finally occurred to Coach Hill or if he wants him back based solely on his previous merits or if he's only

stopping by to ask Klint for his uniform but whatever the reason, I come downstairs after Miss Jack calls me and find Coach Hill standing stiffly in her ornate parlor in his gray sweatpants, team windbreaker, and ball cap; he looks like a piece of gravel that's fallen inside a little girl's jewelry box.

Miss Jack is standing beside him leaning on her new cane. She's not supposed to be standing. She had bad knees to begin with, and she really messed them up running to get to Klint.

Between her arm in a cast and her broken collarbone, she hasn't been able to get back into real clothes yet.

She's wearing a long, emerald green robe and matching slippers. The glasses she keeps on a chain around her neck are perched on the end of her nose. The bruises around her eyes have faded from their original purplish gray to a faint yellow green.

Luis is standing nearby frowning at her. I know he wants her to sit down.

"Kyle, Mr. Hill is here to see your brother," she tells me.

"Coach Hill," he corrects her.

"Oh, I'm sorry. I hadn't realized coach had become an official title like doctor or prime minister."

"Hey, Kyle."

"Hey, Coach."

"Do you think it's a good idea?" Miss Jack

asks me.

"I don't know. Are you here to see if he wants to play on Monday?"

"Does he want to play?"

"I don't know."

"Am I to understand that you're not here to see how Klint is feeling," Miss Jack breaks in, "but only to see if he's still capable of playing your silly game?"

"Silly game?" Coach exclaims.

"He hasn't talked to me at all about the team," I dive in, suddenly realizing it might be good to keep Coach and Miss Jack from talking too much to each other.

I think Luis has the same idea because he tries to get Miss Jack to sit down, but she won't listen to him.

Coach gets right to the point.

"Do you think he can still play?" he asks me.

"Sure. Why wouldn't he be able to play? He's fine."

"I'm not talking about here."

He curls his arm and claps his hand down on his bicep.

"I'm talking about here."

He taps the side of his head.

"He's not the same anymore. He's crazy."

"He is not crazy," Miss Jack says, angrily.

"He's not crazy," I agree with her. "He was crazy before. Now he's okay."

"Okay. Whatever. Crazy then. Crazy now.

What I'm saying is, he was a great ballplayer before. Can he still play ball now?"

"I don't see why not."

"It's a mental game, Kyle."

"A mental game?" Miss Jack interrupts. "Baseball? I thought it was a bunch of men standing in a field waiting for another man to hit a ball to them with a stick. I can't see how that could require any more thought than throwing rocks in a pond."

Coach Hill's face starts to turn the distinctive shade of burst-capillary reddish pink it always becomes before he explodes at a player or an ump.

"She doesn't know anything about baseball," I explain to him, trying to head off an outburst he might regret. "She's never seen a game. Ever."

He stops being mad and becomes dumfounded.

"He needs to play in state finals this year," I tell him, trying to distract him from Miss Jack. "What about his future?"

"I don't know that he's got a future. No college coach wants a kid on their team who might crack under the pressure and try and kill himself."

"Coach Hill," Miss Jack gasps, "I am not going to let you speak that way about Klint."

Luis looks toward heaven.

"Qué mierda," he mutters.

"A criminal record they can overlook,"

Coach goes on, ignoring her, "but crazy . . ."

"Would you please stop using the word *crazy?*" she interrupts him again. "Klint Hayes is one of the sanest people I've ever met. It takes a tremendous amount of mental and emotional fortitude to endure what he's endured."

We all fall silent at the sound of footsteps in the hall.

Klint comes walking into the room. He's in a pair of jeans and a plain blue T-shirt. He still has marks around his neck; they look much better but only to us, I realize as I watch Coach's eyes fasten on Klint's throat and a pained expression cross over his face. They must look horrible to him.

"Hey, Coach," Klint says. "I thought I heard your voice."

"Hey, Klint. We've missed you at practice."

"I've missed being there."

"You have?"

"Well, sure. I've never missed this much practice time in my life."

"You know you were always welcome to come back. No one ever thought you were off the team. I mean, I wasn't exactly thrilled with the way you handled yourself at the Laurel Falls game. It was pretty stupid and you may have lost . . ."

"Coach Hill!" Miss Jack cries out again, her patience obviously wearing very thin.

Coach glances at her and shakes his head

in disgusted defeat.

"What I'm saying is, you weren't kicked off the team because of it," he finishes.

"Thanks."

"Is that what you thought?"

"I didn't know what to think."

"I suppose I should've been in touch sooner but we've been busy getting ready for states. I guess it slipped my mind."

"Your best player slipped your mind?" Miss Jack scoffs.

"Why are you here?" Klint asks.

"Well, I wanted to see how you're doing. Maybe see if you feel up to playing on Monday?"

"Isn't it kind of late to come and ask me that?"

"I went ahead and put you on the varsity roster."

"Thanks, but that's not what I'm talking about. Why didn't you ask me last week?"

"I wanted to give you your space."

Klint doesn't buy it. I can see it in his eyes. He's probably wondering the same things I'm wondering: Does Coach actually believe Klint can't play anymore and that's why he wrote him off, or has he been afraid to see him? Was he so freaked out by Klint's suicide attempt that he was actually ready to jeopardize their shot at the state title rather than face him?

We'll never know for sure. Coach may have

a one-track mind, but that track passes by a lot of weird places. All that matters is if Klint wants to play.

We're all waiting for his answer when he surprises us by turning to Miss Jack.

"Will you come to the game?" he asks her.

She's been standing there glaring at Coach like she might pull a shotgun out from under her robe and blast his head off and now she falls apart into a female fluster.

"Oh. Well. I . . . ," she stammers, then glances at Luis and composes herself.

"Yes," she says. "Yes, I will."

Klint holds out his hand to Coach Hill. He takes it and they shake.

"Okay, Coach," he says. "You've got yourself a second baseman."

"Good. Practice tomorrow and Saturday," Coach says. "I'll see you there."

He starts to leave, then pauses.

"Oh, by the way, Mrs. Hill says she hopes you're feeling better."

We nod and stare at the floor while we wait to hear Luis see him out, then we look up at each other and burst out laughing.

I'm pretty pumped up after Coach leaves. I'd been in a kind of denial where I avoided talking to Klint about finishing the season in case it upset him, but the truth is, it's all I've been thinking about. They have a shot at being state champs this year. It's a big deal, and it's

something Klint has wanted since he set his first Little League MVP trophy on the shelf beside the TV.

Klint's in a great mood now, too. He leaves the room for a couple minutes and comes back with two of his gloves and a ball.

He throws his old glove at me and says, "How about some catch?"

I don't know how many times in my life I heard my dad say those words to Klint. He never said them to me. He never had to. By the time I was old enough to throw a ball around, he was busy with his superstar in the making.

Klint's the one who taught me. We haven't played in a long time. Somewhere along the way, when baseball stopped being a game for him and became a job, tossing a ball back and forth in the yard with his little brother must have seemed pointless.

Today he acts like there's nothing he'd rather be doing.

Miss Jack has hundreds of acres, but we stay in front of the house in the gravel drive. The warm sun on my shoulders and the lazy rhythmic smack of the ball hitting our gloves lulls me into a waking doze. I hear the sound of a car's engine in the distance, but I don't notice that it seems to be getting closer. A flash of red streaking through the trees behind Klint jolts me back to my senses.

Before I can decide if I should run and hide

or stay and be snubbed, Shelby has parked her car and the choice has been made for me. She's seen me and I can't leave without looking like a coward or a jerk.

I'm hopeful from the moment I see her. Gone is the drab disarrayed chic of her Paris wardrobe. She's wearing neon pink Converse tennis shoes, white shorts, and a crisp sleeveless yellow blouse tied beneath her rib cage exposing the flat plane of her belly.

Her eyes are hidden behind big sunglasses set in yellow frames, and I can't tell what's she's thinking or feeling as she walks toward the house.

I never told Klint about Starr and me, but he did figure out something was wrong between Shelby and me. He asked what happened and I told him it didn't matter, the main thing was I got sick of her jerking me around. This seemed to be all the explanation he needed.

The two of us stop playing catch and stand stiffly on either side of Miss Jack's front lawn like palace sentries.

Klint takes the ball and throws it into his own glove. *Thwack!* He does it again. *Thwack!* He watches Shelby suspiciously as she approaches.

I wonder if she's actually going to walk into the house without saying a word to either of us. This would be a whole new level of cold for her.

She comes to a stop directly between us.

Thwack!

"Hi, Klint," she says without making any move to get any closer to him. "How are you?"

Thwack!

"Good."

Thwack!

"Hi, Kyle," she says quietly.

"Hey," I reply.

She takes off her sunglasses and looks at me.

"Could we talk somewhere?"

Thwack, thwack, thwack!

"Sure."

Klint lopes up the front steps and disappears into Miss Jack's house before I can even glance his way.

"Where do you want to talk?" I ask her.

"We can do it right here."

We walk over to the porch and both take a seat on the bottom step. She pulls off a leaf from one of her aunt's rhododendron bushes and starts rolling it between her fingers.

"I like your shoes," I tell her.

"Pretty bright, huh? I got tired of dressing like a cold, rainy day," she says with a sigh, "even if it was tres chic."

"What's wrong with dressing like bubblegum ice cream?"

She smiles at me.

"Nothing."

I don't say anything else. It was her idea to talk. I wait for her. After a minute of staring at her shoes, she goes on.

"I thought I was so mature when I was in Paris. There I was wearing serious dark clothes and drinking wine and being openly seduced by grown men in public places."

"What?"

She waves away my concern with her leaf.

"Then when I got home, I freaked out on you because you had sex with my sister. That wasn't very mature of me. I had no right to act that way. You're not my boyfriend. You can have sex with whoever you want."

"Not exactly. Let's say I can have sex with whoever wants to have sex with me."

She smiles at me again.

"I know Starr's no angel. And she's very hot. What guy would say no to her? You know what the strange thing is? I was always worried she'd go after Klint and instead she goes after you. Isn't that funny?"

"Yeah, that's funny," I say with a nervous laugh.

"I guess I'm trying to say I'm sorry for the way I acted."

"It's okay. I said some pretty rotten things, too."

"I deserved them. Especially when I started going on and on about how much I loved Klint."

Her voice trails off, and I can tell something

else is bothering her.

"When I heard about Klint, I didn't feel as bad as I should have felt," she confesses.

"What do you mean?"

"If I truly loved Klint with all my heart and soul the way I thought I did, when I heard what happened I would've been devastated. I would've been racing to see him. His pain would have been my pain. Instead, the only person I was thinking about was you."

"Me?"

"Yes. I was worried about *you.* And something else. I know this sounds horrible but knowing what he did" — she pauses and struggles with her words — "it changed how I feel about him."

"He's not crazy," I state automatically and defensively, recalling Coach Hill's accusations.

"I know," she replies quickly, her eyes widening in apology. "I don't think anything like that. It's just that Klint always seemed so tough. Like nothing could shake him."

"Now you think he's weak?"

"No, I don't think that, either."

She stops and goes back to staring at the tips of her sneakers.

"What he did makes him seem human."

I can't help laughing at this.

"You were looking for an inhuman guy?"

She laughs, too.

"I could introduce you to Chad Hopper," I tell her.

"Who's Chad Hopper?"

"Someone who fits into that category."

"Maybe inhuman isn't the right word. How about unreal?"

"Well, that sure isn't Klint or me. We're as real as they come."

As soon as I make this proclamation, she reaches for my hand and squeezes tightly.

"Do you remember how we met?"

"Four years ago at the county fair," I rattle off. "You wanted to go on the Zipper and your friend, Whitney, wouldn't go with you. I heard you talking about it and I volunteered to take you."

"I couldn't believe it," she says, grinning broadly at the memory. "You weren't like any boy I knew at my school. They would've stood around in a big, stupid group laughing and making fun of me. None of them would've had the guts to ask me to go on a ride no matter how much he might have wanted it because he'd be afraid I'd embarrass him. But you didn't care about what anybody else thought. You were your own man."

This seems like a good moment so I go for it.

"Since you're not stuck on Klint anymore, does that mean you're available?" I ask, hopefully.

"I don't want a boyfriend right now," she replies, giving me a playful smile. "I like being free."

"Maybe we can be free together?"

"Okay."

She gets up suddenly from the step, and her eyes widen again, this time with excitement.

"You know that bullfighter, El Soltero? The one that's in all those posters all over Aunt Candace's house?"

"Yeah."

"It turns out she was going to marry him."

Her voice takes on the low, hurried, breathless quality I love so well.

"They were madly in love, but the night she was going to accept his proposal, he was killed by a bull. Right in front of her. The bull she brought home with her. Calladito! Ventisco's grandfather! Have you ever heard of anything so romantic?"

I'm not sure I'd call it romantic, but I smile and nod and act like this is the first time I'm hearing about any of it.

"When I went to visit her in the hospital, she told me all about it. She's going to show me some pictures today. Do you want to see them?"

"Sure," I say.

We race up the steps together. At the door Shelby turns to me and holds me in her amber eyes sparked with flecks of spring

green light.

"My aunt Candace was a beautiful woman," she says proudly.

"I'm not surprised," I tell her.

Chapter Twenty-Nine

Nothing can entice Mrs. Hill to a game, not even the possibility of Mr. Hill finally achieving the state title that has eluded him during his twenty years of coaching high school baseball.

If it happens, it won't be today. This is only round one of the western region play-offs. It's the game we lost last year on a Brent Richmond error. A win will take us on to the quarterfinals and then the semifinals and hopefully the championship game.

I explain all this to Miss Jack as we make our way to our seats. She's moving very slowly and leaning heavily on her cane. It's been over two weeks since she got hurt, but old people don't heal very fast. According to Luis, sometimes they don't heal at all. She's still in a lot of pain, but she never complains.

Luis was against this idea. He said it was too soon for her to go out and especially for her to do something as exhausting and potentially dangerous to her old, brittle bones

as maneuver her way through jostling crowds of enthusiastic baseball fans and then sit on a hard seat for hours in the sun.

The more he told her she couldn't go, the more she dug her heels in and insisted on going, until finally it got to the point where I couldn't tell if Luis was telling her she couldn't go on purpose because he knew that would make her go.

Eventually a compromise was reached where Miss Jack promised to wear a sun hat and take bottled water with her, and I had to assure Luis I'd stay by her side every minute.

When I asked Luis why he didn't want to come along with us, he said it wasn't his place.

The only remaining problem was how to get there. The drive to Altoona and the Blair County Ballpark was over an hour and if Luis didn't want to stay for the game, it didn't make much sense for him to drive all that distance, back and forth, twice in one day.

Miss Jack suggested he could drop us off and stay in Altoona and soak up the culture while we watched the game. He said something elaborate to her in Spanish. I didn't understand any of it except the word *cojones.*

Miss Jack and I started joking about who was going to drive — her or me — if Luis didn't want to take us. He said even more stuff to her in Spanish.

Our problem solved itself when Miss Jack

got a phone call from Shelby's mom telling her she'd love to attend the big game.

Miss Jack got off the phone with a puzzled look on her face and explained to me and Luis that apparently Rae Ann was a closet baseball fan and was briefly engaged to a minor-league player in Miami before she met Mr. Jack, a Cuban named Pedro Juan.

Miss Jack and Luis had a lot to say about that in Spanish to each other.

Luis saw us off this morning after sticking some sunblock, a pack of moist towelettes, a pretty Spanish fan, and a couple bottles of water into Mrs. Jack's huge orange straw purse decorated with palm trees and pineapples. I explained about the concession stands, but he insisted on sending their own water.

Mrs. Jack looked and smelled like she was off to spend a day at the beach. She had on a short, sleeveless turquoise-blue sundress and a matching ball cap, painful-looking strappy sandals covered in silver jewels, mirrored sunglasses, and tons of wooden and glass bead necklaces draped around her neck like Hawaiian leis. Her hair was pulled back in a ponytail, and her skin glistened with coconut-scented oil.

Miss Jack looked like she was going to an English tea party with the queen. Her dress was long and loose, made of a gauzy green material the same shade as a katydid's wings,

and her hat was broad brimmed, natural straw, and held on to her head with a sheer scarf tied over it, the same color as her dress but sprinkled with pink rosebuds.

She and Luis debated endlessly about her shoes and her arm and finally decided on a pair of beige canvas loafers for her feet and a cream satin shawl tied at her neck in a makeshift sling to replace the medical supply house one she wore around the house.

I was the only one in our little group who looked like he was going to a ball game.

Miss Jack seems to like the ballpark. As we walked in the front gates she commented on the loveliness of the redbrick façade. She said she expected something cheap and modern. I told her the look of the park was inspired by the old railroad roundhouses that used to be all over Altoona back in its heyday and that even the minor-league team that the park was built for took its name from the railroad industry. Most people think the Altoona Curve is named after the curveball, but the name actually comes from the historic Horseshoe Curve carved into a nearby mountain.

Miss Jack was impressed with my knowledge. I explained to her that baseball can be a long, boring game and you have to find some way to entertain yourself, even if it's only talking to old-timers and reading promotional brochures.

Once inside, she marveled at the cleanli-

ness and the size of the park, but then she got distracted marveling at the size of the people. I tried to regain her attention by spouting more facts at her, like the park seats seventy-two hundred people, and pointing out the big wooden roller coaster sitting beyond the right-field fence. She liked that enough to stop wailing about how people should put down their Big Macs and go for a walk.

We've got great seats right behind our dugout. Bill's already there. He sees us coming. It would be impossible not to. He stands up and waves.

I notice everyone's been watching us and sort of acting strange, falling silent and automatically moving aside when we approach them. It could be solely because of Miss Jack's outfit, but I also get the feeling people might know who she is and the myth that surrounds her. Luis informed me as we were leaving this morning that she hasn't made a public appearance in forty years (except for the one night she showed up very unexpectedly at The Mine Shaft).

She's barely been seated when Tyler's dad leans in from the seat behind her where the Mann clan and their many friends and relations are taking up four solid rows. Almost every one of them is wearing a T-shirt that proclaims: TYLER IS THE MANN.

"Excuse me, Miss Jack, but I have to

introduce myself. I'm Harvey Mann, Tyler's father. I just want to thank you for inviting him to your home. That was a real thrill for him. A real thrill. My family's worked for J&P Coal for many generations. We got a whole new generation now hoping all that talk about clean coal and getting a lot of the mines working again ain't just talk."

Miss Jack insists on getting back on her feet to properly greet him. I help her up.

"Mr. Mann," she says, extending her hand. "I'd recognize you anywhere."

"Well, thank you, I think," he laughs.

He has the same crew cut and the same grin as his son. Hang thirty years, fifty pounds, and eight trips to the maternity ward on Tyler and you have his dad.

"This is my wife, Sally."

Miss Jack takes her hand, too.

"You have a charming son," she says.

"Charming?" Mr. Mann laughs again. "Well, that ain't exactly a word I'd use to describe him."

Mrs. Mann swats his beefy arm.

"He is too charming."

Miss Jack scans the rows of matching T-shirts.

"You have quite a large family."

"Eight kids."

"Goodness," she exclaims.

She gets seated again, and before I can even coax her into having a sip of water, Britney is

standing in front along with a few of her sisters. She holds up a marker.

"Can we sign your cast?" she asks, excitedly.

"Well, I don't know." Miss Jack looks at me.

I shrug.

"Certainly," she replies and returns Britney's smile. "Why not?"

I settle into my seat and finally allow myself to relax a little and soak up some atmosphere. It's a great day for a game. The sky is blue. The sun is shining. The air is filled with the smell of hot dogs, popcorn, freshly raked dirt, and new-mown grass.

There's a big turnout. The two decks of seats are almost full, which is impressive for high school ball. This isn't even the championship game yet, but it's no ordinary playoff game, either. The state's best pitcher and top hitter will be meeting for the first time ever: Shane Donner and Klint Hayes are going to finally face each other across that seemingly endless expanse of sixty feet that the ball's going to sizzle over in four-tenths of one second.

The Blue Valley Cougars finish their warm-up, and the Flames take the field for theirs. Both teams briefly mix on the green diamond, their jerseys creating a perfect red, white, and blue American moment.

"There's Klint," Bill points and gushes proudly to Miss and Mrs. Jack.

Mrs. Jack stands up, claps her hands around her mouth, and yells, "Yay, Klint."

They take their positions and start throwing balls around.

"What are they doing?" Miss Jack asks.

"They're warming up," I tell her.

"Is this where he'll be during the game?"

"When they're not at bat, yeah."

She watches for a few minutes, then announces, "I need to speak with Coach Hill."

"No, you can't."

"Why not?"

"Because no one can talk to him right now. The game's about to start."

"Isn't that him? Right there?"

She points out Coach, who's standing near the third-base line with his fists on his hips, vigorously working a piece of chew in his mouth.

I nod.

"He doesn't look unapproachable. He doesn't even look busy."

"Miss Jack," I start to plead.

"I'm going," she tells me.

I bury my head in my hands and groan.

If anyone else had tried to speak to Coach Hill right now — even a pro scout — he would've ignored him, but when Miss Jack calls out to him and finally gets his attention, he comes walking over like he's in a daze.

I know it's not because he's impressed with who she is. I think it's because he can't

believe she's real.

Despite his unbendable belief in the sanctity of pregame ritual and his own exalted position, I think he's helplessly fascinated by her otherworldly weirdness, like he's stumbled upon an alien life-form.

He comes within a few feet of the fence.

"I don't want you to be too hard on Klint," Miss Jack tells him. "He's still fragile."

The coach screws up his face beneath the shadow of his ball cap in a look of complete bafflement.

"Huh?"

"Okay, Miss Jack," I say as I move her away. "Let's go. The coach has a lot to do."

I'm ushering her back up the stairs when Mrs. Jack suddenly bursts out of her seat and screams, "We want a pitcher, not a belly itcher! We want a catcher, not a belly scratcher!"

She raises her fists over her head and shakes them and her boobs in perfect harmony.

"Woo hoo! Go Flames!" she shouts and swivels her hips.

I'm pretty sure she's not even drunk.

"Yeah!" Bill bellows in response, and they high-five each other.

It's going to be an interesting game.

But not on the field. Not for a while.

The first few innings are a snooze. We can't get a hit off Shane Donner. He blazes one fastball after another across the plate. He's

got a wicked curveball, too, with an unpredictable bend and a splitter that no one even wants to try.

He's the picture of composure as he stands on the mound, chewing his gum, calmly nodding or shaking his head at his catcher's signals before letting loose with a ball that travels through space like it's been shot from a cannon.

Klint's first at bat is a tense moment. The entire crowd becomes deathly still and silent. No one dares to breathe.

He's out in four: a foul tip and three strikes.

Bill gives me a look sick with concern. I tell him not to worry.

Personally, I'm relieved. At least he didn't run out of the park this time.

The Cougars don't have much better luck with our pitcher, Joe.

They only get four hits in four innings and aren't able to put a man on base. Two hits are pop-ups. One's a line drive into right field that the hitter foolishly tries to stretch into a double. Klint tags him out after snagging a wild throw from Cody Brockway. A beautiful play on Klint's part. The third is a hard one-hopper Klint fields and throws to Tyler for the easy out on first.

But the most dangerous difference between our pitchers isn't the few hits that have been allowed; it's that Shane retires one batter after another in usually four or five pitches while it

takes Joe a lot more. By the bottom of the fourth inning of the scoreless game, his exhaustion is beginning to show.

I spend half my time worried about Klint and the other half worried that Miss Jack is bored. She doesn't complain. She dutifully drinks her water, fans herself like a señorita, and keeps her eyes trained on Klint when he's in the field. When he's in the dugout, her attention wanders, and she amuses herself by watching people in the stands.

I wanted her to see something exciting. I wanted her to see something as amazing as her tales of what happens at a bullfight.

Since not much is unfolding in front of us, I try to make up for it by explaining what she's not seeing. I try to make her understand that baseball isn't a game for dumb brutes who stand around half-asleep scratching themselves. It's a game of alertness, quick reactions, and complex calculations.

I describe how a hitter faces a ball coming at him at close to a hundred miles per hour, how it arrives at the plate in less than half a second from the time it leaves the pitcher's hand, how half of that half of a second is going to be taken up by the batter's swing so he has to decide well before the ball gets to him what he's going to do.

I also try explaining the intelligence and agility required to play second base, how Klint has to get into the right position every

time, how he has to cover the base and make the right cutoff plays, how he has to respond instantly to driving, smash hits and slicing drives and uncooperative grounders, how he has to catch and throw the ball instantly with hands so soft that he doesn't grasp the ball completely and how he has to have feet as light as any dancer's.

She listens intently to all I have to say, but I don't know if any of it impresses her.

For all those people present at the game who questioned the existence of a merciful god of baseball who believes in granting second chances, all doubts are put to rest in the top of the fifth when Brent Richmond, the goat of last year's series, drills a high line drive between left and center fields that he's able to stretch into a double.

The crowd goes wild not only because Richmond got a hit but because he proved it could be done.

Even the Cougar fans are happy. One of the problems with having the state's best pitcher is that your games are usually pretty boring. Baseball just isn't as good when no one ever gets a hit.

Donner isn't fazed at all. As if to prove it, he strikes out our next two batters with a half-dozen fastballs that crack so loudly in the catcher's mitt, I see people wince.

Klint's up next.

There was a time in my life when I would've

relished this moment, when I would've glanced back and forth between Bill and my dad, the three of us grinning from ear to ear, knowing that Klint's ability to deal with pressure was what separated him from the merely great and the truly remarkable. He could hit and he could field, but what made him the player that people talked about for weeks afterward was his ability to perform in the clutch.

Now I know that what appeared to be an amazing superhero power of his was actually an outward sign of his inner damage or, as his shrink puts it, a dysfunctional coping mechanism that almost killed him. He never let anything get to him because he was able to keep himself from feeling anything at all.

What is he thinking about now? I wonder as I watch him step up to the plate. Is he thinking about Dad? Does he believe Dad's in heaven watching him? Does he need to believe that? Or is it enough to know that Dad was here with us for a little while, long enough to make us who we are? Now it's up to us to keep moving forward and finish becoming what we're supposed to be.

The first pitch is a ball, low and outside.

The crowd likes that.

Shouts of "Good eye! Good eye!" ring out around the stadium.

The next pitch is outside, too.

Now things are finally getting interesting.

Bored, grumbling fans set down their drinks and their bags of popcorn and start to sit up and take notice.

Working behind in the count is dangerous for any pitcher, even one as good as Shane Donner. On the rare occasion when a hitter puts a ball into play on an 0-2 count, he usually gets on base.

"What's going on?" Miss Jack asks me.

I've already explained about balls and strikes.

"He has two balls," I reply.

"That's good," she says.

"Yeah. Now the pressure's on the pitcher. He needs to get the count even so he can get Klint to start swinging defensively and screw up."

Klint doesn't swing at the next pitch either.

The ump calls it a strike, and the crowd erupts into catcalls of disapproval.

"Are you blind? Are you friggin' blind?" Bills screams at the top of his lungs.

"What the hell are you doing? That was a mile outside!" Mrs. Jack screams standing next to him.

Miss Jack looks up at her.

"Rae Ann," she scolds. "You're a mother. There are children present."

"Screw them," Mrs. Jack says and goes back to shouting at the umpire.

The Mann clan has joined in, and our entire section is accusing the umpire of

everything from needing glasses and taking bribes to having a difficult time getting erections.

Klint steps out of the box.

My heart skips a beat, but it turns out everything's okay. It's better than okay.

He puts his bat beneath his arm and casually tugs at his batting glove, holds the hand up in front of his face, and flexes his fingers a few times as if testing for the right fit.

He takes his time and goes out of his way not to look at Donner or any of the infield. He's doing a psych-out.

He's seen enough pitches now. He's confident.

He fouls the next pitch. It goes flying behind him into the stands and someone gets a nice souvenir.

With a pitcher like Donner who's throwing blazing fastballs at a speed rarely seen at the high school level, the umpire is going to give all the borderline pitches to him and not the batter. Klint can't wait for the best pitch. He has to swing at anything that comes near the plate and keep fouling off pitches until he gets something good to hit.

It's 2-2, and Donner is feeling the pressure. The next pitch is a ball.

The crowd goes crazy as the Cougars call a time-out with a full count, and the coach and catcher join Donner on the mound.

"What's going on, now?" Miss Jack asks.

"The other team called a time-out so they can talk."

"They're discussing Klint?"

"Yeah. He's starting to worry them."

"Good," she says.

Donner's next pitch is perfect. Right down the center of the plate between the belt and knee. Klint gets a piece of it and sends it flying far into right field. Everyone's on their feet but left with nothing to cheer for. It veers foul.

Klint doesn't care. The damage is done. Donner's seen him make contact, and now he knows he can send the ball far enough to put it away. All he has to do is move it a couple feet inside.

The next pitch is a foul tip.

The crowd groans.

Shane Donner has been forced into throwing an eighth pitch to the same hitter, a situation he rarely encounters.

Klint gets into his stance, legs anchored, eyes staring down the pitcher; then he gets ready to swing, his arms pulled back, pushing against nothing but quivering with the power of a loaded catapult, his body coiled for the attack.

Donner throws. Klint swings.

A pure clear crack rings out, that distinctive sound baseball fans know so well: when the ball meets the sweet spot.

As Klint completes his swing, he's already

running to first base, the momentum of the bat pulling his legs into motion.

The ball flies into deep right field. It hits the wall, takes a bounce, and comes to rest without anyone near it.

The Cougars' outfielders had grown complacent and cocky. Even though they knew Klint was a power hitter and Donner had just been forced into throwing a troubling eight pitches, they weren't ready for a long ball. They were too far up and not paying attention.

The right fielder runs after the ball. By the time he reaches it, Klint has rounded second and Brent is on his way home.

Standing spread-eagle, he rockets the cutoff throw to the second baseman in short center field. It takes a bad bounce, but he grabs it and turns to throw.

Klint doesn't slow down at all for third. He picks up his already furious pace, keeping his eyes ahead, pumping his arms and legs, running for his life the same way I'd seen him do it a few weeks earlier, only then he was trying to get as far away from home as he could. Now he was determined to reach it.

The second baseman sizes up the play in an instant and throws to the catcher who's crouched behind the plate waiting for the tag.

Klint launches himself into space, Superman-style, with his arms outstretched. Half the fans scream, and the other half suck

in their breath.

Headfirst slides are never done in high school ball anymore. They're hardly ever done in the pros, either. They're not only more dangerous, but most players are convinced they take longer than feetfirst slides. Common sense says they should be faster because the runner doesn't have to interrupt his forward momentum, but most players hesitate. The fear of diving headfirst at top speed onto a hard surface is a difficult one to overcome.

I don't think Klint has a choice. I think he suddenly becomes airborne the same way a plane does once it gets up enough speed. But if he'd been able to stop and think about what he was doing, I'm sure he would've done the same thing.

If there's one thing both of us know, it's how to survive being thrown to the ground.

The catcher takes the throw high and slaps down the tag.

For a split second the world stops spinning until the ump slashes his arms out to his sides and yells, "Safe!"

I look over at Miss Jack who's on her feet cheering along with everyone else, her face flushed with color and lit up with the delighted smile of a little girl.

"Duende," I whisper.

CHAPTER THIRTY: LUIS

I am a complicated and surprising man. I've had many love affairs, but I've never been in love. I'm lucky at cards, and I'm good at crossword puzzles. I have fantastic teeth. I play the lottery every week. I love basketball and Humphrey Bogart movies. I subscribe to *The New Yorker,* and I understand all their cartoons. I keep a bag of peanut M&Ms in my room at all times. I have a fear of heights and baggy clothing. My feet never smell. I can shoot a gun. *Don Quixote* is *not* my favorite book (but it's a very good one). I cry at the end of *The Wizard of Oz* when Dorothy goes home no matter how many times I've seen it. I was deboning a trout on 9/11 when the terrorists attacked the World Trade Center. I'm an excellent chef. I'm an accomplished horseman. I taught myself English when I first came here, and then I taught myself French in case I ever want to go to France to try the food. (I don't want to be harassed and misled by haughty waiters.)

If I were allowed to clear up three popular American misconceptions about my country and my people, they would be: Spain is nothing like Mexico; Antonio Banderas is nothing like a Spaniard; and Ernest Hemingway knew nothing about bullfighting.

Occasionally a man must examine himself and take stock of his life. I did that recently when Candace was hurt.

I don't think she realizes how close she came to dying. She didn't just break many bones; she had a heart attack, as well.

Her doctor explained to me that this wasn't a sign of poor health. Considering her age and the extreme physical and emotional circumstances she experienced that night, it wasn't surprising her heart gave out.

I'm aware that she's getting old, but I had never thought about the inevitable conclusion of old age ever reaching her, which is death.

It doesn't seem possible that she could die or at least not unless she made the decision. She's too stubborn to be talked into anything she doesn't want to do. Even death couldn't succeed at this. Maybe death doesn't want to argue with her and that's why he's stayed away so long.

I've been taking extra good care of her since she came home from the hospital. She is not an easy patient. Every time she makes me want to scream in frustration, I must remind

myself of the sacrifice she made and the pain she is in.

Kyle has described to me everything that happened that terrible night. He told me about the unbelievable strength she showed for a woman of her age and size and how fast she ran down the road after him. He said she looked like a frightened ghost.

The only time I have ever seen Candace Jack running was across the yellow sand of the plaza de toros in Villarica to get to her dying lover. That day she looked like an anguished angel.

I've come to the parlor to check on her. Shelby and Kyle have just left after yet another afternoon of Candace regaling them with stories of Manuel. Her brush with death has been the key to opening the glass box where she's been living with her memories all these years. Or maybe it was the trauma of seeing a strong, young man almost die before her eyes again.

Emotionally, she seems happier than she's ever been, and mentally, she seems as strong as she's always been — but she hasn't recovered physically. Her progress has been very slow.

Miss Henry is carefully situating pillows around her. Miss Henry has shown a remarkable aptitude for tending to people with broken bones.

She picks up her feather duster as she's

leaving and completes a few departing swipes at the objects on the mantel, including Klint's state championship trophy.

Now the golden torero on Candace's clock has a golden baseball player to keep him company. They face each other, one with his cape raised and the other swinging a bat.

"Qué estás haciendo?" I ask Candace.

She gestures at the table in front of her where there are dozens of pictures spread over it. Old black-and-white photos of her and Manuel. Of me and Manuel. Of the cuadrilla parading into the ring with Manuel. Of Manuel and Carmen del Pozo. Of all of us having a meal together at a hotel, Manuel smiling around a fat cigar clamped in his mouth with his arm around his beaming Candy. Of Manuel and Paco. Of Manuel alone. Of the Spanish countryside. Of cramped stone villages huddled against hillsides. Of orange earth dotted with green trees. Of massive, carved wooden church doors and shop front windows hung with cured hams. Of toros.

I stand in front of her, then I begin picking up the photos one at a time, reliving my wonderful, ill-fated youth.

Candace picks up a photo of herself, Manuel, and me. It's after a bullfight. Manuel is wearing his *traje de luces.* He's spattered with blood and his hair is damp with sweat. He's smiling grandly for the camera while clutch-

ing Candace to his side; she is smartly dressed in a polka-dot dress, white gloves, and a hat. She's smiling adoringly at him, oblivious to the blood and mud.

I'm standing on the other side of Manuel, only twenty years old: a boy who think he's a man; a man who still thinks like a boy.

I'm not smiling.

"You never liked me," Candace comments, slyly.

"Who says I do now?"

She puts down that photo and picks up one of the two of them sitting at a café in Madrid.

"Do you miss Spain?" she asks me.

"Yes, sometimes."

"I was just thinking if Manuel had lived and I had married him, I would have lived in Spain for the rest of my life. Our places — yours and mine — would have been switched."

"Not exactly. I doubt you would have been my slave."

"You know what I mean. I would have been the immigrant. Not you."

She puts all the photos down and stares straight ahead, thinking.

"I've never really tried to understand why I clung so to Spain, why I filled my home with Spanish art and objects, why I only want to eat Spanish food and speak Spanish to you."

"And why you have a descendant of one of the finest bulls Spain has ever produced

romping around your backyard," I add.

"The obvious answer has always been that it's some kind of ongoing homage to Manuel, but I think it's something else. I think I created a Spain for myself because it's where I was supposed to be living. I've made myself an immigrant in my own home."

She pauses and looks up at me.

"Do you consider America your home or Spain?"

"They are both my home, yet somehow neither is my home. I like to think of myself as a flower — a strong, handsome flower — that's been picked and put in a vase while my roots have been left to grow a new flower."

"That's a lovely thought. So you're saying there are two of you?"

"Yes, I suppose I am."

"But the one in the vase must eventually die."

"I'm a sturdy flower."

"Yes, but even so, the one with the roots will still live much longer."

"Not if there's a drought."

"You're impossible," she scolds with mock frustration. "You have an answer for everything. Then answer this for me: If I were gone, would you stay in America?"

"What kind of question is that?"

She sighs and for a moment, she looks every one of her seventy-seven years.

"I won't live forever, Luis."

She returns to looking through her photos and my thoughts travel back to the day Manuel told me he was going to ask her to marry him.

It was before a corrida in Sevilla. We were in his hotel. He had just woken up from his siesta and the curtains were still drawn and the shutters closed. The room was dark and quiet. He would keep it this way until he was fully dressed and had finished praying, then I'd open both the curtains and the windows to let in light and noise before we made our way downstairs through the group of reporters, fans, and well-wishers to the van that would take us to the ring.

He had already put on his tights and undershirt. He had pulled his salmon-colored bullfighter's socks up over his knees and fixed them in place with garters. He had crammed his legs and genitals into the skintight knee-length breeches of his suit and buttoned up the fly. He had stepped into his black leather pumps and set his skullcap on his thick black hair. He had slipped into his tuxedo shirt, tied a thin black tie around his neck, and pulled up the braces attached to his pants.

He had his arms held up in the air as I was winding his sash around his waist when he announced to me, out of the blue, "I'm going to marry Candy."

The shock momentarily froze me in my duties.

I knew he was serious about her. He had never stayed with one woman for so long and yet, in my opinion, they hadn't been together long enough to make a decision as important as marriage. And there were other problems, too. For one, she was American. Two, he was El Soltero.

My thoughts flew back to the momentous day he called me up to the room where he was staying above my father's restaurant and asked me if I wanted to work for him. He joked with me that he could never get married because he would have to become El Esposo. It was still true. How could the Bachelor take a wife? And how could one of the most brilliant stars in the firmament of Spanish heroes even think about taking an American wife?

All of it was blasphemous.

I got over my astonishment and continued wrapping. Then I went to get his vest.

"You have asked her?"

"No," he said.

I laughed, mostly out of relief.

"Then how do you know you will marry her? Maybe she'll say no."

As soon as I said these words, I knew they were a mistake. His face turned dark and sullen. What kind of idiot would ever dream of suggesting to Manuel Obrador that there

could be a woman in the world who would refuse him?

"She'd be crazy to say no," I said nervously, trying to recover, "but women are crazy. And she's not one of us. She's American. Would you live in Spain?"

"Of course, we'd live in Spain," he said irritably.

I walked over to the bed and picked up the final and most stunning part of his costume: the heavy waist-length jacket with wide epaulets covered in gold filigreed embroidery, tassels, and beads. This night he was wearing the color *sangre de toro.* Bull's blood.

I returned to him and held it up for him.

"Maybe she wouldn't want to," I said.

He slipped one arm into the jacket and then the other. I let the heavy weight of it settle onto his shoulders.

"I'm surprised at you, Luis. You of all people should wish me happiness."

"I do."

"You should want me to get what I want."

"I do."

He walked over to the mirror to check his appearance. No matter how many times I'd seen him dressed in his suit of lights, I was always struck dumb by his beauty.

"Ah, I know what it is," he said, turning around suddenly, and fixing me with a mischievous smile.

"The other men, they like Candy very

much. They respect her. They think she is very beautiful. But they say you don't like her."

"That's not true."

"I suspect it's not. You act like you don't like her, but I know the real reason behind it."

He turned back to the mirror a final time, but the grin never left his face.

"You want her for yourself."

Sometimes I wonder what Manuel would think of us. Would he find it funny or tragic that I did end up getting her for myself, only to find out I could never have her because we each loved him too well.

She lifts her chin and fixes me with her eyes of green thunder.

"I think you would miss America," she tells me.

"Not the way you think."

The rest of the words I want to say to her spring to my lips but I won't let them out: You are my America, Candace. As Manuel was my Spain. Once I've lost both of you, the concepts of country and home will no longer matter to me. I will be a nomad looking for a safe place to pitch my humble tent.

■ ■ ■ ■

Part IV
La Vieja Compañera

■ ■ ■ ■

Chapter Thirty-One: Candace Jack

Rafael had a wonderful season this year, and I'm happy for him. It seems he may have finally been able to shake off his own insecurities and doubts and get out from under the burden of sharing Manuel's blood.

I just finished reading his latest letter before starting off on my walk. He still has his final two corridas left in the middle of October, but he seems confident of their outcome.

Along with his clippings he also sent an article about a recent study performed at a university in Spain where it was determined that fighting bulls have special hormonal mechanisms that allow them to block pain by releasing high levels of beta-endorphins.

With each spike of the picador's lance or thrust of the torero's sword, the bull is saturated with hormones that switch off pain receptors and produce pleasure.

In other words, he's having a good time.

I wonder if Rafael sent the same clipping to his American actress.

I wasn't able to walk much this past summer. My bones have healed. My cast was removed. But I still hurt everywhere, and my knees have never fully recovered.

I've set out on this walk alone with my cane and the cell phone Luis and the boys insisted I get so I can call in an emergency. I don't know how I'm supposed to call using a device I have trouble turning on, but it makes them feel better.

The boys are at school. Luis is taking his nap. He won't admit to taking a nap, but I know that he does.

I decided to sneak out on my own. I don't know what possessed me. I see the potential danger, and after only five minutes, I feel the encroaching pain but onward I go.

I didn't get to see much of the boys after Klint's team captured the state title. He and Kyle spent the rest of the summer traveling to tournaments.

Since coming home again in the fall Klint's been pursued by colleges and even some professional teams, although Kyle has explained the dangers to me in a player turning pro too soon. I've had scouts to tea, and I've been given tickets to games that I've passed on to Jerry that brought tears to his eyes. I've discussed everything from signing bonuses to freshman curriculums.

Klint seems to find my involvement extremely amusing while Kyle has told me

many times how much he appreciates my help. He's been amazing. He has single-handedly overseen every aspect of the overwhelming process of helping Klint consider all his options and what they entail.

For my part, I've talked extensively to Klint, and he knows what I think should be his most important consideration.

They've both been back in school for almost two months now, and things have calmed down. We've fallen into a pleasant routine.

I don't know why lately, these past few days, I've felt restless.

I'm sure to a bystander I'd hardly present a picture of restlessness as I hobble at a turtle's pace down a path through the woods to the bottom of one of my pastures.

I stop to rest and lean against the fence.

It's a blustery, gray day, but it doesn't stop me from admiring the scene before me. The dying autumn grass stretches out in rolling hills of lemon-green that are eventually blurred by the deep blue shadows cast by the distant mountains.

The sky is a solid grayish white except for a patch where it looks like the clouds have been worn too thin and are pulling apart into shreds. Hints of the softest blue can be seen behind them tinged an amber-pink from the weak light of a hidden sun.

I'm watching this spot above me when I

hear a crashing noise in the underbrush not far from me. It stops then starts again.

I wait with my heart pounding to see if it's a deer or a wild turkey or even a black bear.

I catch my breath when Ventisco steps out into the field.

He's only thirty feet from me. Safely on the other side of the fence, I assure myself, knowing if he truly wanted to get through the fence, he could.

I haven't seen him for a year, and I've never seen him this close to the house.

He marches farther out into the pasture, fearlessly, nobly, no different than he would have galloped into a bullring if he had ever been given a chance.

I wonder if I've been right to deprive him of his destiny.

The fighting Spanish bull has a different lineage than any other cattle. He is descended from ancient strains of wild stock that once roamed Europe. He is fiercer and more aristocratic than his domestic counterparts and perhaps the most dangerous animal in the world.

Looking at him now, the power behind his loose-muscled gait, the enormity of his neck and shoulders, the perfect balance of his lethal horns, the deep dark glossiness of his jet-black hide, I'm quite sure he was meant for something much greater than this quiet country life in a Pennsylvania valley.

He senses me and looks in my direction.

I'm not afraid. I'm fairly certain I wouldn't be afraid even if there wasn't a fence between us. If he were to come charging at me, I would stand still and accept what fate brought me, knowing it was my time.

He stands like a statue and watches me intently. There's intelligence in those fathomless black eyes calling to me the way a wishing well calls to a child to cast all his coins until penniless.

I remember Manuel's warning: he is not a dumb animal. A bull thinks, but no man can ever know what he's thinking.

Maybe a woman can.

"Is this what you wanted, Ventisco?" I ask him.

He continues staring at me but doesn't move.

"Or would you have preferred the ecstasy and glory of the ring?"

A ripple travels through the muscles on his side. He gives me one snort.

"I suppose I've kept you from the bull's equivalent of a man having a fatal coronary during orgasm. Men say they can't imagine a better way to go."

He snorts again and takes a few forceful steps toward me and stops.

"I've doomed you to the ravages of old age. To watching your strength and beauty fade. To die lying down."

He tosses his head and I think he may charge, but he hesitates, then turns and trots away.

I watch him pick up the pace until he's charging across the field in an easy loping gallop, showing off. He stops once and looks back at me from far away, then he disappears over a hill.

Crazy old woman, he was probably thinking.

"Conceited old bull," I say out loud.

I'm strangely elated after seeing Ventisco.

I head back toward home no longer feeling the aches and pains in my bones as badly as I did before our meeting, but once I reach the house, I'm suddenly exhausted.

Jerry's standing in front of it in his familiar red-and-black-checked coat studying a second-story window. His arms are crossed over his chest, and his jaw is methodically working a wad of tobacco tucked inside his lower lip.

"Hello, Jerry," I greet him.

He turns, pulls off his cap, folds the bill, and stuffs it in his pocket.

" 'Lo, Miss Jack. You supposed to be out here walking around by yourself?"

"Please, Jerry," I reply, gruffly. "I'm not an invalid."

"I know. It's just Luis . . ."

"Don't talk to me about Luis," I interrupt him. "If it were up to him, I'd be one of those

people living in a bubble."

"Prob'ly."

"What are you looking at?"

He extends a finger toward the house.

"That window there. The paint's flaking on the trim. Don't know why. It's the only one. Thought I should take care of it."

"You?" I wonder. "Don't be silly. We can hire someone. You shouldn't be climbing that high at your age."

He doesn't look at me and his expression doesn't change. I can't tell if I've offended him.

"There are a lot of things I shouldn't be doing at my age. Like waking up in the morning. But I'm still doing 'em."

He chews and chews and contemplates the window further.

"If it'd make you feel better," he tells me, "I'll get someone else to do it. You're the boss."

I glance at him again. His face remains neutral.

We both continue to stare up at the window.

"It's a beautiful house," I state.

He squints at me.

"Yep. It is."

"I can't tell you how much time I've spent agonizing over what would become of this land and this house if something were to happen to me. I don't have any children to pass it on to, and I can't stand the thought of giv-

ing it to Cameron since I know he would never appreciate it; yet the thought of it being sold to strangers is horrifying to me. But just recently, the answer became so obvious to me, I couldn't believe I never saw it before."

He nods and turns and spits into the gravel.

"My mother used to say old age was the loosening of the bonds of the flesh that make us cling to false hopes. She said getting old wasn't about the decay of our earthly bodies but about the deliverance of our souls to a place where we could finally see earthly matters clearly and make our peace with them before becoming one with the natural world."

"Your mother said that?" I ask, rather impressed.

"Yep."

"She was a wise and eloquent woman."

"Yep."

He retrieves his cap and puts it back on his head with a tug at the bill.

"Afternoon, Miss Jack."

"Good afternoon, Jerry."

I go inside and think about sitting down in the parlor to rest but decide to drag myself upstairs for a nap instead.

I don't realize until I'm standing in my room that I forgot to take off my coat and shoes. Kyle's scarf is still tied around my head.

Suddenly, I can't perform even these simple

acts. I'm overcome with an exhaustion that tugs at me like an undertow. A moment of green silence passes as I'm submerged in calm water and my body begins to dissolve like sugar.

I'm falling in slow motion, the way everything happens underwater. My arms are suspended next to me, but I'm not holding them up. I watch them curiously, wondering how they can feel so light. Now my legs are rising, too. I see the tips of my shoes.

Then suddenly I hit bottom with a bump. I come bursting back to the surface, gasping for breath, while the hypnotic liquid falls away from me in a shower of lacy droplets.

I'm sitting on the edge of my bed. My heart is racing too fast. My lungs ache. I lie down very slowly.

I wonder if I should be afraid, but before I can fully explore this thought, my head fills with a wonderful memory I haven't recalled for ages.

We were at Carmen's finca, and Manuel was putting a young calf through her paces to see if she was worthy of being released into the fields to mate and produce champion bulls or if she would be sent to the slaughterhouse for meat. This was a traditional way of testing stock for quality and also for bullfighters to practice their technique.

Carmen and El Gato were both there watching along with Manuel's sister, Maria

Antonia, her husband and son, Juan Manuel, and a group of Carmen's rich friends.

We stood on one side of the whitewashed practice ring while a group of sunburned, fierce-eyed men wearing tweed caps and dusty breeches smelling of tobacco and wood smoke stood on the opposite side. These were the ranch hands and bullfighting professionals who had come to see for free a little of the magic other people would be paying to see at a corrida a few days away.

Manuel had just finished his session to a round of appreciative applause and walked over to us, leaving the bewildered, conquered calf standing in the middle of the ring breathing heavily.

He was in his usual practice garb of high skintight pants, leather boots, and a white button-down shirt beneath an old cocoa brown sweater.

He was smiling, relaxed and happy with himself. He came straight to me for a kiss, and I breathed in the earthy scent of him and thought of the leisurely lunch and the delicious siesta we'd be having soon.

Upon seeing his famous uncle so close, little Juani held out his arms and began chanting, "Tío, Tío, quiero torear."

Manuel's smile broadened, and he put his muleta under one arm and reached out for the boy. A panicked look came across María's face, but there was nothing she could

do. Everyone else had started laughing and clapping.

He took the child, a miniature of himself with big dark eyes and thick black hair, hefted him onto his right hip, and walked back into the ring where he made a few casual passes with his cape. The cow charged and Juani squealed.

I think I feel something lying next to me, but I'm too tired to open my eyes. I'm sinking again back into the cool, quiet green, only this time it presses uncomfortably against my chest.

I reach down and stroke the cat's fur. I still have the presence of mind to know I don't allow him in my house. I wonder why. It seems silly to me now. He burrows closer and begins purring.

With my memory interrupted, my thoughts drift to the words of Jerry's mother, and I think I can actually feel the loosening of my bonds of flesh. All the pain I've known is unimportant now. All I feel is love.

Manuel lowers his nephew but he's no longer Juani; he's Rafael. The little calf grazes his little legs on one of her passes. He shrieks with delight, and I smile.

In the midst of the small crowd leaning against the fence is Luis. So young. So controlled and contained yet so generous. The boy who would save me.

I see the flutter of the cape, too, and I run

toward it as any toro bravo would . . . with joy.

Chapter Thirty-Two: Kyle

Our stuff is packed. It didn't take long. A few suitcases and a couple boxes sit out here in the hall along with the smashed chrome antlers off Dad's truck grill.

For the time being, Klint and I are going to stay with Bill. Cam Jack didn't waste any time kicking us out. The very day Miss Jack died he told us we had to leave.

Luis got furious. I'd never seen him confront Mr. Jack before. Even so, he remained polite. He explained in a low, controlled voice that we couldn't be expected to leave immediately. We would have to make plans. There was plenty of room in the house. It wouldn't hurt anyone if we remained a few days. Plus he had many household arrangements to make.

I realized as he was talking that he included himself in the "we," and I understood in a flash that Mr. Jack had kicked him out, too. Luis, to him, was the hired help, and he'd been fired the moment Miss Jack took her

last breath.

Mr. Jack said we could stay until the funeral and the reading of the will. At that point, the house would be legally his and we would have to go. Luis thanked him, then the minute he left the room, he began ranting toward the heavens in Spanish; but then his eyes suddenly filled with tears and he excused himself and rushed from the room.

At least I know Mom can't make us live with her anymore. Miss Jack was made our legal guardian and she explained to Klint and me that we don't ever have to see Mom again if we don't want to.

It's been almost five months since Klint tried to kill himself, and we haven't heard anything from her or anything more about her plans to move back here. We also haven't heard anything about Krystal.

I finished her fairy painting but never got around to sending it to her before all hell broke loose. It's sitting here on top of the boxes along with Dad's antlers. Someday I'm going to find her and give it to her. It's one of my goals.

I check my reflection in one of Miss Jack's mirrors. I had to buy a new suit. In one year, I outgrew the one I wore to Dad's funeral.

It's black, the way it's supposed to be, but I wouldn't compromise on the tie. I picked out a colorful one with a mosaic pattern that reminds me of Miss Jack's candles.

I hear Klint trudging up the stairs. He comes around the corner.

"You ready to go? Luis is looking for us."

We stare at each other in our suits, and I know we're both thinking the same thing. We're both remembering the last time we put them on.

It's only been a year between the two funerals, but I've done a lifetime of growing up. I wish I could hug Klint. It's the same wish I had the night Dad died. Seeing him now, I'm filled with the same need I had then to take him in my arms just to know he's really here and to feel his arms around me just to know I'm really here, too.

He's done a lot of healing, but he still can't handle physical contact. Mom took that away from him.

Luis is waiting along with Mr. B, who's sitting at the bottom of the stairs cleaning his face with a big orange paw.

He's had the run of the house ever since Luis found him curled up next to Miss Jack with her hand resting on him after she had passed away.

Animals are supposed to sense things better than people, and I think he was the only one of us who knew she was dying. He went to her that day to give her comfort. Luis agrees. That's why his status has been elevated.

Mr. B seems to understand. He has an even

more superior slink to his walk and glint in his golden eyes than he used to, and he hardly wants to go outside at all anymore. He's taken to lying on Miss Jack's favorite chair in the parlor and spends most of his time there. At one point, Klint suggested maybe Miss Jack's soul passed into Mr. B when she died.

Luis said that was nonsense, but I notice he now crosses himself every time he walks by the cat.

"It's time to go," Luis says when he sees us. "Klint, do you mind driving? I don't want to take the Mercedes."

"You want to go in the truck?" Klint asks.

"Yes."

He shrugs.

"Sure."

Luis leads us outside. He's dressed entirely in black, including his shirt and tie, but has a splash of scarlet on his chest where the tip of a red handkerchief sticks out of his breast pocket.

I don't know what Luis is going to do now that Miss Jack is gone. Maybe he'll go back to Spain. I'll miss him, but I'm not worried about him. It may be selfish, but I've been too worried about my own situation to give much thought to anybody else.

Klint will be moving away to college next summer. He's had a lot of offers. He still hasn't signed his letter of intent, but all the schools he's favoring are far away from here.

I don't know what's going to happen to me.

We're probably a funny sight, the three of us crammed into the cab of a truck, pulling up to the biggest church in Centresburg where tons of expensive cars line the street and fill the parking lot.

I don't know where all these people are coming from. We lived with Miss Jack for a year, and outside of her family and Bert Shulman, she never had any visitors or left the house to visit someone else.

I guess she was famous, in a way, and I've heard funerals for the rich attract all kinds of people who didn't know them very well. They come as much for the spectacle as they do to pay their respects.

I ask Luis about it, and he says she knew many people and she touched many lives.

We're running a little late, and we have to park a couple blocks away. As we're walking up to the church, I wonder again at Miss Jack's insistence that she have her memorial service here and not in a funeral home the way my dad did. When Luis told me this the other day, I was kind of confused.

I know she wasn't religious, and she never went to church. But now that I'm standing before the massive gray stone building with its impressive red doors and jewel-colored windows and angels carved into its façade, I think I get it.

I can't imagine Miss Jack's farewell to this

life taking place among beige carpet, folding chairs, and fluorescent lighting.

She didn't choose this church for its spiritual advantages but for its grandeur.

Tyler and his parents are the first people I see who I recognize. During the last few games of the state championship series, we always sat in front of the Mann clan, and Miss Jack got to be pretty friendly with them. I think she was fascinated by the size of their family and their obliviousness to the fact that they should be troubled by it.

Tyler sees us, too, and waves. Klint starts off in his direction, but Luis takes me by the arm to stop me.

"There's someone I want you to meet," he says.

I search the faces of the whispering people in their somber clothes filing into the church and try to guess who Luis means.

A few remain outside, hiding themselves in shadows, having a last cigarette before the service starts.

One of these men stands out. He is obviously foreign, but I can't define why. He's not dressed any differently than the others. He's not different physically. Our left fielder, Matt Martelli, is just as dark-skinned and dark-haired. They could be brothers except this guy is much better-looking.

It might be the way he's smoking. Americans smoke guiltily or defiantly. He's doing it

casually and elegantly, leaning against the wrought-iron railing on the stone steps in a patch of clean fall sunshine that's been filtered through the remaining bright orange leaves of a shedding tree.

I'm right in my choice. When he sees Luis, he drops his cigarette, crushes it with the tip of his glossy black leather shoe, and flicks it off the step behind some bushes.

He walks toward us with his shoulders back, chin up, eyes forward, and I realize what sets him apart from everyone else here is his composure.

"Kyle, this is Rafael Carmona." Luis introduces us. "He is the grandson of Manuel's sister, Maria Antonia."

Rafael extends his hand to me.

"It's very nice to meet you," he says. "I've heard a lot about you."

"You've heard about me?"

"Aunt Candy and I wrote to each other frequently."

His English is very formal, but this just adds to his regal air. His accent is much thicker than Luis's.

"You're a bullfighter, too? Right?"

"Yes, I am."

Knowing he stands unarmed face-to-face with large and mythically murderous beasts and knowing he's related to El Soltero makes him seem like a character who's stepped out

of a fairy tale. I don't know what to say to him.

"And you are an artist, too?" he says to me.

"Yeah. I guess so."

Rafael smiles.

"You are very young. Soon you will accept it. I hope you are not too sad at Aunt Candy's passing."

"I'm a little sad."

A lump catches in my throat, and I have to stop after I say these words. I've been trying to pretend I'm not upset. I keep telling myself it's not possible for me to care that much. I didn't know her long enough. Plus her death wasn't a tragedy like Dad going over the mountain or Manuel being killed by a bull's horns. She was old. She lived a long life. It was her time. We're not supposed to feel bad. At least that's what everyone keeps saying.

I blink back some tears and tell myself again that it doesn't make sense to be sad.

"You must try and think like a Spaniard," Rafael says encouragingly. "A Spaniard lives only to die. We're not frightened or horrified by death. On the contrary, we are always thinking about our own deaths. We wish them to be lovely and honorable."

"Like death in a bullfight?"

He smiles again.

"Yes. There is a poem I like very much by one of our most famous poets, Jorge Manrique: Nuestra vidas son los rios / Que van a

dar en la mar / Que es el morir.

It means, our lives are the rivers that go to the sea, which is death."

"It's nice," I tell him, "in a creepy way."

He laughs at this.

"I know it is hard for you to understand. Americans are only concerned with living well; Spaniards want to die well."

I wonder if Miss Jack died well by a Spaniard's standard. The doctor said she passed away quietly. I think that might even be better than dying instantly.

"You should come for a visit to Spain," he tells me.

"I'd like that."

"Would you like to see a bullfight?"

"Yeah. That would be cool."

"Do you write letters?"

"Well, I can. I've never done it because I've never known anyone who would write back."

"I'll miss my letters from Aunt Candy. Maybe you and I could write to each other?"

"Sure."

"We should go inside," Luis announces.

Rafael leaves us. Luis gestures for Klint. We wait for him and then we go inside together.

The church is packed. We stare at the rows of pews stretching away from us filled with the backs of people's murmuring heads.

I don't know where we're going to sit.

"I wish to stay behind," Luis tells us.

"Klint," he says, "you know where you

should be."

Klint doesn't say anything to me. He just starts walking down the red-carpeted aisle toward the front of the church where Miss Jack's closed casket stands. I knew she'd insist on this. She would never tolerate having people look at her when she couldn't look back at them.

I haven't seen Bert Shulman yet, but his presence is felt by the amount of yellow roses everywhere. There are dozens of vases of them, wreaths and garlands, and hundreds heaped on the coffin. He must've bought every yellow rose in the state.

As we near the front pew I can make out the heads of the Jack family: Cam Jack's slick pewter cap of hair and his wife's teased blond mane; then Shelby, the shiny new penny; Starr, the tawny beast; and Sky, the golden princess; and a man sitting next to her I assume must be her prince.

There's a man crouched down in the aisle next to their pew talking to Mr. Jack. He's Chip Edgars, the lawyer who advertises on TV. I've seen his picture on billboards, sides of buildings, flyers stapled to telephone poles, and even a few barns.

It takes a special kind of ego to want to see your own face that much.

He stands up, claps Mr. Jack on the shoulder, and starts walking back down the aisle in our direction. As he passes us, he gives us a

funny look; for a moment I think he's going to say something to me, but he keeps walking.

We reach the family pew and stop.

Starr looks the worst of all of them, tired and faded. My heart goes out to her, and I don't even know why. I'm supposed to be consumed with feeling sorry and scared for myself. I wish I could comfort her, although I don't think I have the ability. Maybe someday I'll paint that picture of her we talked about. She doesn't have to pose for me in the flesh. A painter works not only from visual images but from emotional stores, and I'll never forget how she made me feel that day.

Skylar's on her cell phone and is dressed in a skimpy black dress and a lot of jewelry that makes me think she and her boyfriend are heading for the nearest city after the funeral for an expensive dinner and a night of clubbing.

Mrs. Jack is a wreck. Her eyes are red and swollen and rimmed with bleeding mascara, and her lap is littered with wet, crumpled Kleenex. I do a double take when I notice her purse sitting between her and Shelby.

I'm not mistaken. Baby's bulbous eyes are peering out from its depths.

Shelby's sniffling into a tissue. She looks up at me. A range of emotions play over her tearstained face: relief at seeing me, her ongoing grief, then something like fear.

I realize where this is coming from.

Mr. Jack immediately gets to his feet to block us.

Klint stands his ground. They face each other, nose to nose. The church falls completely silent except for the melancholy soundtrack provided by the organist.

Mr. Jack is distorted with rage. He clenches his fists at his sides. Sweat beads pop out along his hairline. He clamps his lips in a tight, trembling seal against the poison he wants to spew at us.

Klint remains calm. I'm probably the only one here who's aware of the terrible trembling coursing through his body. I don't know if he's trying to restrain his anger and disgust or if he's truly frightened.

They stand this way for an eternity that lasts a minute before Cam Jack, the richest, most powerful man I will ever know, a captain of industry, and heir to a ruthless bastard's legacy crumbles beneath the flame blue gaze of my brother, a janitor's son and heir to nothing except the pain of family secrets and sudden deaths.

Klint and I walk past him to the end of the pew where we take our seats with the rest of Miss Jack's family.

I reach for Shelby's hand.

Miss Jack is going to be laid to rest next to her brother and his wife. When the church

service is over, we drive to the cemetery.

At first I'm surprised to find out Stan Jack was buried on this unremarkable hillside among cashiers and truck drivers and laid-off coal miners, but then I remember how he chose to build his homes here and raise his son here no matter how much money he made.

His headstone is big but square and simple and comes across as humble compared with the five-foot marble cross marking the grave of a well-known car dealer or the sword-wielding avenging angel standing guard over the final resting place of the local Mattress King.

I finally catch sight of Bert Shulman. He's in a charcoal suit with a bright yellow bow tie that matches the single yellow rose he's carrying.

He musters a smile when he sees me and Klint and nods in our direction.

I also see Jerry for the first time today. I almost don't recognize him. Working around Miss Jack's house in his gray work pants, flannel shirt, and ball cap, he always seemed all-powerful and indestructible. There was no problem he couldn't fix. In a suit and tie he looks like an ordinary old man.

He's standing far away from everyone else, almost as if he thinks he shouldn't be here.

I'm thinking about walking over and saying hi to him when I feel a tap on my shoulder.

"Hey, Kyle."

It's Bill, another guy who loses himself when he puts on a suit.

"Hey, Bill."

"How're you doing?"

"Okay. How about you?"

"I'm okay. She was a nice lady."

"Yeah."

That same lump comes back into my throat again, and I have to swallow hard.

"You got a minute?" Bill asks.

"I'm at the same funeral you are. What do you mean?"

"Come here."

He starts limping away from the crowd back toward the road where the cars are parked in a seemingly endless line.

"I told her this might not be the best place to talk to you, but she insisted," Bill starts explaining. "I kind of got the feeling she wanted to pay her respects to Miss Jack, too."

He looks toward a lone woman in the middle of the road who's pacing and frantically smoking. I'd know the spidery jerky movements of her arms and legs anywhere.

"Hey, Aunt Jen," I say to her.

She came to see Klint once after he got home from the hospital. She brought him an ice cream cake and a deck of cards and couldn't make eye contact with either of us. She left right away. We haven't seen her since.

"Sorry about all this," she says to me when

I get close enough to see she's in a torn pair of jeans and a beat-up leather jacket.

She's definitely not dressed for a funeral.

"Yeah," I answer her.

"I hear you and Klint are going to live with Bill for now."

"Yeah."

"I hear Klint's been getting a lot of college offers already."

"Yeah."

"Has he decided where he wants to go?"

"No. Maybe Kansas or Florida or even Hawaii. It's all the same to me."

I plunge my hands in my pants pockets and rock on my heels waiting to see if she has anything else to say. It's strange that she came to Miss Jack's funeral just to make small talk with me.

"I want you to know I didn't know about anything," she says suddenly, her words choked off by an unexpected sob.

She composes herself quickly. I try to read her expression through the fog of cigarette smoke hanging between us. She looks startled by her own admission.

"It's okay," I tell her. "You want to come over to the funeral?"

"No. No, I hate funerals," she says, shaking her head vigorously. "I went to my mom's, and I told myself that was the last one I was ever going to. Besides, I'm pretty sure Miss Jack hated me."

"She was probably just disappointed in you. It took me a while to figure out there's a big difference between the two. I don't think she hated anybody."

She seems to think about what I said, finishes her cigarette, and tosses it into the grass.

"Well, I'll let you get back but before you go, there's someone here who wants to see you."

I look around me in all directions, but all I see is the flaming October countryside and a road parked full of cars and trucks.

Aunt Jen starts walking even farther away from the funeral, and I helplessly follow.

Soon I recognize her car, and I notice there's someone small sitting on the passenger side.

She looks up and sees me.

I rush over to the car. She doesn't open the door, but her window is down. I lean inside it.

"Hey, Krystal. What are you doing here?"

"Hi, Kyle," she says in a chirpy, normal little girl voice. "I'm visiting Aunt Jen."

She's in jeans and a T-shirt, with her hair in a ponytail, and has dirt under her fingernails like she's been playing outside. She's reading a paperback book with a girl and a horse on the cover. I can't find any sign of the hateful little woman she was at Dad's funeral. Even her freckles are starting to come back. Relief

rushes through me.

"Krystal's staying with me for a while," Aunt Jen explains. "I wanted to let you know so you can make plans to see each other."

"I'm sorry your old lady died," Krystal says. "Did you like her?"

"Yeah, I did."

"Aunt Jen says we can go out to dinner tonight if you want. And Klint, too."

I glance at Jen, who seems to have calmed down a little if the reduced speed of her smoking is any sign.

"I didn't know if you'd be busy."

"No. We can do it."

I pull the tiny silver shoe from my pocket and show it to Krystal.

"Do you remember? I gave it to you at Dad's funeral, and you said you didn't need it and threw it away."

"Why do you have it?"

"I kept it."

"Why?"

"To remind me of you."

"You're crazy, Kyle," she says, rolling her eyes like I'm already annoying her, exactly the way a little sister should act.

I put it back in my pocket and smile to myself.

"Okay, hon. Give me one more minute to talk to your brother," Aunt Jen breaks in on our reunion. "I'll be right back."

She leads me back down the row of cars.

"I haven't told Krystal yet, but she's not just visiting me. Your mom dumped her on me. Maybe for good. I don't know. She's run off with some new guy."

"Are you serious? I can't believe it."

"Believe it."

"Are you going to be able to take care of her?"

"I don't know. I'm gonna try. It would be nice if you boys could help out. You know. Visit her and stuff."

"Sure."

I give her a quick, awkward hug.

"Everything will be okay," I tell her.

She doesn't look convinced.

I decide to wait and tell Klint about Krystal when the funeral's over. I join him where he's standing with Tyler, his parents, Bill, and to my surprise, Coach Hill.

The Jack family is seated in a row of folding chairs set up beside the coffin where it's waiting to be lowered into the ground.

Klint and I stand on the other side of the coffin.

I look around for Luis as the preacher gets ready to say his final words and find him standing at the edge of crowd with Jerry. They're shaking hands, but Jerry's head is bowed down and Luis has his other hand bracing his shoulder like he's holding him up.

There's always been a mild antagonism

between the two of them, just like I suppose there should be between any two knights serving the same queen. Now that she's gone, for today, their duty is to each other.

The preacher's comments are brief. He says a prayer.

Bert steps forward and places his last yellow rose on her coffin.

Rafael crosses himself and gives her a string of rosary beads.

Luis takes the red handkerchief from his pocket, dabs his eyes with it, and lays it over her.

Next Klint steps forward.

He pulls a folded piece of paper from inside his suit jacket and puts it on top of the coffin, too.

I don't know much about funeral etiquette. I've never seen this done before. Nobody put any precious mementos in with Dad. In hindsight, I'm sure this was a good idea as I picture the inappropriateness of a coffin covered in baseball cards and empty beer cans.

A part of me hesitates, wondering if I'm doing something wrong, but a bigger part of me pushes me forward and I walk over to the coffin and take back Klint's piece of paper.

I have to know what it is.

I unfold it and see the Western Pennsylvania University letterhead across the top.

My hand starts to tremble as I begin to read it.

Dear Klint,

On behalf of the Western Pennsylvania University athletic department, I'm very happy to accept your letter of intent and look forward to welcoming you as a member of our 2009–2010 varsity baseball squad. As discussed earlier, you will receive a full scholarship with . . .

I don't finish reading it. I drop it and run. I only have ten feet to cover to reach my destination, but I do it at a sprint.

I throw my arms around Klint and hold on to him for all I'm worth while I blubber, "thank you," over and over again.

I'm not just saying it to Klint; I'm saying it to Miss Jack, too. I thanked her for saving my brother's life, but I never got around to thanking her for saving mine.

Klint's as stiff and unyielding as a board, but he doesn't pull away. He lets me cling to him and cry against his shoulder until his surrender.

His arms wrap around me and I hear him crying, too, and I know my brother has finally come alive again, instantly.

EPILOGUE: THE TEMPESTUOUS ONE

"This is it, then," Cameron says to me.

"Yes, I suppose it is," I reply.

We both look around the grand foyer at Candace's paintings. My gaze comes to rest on the entrance to her parlor. Inside the room, I spy Kyle's cat sitting on her favorite chair.

Cameron notices, too. He starts to say something, then stops himself.

"You're sure you know what you're doing?" he asks me.

"I appreciate your concern, Mr. Jack, but yes, I'm very sure."

His face darkens at this response.

We both turn and walk slowly to the front door. I arrive first and open it for him. He steps outside and I follow.

Kyle and Klint are helping to unload some boxes from their aunt's car. Their sister, Krystal, is sitting on the porch in Candace's favorite chair, fanning herself with one of Candace's Spanish fans that I gave to her.

She smiles at us.

"Buenos días, señorita," I call out to her.

"Buenos días," she returns the greeting with a giggle.

Cameron ignores her.

"Shall I walk you to your car?" I ask him.

"No, thanks."

He starts down the stairs, then pauses to look back at me with malice twisting his features.

"I'll fight this."

"You will lose," I assure him. "There are forces at work here that are greater than you and me."

I wait for him to depart and the boys to pass by me with their boxes before I join Aunt Jen.

Not surprisingly, she's in the process of lighting a cigarette. She's wearing cutoffs and a tank top, and her exposed legs and arms are painfully skinny.

"You should stay for lunch," I tell her.

She glances at me suspiciously.

"Why?"

"Why? Because I've asked you to stay and because it will be the best lunch of your life. We're having croquetas de pollo," I entice her, remembering how much she loved them before. "Y ensalada de codorniz escabechada con vinagreta de piñones."

"What the hell are you saying?"

"A salad with tender, sweet, pickled quail

meat and a pine nut vinaigrette."

"That's one of the weirdest things I ever heard of," she says with a derisive laugh, but I see hunger burning in her eyes.

"And flan," I add.

"What's flan?"

"A sweet custard with caramel and if you like, I will top it with a little rum."

The tip of her cigarette is burning down without her placing it into her mouth.

"You sure you want me to stay?"

I gesture at Kyle and Klint who are on their way back to the car.

"They are your family. They need you."

Candace left me everything with the stipulation that upon my death it will all go to Shelby. I wonder if I will ever get over my astonishment at this. I wouldn't have even attended the reading of the will if Bert hadn't insisted that I go.

Her nephew did not take it well. I think I have a very good command of the English language, but he introduced me to some words I've never heard before.

Along with the house I also inherited legal guardianship of Kyle and Klint, and since we have so much room, I thought it would be a nice idea to let Krystal come live here, too, upon the approval of Aunt Jen.

I suppose it is wrong to say Candace left me everything. She made sizable trusts for

her three grandnieces and also for Kyle and Klint and Rafael.

She also left some money to Bill Fowler and the Mann family.

She provided Jerry with a very generous retirement package and gave him the house he's always lived in, along with ten acres of property. Even so, he has agreed to continue to work here. He is the kind of man who will always work. I'm sure that even his vision of heaven includes a few wheelbarrows of celestial mulch that will need to be spread.

Miss Henry has agreed to stay on, too, but I've asked her to get a more becoming uniform.

I'm happy with my good fortune and hopefully someday I'll be able to enjoy it, but for now I'm numb with loss. Each day without her drags on endlessly. I'm grateful to have the boys and their sister around. They keep me busy and my thoughts occupied. But nothing and no one can ever replace her.

I've spent as much time as possible these past few days searching for Ventisco. It's a foolish pursuit. His domain covers hundreds of acres of fields, mountains, and forests. My chances of finding him are next to nothing, but I feel an inexplicable, desperate need to see him.

I let the cows out into the many pastures hoping their scent would attract him, but he continues to stay away.

Does he know she's gone? I wonder.

Ventisco will be the last of Calladito's descendants that I will ever see. I'm not saddened by this. Like all good stories, theirs must also come to an end — but only the acting of it. The telling of it will go on forever.

I hope she has found him. I hope they are at peace.

As for me, I am still part of the land of the living. I must go. I have nuggets to fry.

ACKNOWLEDGMENTS

Writing a novel is a solitary experience filled with frustration, bewilderment, and the constant nagging feeling that you should be doing something else. Each day you are alone in your head struggling to convey a fictitious story using words you hope will stir a bunch of people you will never meet while never fully understanding why you want to do it. This is the fourth time I've sat down to pen acknowledgments for a novel, and each time my initial reaction has been to write: I'd like to thank myself for writing a book all by myself for no good reason.

But then upon closer inspection of my life, I always come to realize that even though the work is solely mine, I'm surrounded by people whose love and support enables me to do it. So once again I'm rounding up the usual suspects who deserve my thanks.

One of the greatest gifts a writer can have is a good agent, someone you trust implicitly, who understands your work, and if you're

truly lucky, someone who is a wise, cool human being you like to talk to. I have all these things in Liza Dawson, and I treasure our relationship.

Many thanks to my editor, Shaye Areheart, who has shown boundless enthusiasm and respect for my books. She is quite possibly the funnest (why isn't "funnest" a word?) editor in the world but also a wickedly accomplished woman in the publishing biz, a rare and wonderful combination.

To Molly, who is armed, dangerous, adorable, and loves me in the reverent way that only a little sis can love a big sis. Thank you for always being there for me and letting me be there for you. To my mom who is simply my best friend. (Is that corny enough for you, Mom?) I don't know what I'd do without you. And finally, to my children, Tirzah and Connor, who are my Everything, y el amor de mi vida, Bernard, who has given me so much, not least of all España. *Te quiero, Nardo.*

ABOUT THE AUTHOR

Tawni O'Dell is the author of three previous novels including the *New York Times* best-seller, *Back Roads,* which was also an Oprah's Book Club selection. She lives in Pennsylvania and Spain with her two children and her husband, literary translator Bernard Cohen.

The employees of Thorndike Press hope you have enjoyed this Large Print book. All our Thorndike, Wheeler, and Kennebec Large Print titles are designed for easy reading, and all our books are made to last. Other Thorndike Press Large Print books are available at your library, through selected bookstores, or directly from us.

For information about titles, please call:

(800) 223-1244

or visit our Web site at:

http://gale.cengage.com/thorndike

To share your comments, please write:

Publisher
Thorndike Press
295 Kennedy Memorial Drive
Waterville, ME 04901